A Dry Patch *of* Skin

A Dry Patch *of* Skin

Stephen Swartz

MYRDDIN PUBLISHING GROUP

UNITED STATES · UNITED KINGDOM · AUSTRALIA

ISBN-13: 978-1-939296-32-0

ISBN-10: 1939296323

www.myrddinpublishing.com

Cover design by Marta Swartz

For the arrows of the Almighty are within me, the poison whereof drinketh up my spirit: the terrors of God do set themselves in array against me.

Job 6:4

Part One

1

AS A CHILD, I WAS NEVER ALLOWED INTO THE CHURCH. My aunt thought I carried some curse and she didn't want me to ruin it for everyone. So I stayed outside and usually read a book. That haunts me as I pause before stepping inside this chapel.

The priest stands in his black suit and white collar. His eyes study me as I approach, strolling quietly up the aisle. This small church is set high on a hill overlooking the resort town of Makarska on the coast of Croatia. Far below its open doors stretches the picturesque town of red tiled roofs and gray-plaster buildings. There is a sandy beach caught between granite cliffs. Already at this morning hour a dozen vacationers take in the sun or swim in the turquoise sea.

With a curt nod to acknowledge our meeting, the priest starts to speak, can not find the words, then recovers.

"Mister Székely," he says, "I'm terribly sorry for your loss." Then, as if only at that moment remembering, he hands me a beige envelope with elegant black writing on its face. The logo of a Hungarian law firm is printed in the corner. "This is from your parents. I am to give it to you as soon as you arrive. Before the funeral service. I hope it is not rude of me."

"No, not at all, Father."

"Thank you." He gives me another curt nod.

"I'm sure glad you speak English," I say sheepishly, "because I don't know any Croatian."

I take the envelope, glance at it, and wonder what value it might have. Mother was always fond of writing letters, sending cards, but during the past dozen years she had dwindled down to only birthday and Christmas.

I turn the envelope over in my hands, feel how thick it is, which can only mean it is longer than most of her letters.

"Does this letter explain what happened? I mean, why they committed suicide?"

"I do not know the content of that letter," says the priest with a frown. "They only wished me to give it to you. Also, they wish for you to take a week and enjoy a richly deserved vacation. Your room has been reserved and everything is paid for the week."

"How kind of them. They must have believed I would travel all the way here to see them off."

"You work so hard, they always told me, thus you need a good break."

"But there was no need to kill themselves just to get me to fly over to Croatia."

I tear open the end of the envelope and pull out the tri-folded letter of three thin pages wrapped around a generous gift of cash. The letter, written in my mother's hand, will take some time to read.

"Yes, I supposed it's my duty," I say, looking up from the letter and casually folding the cash into my front trouser pocket. "Me being their only child.... It's an obligation. So...."

I take a few deep breaths.

"You're a good son," says the priest.

I frown at his remark. "At least they were old—old enough for death, but not too old to be able to make a rational decision. Probably they were simply tired of all they had endured."

"Indeed, Mister Székely. I'm sure it was for the best."

"Please, Father...call me Stefan."

We shake hands and he assures me that everything will be ready for the service the next day.

Reclining on the bed in the hotel room they have arranged for me, I reread the last letter.

ᎧᏗ

It was not that I mistrusted the words of Mother and Father. It was not that I doubted what society itself had shown me. Indeed, I got up from the bed and stood staring into the mirror on the wall and wanted to deny everything, yet I knew deep inside there was a bomb, a time bomb of sorts, ready to explode when just the right elements came together. And I could not know when that would occur.

For my parents, stuck in upstate New York, it began rather late, after age fifty—or so they confessed; I had not seen them face to face since I left for college and even then my view was from across a parking lot. Thus, I had no incontrovertible visual confirmation of their plight. They also had begged out of my graduation ceremony and then I took a job far away from them. And much later, they died.

Before that, there were plenty of letters and phone calls, and with advancement in technology, also emails and text messages. When finally they succumbed to their own time bomb, it was my mother who dared leave a note outlining what I should expect. She was careful to add that my father did not approve of such a warning, considering it a black mark or a red flag that would ruin my life, keep me from enjoying the good years I had. However, she had deemed it a necessary kind gesture, something that any mother should do for her son.

Then they took their pills, far too many of them, and died in peace, the full afternoon of sunshine raining upon them. Perhaps it's only rumor that the maid found them, sitting in their balcony lounge chairs, already decaying and covered with flies.

I attended their funeral—closed coffins, of course, as befit their deplorable physical condition—and I gave the eulogy to a gathering of twenty empty pews. They were not known in this town, which likely suited them. The priest showed no emotion; it was simply a duty to be performed. He praised the irony in my speech, then remarked how much I resembled my parents.

The Dalmatian coast on the Adriatic Sea was certainly not what I would have expected as my parents' choice of destination. The town of Makarska, just south of Split and a hundred miles north of the more famous Dubrovnik, should have been a lovely choice for retirement: close to the sea. We are of Hungarian heritage, that is, from a land-locked nation, yet they craved the seashore. They had their life and I had mine. I never thought to question them since they continued shuffling money to me on special occasions.

As they wished, I took a few more days in that resort town, with the cedars and cozy beaches nestled between rocky hills, stretching far in each direction from my hotel balcony. After a long nap and the bottom half of a bottle of Merlot, I set out to enjoy myself the rest of the week. After all, I had gone to some trouble to take off from work on short notice and make the long trip from the States to Croatia. It had to mean something.

Once I was home again, I did what my parents eventually did. I removed all the mirrors from my home—except what was fixed to the wall in the bathroom of my apartment.

Mirrors are such odd devices, and whoever invented them should have been killed. They purport to show us the true state of affairs and yet everything is distorted. In the distortion is our faith. We believe what we see, what we want to see, and fool ourselves that it represents reality when, in fact, it is all pretense.

For me, especially. I stare and stare, day in and day out, and all I ever see is the mask I wear. (I do not intend to be morbid; I mean 'mask' as metaphor, not as a covering for the face such as one uses for Halloween celebrations.) Yet the face I see there is not me; it is a veneer that hides the truth. Granted, I am pleasant enough to gaze upon, as amorous friends have stated over the years. However, I know the truth, and so I search for it every day. What will be the first sign? Will it simply be a dry patch of skin? An odd blemish? A discoloration? With the close attention of a pimply teenager conducting surgery upon an inflamed pustule, I search for any sign that the time has come, for the ticking must surely have begun by now.

But I digress....

Indeed, I found my calling early on and have stuck with it. Something simple. Something I could do quite well with minimal supervision. Work my own hours, for the most part. I had no idea why I was drawn to phlebotomy, but working as a white-coat technician in a medical laboratory seemed to fit my quiet temperament. Once I completed my training and endured some probation under the tutelage of a string of demonic supervisors, I was able to choose my own schedule. I grabbed the graveyard shift. No pun intended.

Throughout my childhood I played various games with other children of the neighborhood. Day after day, the same. Our play was fueled by the daily afternoon movies on our televisions. We had that entertainment in common, all arriving home at the same time and tuning in. We knew and worshiped the chief deities of our horror-filled afternoons: Frankenstein, Wolfman, and Dracula. We knew their adventures well.

"It's Stefan's turn to be Frankenstein," a friend would call out. I didn't mind; tomorrow I would play a different monster. More often than not, given my lanky physique and dark hair, they assigned me the role of Dracula. It was all make-believe.

In my high school days, an English teacher demanded that I read the novel *Dracula* for class. I struggled through fifty pages before putting it aside. Later, I watched a film of the same story. My thoughts were uncomfortable. I could not understand how someone could live so long with so many biological flaws. It made no sense medically. The *undead*, some called him. He was dead yet not dead. Merely clever word play, I thought. In medical school, I became aware of the kind of animated effects a non-living organism could display. A brain-dead patient, one who had lost consciousness, sense of self, and independent agency yet whose body still functioned, could be said to be undead—yet hardly like this dapper Dracula, Prince of Transylvania, who slept in a dirt-filled coffin by day and ventured out by night in search of a sip of blood. Odd lifestyle. And medically impossible.

But I digress....

So there I was: a fully fledged adult with a credentialed job, a decent place to live, an automobile to transport myself between the two, and time enough on my hands. I was dutiful and took small pleasures where I could: in sports, drama, art, literature, nature, science and technology, and what could pass for love in a singularly physical sense. I was not a playboy but definitely a cad. There were no classes on this facet of humanity, so I was forced to learn by trial and error. Often.

However, it was only a few months after I moved half-way across the country to take a new job—from cold, cloudy upstate New York to hot, sunny Oklahoma—that I met Penny.

Yes, Penny Park, ace news reporter, who I call *my Beloved*. And she is the reason for everything I have done.

It happened like this: Oklahoma, middle of May. Tornado coming. A big one.

As a besotted old fool who had moved from the Northeast to take a job here, I found myself in the wrong place at the wrong time. Not much had changed for me with this move, apparently. I still lived alone, had a phone no one called, an email address no one used, and I did not know my neighbors—or anyone, for that matter, in this new city. I had a good job. But I had to get away from that city of my birth.

I hunkered down like everyone else when the sirens sounded. I didn't have much to worry about, not much the world would lose if the tornado singled me out for destruction. I watched the television reports, flipping wildly from one station to the next, examining radar maps, calculating my odds. I packed away my important papers and a few precious personal items, just in case.

Landing on one live video feed, I saw what at first seemed to be a little girl driving a big truck with the remnants of a barn flying past her. Not a little girl, of course, but a woman, hunched over yet driving with a competence I could never have predicted. She was being chased by the storm! She turned to the camera at that moment and described what she had experienced with the tornado coming so close. With her heart-shaped face, piercing brown eyes, pink lips, and a swath of coal-black hair, I was immediately in love.

Not really.

I know that sort of thing happens far too easily for me, so I quickly discounted my feelings.

Even so, I searched for her—purely out of curiosity—on that television station's website, innocently wondering who she was because I had never seen her reporting before. By her name, I guessed she was Korean. I searched all the popular social media. We can do that now, although it might be called stalking. When I was young, there was a fortified wall erected between celebrities, even local ones, and their viewing public. Other than special publicity events at the mall, we could never speak directly to them. Now, however, these online sites made it easy: you 'follow' someone or request a 'friend' link or send a message. No harm; just being a fan. A groupie. I got on that website that's all about faces. You know the one. I found her page, clicked 'follow', sent a 'friend' request and a cleverly-worded message in praise of her decorum during her dangerous mission.

Did I mention I survived that tornado? I did, but I was called in to help handle the supply for the blood bank. Poor survivors. Nine did not survive.

Late in the evening of the day that F5 monster swept away hundreds of houses just 15 miles south of me, I was online again to follow the latest reports. Curiosity. I hated to see the death toll increase, but there it was. Everyone was posting about their experiences with the storm, what damage they had, who had been lost, and what they would do next. Community. We needed to share our feelings.

And I noticed the red flag: I had a message.

It was *her*: she sent a reply.

She remarked on my typo with an LOL. So I wrote a reply.

Immediately she responded. Amazingly, she was online.

So I responded again and she responded again.

And I responded and she responded.

And this went on for more than an hour, messages passing between us every minute, a sentence or two at a time—as though we were having a real conversation, two strangers becoming less strange.

She appreciated my sense of humor in such difficult times and liked my recognition of her professional efforts reporting the storm, even though she was not actually on the weather team. Sense of humor? Me? I tell jokes to get people to relax as I draw their blood.

And our messaging continued late into the night.

The last messages we exchanged were to arrange a meeting the very next day at the Barnes & Noble bookstore between the station and my apartment. In the café area. Lattés would be my treat. Just a chat, nothing more. No obligations, no contract. Before the final smiley face, I dared type: *You can leave if I look scary.*

I had no realistic hope of anything, but I went anyway. I went early, browsed a bit, pulled a book and a magazine out and took them to the café, sat and pretended to read, even as I constantly spied on the door, looking up with each entrance or exit.

Time passed; I am perpetually early while the world is notoriously late. So I remained patient.

Then I decided, fifteen minutes after the appointed time, to have a go of the evening by myself. I rose to get my latté.

Two people stood in front of me.

With my back turned, I heard a voice call my name. I blinked, now next in line to order. Money in my hand, I was ready to pay.

I spun around and there she was: my favorite reporter, Penny Park!

Despite the late spring warmth, she was bundled in a red vinyl jacket, her black hair draped about her shoulders, the same face I'd seen on television now aimed at me, her eyes sparkling. She recognized me from my profile picture on that website.

Because I stood in line to get my coffee, she could have made a U-turn and exited but instead she came up to me. She said my name: "Stefan…?" with a perfect degree of inquisitiveness, the kind a child displays when he or she is anticipating a wonderful Christmas gift: Can it be real? Is this what I asked Santa for? And he actually brought it for me?

She continued, straight to my face: "Are you Stefan?"

"Penny!" I exclaimed. Of course I recognized her. I did not act surprised; I was elated.

My hand shot out and she started to take it, pausing to be sure my hand was ready to receive hers. Then her hand slid into the crux of mine. My hand hesitated releasing hers.

I asked what she would like to drink and settled the order, invited her to sit at my table: that one, over there in the corner.

She made a joke about us needing privacy.

I brought our lattés over to the table where she had taken off her coat and sat. In her black sweater, white blouse collar poking out through the V, she looked beautiful.

We proceeded to talk as though we had just finished our long online exchange only a few minutes earlier. Sipping our lattés, laughing at things mentioned in our messages, then dropping into serious mode to discuss the state of the city following the tornado. I wanted to take her hand then as it lay on the table top, but I dared not.

After an hour, the moment finally came. She checked her watch, suggested it was time to go. Not making any excuse, just offering the idea, announcing that we should say goodbye. It was not any kind of date; I knew that going in. But the way we talked left me desiring more. What more could there be? I would always be able to see her reporting on television. I had internet access, too. Plenty of ways for me to see her again.

"It's been nice," I said as we stood and went slowly among the little tables over to the doors.

She agreed.

I held open the door for us and we stepped outside.

"If you like, I could call you and text you and send emails and messages almost every hour," I said with a chuckle. "If you like."

She held up her cell phone, tapping it. No doubt she had missed a lot of messages while talking with me.

"Maybe not every hour," she said, fiddling with her phone.

"Of course. My bad." Yes, I said that slang expression, just to further invest her with my sense of humor.

"What's your number?" she asked—instead of checking her messages or getting ready to respond to a text or call from one of her many friends, colleagues, or family members.

"My number?" I asked, wary. Was I about to be reported for misbehavior?

"Sure," she said. "I'll text you."

And the number slid easily, digit by digit, from my mouth.

"Thanks," I called as she walked to her SUV, serendipitously parked next to my car. Same color, same brand. Good omen.

"See you!"

As I watched her drive away, a flash of memory struck me: a nondescript moment in our conversation when she apparently felt comfortable enough to reach across the table and flick a spot of coffee foam from my cheek. Just a quick swipe of her fingertip. She could have put my eye out if she had wanted to, but she had instead given me another omen: she had identified the spot on my face that would soon bear the first sign of my affliction.

2

Penny invited me to church. That was unexpected. We had not yet had the traditional dinner and a movie date. We had only been sending messages back and forth by text message, social media, or a rare email, but not much in the way of actual phone calls. She was more the texting type, but I wanted to hear her voice.

I met her at the designated church and immediately I had the willies, the heebee-jeevies, a dark premonition that my soul was about to be found wanting. My veins ran cold as I parked, again early, and stared at the building: the Korean Christian church. The sign was in English and Korean.

As the name suggested, the service was entirely in Korean.

"But you were born in America," I pointed out later.

She liked to go to church once in a while to clear her head of all the tragedies she reported on. When she found this Korean church shortly after moving here, she knew it would be the one. Her parents and grandparents had taught her Korean and she had spent a year and a couple of summers over in Korea working as an interpreter and translator. It was still part of her heritage.

"That's rather charming," I told her.

We sat in the middle, half way between front row and back, right where the minister could focus on us during the sermon—in Korean. Everything sounded to me as though I was full of sin. I kept sneaking glances over at my "date" and saw how her lovely dress stopped at her knees in a spring Easter parade kind of way. I was caught looking twice but only suffered a wary grin.

Evidently, I passed the test. I went to church with her, no questions asked, no complaints, no trying to grab her during the hymns, contributing to the offering plates. I put in five dollars. For that, our encounter went on.

We grabbed some take-out lunch, nothing fancy, and went to the park surrounding a huge lake I had seen on a map but had not yet visited since moving here months earlier. Lake Hefner. She seemed to know her way around the area; I followed in my car. We parked side by side at a shelter and ate our sandwiches there. We talked about life. And living. Almost a recap of the sermon. And we smiled.

I joked about the church, the partly cloudy Sunday afternoon, warm and humid, and our day jobs sneaking up behind us, just waiting for the crack of dawn to strike.

Instead of laughing, she got serious, talking about her move from Colorado where she had, as her career highlights, covered wildfires and a shooting at a movie theater. Oklahoma only had tornadoes to report on—the only bad thing, right?

"Well, honestly, I'm almost as new as you," I said. "But I'm sure there are a lot of good human-interest stories out there in the naked city."

She laughed at that. I wasn't trying to make a joke.

We walked around the lake, or a good portion of it, before doubling back. Our steady conversation continued and at one point our hands touched, clasped. I think we both realized things were moving too quickly and let go without a word.

Back at our cars, while saying goodbye, we hugged. It was so innocent, so puppy lovish. Perfect for that moment in time, that brief sliver of my life.

I only mention this because the way our relationship began was so different from my usual way. In the past, I would meet someone and we would be in the sack fairly quickly. You see, my parents blessed me with both handsomeness and a charming temperament. I was fit, on the thin side by nature, and physically active. I fenced in college, won awards with epée, being a lanky fellow. I could talk a good seduction, too. There was something about my eyes, ladies often remarked, a steel blue-gray that penetrated their souls. Whatever worked worked. They never lasted, but I got what I wanted, what I needed, and I presume so did they. A casual exercise in harsh reality. Some call it recreational dating. Others jokingly refer to it as the meat market. Don't they realize it's all about blood and fluid exchange and chemical reactions and so many psychological twists and social customs bent by biology? There is no free will.

Despite all of my clever posturing and indulgences, however, I never found the One. Never was quite sure I was looking for the One. The thought crossed my mind more often as I grew older. Somewhere in all of that business I had gone to see my parents off, to wish their souls some peace, never thinking anything was odd about their demise. Or my existence.

Was I wasting my time on this Earth? Was I getting too old to start this family thing everyone insisted was the norm? The usual track, the American dream? I had no answers.

So once more I sought to distract myself with brief, useless dalliances. Eventually, I reached a point where I wanted to get the hell away from everything so I accepted a new job far away. A fresh start, I told myself. Forget everything before; this would be like being born again.

And Penny Park became my midwife!

The next few weeks were a mad whirl of text messaging and social media connection. It was fun. Enough of that basic ritual and we could stay in touch without really having to engage each other in conversation. In that way, she would keep me updated on her whereabouts, what incident she was covering, whether or not her report would be on the broadcast at 6 or 10, and when she arrived home, always after midnight. At least our schedules seemed to fit, though hers was likely because of the crimes and crashes she reported on happening later.

It was summer and we met for dinner—mostly sushi, or a Korean restaurant with the fifty-five tiny bowls of different food items spread across the table, green tea in a pot, white rice in a communal bowl. When we decided to see a movie, I argued for the romantic film while she insisted on the zombie flick. Of course, she won; we know how dating works.

Other days, she would send me a text asking me to grab some food and meet her at a certain location because she had to stay there for a story and was hungry. I complied, and felt happy at being invited to assist her. She usually had specific requests so even if there were a restaurant *per se* nearby, that food would not be what she wanted. She also called me on occasion to bring something for her to eat to the station. As her personal delivery boy, I went right in, carrying a bag or box—the receptionist knew me by then—and upon handing over the goodies, I would receive a pat or a quick hand squeeze as though a deal had been made. Yes, I understood it was her workplace and we could not simply throw everything off the desk and make love right there—

Did I mention making out?

After that zombie movie and a late latté with dessert at the Barnes & Noble bookstore near the theater, we returned to her apartment and just went crazy. That made everything I did for her day in and day out completely worthwhile. That was also the first time I felt self-conscious about my body and my ability to do what had always been so easy for me. I didn't know whether I should have pressed for more or if that assertiveness would have ruined our relationship. Or, perhaps, my hesitancy would signal I was not really "into" her as much as she thought I was.

So I panicked. I went on a trip, just to clear my head. I drove north, initially to escape the heat of Oklahoma, but gradually I decided on a destination: Winnipeg, Manitoba, Canada. It was there. It was somewhere else. I drove and arrived. I bought some souvenirs, visited the lake, and drove back.

In the middle of my trip, one evening in my hotel room in Gimli, a village on the shore of Lake Winnipeg, Penny texted me. She wanted to set up our next date, asking when I was free. I had to text back that I was in Manitoba.

WTF??? was her reply.

I texted her that I would return in a few days. Then we could meet again, have some fun, start to get serious.

Serious was the operative word. I was serious. More serious than I had ever been in my life. I thought she was serious, too. There was definitely chemistry between us. We were building a whole laboratory together. We were so comfortable; we could kid around and we could be quietly contemplative. We had a wonderful sixth sense between us, although we were not yet finishing each other's sentences.

Yes, we belonged together.

Penny Park was my One. I was late, certainly, but I had finally found my One.

Nothing truly worth having ever comes easily, fortune cookies have suggested.

After I returned from Canada, we met and I was surprised by how excited she was to see me. We picked up where we left off, only now I had no qualms about showing her exactly how I felt. We believed in a slow relationship but now it turned quicker. We spent more time at her apartment, sneaking affectionate gestures while cooking together, very lovey-dovey, discussing life and all of its convoluted meanings as we watched DVDs, cuddling on her sofa, sensing the quickening of our blood flow as our lips merged—until we couldn't stand to hold back any longer.

"You really want to do it?" she asked one night. "Are we ready for *that*?"

I repressed a chuckle. Here we were, stretched out in bed, the sheet already hot and moist, having stripped ourselves piece by piece down to our undies. We had been embraced for an hour, caressing and kissing, and getting quite hot. Unbearably hot. We paused for a breath, and she glanced over at me.

"What do you mean?" was all I could muster.

She knew I wanted more. She had noticed my erection. I had been pressing up against her, so she knew where I was coming from, where I wanted to go. And yet, I could not push her, could not take command. I could not just take what my body wanted. That is how the soul works when it's infected with love.

I could only utter one syllable: "Oh."

Her face was a mask of neutrality.

"I think I'm ready," she said, perhaps not wanting to give full commitment to the idea. After all, who wants to own that kind of responsibility? Not me. And apparently not her.

Yet it had been so many weeks of *almost*, of walking gingerly along the edge while staring across the abyss to the heavenly garden on the opposite shore.

"You are giving your consent?"

"Yes," she said with heavy breath, then rolled against me.

So we did it. What the missionaries ordered of the savages. The best part was the way our eyes locked together through it all—except at the very end when we were forced to close our eyes during the final ecstasy. With that sensation I finally recognized what could only be classified as *passion*. Many have written about it, poems to its bliss, explanations, definitions, serious attempts to categorize and explicate the vagaries of such a strange, inhuman experience—yet we both knew without words what it was in that blink of exploding chemicals!

Much later, we greeted the dawn with smiles of joy.

"You know," she said, "you look very good this morning."

Of course, that was before my body started attacking me.

We sat at the breakfast table, and she caressed my shoulders each time she passed me as she prepared our meal. A kiss on the cheek when she served it. Furtive glances crossing the table between bites. Small talk about anything but what happened the previous evening. Afraid to mention it, afraid it wouldn't be real, that it would no longer be our secret.

"That was good," she suddenly said.

"Yes, delicious omelet," I responded. "You are a great chef."

"I meant the sex."

"The sex...?"

I watched her thinking, gathering her words. I waited, eager to hear them. Instead, she returned to the last bite of egg, took it into her mouth and chewed, swallowed, as a smirk played hide-and-seek in the corner of her mouth.

"I never experienced anything so...profound."

She was grinning.

"Uh...profound?" I asked.

"Not what I expected," she continued. "Just from what I know about you, I guess I expected something rough, maybe painful. But you made me feel comfortable. Like I knew you could never hurt me."

"Why would I want to hurt you?"

I was, of course, flashing back to those days when I did not care if I hurt anyone. That was safely in the past.

"I know you wouldn't. That's why I gave consent."

Smiling, I nodded like it was a ritual. "I'm happy you did."

She reached across the table and took my hand.

"I'm glad we waited."

I squeezed her hand. "Yes, slow is better."

"Slow *is* better."

To prove our theory, we decided to take the rest of the day to repeat the experiment, trying to make what was basically a ten minute exercise last as long as possible.

That was the last thing that was slow. In my bloodlust, I had to secure this One for all time. I had to be sure Penny would always be with me. I became worried that she would grow tired of me, of us, of everything we were doing, so I pushed us along at an ever-hurrying pace, along to what I now simply call the "ring" episode.

It is embarrassing, I must admit, in hindsight. I overreacted. Rather, I acted—I overacted.

Suppose there's this guy who is a little bit like me. He meets somebody by accident who is so completely wrong for him—or, more accurately, he is so completely wrong for her. Nevertheless, there is a click, a connection.

Let's say the two of them believe age difference isn't an issue, that no future need concern them. It's just for now. However, little by little, it happens. There are dinners, movies, walks, talks. The evenings run late, slip into sleepovers. Just friends hanging out, getting sleepy, and the sofa is right there. Then a mysterious thing happens: affection. There's a realization that it's no longer just having fun for now. What's the harm in making plans? If they like it, why panic and fear it will go away?

And so they stroll through the mall and pause at the jewelry store. Suddenly just having fun for now becomes *are you serious?* Playing along, pretending, dreaming. They play the game and believe in the dream. There is, indeed, one ring to rule them all. And that is magic in the first degree. Nothing can take back that moment, those feelings, when a future coalesces from the mist and becomes concrete.

But concrete is hard and inflexible and it's scary. Too many thoughts of falling and cracking a head open against the stone. Fear unfolds. Doubt forms. Everything adds up, overwhelms. It disturbs day and night, finally erupting in the classic medium of text message:

Sorry- I just can't do it

And winter arrives early, blows cold, freezes reality into a hoarfrost statue of Defeat personified.

So this fellow who was a little too much like me wonders what to do with a ring that has been sized for one particular finger in the universe. Save it for a rainy day? Go all Prince Charming-like in search of another finger to fit the ring? Or get on that phone and beg, beg, beg? No, that's not actually, umm, dignified, so don't. Wait. Could do that. Life goes up and down, everyone knows. This is down. Next comes up. The Earth still spins, the sun shines, the night comes and goes.

If u wanna meet at church I can buy u lunch after reads the text message early one Sunday morning after a sleepless night.

There is nothing quite like sitting on a hard pew next to the lady with the naked finger, listening to all those instructions, chiding one to keep it fun, that life is not intended to be hard, though hardship does come, will always come, to those who fear having fun just for now.

She's in a flower-patterned dress as fresh as springtime; he's in a suit, serious for once, as they walk around the lake. Warm sun, cool breeze, and somewhere along the shore, where the trees offer shade, there is a pause for explanation.

"Then let's go back to having fun for now," I said. "Like you suggested. I can do that."

21

My Beloved refused the ring, gave it back, broke my heart in a thousand different ways. All my fault, of course. I overacted—

Days later, I returned to that mall, to that jewelry store, with my Beloved, as though nothing disastrous had occurred. We are cordial, friendly though not exactly loving. No longer holding hands, no longer smiling, we are simply undertaking a task that is required of us yet one neither wishes. Returning a ring?

We stood before the counter once more, sales person smiling and bowing and waiting for his commission, while we make up our minds—as though minds could ever be rearranged into something that made sense. People do what they do; most acts are inexplicable, condemned to categories and classification or piles of evidence sitting in judgment and/or social media's 'like' or 'favorite' clicking quirks.

After we parted, I went to the mall's restroom and stared hard into the wide mirror, lit up like some kind of inquisition. I was haggard. Too many sleepless days. I could not concentrate on my work at night, either. I watched the TV news religiously, eagerly awaiting a report by Penny Park. It did not matter if it was a peeping tom or car chases or a bee infestation or a veteran coming home. I always focused on her eyes as she spoke into the camera.

Staring into that mirror, however, alone in that restroom at the mall, the miscellaneous sounds of shopping outside dulling my mind, the first thought to enter my mind was of ending all this pretense of life meaning something. What was the point of anything if nothing mattered? I do my job and people benefit, so I am a saint. My own life is nothing. Every day I go through the motions of being human, of caring, of believing, of expecting my situation to somehow get better. Someday I will reach a place of reward. Like my parents did? There had to be some purpose to all this madness, this relentless repetition of rituals and recited scripts—

A brownish spot on my cheek caught my attention. On the side of my face, at the edge of my sideburn, I had not noticed it previously. In the bright lights of that restroom, studying my face like so many floating cells in a petri dish, I saw it clearly.

I touched it with the tip of my index finger.

Either I was getting old, finally, enough to start showing my age, or all the worry Penny had caused me was now manifesting itself in physical symptoms. That could happen. Sure, my body had clocked over another thousand miles since we first went to the mall and I'd nudged her over to the jewelry counter.

She thought I was joking, because I was always joking. When the seriousness of my suggestion hit her, she became paler than me. Not what she was expecting, I knew. She had not entertained such thoughts. Yet she played along, allowing the salesperson to show us a collection and, at my insistence, choosing one set of matching engagement ring and wedding ring.

"Are you serious?" she had asked eleven times while we stood at the counter.

I responded in the affirmative for the first five questions, then nodded to the others.

Mirrors do not lie. I stared at this person, a perfect double, a mannequin of someone who is a fool. At *me*.

And that spot—the discoloration, the dry texture, a simple skin blemish. It was the mark of Cain to me. Was this what she saw? Did I now have a sign of age that made the situation clear? There could never be any permanent union for us. That was her decision. It was all for now, for fun, just for fun, just for now. Nothing more.

There is no future for you, man with the spot on your face!

Accept it.

3

It's raining. The most profound metaphor of literary existence. It's worse if it's happening to you in real time. November rain is the best. By best I mean worst. My sarcasm increases in autumn.

I was not sitting and waiting, not observing faux people at the mall, as before. What else is there to do late on a rainy Saturday afternoon? I was free to go, after all. The papers were signed and the nurses thanked.

Someone found me passed out in the lab, down on the floor, and called an ambulance. No, it was not suicide. Not then. I did not remember much. I felt light-headed. I was holding a vial of blood in my hand, raising it to the light to read the label, and the room began to spin. I grabbed the counter but not tight enough, so I fell and the vial broke, spilling blood across the tiled floor.

I chalked it up to stress. I was not sleeping, not eating right. My blood was not iron-rich enough to sustain me. I had simply fainted. Happens to lots of people.

However, that got me a couple nights in a hospital, checking me out, getting me back to proper condition for a person of my age and disposition. Yes, I gave blood, and they were sent off to the same lab where I work. I felt the irony from my bed. As I came to the hospital without a bag of supplies, I had nothing to do but stare at the ceiling and brood. I realized I am a champion brooder. Nobody can out-brood me! Set up a contest and I will win easily. Put your money on me.

I know only one person in this city of 600,000 people—not counting my coworkers, and they wouldn't do me any favors but call 911 if my comfy graveyard shift could be stolen from me. That one person was Penny Park, my Beloved, the love of my life, she who refused my ring, rejected my love, took my heart and squeezed out every drop of my essence. That likely was why I was found to be low on blood; I got a transfusion. Penny was the only one I could call for a ride home from the hospital.

Sure, it was afternoon, working time for her, gathering news stories like groceries before a family feast, but I dared to call her. Not send a text but call. No answer; voicemail. So I left a message that I had been in the hospital and needed a ride home. I was certain that, despite our tiff, she was a compassionate person who would help this broken down piece of man.

I waited for a ride and after one hour and twenty-five minutes decided I could walk the three miles home. It was a straight line. The exercise would do me good.

So I left the hospital and walked home. The rain started half way, light but steady. I didn't have any bag, no suitcase to drag, just the clothes I'd been wearing a few days before. They dressed me in a gown while I was their guest.

What had I done wrong this time? Wasn't it obvious? I simply tried too hard.

It seems ironic, of course—irony being my middle name: yes, I'm Stefan I. Székely officially—because I always believed I had been a good person. You know: a kindly nature, a live and let live personality, spiritual but not dogmatic, friendly, happy-go-lucky, imaginative, romantic, always looking at the bright side of things even as I expect the worst. Not even interested in zombie movies or vampire TV shows. Only the monster games of my youth to corrupt my soul. Never dwelled in dens of iniquity. Never had the vices of smoking and drinking. And for the past many years did not really indulge in the poor quality diets that many of my fellow citizens did. I like veggies—even broccoli, even Brussels sprouts and beets. And *oh my god* do I chug the paprika! I turned to my genes, family history, and serendipity—all less than ideal. So was it stress? Something I ate? My mood?

I thought back to the first time I stayed in a hospital. It had seemed quite serious at the time. I was a boy and a neighbor's dog bit my leg. Not wanting any harm to come to the dog, I kept quiet. I had been teasing the dog, after all. The spot of the bite turned yellow and purple, and was eventually discovered by my aunt. She took me to a doctor. I was hospitalized and tested for rabies. I did not have it. The strange thing was that the dog died a few days after biting me. It was as though I was the one with rabies. Apparently my blood was toxic to the dog. I was advised by Mother not to donate blood. Only much later did she reveal that it was a sign she had dreaded: that I was part of the family legacy, despite her prayers.

This time, being older and losing consciousness, the episode was more frightening. I did not fear death, only the entertaining things I would miss by being dead. My mother's words returned to me: I might still be able to enjoy my entertainments even after death. A religious declaration? I thought she was joking, saying whatever might get me out of my boyhood funk.

I was not sure it was good to be home, but it did signal my ability to walk three miles, half of it in the rain. I hate to say it, but the only person I really knew here, the woman with whom I had shared my soul, did not pick me up, did not give me a ride home from the hospital.

Later I learned she was down in Norman that day, following a story, that college town a good hour south from the hospital. By the time she noticed the message I had already waited an hour. She believed I would call someone else. She did not remember that, to me, she is the One—my only One.

Perhaps it is enough for me to simply say we made up. After all, many people have similar experiences so I do not need to go into detail. The only difference might be the imposition of certain rules for us to follow. Indeed, for *me* to follow. I agreed to them straightaway.

First was that I should not push my Beloved again toward any kind of marriage. No signs, no symbols, no talking of such an arrangement. Fine, I thought. It didn't matter very much. As long as we could be together, what did a piece of paper matter? The truth was that she was devoted to her career and had never given any thought to finding some guy to marry, much less go through all the silly rituals required of a marrying couple. She was not a bride kind of woman. She was complete already.

The second rule was that I must accept our time apart during the week. We each had jobs to do. Hers was a 24 hour on-call kind of work. She needed to be free to answer the call, whether it was to report a crash, a crime, or something else awful. Between ambulance chases, she would be creating her projects: human-interest stories. (I suggested she interview a phlebotomist.) We would be together only on weekends—unless it was her turn to anchor the early morning broadcast. Getting up and ready for a 6 a.m. show would require a good sleep—that is, solo sleeping, no partner to snuggle up with or kiss goodnight.

The third rule, if we were to continue our bedroom activities, was that I would henceforth always employ a condom whenever we desired to make some of that love together. After my hospital stay, I had to agree. I did not let on about my condition; it was not anything contagious, not a sexually transmitted infection. It was genetic. And it might not even manifest itself in my life. My parents' genes had cancelled each other out.

For my Beloved, however, the main reason was her insistence on not having children. Career again. Nothing against children, no hatred of babies. Motherhood was simply not her calling, she explained. Her parents wanted grandchildren, sure, so she was under pressure to meet someone and get married, start a family. When she had resisted to the limits of politeness, she demanded that they accept her choice not to have children in favor of a career in broadcast journalism.

That fit my plans, too. At forty-five, I was well past chasing children around a backyard.

So we were together again—just as Fate would have it. And Fate sent Penny away for the winter holidays, back to her family in Colorado. Too late for me to accompany her—too late to purchase tickets and get on the plane, sit next to her and smooch the whole way. No, it was not to be.

You see, the final rule, number four, was that I could not, should not ever meet her parents. I wondered how that would work. They would see me eventually. They'd have to. If we ever do get married...?

"Not a chance," Penny reminded me.

"How about if they visit you?"

"You got your own place, right?"

"Well, yes. But I thought we were going to move in together."

"You are working quick, aren't you?"

"Sorry. It's just that—"

"We're back together again—with rules—and you're breaking the first rule already. No marriage talk. And no pushing for more than whatever happens."

I bowed my head. "Sorry."

Her father was in real estate and quite successful. He also was very insistent that his daughter meet and marry a man of Korean heritage. That included such a fellow being closer in age to his daughter than I was. He was the stern parent. Tae Kwon Do champion, too.

Her mother was the opposite: friendly, outgoing, tolerant, and often scatter-brained (Penny's words, not mine). Penny said her mother would like me, except for the fact that I had slept with her daughter. Or maybe she would take that as a good sign. Penny laughed when telling me how her mother had begun to suspect her daughter was a lesbian.

"I hung out only with other girls," said Penny.

"That doesn't mean you're a lesbian. It just means you have friends. Unlike me, poor me."

"And I didn't date any guys. Except for whoever my Dad set me up with. Boys—little boys, not men. They couldn't deal with me. I didn't make it easy for them so they didn't like me. Not sexy—you know, boobs? And not submissive enough. Not girly enough for them."

"I like you just the way you are."

"Hah. You have to say that."

"No, I mean it."

"Ah, you're so baby-brother sweet."

"You didn't have to say *that*."

All right. I relented. I wasn't marrying the parents.

Glad to be back together, I could sit out a couple weeks. I had work to do. Lots of accidents happen during the holidays. People in car crashes, domestic disputes, shopping crimes, gift thievery, whatever. Blood would be needed.

I took her to the airport and swore I'd be there to pick her up when she returned, saving her the cost of parking.

We stood on the curb and I dared kiss her. I caught her by surprise and she shifted awkwardly into my arms. Her hands went to my face, held my head in place as she took the initiative and drove forward, then rubbed her hands on my cheeks.

"You need some lotion," she said, parting from me. "All this cold, dry air."

I wasn't sure what she meant. She explained that my cheeks were rough. My skin was dry, felt scratchy against her hands, like the wind had dried it.

"Got to stay hydrated, especially in winter," she said as she grabbed her carry-on and wheeled it away.

I followed with her larger suitcase, brought it up alongside her in line at the check-in counter.

"I'll take care of it, don't worry."

"Good," she said, grinning. "I want to kiss those cheeks some more when I get back."

"They'll be soft as a baby's bottom."

"Remember, no baby talk."

"It's just an expression."

She laughed.

One more kiss at the security checkpoint, then into the line for her. I waited.

The line moved slowly. I checked my watch. I glanced at Penney, also checking her watch.

I stepped over and gave her a sip from the water bottle I'd purchased—she insisted on staying hydrated, right? She took a few swallows, thanked me.

"You can go now," she said with a little edge to her voice.

"I have to see you go through. It's the rule. One of the rules."

"I won't go through if you're standing there watching me."

"Please let me stay."

"Go home, Buddy Bear."

I pouted. Reluctantly, I turned and stepped away. From a safe distance I spun around, fixing my eyes on Penny as she advanced in the line.

There she was, watching me watching her. Her hand gave a quick wave, ushering me away.

I left when she arrived at the checkpoint and handed over her passport. Then she went out of view.

Be good BB came her text message a few minutes later. The BB meant Buddy Bear. I smiled.

You too PP

We r good 2gethr

I <3 U

U2! And a moment later: Not the band.

A brisk wind was doing its best to hold me back as I crossed the parking lot. My cheeks felt like they were burning. So raw, like a few layers of skin had been seared off. My hand went to my cheek and felt it: rough, dry, scaly.

In my car, I reached in the glove compartment and retrieved the small tube of lotion left from the previous time Penny had remarked on rough skin. I applied the lotion liberally, from my hairline to my chin and from ear to ear.

I studied myself in the rear view mirror: a gooey, goopy goblin stared back at me. That monster seemed to be suffering from some dreaded disease. His skin was in globs, melting off his face. Horrible!

Suddenly the future seemed to flash before my eyes. Just a flicker. A flit. A wave of nausea passed through me and I had to pull over and wait it out.

4

The lotion worked. Penny thought I looked good when she saw me at the baggage claim and ran up to me like a smitten school girl greeting her rock star. We hugged tightly like we had really, truly missed each other. Her hands on my cheeks did not elicit any complaint.

Driving home, we stopped at the Barnes & Noble bookstore and she explained the gifts she had for me: Korean delicacies, specialty beverages, and a gift from her mother intended for "that boy you're seeing but you won't tell me about even though I can see it on your face when I ask you what's going on down there in Oklahoma"—that boy she finally gave a name to: Stefan.

"Stefan? What kind of name is that? You mean Stephen?" her mother had asked.

"No, his name is Stefan," Penny had replied. "His family's from somewhere over in eastern Europe."

I laughed at her recounting of the episode.

"Yes, somewhere," I confirmed.

Penny continued: "So he's a foreigner?" her mother asked.

"No more than we are."

"Your father and me were born here. You, too. We are all American."

"He's American, too."

"What's his eastern European name then?"

"His name is Stefan Székely."

"Zay-kelly? What is that?"

"I dunno, maybe Romanian. He doesn't talk about that sort of thing. He's American."

"Does he speak with a sexy accent?"

"No, Mom. He speaks good old American English, like you and me."

"Maybe he's from Transylvania," said her mother with a quick laugh. "There's a vampire named Stefan on that TV show, you know. He's so handsome. They're all so sexy, those vampire men. Lots of sex on that show, too."

"Mother!" Penny had snapped.

"You and your boyfriend...you two have sex yet?"

Again she had snapped at her mother.

"What did you tell her?" I asked.

"I told her once or twice."

"Well, which is it? Once or twice?"

"Once or twice a weekend."

"I bet that shocked her."

"Yep. Almost had to call an ambulance."

I grinned, set down my latté, leaning back. "She sounds like a real hoot. I like her."

"Then you marry her." Penny sipped her latté, apparently pondering that possibility. "So now she knows about you. It's only a matter of time before my dad will know, too. He'll want to meet you and he will reject you."

"Why? I'm a nice guy."

"You're a white guy. And you're almost his age."

"Two strikes...."

She told me how her parents were separated, how her mother was ready to start dating. Father had concentrated on building up his business. Mother took care of the house and raised the daughter and son. Eventually they both realized they were bored with each other. The break was amiable and her mother was well cared for financially but free to engage in a career of her own: catering. She was quite the cook, according to Penny. And, lucky us, she would be visiting soon. However, it would be best, she informed me, if I bowed out and not expect to be introduced to her mother. Life would be simpler that way.

"You want to hide me?"

"If you don't mind. It's just a week or two."

"Like I'm your secret lover?"

"Yes, like that. Secret lover."

"I visit you only at midnight, then make exquisite love to you by moonlight, like a...."

I hadn't planned to go there but I had taken a dangerous step in that direction already, heading down that path. I almost bit my tongue, wishing I could take it back. Nothing could make me say that word.

"Like what?"

"Like one of those people...those kind of people...who make love at night...in the dark...secretly."

Penny laughed like a chorus of fairies. "You're so funny!"

Until that particular Saturday, I had always been rather nervous shopping at the Target store near where I lived. That store was filled with soccer moms, most of them dressed in their workout attire, sport tops and stretchy yoga pants, fresh from one of the three fitness centers within a mile of the store. Some of them had children in tow, or pushed baby carriages. It was a store full of life.

On this early evening, however, I went with Penny to gather groceries for dinner. We planned to stay in and cook together. She had something in mind but wouldn't reveal it to me, so I was content to follow her down the aisles. I thought of something I needed to get and told her I'd be back.

Half-way across the store, passing the shoe section, a child darted out into the aisle right in front of me, out from between the stacks of shelves. Not only had I stopped suddenly to keep from crashing into the child, who seemed about eight, but I stopped because of the child's appearance.

At first I wasn't sure if the child was a boy or a girl, dressed in t-shirt, jacket, jeans and sneakers. The child's blond, curly hair was long enough for a girl but not too long for a boy. The child seemed frightened, then, realizing I posed no danger, relaxed and displayed a grin which showed the child's teeth: rough, uneven biting tools, gnarled yet sharp. Fangs would be a better description. And the child's face, besides being ghostly white, was tight, pulling back against the skull beneath. That made the eyes bulge, the cheeks flat, the nose withered down to cartilage. Seeing my startled reaction, the child tried to cry—that is, let out crying sounds but no tears came.

The mother appeared and calmed him/her, alternately giving me a dismissive glare. How dare I frighten her child! What right did I have to be in that store on that evening and come rushing down the aisle, nearly crashing into this sweet, innocent child?

"Sorry," I muttered, not knowing what else to do.

Returning to Penny's grocery cart, unable to remember what I was looking for, I told her about the encounter with the child, the hideous child.

"That's not very polite," she scolded.

"It's true. I'm not being rude. The child was ugly—in a poor unfortunate way, like he or she had a disease."

"That makes it more awful."

"I know, I know."

"You're in the medical field. Aren't you supposed to be compassionate?"

"I was surprised, that's all."

We were nearly finished filling the cart when the lights flickered.

"Here we go again," said Penny.

While I was on the other side of the store, the lights in the meat cases had flickered and gone off, she said. They put up signs saying not to buy anything from those cases because they could not guarantee the freshness. The power had been going off all day.

When the lights flickered again, I panicked. I did not want to be stuck in a dark store with that devil child running about.

Then the lights went out completely.

Penny grabbed me and I held her in my arms. Within a minute emergency back-up generators brought the lights back on but at only half the usual brightness. She pulled away, like it had been a mistake to show her fear of the dark.

"I don't mind holding you," I said.

The lines at the checkout were long, had been long since we entered the store to start shopping. Now that the meat cases had lost power, the meat going bad, the cash registers could not take credit cards, either. More than an hour in the store filling a cart with food that may have turned bad. What a waste!

So we parked the full cart of food in a narrow, out of the way aisle in the automotive section and walked out.

A few minutes later and we were again dining at our usual place: Sushi Neko. They knew us and served us our favorite fare. It was pleasant but becoming routine.

After dinner we returned to her apartment and watched a DVD, a romantic comedy, and when it became predictable, we began making out. Before it ended, we were in bed doing things she would never tell her mother about.

CR

I could not get that child's face out of my mind, however. After Penny and I made love, I lay there thinking, trying not to picture that child in my mind. I wondered what disease could cause such disfigurement. I wanted to jump up and grab one of my medical books but they were all back at my little apartment, a place too small and too unkempt for a good date night. Besides eating and sleeping, I was hardly there. But I could not stand it and got up and went to the bathroom.

Not wanting to awaken Penny, I kept the light off. But when I looked into the mirror and saw only my dark hulking self framed there, I startled.

Frozen before the dark mirror, I felt a presence behind me, then hands on my hips.

The lights flicked on and I instinctively closed my eyes.

"What're you doing?" asked Penny, hugging me from behind.

I opened my eyes and stared ahead at the naked figures of me and my Beloved. She moved from behind me, both of us naked in front of the lighted mirror. It held a grim fascination for us, we both seemed to realize at that moment. Our bodies, flaws and all, were presented so plainly there in the frosted glass.

"Look at me," she said. "Too skinny. And I got tiny tits and no curves." Her arm relaxed around my waist, then fell to her side. "I'm a boy—a boy with a vagina. You know?"

"And it's such a lovely vagina."

"Come on, Stefan. Why do you even sleep with me?"

"Well, you're very sleepable."

"Sleepable? No, why?"

"Because I love you?"

"Forget for once you have to say that. What is it about me that obsesses you so much?"

"I like the whole package. The body, the face, the mind, all of that stuff inside you that makes you who you are. It's really a potpourri—a mélange of flavors, textures, scents, and so many tactile pleasures."

"It's got to be more than fucking—excuse me, making love."

"Yes, I prefer making love."

"Me, too. So come back to bed. I'm already awake. We might as well do something."

"Yes, might as well do something."

She glanced at me, the mirror image of me, speaking to that two-dimensional person. "You're upset about something. Was it something I said?"

"No, Penny."

"Then what's the matter?" Her arms encircled my waist.

"Oh, I'm still thinking about that kid at the Target store."

"Forget it. Just a casual mistake. You apologized for bumping into her, so forget it."

"No, that's not it. I never bumped into the kid. The mother thought I did, maybe, but I didn't. The kid started to cry, seeing my reaction to seeing that ugly child."

"How ugly?"

I shook my head, unwilling to entertain further thoughts. But she pushed me. So I described the child in horrific detail. Penny was shocked.

"Geez, what could be wrong?"

"Some terrible disease. Obviously."

"And the mother took her out in public? That's kinda cruel. Expose the child to...to your kind of reaction."

"I would've not looked but she was right there in front of me."

"All right, all right. Now can we forget it?"

I had to smile, loving the way she always makes things better. Probably part of her reporter training. How much awfulness can a person report on without it affecting the reporter? So she visits church once in a while. And she has a boyfriend who sleeps over on weekends. A little playfulness, a little sex, a little cuddling and comfort. Then back to the realities of life.

Her hand slid slowly up my bare back, pausing a few times to run her fingernails against my skin.

"What's that?" she asked. Her fingernails stopped.

"What's what?"

She turned me to the mirror. Reddish-brown patches marked my back, just dark enough to notice them against my otherwise fair skin. The patches were dry, scaly, and after she ran her nails over them they felt itchy. I tried to scratch but could not reach the worst one.

"Do you mind?" I asked, then begged. "Please?"

"I really don't like digging my nails into your scales."

"I'm sorry."

"You need to hydrate more. You never drink enough water."

"I drink enough. I'm always running to the bathroom to pee."

"Then maybe it's something else. A skin disease of some kind. Psoriasis? In which case, I don't want to be scratching it."

"Could be eczema."

She went to the basin, ran hot water and soaped her hands.

"I don't know what it is. I thought it would go away."

"Maybe you should get that checked out."

"I will. I definitely will."

"And maybe we shouldn't, you know, make love any more tonight. Not until you know what it is and get it treated. Besides, I think that was the last condom. Put that on the shopping list."

My mouth fell agape. Being dismissed as easily as adding an item to a shopping list.

"What?" she asked, seeing my shock.

She dried her hands on the towel and faced me. She didn't seem angry or disgusted, just being practical. As always.

"Can I still sleep with you?" I asked.

"Sure." She stepped out of the bathroom. "Then again.... Can you wear a shirt? So any loose scales won't get on the sheets?"

"If you like." I stepped into the shower—since I was already naked. "Let me get a shower to wash away all your scratchings." I turned on the water. "And thanks for caring about me."

She didn't seem to hear me over the water noise.

"Thanks for caring about me," I repeated after the shower, towel wrapped around my hips, coming into the bedroom.

I found a t-shirt in the one dresser drawer she let me use, my weekend drawer, and pulled the shirt on. I added a fresh pair of boxers from the same drawer and slipped into bed beside her.

"I do care about you," she whispered.

"Thanks," I said, trying to sound positive. "We can't let a dry patch of skin get between us, now can we?"

It felt strange to be sitting in the waiting room as the patient this time. I glanced around at the cohort of flawed humans. I could identify some of their afflictions by sight, others not. I wondered if anyone wondered what caused me to show up at this clinic this morning. Was my flaw so obvious? Could anyone detect it on my face?

"So...what brings you here this morning?" asked the perky physician's assistant, blond and leggy.

"A dry patch of skin," I said glumly.

She turned from her clipboard and regarded me. She stared right at my face, though not into my eyes. Apparently searching for that spot without me even suggesting it was on my face.

"I see," she said without seeing it.

So I showed her. I stood and pulled off my knit shirt over my head and posed for her. She remained seated on that round stool and, with latex gloves on, poked at the patches I pointed out to her. Chest, mostly. Some on my upper back. No apparent pattern to any of it. From nickel to half-dollar size, squarish or diamond-shaped, jagged-edge borders. The healthy skin ran right into the slightly browner patch of dry, rough skin, which flaked and fell if scratched.

She agreed such a patchwork would not be caused merely by winter wind, dry air, or a lack of hydration. I could win that bet with my Beloved.

"No, it doesn't hurt," I responded. "But it does itch from time to time, especially if it gets scratched. Then I have to scratch it more and that causes more itchy feeling."

She thought it was simply a skin disease, a rash like a child might experience, such as poison ivy—though she could not speculate how it would present in such an irregular fashion. The right topical ointment and a protocol of pills would do the trick.

Off I went to the Walgreens on the corner near my apartment to fill my prescriptions.

Back in my own abode, away from the luxury of my Beloved's apartment, I applied the ointment to spots I could reach. I got creative and dabbed some on the end of a bamboo backscratcher device, then applied the backscratcher to all of the hard to reach patches. I stood stiffly before the bathroom mirror and applied the ointment to my face. And neck. There was a small patch starting on my shoulder. Another on my upper arm.

Geez, I'm falling apart. I moaned.

Standing naked in the bathroom, I waited for the ointment to be absorbed, resisting the urge to scratch myself in a dozen different places. I just hoped that my Beloved had not picked up my problem, what with us sleeping in the same bed, rubbing against the same sheets, even making love, or trying to, without the distraction of worrying about my dry, rough skin.

Fifteen minutes later I carefully wrapped myself in a bathrobe and put myself to bed. I'm a night shift person, after all. I had stayed up after work to visit the clinic first thing in the morning so it was way past my bedtime. I fell asleep quickly, awoke twice to adjust the curtains against the spring sunshine, and later turned on the fan to create some white noise to shield me from the lawn care crew working outside.

Getting up for work again, I pulled off the robe and did not notice much improvement. By the end of the week, repeating the ointment process on schedule and taking the pills, it seemed that most of the brownish patches had softened and faded back into my natural color. I could still find them on my body and they still itched somewhat, but I decided the problem had improved.

I thought I was on my way back to optimal health.

5

I could guess what was happening. He appeared slightly younger than me, husky and tanned, rugged like he worked construction, but for this evening he dressed in a pressed t-shirt, hanging his sunglasses from the V-neck. His blonde hair had been tussled by the wind. The woman who was his guest dressed in baby blue sweater and tan slacks, heels for her office job, I surmised, and her dark hair was clipped back into a ponytail. From behind, she appeared young yet when I got up to toss my latté cup in the trash, her face appeared the same age as her gentleman friend's.

"You know what they're doing?" I asked Penny. She did not know, so I told her. "They're on their first date. Probably they met online, struck up a conversation that led them to trust each other enough that one of them suggested they meet. Of course, they would meet in a public place such as the café section of this bookstore." I grinned at Penny.

"That sounds familiar," she said.

I glanced askance at the couple. I could hear them clearly. In turn, each was answering questions posed by the other, telling the details of life histories that extended decades, focusing on a few minor incidents which they believed would show themselves in a good light, make themselves seem a bit more human.

"So what are you saying?" asked Penny. "Is there something wrong with that?"

I stared at her cell, set on the tiny table, poised as if she were expecting to receive or make a call or text message in the next few seconds. I sighed, as immaturely as possible.

"Nothing wrong, nothing at all. I only thought to find some disdainful amusement from the serendipitous coincidence."

"Using big words again," she said. "You know, you have to stop that." She looked up. "I know your secret: you use big words, trying to sound like some professor, whenever you get upset."

"Or whenever the 'big word' is the most *judicious* word."

"There you go again," she said, and returned her gaze to her magazine. "And no more air quotes, please."

I smiled, nodding, because that is what I do.

We had been shopping earlier, which was sheer terror for me. I stood dutifully beside my Beloved as she flipped through racks of blouses, dresses, and slacks. Career women, right? Need to look businessy. I would never have missed the opportunity to spend an afternoon with her—now that my skin problem had been resolved. And yet, there I was: standing.

And standing.

Standing here, standing there, standing over there.

Sometimes pretending to sit with my back pressed against the wall outside the fitting room.

"So what do you think of this?" she would ask each time she came out. I gave my honest opinion; she had good taste.

Yes, dear, you look marvelous, simply marvelous.

Of course, my Beloved, it flatters your figure to no end.

No, how could that make your butt look bigger? You have the smallest butt I've ever seen.

For my patience, I was rewarded with a trip to the swimsuit department. Certainly I could withstand a bit of waiting there. Suits were selected. I recommended the small pink one, the two-piece. No, not my choice; hers alone. I queried her upon exiting the fitting room: she had selected a one-piece in blue. I would be allowed to see it once we were on the beach for our summer getaway. I cringed a little, unable to conjure enthusiasm for a day at the beach. I am sensitive to the sun and really would prefer an indoor pool.

So, having finished the shopping, my Beloved offered me the chance to peruse the books for something new. For her, an iced coffee, what is called a Frappuccino, would be the lure.

"Thank you for coming with me," she said.

"My pleasure."

At that delightfully fragrant moment, a genuine smile spread upon my face, a register of pleasures compounded by the hours we had spent together.

"Are you finished?" I asked in a cheerful tone.

The final slurp of her drink was an echo. She nearly laughed, seemed to want to repress it but I insisted she let it go, and it went bouncing about the café like a rubber ball filled with fairy dust, bouncing against each and every table and returning to ours with such a delicate spring that I had to laugh as well. My laugh, however, did not spring; no, it went *thud* against the wooden floor, like an unwarmed day-old muffin, and rolled among the feet of that dating couple sitting beside us, much to their chagrin.

"Ready to go?" I asked Penny.

"I guess so." Such a delight, she is. "Your place or mine?"

"Oh, your place. Definitely your place. That's the only place where I feel at home."

"But you can't move in 'til next month. After my mom visits."

"Can't have Mother Dearest see you with an older man."

"You're not old." She had to put her mind to the math. "Not *that* old."

My Beloved was scheduled to anchor the weekend morning news broadcasts, her Holy Grail. Her turn came up every four or five weeks. That rare honor required her to be at the station at 4 a.m. for an opening at 6 a.m.—which further required her to go to sleep much earlier than I could have managed.

Her weekend broadcasts also coincided with the arrival of her mother for a two-week visit. I remained on lock-down, limited to text messages to keep in touch. Although I offered to help in any way I could, her advice was simply to stay out of the way. I took it in a light-hearted manner. I knew how parents could be.

Then I let slip that my parents had died a year before.

I had not meant to say anything provocative by that remark. It was not that I wanted her to feel guilty for still having parents alive and well. It was not that I was trying to push my way into her family, like an adopted son. No, it was a pure slip of the tongue. She mentioned parents and my mind locked onto that word and out came my remark.

"I'm sorry for that," she responded.

"Be happy you have your parents," I said, mostly to recover from my faux pas.

"You're right. I love her, but she can be a pain in the ass."

"She sounds wonderful."

The night before Mother Park arrived, I met my Beloved for dinner. We kissed goodnight but I did not sleep over. I removed my meager sleepover belongings from her apartment, lest they be discovered by a snooping mother.

I was not too disappointed to be left out. Besides, some skin discoloration was returning. I refilled my prescriptions. Perhaps I was not yet ready to be put on display.

Contrary to her original declaration, I was eventually invited to join them for dinner out one evening. Her mother insisted. I held up my end of the conversation. My Beloved was glowing, smiling at everything I said, and it was clear her mother noticed.

Another evening, I was invited for dinner at her apartment. It was Korean food, courtesy of Mother Park. It was quite delicious. Penny was correct: her mother was a fabulous cook. Previously, I had only sampled Korean food in a restaurant but Mother Park's cooking was much better. I told her so. She blushed and waved off my compliments. Not only was my assessment true, but I had won a whole bunch of points—which would translate later into a wealth of favors from my Beloved.

Mother Park inquired about my ancestry, amused that my name was, for her, unpronounceable. She alluded to the *Twilight* books, suggesting I looked like that Edward Cullen character but with different hair—better hair. She went on and on about that series, practically telling me the whole story, as we consumed our dinner. Penny tried to intervene.

"He doesn't want to hear about that vampire stuff," she said, flashing me an expression of sympathy.

"I'm only saying there's a resemblance," said Mother Park.

"There is no resemblance," Penny countered.

"If not that Edward then his father, the doctor, Mister Cullen. Since your boyfriend is older, he could pass for Mister Cullen. He's a very handsome man—I mean, vampire. They're all popular now."

"No, it's zombies that are popular now. Not vampires. That trend has passed."

When they paused to take a breath, I spoke up:

"I think both of them merely play to humanity's fear of the unknown, especially that age-old concept of the abnormal couched within the normal. That is, a real, biologically viable man who is yet again not a man but something undead. It's the same with zombies: they're normal for the most part yet they're infected with some fatal flaw that renders what once was a perfectly normal, lovable family member into an unexpected, unthinking evil. That's what scares people. That something normal can so easily be transformed into something abnormal. It's got nothing to do with some disease or a weird appearance that someone might have. It's the visceral fear of transformation into something hideous—and with no cure—that forces us to irrevocably face our mortality."

They stared at me and we could hear the crickets all the way over in Korea warming up for the night's chorus.

"He reads a lot," said Penny.

Mother Park seemed amused, decided to change the subject to...cooking.

That kind of drama was not what I intended to riff on. Like most people in America, I knew about the *Twilight* series, and I respected the author for coming up with a suitable story for such a successful marketing juggernaut for teen girls. If that was her plan. Who wouldn't have fallen in love with a brooding, pale, square-jawed, sparkly-skinned undead fellow? I could see the attraction. In the film version, I appreciated the gloomy locale of Washington state, the moody disposition of the heroine, Bella, and her obsessed vampire protector, Edward. I knew it was all a set-up. If two such people were actually put in a room together in real life, what would they discuss? Would they get along? Would they share their blood? Too many questions to answer in a single evening, though Mother Park had plenty. She seemed to be a fan of the series, and was pulling quotes from the books as quickly as Penny could say something negative about them.

However, I knew about Dracula, the character in the novel of the same name and in the countless film and television versions: serious, comedic, farcical, or ultra-violent. None of those fellows were sparkly, none of them so lovable. They were hunters, always seeking their next meal. Desperate to die and rid themselves of their pain, yet unable to die. The undead. They were perfectly suited for paralyzing their prey with a glance, with seductive words. Then came the bite to the throat.

Now the idea is to have "the lion fall in love with the lamb"—the famous quote from both book and film—but that seemed quite obvious to me: Why shouldn't a lion fall in love with a lamb? Weren't lambs tasty? The fact that he never did "eat" his girlfriend was illogical. Did he starve? No, he and his surrogate family apparently hunted deer, which were not as delicious but allowed them the moral high ground compared to other undead.

I tried to ignore Mother Park's agitated remarks.

Penny defended me and I loved that about her. She grabbed my hand.

Why did I need defending? I am not a vampire.

What did Mother Park see in me? Something sinister beneath my skin? Or on my skin? A certain look in my eyes? The tone of my voice? The fact that I had slept with her daughter? Or was it something more? I had made sure no dry patches were visible when I left home to meet them at Penny's apartment.

Was it my name? Is Székely really a "vampire" name?

While I was a boy, my mother once told me about our family. Although we were of Hungarian heritage, we were some of the Hungarians who had lived across the border in Romania prior to their immigration to England in the early 1800s, then to the States in 1898. She had shown me a chart of everyone. I saw I was connected to something larger than myself: an amazing fact to a young only-child. She pointed to the red stars by certain names. Those relatives had died of the disease, she explained.

I had to pause—Mother Park and Penny were in a hot debate anyway, something about the family's *kimchi* recipe and the split between family members over the change of a few ingredients.

My skin suddenly felt itchy and I had to excuse myself.

I went to the bathroom, feeling Mother Park's eyes following me, no doubt wondering how I knew where the bathroom was. Obviously, I had slept over a few times, she had to understand.

I pulled off my shirt and stared at myself in the mirror. My skin was checkered, brown and beige, across my shoulders and chest—out of sight while my shirt was on. The brown patches were dry, scaly, itchy, and had developed a raised texture like burnt toast. The unaffected skin remained supple and smooth. What was causing this? Was it all psychological? Could Mother Park's suggestions be playing with my mind, making my skin become dry and scratchy? Could I be that susceptible to the power of suggestion?

After taking a few minutes to scratch myself, to get rid of the itch, I applied some of the white lotion Penny always kept in her cabinet—for when her hands got too dry from the winter wind while outside reporting on the snow or an icy crash scene. I had no such excuse. I only handled vials of blood in a laboratory, a controlled environment. I poked people with needles. I labeled samples. Nothing stressful at all.

Penny was calling to me, asking if everything was all right.

"Everything's fine," I responded, coming out with my shirt on again.

She seemed to know what I had been doing and stood as I approached the table. Moving so her back blocked her mother's view of me, Penny deftly rubbed away a glob of lotion from my throat. She did so by kissing me, full on my lips while her hand curled gently around my Adam's apple.

"I see, I see," said Mother Park. "It must be official now. You two are in love!"

"Yes, we are," said Penny, parting from me.

I apparently was blushing. "Yes, in love."

"Your father's going to want to know all about him."

"Please hold off as long as you can, okay?"

Oh, why couldn't we just be married already and settled into our domestic bliss? We fit so well together. We are so right for each other. And with Mother Park's blessing, it was a done deal.

A couple days later, I went with them to the airport to see off Mother Park. When the woman was safely through the security checkpoint, my Beloved let out a long sigh. I patted her back.

"Glad that's over," she mumbled.

"Aw, she's not so bad. I like her."

"Try living with her for twenty years."

"I'd like to do the next best thing: live with her daughter for twenty years."

She glared at me as though she doubted I had that much time left. Twenty years? I could make it. I might not be quite so lively or handsome by the end but, until then—

"Yes, I could please you for twenty years," I told her, feeling the urge to scratch myself.

"You promise?"

"I do."

"Oh, stop that!"

6

Another weekend: me on the sofa reading some Heidegger book, thinking about my existence, and my Beloved across the room at her computer editing a video for some report she had coming up, speaking the voiceover narration into the mic. Domestic bliss.

Whenever we didn't go to church, Sunday mornings were when we felt the love. We liked to wake up in each other's arms and kiss right away, even before mouthwash. Eventually, we would think of having brunch. However, sometimes excitement occurred and we took care of it as lovingly as possible, then had brunch.

This Sunday, however, I slept in sweatpants and long-sleeve t-shirt, trying to protect my skin. We did not make love. I tried to get cuddly, but Penny would have none of it. I could tell she was afraid of the skin problem I had.

I got out of bed, escaped to the bathroom.

Sensing my disappointment, she came in wearing nothing but birthday suit. My eyes widened.

"I'm sorry," she said, standing beside me, her golden-beige skin contrasting with my gray sweatsuit.

I nodded. "We must be careful."

She reached for the hem of my sweatshirt, started pulling it upward.

"Here, let me help you with that."

She proceeded to remove my shirt, leaving me topless before the mirror. I looked at myself as she knelt to help remove my sweatpants. When they were gathered at my ankles, I stepped out of them and stood naked beside her as she straightened up. We stared at the two of us in the big mirror. It was the measure of our existence: here are two humans, one male and one female, of average attributes, two examples that have copulated previously and might copulate again if not for a dry patch of skin or two. Or thirteen.

She moved behind me, let her arms come around to the front and clasped her hands over my belly.

"Does it hurt when I hug you?" asked Penny, my Beloved. Only a Beloved would ask such a question. Her arms ringed my torso, snug but not pressing. My skin welcomed her arms. She tilted her face against my back, nestling her cheek between my shoulder blades. "Still okay?"

"I'm all right."

"Good. I don't want to hurt you."

"I don't want to *be* hurt."

"Maybe you need to check into it."

She released me, stepped back. I could sense her mentally checking herself, making a list of points on her body that had brushed against mine. Perhaps, she would need to tell a doctor someday.

I turned to her, glad to be out of sight of that cruel mirror, feeling as though I was about to lose the love of my life by being honest. I had not yet lied to her in our almost one year together. However, she deserved to hear the truth.

"I'm sorry, Penny. I don't know what it is. But I'm sure it's something simple, you know, easily explained. Just need a doctor to explain it. I don't think I did anything wrong. I mean health-wise. I've been completely faithful to you. And no new foods or strange herbal supplements. I live a clean, happy life. You know that."

"Change of laundry detergent? I heard sometimes people are allergic to their clothes, from the detergent they used."

"No, I'm using the brand I've always used."

"Try changing it, see what happens."

"Sure." I reached for her but did not expect her to accept my embrace. "Thank you for being patient. Now—and when your mother was visiting. I love how you stood up for me, and how you defended me when she was talking about *Twilight*."

"But you're not one of those stupid characters."

"And yet...I seem like one of them. She said so."

"Listen to me, Stefan. I defended you for two reasons. First, she was wrong and it was making you uncomfortable. I saw that. And two: seeing you uncomfortable got me upset. I didn't want you feeling uncomfortable. That's because...I love you. I don't know how but, hah, the lamb fell in love with the lion."

"Wow, you said it. Actually spoke the words."

"It's not an easy thing to say. You'd better appreciate how difficult it is."

"I do, I do." I had to grin. "Remember those words: I do."

She laughed. "There won't be any wedding, Buddy Bear. I like having you in my life but a wedding won't make it any better. We can live together, but no wedding."

I moved many of my things into her apartment, the nicer of our two. Mine was a dump, I readily admitted, but that was through no fault of my own; it was too small to hold my books and leave room for leisure activities. She dared stay over with me there a couple times but I became embarrassed and relented to spending weekends at her place. My bed, a glorified futon, was also old. Hers was a lovely queen-sized playpen.

During the week, I slept in my own apartment, from dawn until late afternoon when the neighbor kids arriving home from school made too much noise for me to sleep longer. I could go to work, catch her reports on the 6 and 10 broadcasts, then work through the night, knowing she would arrive at her apartment by 1 or 2 and send a text message to let me know. We exchanged texts through the evening, some pure comedy, others innocent flirtations, some downright passionate.

Then one afternoon, on the way to my job, I stopped in at the usual Barnes & Noble bookstore for a latté and muffin.

And here comes Penny with some guy: tall, rugged, with jean jacket and scruffy beard, holding the door for her, letting her enter, and sweeping his arm up behind her. She didn't see me in the corner with my magazine and latté. They went to the counter to order something.

I checked my watch: 3:33. She must be working now and just stopped off for an afternoon pick-up. I wanted to chuckle but I swallowed hard. Yeah, pick-up. Who was that guy? By pick-up, I meant caffeine stimulation, but it hurt me to think she picked up this guy, this man who was younger than me, more fit, possibly more handsome. I'll admit it. I'm not jealous. Not really. Not much. All right, in a few circumstances, I am able to feel that emotion. One of them was now. Who was that man?

With drinks in hand, they took a table, sitting perpendicular, leaning forward, elbows on the tabletop. His aviator glasses hung from his open shirt collar. His ball cap was pushed back, bill forward. She kept her coat on; she is usually cold whenever I am comfortable. It was a cool May day, rain earlier.

They chatted—something about a crash on the highway.

And then she caught me in the corner of her eye. At least I thought she must have caught me even though she gave no indication. Perhaps she did not recognize me. Perhaps she was deliberately ignoring me for the sake of this companion.

Then she turned.

Her face lit up suddenly as recognition splashed over her. She turned back to say something to the guy, and stood. She came over to me. She came to me!

"Well, hey there, stranger! What're you doing here?"

I ripped open a toothy display, my genuine smile because now I felt relieved she chose not to ignore me in the presence of that handsome fellow.

"Same ol' same ol'," I blithely muttered, affecting a calm demeanor while nerves rumbled beneath my skin. "Waiting for Fate to move me to my next assignment."

She laughed and I loved the sound. She asked me about work and I said I was heading there soon. Calling her gentleman friend over, I stood and he and I shook hands. She introduced us, him to me: her new coworker, team member on the mobile reporting vehicle, the photographer, "photo-journalist" in proper parlance, the dude named Tommy.

And me to him she said: "My boyfriend, actually."

Yes, she called me her boyfriend. I melted a little, grinning. She took my hand, gave it a squeeze, something to reassure me.

"Good to meet cha," said Tommy. *Cha*, he said.

"Likewise," I said, but it was a complete and bald-faced lie.

But I was the boyfriend; she said so, announced it to everyone sitting in the café. Everyone knew I was the boyfriend, Penny's boyfriend. I was ace reporter Penny Park's boyfriend. And I had sleepover privileges.

We chatted a few minutes more, then they had to leave but before exiting, my Beloved gave me a great hug, full arms, and a sloppy wet kiss, ending with "See ya tonight" even though it was the middle of the week and I usually would be sleeping in my own apartment. Perhaps she said that for *his* benefit, to let the team member know I really was with her.

I stared as they left, got in the news vehicle and drove off—she drove it, the dude riding shotgun. My heart buzzed with excitement. I typed a long text message expressing my thanks for how she had introduced me and treated me in front of her more attractive co-worker and how I appreciated it and—

With a thought to how she disliked expressions of romance, I deleted that overwrought prose and typed a simple I <3 U and sent it out into the chilly rain, hoping she would not crash while retrieving her phone.

I went about my work that night, and the nights that followed, with half my mind focused on my condition. It was irritating, not only in an itchy way but also in a *get out of my life already* way. If it was something simple, it should be gone by now. If it was more serious, then let's get the diagnosis and start treatment. I need to be free of this problem so I can be with my Beloved.

However, Penny hesitated the next few times we tried to be intimate. With my skin not 100% I relented and slunk away for a while, hiding my misery on the graveyard shift and in my dark hovel. She was as kind as she could be, working on some reports she needed to finish. She did not need to say she feared catching whatever I had.

And each dawn, as I crept home to sleep, I stripped down and stood before the mirror of judgment for yet another inquisition.

I hate mirrors. However, I think we are meant to be mirrors. We reflect the world around us as surely as if we were made of glass ourselves. When two people meet, they see each other first: the outer facade. They size up each other: Who is this person? What characteristics of normalcy does this person exhibit? What hidden flaws might there be? We look and examine and assess and make a fistful of judgments in the blink of an eye. And we compare that person to ourselves, to the reflection of the person we think we are.

And if we dare become a unified entity—the couplehood to which philosophers and Valentine greeting card writers refer—we use our Other as a stabilizing reference, a harbor to tie up our ship, a weather pattern for the day.

I look at my Beloved and she is perfect. I can say perfect even knowing that it is not statistically possible to be without some flaw however minor. Who can state with any accuracy or moral authority what is normal? I learned in medical school, and it's the same with any scientific endeavor, that normal is merely a statistic. Majority rules.

Unfortunately, mirrors do not lie. Sure, there are lighting tricks, and the basic principle of optical illusion always reverses what you see. It is the eyes which lie. It is the mind that invents a comfortable version of the truth and blames the mirror for any arguments to the contrary.

I stare at the mirror—not at *myself* in the mirror—and I see the truth.

What once was a cheek of pleasant Caucasian pink, smooth and moist, full and curving outward, now has sunken, become flat and gray, and the dryness shows even at arm's length. Lotion no longer helps. In fact, the situation is beyond mere cosmetic appearance. It hurts. I can feel the awful tightening as the skin dries. It becomes brittle, wants to flake—and soon will, like a bad sunburn. Or chapped lips that crack open and bleed. But all over my body. Flaking and peeling, and continuing to dry out, like the husk of some dead plant.

I lean in and stare at my face. The whole patch of skin. Right cheek. Left cheek. Over the bridge of my nose. My chin. Across my forehead. There is no oil for pimples. My skin is abnormally dry, cracking, bleeding, hurting.

I could claim sunburn, but I am not red, not even pink, rather a solid, pasty gray. Like clay. Like fired clay: a statue. Not a living, breathing human being.

And yet I breathe.

I take a long, deep breath and remember what my Beloved said: "Ooo, what *is* that?"

Try to imagine her voice: whiny and agitated as though she had seen a mouse, spider, cockroach, and snake all in her bed at once. Only it was me. Even overnight, the ugly transformation continued unabated.

A few times early in our relationship—between all those early coffee dates and eventually having sleepovers on the weekends—she had playfully applied her favorite green "mud mask" to my face. It was a game. She applied it to herself, too. We laughed, poking each other's face. We let it sit, let it dry until it flaked and cracked. We watched ourselves turn into clay masks. When enough time had passed, she announced we should wash it off. The result would be significantly moister, fresher skin. The television spokeswoman confirmed it. We washed. We gazed at each other. We were moist and fresh, all right.

Moist and fresh. I'd kill for that now.

7

I took a flight through Chicago back to my previous home in upstate New York. I stayed at the Holiday Inn Express by the college and called my friend, Leslie, the dermatologist. We'd had a fling back when I worked there and I knew she would give me the straight answers I was seeking.

"Sure, come on over," she said over the phone and sounded neither happy I was visiting nor afraid of what I'd become.

Officially, I made an appointment. Unofficially, they were full so my time was the last. That had been our usual way of getting together. It's strange how horny medical technicians and doctors can be. Well, then again, everyone knows from all those dramas on television: doctors fixing hearts between sex sessions in the on-call lounge.

In fact, that was one of the reasons I had to leave. Leslie was divorced and looking for a rebound sex toy. We had been fooling around in the lab and in our passion had knocked some vials of blood off the counter. They fell to the floor. Thank goodness they landed on our pile of clothing instead of crashing and shattering. It would have been terrible to have all the broken glass on the floor. And the blood spilled. Worst of all would have been calling the patient in to give another sample because the lab technicians were too stupid to watch what they were doing.

But I digress....

I went through the doors when my name was called, the last person in the waiting room. A young, plucky nurse ("So how're you doing today?" "I guess we'll find out, won't we?") led me back to an examination room and took my vitals. All those were well in normal range. I had lost twelve pounds since I last lived there, however. Leslie, still wonderfully blond and buxom in a classic pin-up style but dangerously intelligent, noted my new thinness, reminding me that I had never been especially chunky.

"All right, Stefan, let's have a look."

I unbuttoned my shirt as she looked over my chart. When she turned, I had my shirt off.

"Oh, you dirty boy," she said, looking me over. "What have you gotten yourself into?"

"Give me a break," I said.

"Sorry, it's just you always have something going on."

"This is serious."

"It's always serious with you."

"I'm in a committed relationship now. I'm not fooling around. In fact, she knows about this skin problem...but, as you might imagine, it's ruining our sex life."

"Yes, I can imagine." She held up her examination tool in her latex gloved hand.

She poked and scraped at several patches of dry, rough skin across my chest and said nothing. She turned me around and continued down my back. She let loose a few *hmmms* this time. She lifted one arm and had a look, then the other arm.

"Does it, uh, go on down?" she asked, her eyes falling to my crotch. I chose to believe she meant my legs.

"Yes."

"Then I'm gonna need to see that, too."

I reached for my buckle and her hands intercepted mine.

"Allow me," she said with a seductive grin, as though she had not just been examining my unusual skin disease. "Just like old times, huh?"

She undid the buckle and unzipped my trousers, then slipped them down to my ankles. Kneeling in an uncomfortable position before me, she examined my thighs. She turned me around to continue her examination. Returning me to my original position, she checked down my shins and calves.

"And...there?" She nodded to my bulge.

"No. Thankfully, no. Not yet...that I've noticed."

She smiled, but not in a reassuring way.

"Well, Stefan, you certainly got something. Have you noticed anything about how it spreads?"

I explained how the first patch had been on my cheek and I used ordinary skin cream to moisturize it. That seemed to work but it came back after a short time when I stopped using the lotion. Then it appeared on my chest. And on my upper back. I shared my hypothesis that it was the clothing I was wearing, using Penny's idea about the wrong detergent.

"It could be an allergy," said Leslie.

"But I haven't changed anything in several years." I hitched up my trousers, buckled the belt, safe once more. "So why now?"

"Allergies can pop up at any time, and for no apparent reason. Could be environmental factors, too. You do work with people's blood, right?"

"It's not like I drink it, though. Stop being morbid. I work in a lab. It's a sterile environment. There's got to be a real reason."

"Well, what's changed recently?"

I thought for a moment but it did not take that long to come up with the answer.

"My girlfriend is Korean. I mean, she's American but she's of Korean ancestry. Like my family way back is Hungarian."

"And you think you're allergic to Korean girls?"

"No, but maybe...Korean food. See, her mother visited not long ago and she was cooking all sorts of Korean food. I ate more of that during her visit than all the rest of my life."

"Could be an allergy. What's in Korean food that you haven't eaten a lot of before?"

We looked at each other only a second and simultaneously spoke: "Garlic."

"That's it. I'm allergic to garlic! Or whatever is in that food. Who knows what's in it? She's always eating kimchi. Now I am."

"And you flew all the way here for that insight?"

"It doesn't matter now. What can I do about it? Stop eating Korean food?"

"Hey, you know who else is allergic to garlic?"

"No, who?"

"Dracula."

She burst into laughter. Until she saw my stern face—with the dry patch of skin on my cheek.

"Sorry. It's just a story. Lighten up. But...actually, I read about people who actually have that allergy. Where they get freaked out by even the scent of garlic? You know?"

Despite her cute face all lit up in gustatory revelation, I tried not to think of her diagnosis.

"We don't know for sure that's it," I said. After all, I had come a long way for an examination. "Can you run some tests?"

"There are plenty of tests I can run, but we want to know what we're looking for. We need to narrow it down. Can't be running tests for all two hundred and thirty-eight known skin disorders. You'll be here for months."

Then I had an idea, a bad idea. I cleared my throat.

"Is it possible...? I mean, have you ever heard of someone who is allergic to...umm...vaginal fluid? Is that possible? Could a man get rashes from...you know, being down there? Like face-first?"

She laughed. "Oh, anything is possible. Is that something we should seriously consider? You do that often? I don't remember you really getting into that when we were together. But you've taken up that hobby now, huh?"

"Is that something I could be allergic to?"

"I suppose. But not all over your whole body. On your face, maybe. I'd believe that. Mouth sores, thrush in your throat, stuff like that. But if your girlfriend is eating a lot of garlic, like you say, it could translate into her fluids. Just like what a guy eats can affect the taste of his semen. You still eating asparagus?"

"No, I'm not. I apologize. I didn't know about that before. I've followed your recipe ever since: pineapple all the way."

"And a dash of coconut and cinnamon."

"Tropical delight...."

She smiled in a whimsical manner, as though she wished to try the new me. Then her face turned serious again.

"No, it's probably not that. We'll run some tests."

She sat and stared at me, zeroed in on my cheek.

"It's definitely not acne. Not psoriasis, not with that irregular pattern. Not eczema. Shingles, no.... No pain, right?"

"It just itches and makes me scratch like crazy."

"Dryness seems the main symptom, right? How's your diet? Staying hydrated?"

"She keeps asking me that! Am I hydrated? Am I drinking enough fluids? Geez, I'm peeing a gallon every hour, I'm drinking so much. But it doesn't do any good. My skin is still dry. It dries out in patches, as though one field of crops out of the whole farm is not getting irrigated properly while the other fields are okay."

She had grabbed a thick book from the shelf as I ranted and was flipping through it. I could see it was a reference manual: skin diseases of the world. Many of the pictures were not suitable for general viewing. I was glad I had not chosen that specialty. Thank goodness there were people in the world like Leslie who did not mind treating skin problems.

"Could be Sjögren's syndrome," she mumbled, reading, "but that's more for women."

"What's that? Never heard of it."

"It's an autoimmune disorder—a syndrome—that targets the moisture producing glands of the body, resulting in excessive dryness in the eyes, mouth, and other areas which have mucus membranes. Like the vagina."

"You're right: for women."

"Are you dry?"

"Yes. I think my mouth is dry more often than a few months ago. I thought it was normal. Me getting older."

"How about your eyes?"

"My eyes are the same. I think they are. Maybe a little drier. However, everything is drier in Oklahoma. It's hot and dry all the time. Except winter. Then it's cold and dry. That would account for my dry eyes and dry mouth, wouldn't it? I've been there a year—and my symptoms began a few months after arriving."

"You're such a good detective. That sounds very reasonable. Maybe you should move some place more humid."

"So now that I flew all the way here for this insight...."

She closed the book and held it in her lap as she gave me a run-down of the likely suspects, cataloging the symptoms for me. It could be *this* but not if *that* is occurring. Or possibly this, but you haven't been down to South America. And so on. Process of elimination. There were simply too many to have to eliminate. She had marked off thirty of the more common problems when she paused to yawn.

"Sorry," I offered.

"Probably we need to take some samples and send them to the lab. Then we'll know for sure."

"You don't know? Not even a guess?"

"It looks like a lot of different things. Hard to just say it's this one or that one. We ruled out a lot of the most common ones just by their symptoms and your history."

"Is it some kind of skin cancer?"

"I can't say. Probably not. What I mean is—and I don't want to worry you—it's not anything I've ever seen before."

"It can't be skin cancer. I looked that up for myself already and I couldn't find any pictures that matched what I have. And, besides, I've always tried to stay out of the sun. My aunt never let me outside if it was sunny."

"I get that, but sometimes other things cause problems. We'll see what's going on with you. Then we'll know. Then we can treat it. Then you can get back to your committed relationship."

"Thanks for the reassurance."

She wrote up some paperwork and called in a nurse to draw my blood and gather a few skin samples. That was awkward. The nurse was not as gentle as I am. She didn't tell jokes to relax me. It hurt. She did apologize for it and I believed she was sincere. The skin samples hurt more: a snip here, a snip there. I was bleeding and got some Band-Aids applied. I felt like I got my money's worth.

I put my shirt on while I waited for Leslie to return. I thought she would return to usher me out as the final case of the day. It was well after closing time. When she did not reappear, I called for her.

"Are you done?" she asked, puzzled. Her hands were shoved into the side pockets of her white coat.

"Yes, I've been sampled thoroughly."

"So any problem?"

I leveled my eyes at her, affecting as solemn an expression as possible.

"This has to remain hush-hush, of course," I told her. "I don't want to lose my job over it. If they thought I had some rare skin condition, they wouldn't want me mixing with patients."

"You *shouldn't* be mixing with patients, Stefan, if you have a skin condition."

"All right, but I can still do my work in the lab. I don't have to touch anyone. I can hide in the lab and do the work and go home at dawn and get some sleep before I do it all over again."

A smirk erupted in the corner of her mouth. "You go home at dawn? Are you serious? Do you hear yourself?"

"What? I'm not being funny."

"You're allergic to garlic, you work at night and stay indoors during daytime. You've got excessively dry skin. You work with blood. You tell me what it all means."

"What? I don't know. That's why I'm here."

"You don't get it?"

"No, what is it? What skin disease do I have?"

She lifted a hand and placed it on my shoulder, the typical doctor-patient confidentiality pose. "I hate to break it to you, but it seems that you are a vampire."

"A what...?"

"It's circumstantial, obviously."

She saw that I was not amused.

"I'm kidding," she said, removing her hand from my shoulder.

"I hope you are."

"It's all those *Twilight* movies. And then they got shows on TV. Lots of rip-offs. It's all pop-culture now. Can't escape it. So many sexy vampire hunks and sexy vampire vixens. *The Vampire Diaries*; that's what it's called. Ever see it? Oh, and another show: *True Blood*. And I got a paperback out in the car that's a vampire story. *Heart Search* is the name. Vampires in love."

I remained unamused.

"Don't worry, Stefan. I didn't mean to tease you. It's just a...a trend society is going through. You know, one of those vampire hunks is named Stefan, also?"

"So I've heard. Is he also Hungarian?"

"If you're Hungarian, you got nothing to worry about. Real vampires come from Transylvania, right? That's over in Russia, I think. All I know about geography is from TV. But I'm sure it's far from Hungary."

I bit my lip. Not really; it's only an expression. Didn't want to draw blood, after all. I did, however, hold back from responding to her comments. Leslie did not ace geography. Hungary borders Romania, especially the Transylvania region. And my family, my mother informed me, lived there. No wonder they immigrated. Or they might have been thrown out. Driven out, more likely. Torches and pitchforks, angry villagers with silver bullets and wooden stakes.

"Leslie, dear Leslie, please stop this line of supposition."

She waved me off, chuckling. "Line of supposition? There you go! Stefan, the wordsmith. You still writing poetry? You know, I kept all the poems you gave me."

"You kept them?"

"They're lovely. You still write?"

At that moment it occurred to me that I had not written any poetry for my Beloved. Perhaps that was because Penny was such a modern woman and serious about her work—work which was about the serious events happening every day. I had not thought she would appreciate poetry. I vowed then to write her a poem on the flight back.

"I put it off since I moved west. Lack of inspiration."

"Your new Korean girlfriend doesn't inspire you?"

"She does. She definitely does. Not for poetry, however. I just haven't written anything. But I will."

"After you get this skin thing figured out, I want you to write her some really sexy poems, like you did for me. Promise?"

I remembered Penny's question, the same question, when we had delivered Mother Park to the airport. Now I wondered if I had any hope of ever marrying her, of boldly declaring the sacred words. First things first, I knew. Get treated, then....

"I do."

"Great," said Leslie. "That's the Stefan I used to know!"

8

And then, just out of my shower, my very careful shower, not too hot and not too cold followed by a careful pat-down so as not to disturb my delicate skin—my Beloved called me.

"No, I'm in Utica," I responded when she asked if I would be coming over tonight. "Utica in upstate New York."

"Where?"

"Where I lived before coming to Oklahoma."

She made a noise. "You just took off again?"

I had nothing to say. Of course, I knew I was not abandoning her. Going to Manitoba was a fluke. As busy as she was each day, she need not spend time worrying about me. It might have been a bit extreme to fly half-way across the country for an exam but I was not sure what I was dealing with and wanted to be examined by someone I could trust.

"Not *just* took off. Took off. I had an exam today. Saw a real dermatologist. A specialist."

"In Utica? Where is that anyway?"

"Near Syracuse. It's my old stomping grounds. Before I came to Oklahoma, like I said."

"Don't you trust me?" she asked in a tense voice, one that worried me.

"Don't you trust that I will be there for you? Here, there, wherever you go?"

"Yes, I trust you." I took a breath. "I don't want to hurt you. That's why I came here. I trust this doctor to give me the truth. And to let me know what I've got."

I stopped talking and expected Penny would come back with another question, but there was silence.

"So do you know?" she asked finally.

"We ruled out some possibilities. I'm waiting for test results now. Biopsies."

"Biopsies? That's like for cancer...isn't it?"

"The doctor doesn't think it's cancer. Not by the pattern."

I went on explaining some of the possibilities and dismissing them. I wanted Penny to have hope for me. It would be very easy for her to decide my skin problem was too much to deal with and walk away. Of course, I could not fault her for doing that. It would be just one of those things. You wake up one morning and everything has changed. Fate.

"I need to get this problem fixed," I said, cutting off whatever she was saying. "I don't want you to catch anything—whatever it is. Let me get this condition treated and I'll be back with you real soon."

"Are you sure your problem isn't me?—us?" Her voice was different, like she was reporting on a car crash, maybe a seven vehicle collision with fatalities. I had only heard that voice when she was on TV. "Are we really as compatible as you said we were when we met?"

"Yes, absolutely."

I had to stop and think. It had all been so miraculous, how we met, I accepted the inevitability of our relationship. We had to be together or else Fate was wrong, and Fate was never wrong. It would have been a slap in the face of Fate.

"We do belong together," I said. "But I want to make it easy for you. I'm trying to heal myself."

"It's already easy. Okay, easy enough."

"I'm doing this for you. For us. For us to be together...like we were meant to be."

"You have it all figured out, don't you?"

"Nothing is figured out. I want to be with you so badly...."

"You're perverse, Stefan."

"I simply want you. I need you."

"To *complete* you?"

"No, not that meme. Please, no memes today. I need you in order for me to go on living."

"I can't have you running off all the time with no message."

"Listen, Penny, I'll be back in a few days and I'll tell you the results. Meanwhile, you get a break from me. I'm sure you can use a break from me."

"No, you're not my mother. I don't need a break from you."

"You are so sweet."

Yes, we really did say those words, that romantic sentiment, exactly like that. That was the game we played. One of us would shift into romantic style and the other would follow—or resist stubbornly. This time, the romantic style was working well.

We ended the call with promises for a hot time followed by a good dinner out and then more hot time. I think that's what our final words meant. They could've meant that. I wished I could be sure I would be suitably refreshed for an adventure like that. And equally sure that my Beloved would welcome me back into her arms. Or let me buy her a latté, at least.

There was a Barnes & Noble bookstore in the shopping enclave near my hotel, so I got my usual latté and browsed the shelves. I came to the Health section. Some shelves were labeled Self-Help, but what I had sadly could not be helped by myself. Addiction and Recovery did not apply to me, either. I passed New Age and found myself in Sexuality. Lots of how-to books there.

I recalled the time Penny and I were arm in arm in our own Barnes & Noble and wandered into Sexuality. It was weird but fun examining one book then another, flipping pages of naked performers in all kinds of positions. I felt as though she might have been seeing something for the first time. Some were new for me, as well. What was fun about it was the suggestive banter we slipped into, especially when someone else was nearby. "We got to try this!" she would exhort while the elderly couple passed us. Or, "You think you're ready for that?" she would ask to try to stay ahead of the teen couple shying away because we stood there. It was simply fun being there with her, her hand on my butt and my arm around her shoulders, both of us wishing we could try something new right there between the shelves.

I realized something had happened as I stood reminiscing. I dropped my hands from my hips and shielded my bulge until it subsided. That part of me worked well enough. Please, I prayed, do not let this problem spread to my penis. At least not there.

I had my lunch at the Panera next door: the Italian combo sandwich with a Greek salad.

After they called my order, mispronouncing my name, as usual, I sat and ate slowly, watching the other customers around me: professionals, groups of mothers with toddlers, college and high school students meeting and studying together. All of them looked normal, healthy, fresh-faced. I put myself away in the back corner where I could stay out of sight.

When I had placed my order, the cashier girl seemed to stare a moment too long at me, at my face, at that dry patch of skin on my face, possibly wondering what the problem was, what my disorder might be, and whether or not she could be harmed by it just by standing before me, as though the virus or bacteria could leap from my skin and strike her there inside a nostril or within the slip of her eyelid and thereby cause her to suffer the same ugly affliction as this old man standing here before her.

But I digress....

Saturday, I walked around, crossing the Utica College campus where I had taught a class in phlebotomy for nurses. The sun grew warm and I found some shadows to sit in as I gazed out at the world.

Sunday, I slept until noon. I forgot where I was, opening my eyes, expected my Beloved was in the bathroom, preparing herself for our afternoon delight. No, I was completely alone. The maid knocked but I announced I was "Okay" even though I knew I was not. The sheets definitely would need changing, the way my skin was flaking. Another lost weekend.

Monday afternoon I got the call I was waiting for.

"We're going to need to get a fresh blood sample," said Leslie.

"Drop the vial?" I laughed.

"No, not that." There was an ominous pause. "Something's wrong with the tests. Wrong results. We need to try again."

"What's the problem?"

"Nothing about the ANA test," she said, speaking slowly, "or the serum protein electrophoresis test."

"Then what is it?"

"We could not get a match with your blood type."

"My blood type?"

She paused. I heard a deep breath. "What is your blood type? Do you know?"

"*Pfft!* Do I know my blood type? It's AB last I checked. I know it's rare, the most rare type, but I always have been special."

"Really? AB? I always thought you were O."

"No, I'm AB. Why? What's the problem?"

Again a drawn-out breath. "Why don't you come in and we'll get a fresh sample and run the tests again."

"Come on, tell me the problem."

"The problem is...you don't have any blood type."

It was my turn to give the long breath, an exhale.

"That's crazy."

"What we got from you is not O, not A, not B, not even what you claim should be AB. You have no type, Stefan. Or, you are somehow.... Let's call it type X."

My business is blood, and I know about blood types and blood type testing. Leslie could not fool me, though she had often tried in the past. I was not sure if she was trying again to tease me or if it could possibly be true that I did not register as one of the common blood types.

Humans are continually evolving. At one time in our distant past all humans were all of one blood type: O. Migration and intermarriage produced eventually the four we have now. It's all defined by the antigens in the blood; antigens ride on the surface of the red blood cells. The ABO test checks which type you are. If you have antigen A, your blood is type A; if it's the B antigen, you have blood type B. There is a rare type which is a combination of A and B antigens called type AB. If you should happen to have neither the A nor B antigens, your type is O, the universal donor, thank you very much. It is important to match the types when any blood transfusion is done or else the body rejects the new blood, or the organs, in the case of a transplant.

The first thing I do when involved in lab testing is check the patient's blood type, even if it is written on the chart. People make mistakes, so I always check again. I've known mine was AB since my high school days, the check-up for playing sports. That did not seem to mean much until I started med school. Later, when I learned it was popular in Japan to associate each blood type with certain personality traits, I tried to date only A types, sometimes B types. The odds of finding another AB were like the odds of winning a lottery prize. Experience proved me right: relationships with O type women never lasted long, nor did we get along well. Good that a transfusion was never a part of our dating regimen.

So I was not shocked when Leslie accused me of changing my blood type. They *can* change, and AB changes most often but usually from more of an A type to more of a B type, depending on the individual and other factors. With AB occurring in less than five percent of the world's population, I was indeed special. So were my parents; perhaps mother was A and father was B. Then presto: an AB baby is born. I also knew that, being East Asian, Penny Park, third generation Korean-American, was A-type without any doubt. An AB gentleman and an A lady could be compatible, and any offspring born from their lust would likely be A.

I sighed, thinking of the last time Penny and I made love—so passionate, slow and deliberate, eyes to eyes, like we wanted to make a baby right there and then.

But I digress....

To humor Leslie, I returned to the clinic and gave her nurse a fresh sample of my precious blood, as purple as always. Leslie stopped by to greet me but with a full schedule we did not chat long. I made an appointment for a few days later, when the lab results would be ready. I swore I could do the tests myself if they let me have lab privileges at her clinic. Too much paperwork, however, so I trusted her staff to get it right. I gave her nurse a few tips on drawing blood, too.

9

War erupted in the former Yugoslavia in 1991 as the nation broke into its ancient ethnic regions. It was quite harrowing at its peak; the cruelty humans can do to each other was shocking. Given the modern arsenal nations had at their disposal, it was the barbarity of ancient rites of warfare that captured the world's horror. The rape of women was used as deliberate acts of terrorism. Women suffered greatly. Their family members suffered. Eventually, the United Nations got into the refugee business. Many of them ended up in Utica, in upstate New York, at about the time my parents were packing up for their retirement.

Yet my parents had a chance to work with the refugees, and they had poor impressions of the low-class folks settling into the life of the welfare recipient who had nothing to do each day but get into mischief and cause whatever trouble could be found. At the beginning of each month they stood in line at the banks to cash their government checks; mind you, few deposited any of the checks. Better to convert it to cash and go drinking and whoring. Like back home. If war does not kill the body, it kills the soul. It turns humans into creatures of bad habits, into automatons of self-destruction.

I saw many of them as I strolled around the downtown streets of Utica. Huddled on street corners like gangs, they smoked and joked, staring at me as though I were one of the Serbian guards at a camp. I had no hatred for them; I pitied them, lives now ruined. How could anyone whose lives were so disrupted ever start again, or start over at middle age or older? Some did, true. The ladies working at the Panera café spoke with accents, had Bosnian names on their name tags. They were happy to have their jobs while the husbands and sons languished in self-imposed indolence. Not many jobs available for them: factory workers with no factories, farmers with no fields, merchants with no inventory, soldiers with no guns.

I recalled as I walked the streets how I'd read news reports of some refugees being hated by both sides, left to rot in the ravaged countryside. Both Bosnians and Serbs thought of them as simply the inevitable result of the years of war. The lost ones, a wandering individual or family group, living off the scraps of the landscape, themselves wrecked in body and dulled in mind, the symptoms of war-weariness. They lived like zombies, I read in one quote. Searching for food was their daily occupation. When none could be found, cannibalism often ensued. Even family members would share themselves: an arm here, a chunk of buttock another time. Until nothing more could be salvaged. The winters came and went, the summers stretching without bounty, the war here or there, and these "zombies" traipsing over the battle-scarred hills in search of the sweet kiss of death that would end their pain.

My footsteps had taken me to the environs of psychiatry, I realized, as though they knew the way. I had been there before, of course. Between my earliest years and returning in adulthood as a credentialed medical technician, I had tried to avoid this gray monstrosity, though it held significance for me.

Utica was home to a massive stone building in a decidedly governmental style of preponderance, once officially called the New York State Lunatic Asylum, then Utica State Hospital, yet lovingly referred to as Old Main. It was the collection point for the state's abnormal horde. Taking in its first patients in 1843, the somber gray façade of the huge structure held no hope for those entering. The first permanent housing for the insane in New York state, among the first in the nation, in its heyday housed hundreds of patients: those with legitimate mental illness as well as those who merely acted differently than the norms of polite society dictated.

Until the facility closed in 1978, and for a few years after in newer buildings set on the same grounds, my parents worked with them: Father addressing the medical side, Mother, the psychiatric side. Family gossip told me I was born there among the denizens of destitution. Certainly I visited often, carried by one or the other parent. The truth may be closer to the plausible situation where Mother was fully engorged with me and forced to give birth during her daily shift. Nurses accompanied her to a cloistered room and there she presented me to the world. Thus, if anyone were to inquire, I could rightly say I was born in an insane asylum.

Another rumor held that some of Old Main's inmates were incarcerated because of their unseemly appearance. Diseases and accidents left many disfigured even as they remained intelligent and fully cognizant. They earned the hatred of their neighbors. Rounded up, many ended up in one asylum or another. If one looked weird, one must also have an abnormal, certainly deviant or criminal mind. And we cannot have such people roaming the streets of our fair city—anywhere in the state. So off to the Utica State Hospital they went: the few who were cursed by afflictions not of their choosing, only the ravagement of a god who cared not for what had been created, what had been relegated to the scrap heap of humanity, for they were never meant to be born, or so it seemed to all save those who dared treat them out of sight of society's stern eyes.

I don't recall much from my short time in Utica. Only vague impressions like any baby, any young child would have. I was sent to live with an aunt in Pittsburgh and it was there that I grew to adulthood, attended college, got my degree and learned my trade. I corresponded with my parents. They traveled about the world. Postcards from many countries. Since then, I have learned of their actual itinerary. It seems they went to a variety of spas and baths, mostly in Europe, but also in South America and Asia. All the information passed via Mother; Father never had anything to say. As Mother wrote in one of her last paper letters before email became common, they were enjoying mineral treatments which revitalized their skin, made them appear much younger than their true age, and which gave them renewed vitality, all the better to live longer lives. I was happy for them.

My aunt always explained that my parents were working in a hospital for terribly afflicted patients and they preferred I not visit them there. They sent money for my expenses, and they paid for my studies at Duquesne University. It seemed odd, yes, but I respected the distance they imposed. My parents were protecting me from their kind of career; they were dedicated and felt it was their duty to finish what they had begun. It was their calling, like missionaries. However, they did not wish that kind of desperate life for me. A few times something was mentioned in correspondence that caused me to guess they had contracted some disease from one or more patients and were likewise suffering themselves. That made sense as I studied diseases throughout medical school.

With time to await test results, I walked the grounds of Old Main, half bemused at the condition of the place, still cold, gray stone yet abandoned, too expensive to tear down—and half frightened by what it portended for so many. There are records somewhere of who entered and who died, who were treated, and what methods were used for treatment, some highly innovative for the time but ultimately barbaric.

I could imagine my parents standing at this window or that doorway, looking out at a world they seldom joined. Their lives were spent at the State Hospital, serving humanity in ways no one else would dare. I stood before the entrance, the mighty columns suggesting justice, as though entrance would cause the clouds to separate and sunshine to bathe the patient in some kind of blessed light, cleansed and healed in one great flash of a holy tanning booth.

Didn't happen.

Meanwhile, there I was walking the streets of Utica, my clothes rubbing against my skin, my exercise heating my skin, the fabric scratching my sore spots. Finally I had reached my threshold. I could take no more, yet I was not back to the hotel.

I was on Genesee Street, less than a block from the Munson Williams Museum of Art, so I ducked inside there and found a restroom. I hurried into the back stall and stripped myself down to my socks. Completely naked but for shoes and socks, although I slipped out of my shoes to get my trousers off.

I wanted to rip into myself, fingernails gnashing at my itchy skin. Looking down, I could not see much that was different, but my skin seemed redder, not surprising considering my exercise. My armpits were quite raw, having been suffering the worst of fabric friction as I casually swung my arms with every step. My crotch was a mass of flaming epidermis, as well.

Standing in that stall, I shuffled with nervous irritation. A few minutes like that and I could not keep myself under control. I had to cool the fire and so, other visitors be damned, I stepped out of the stall. I ran the cold water and slapped handfuls of it over my skin, much of it landing on the floor or running down my body to the floor. It helped, but not much. My skin was quite red. My skin itched and beneath my skin there was a steady sizzling sensation, like the under layers were literally frying in a pan. I splashed more water over myself.

The door opened partly and then abruptly closed. Someone must have seen me standing there naked and refused to enter. It was so quick, that was all I could ascertain. I expected some authority figure to bound in at any second, so I returned to the stall and shook off the water from my skin.

I did feel better—but only in rough comparison to the worst moment of discomfort.

"...and he was naked," said the boy who entered the restroom with two adults.

I guessed one was a museum guard and the other was the boy's father. They discussed what the boy had seen, noted the watery mess on the floor and the counter, then became aware of someone occupying the stall.

"Sir, are you all right?" asked the authority figure, tapping on the stall door.

"Feeling a little sick, is all," I replied with a gravelly tone and a cough for effect. I was still standing, afraid to place my naked buttocks on the toilet seat, not for fear of germs so much as the irritation that the porcelain might ignite.

"Were you standing at the sink a few minutes ago?"

"I'm not sure what you mean."

"This boy said there was a naked man standing at the sinks."

"I'm sure the man was not doing anything perverse."

"Was it you then?"

"He probably was trying to alleviate some medical concern. That happens sometimes."

"Sir, can you come out of the stall?"

"I'm not well, as I indicated previously. If you could give me a few minutes, I shall be able to discuss the matter at length."

Long story made short: I dressed and cleaned myself up, tried to swab up the water on the floor and counter with handfuls of paper towels, then exited and found the trio waiting for me.

I willingly went with them to some back room and explained myself. The boy was not damaged by the sight; he would admit to only seeing my posterior. The father thought I was stupid but not dangerous. The guard, in consultation with his supervisor, elected to send me out with chastisement and the warning not to return to the museum.

Outside, I hailed a taxi and crawled in despite my still damp clothing.

Back in my hotel room, freshly made by the lovely maids, I stripped again and drew a cold bath.

In the morning I rose and when to the bathroom to prepare for the day. I shaved and cut my chin. I suppose I was nervous: one more check-in for the test results. It was a rather good swipe; I smiled at the wrong moment and *swish!* A line of blood. I dabbed it with a tissue. I dreaded the unsightliness of a blood scab or a piece of tissue stuck to my chin. I pushed my fingertip to the cut and held it, waiting for the blood to clot. After a couple minutes, the bleeding stopped so I removed my finger. Regarding my soiled fingertip, I did what most people would do: I put it in my mouth and licked off the blood. It was my blood so I was only sending it back whence it came.

"I've looked over everything three times, Stefan, and I cannot find anything significant." Leslie put on her best doctor face. "On paper you are normal and healthy. Your tests show nothing is wrong with you."

"Except I have no blood type."

"Except for that."

"But it's not that I have no type, it's that it's a type nobody else has."

"Yes, you could say that."

"I did say that."

We stared at each other a moment and I thought I could feel her heartbeat tapping my chest. She scooted closer on her doctor stool and reached for my cheek. Her finger, ungloved, hovered over my dry patch of skin there.

"It looks better," she said. "May I?"

"That depends what you have in mind?"

She reached back and yanked a pair of latex gloves out of a box and pulled them on, then returned to her examination of my face, one hand holding my chin, the other poking at the patch of dry skin.

"It looks different—better, I mean."

"I had a scare yesterday," I said and explained my walking tour of Utica, including my run-in with the long arm of museum law. "Perhaps too much exercise made my skin flush. It actually burned. Like a sunburn. It does not look red this morning."

She sat back. "I don't think you have a skin disease."

I laughed: part real, part fake to show my contempt.

"Seriously. I'm thinking you probably have some autoimmune disorder which is presenting as this skin problem. The sunshine probably affected your skin."

"I did wear a short-sleeve shirt." I held up both my arms, side by side at the elbows. "My skin is not more red on my arms than the rest of my body."

"I can't put my finger on it—"

"Why would you want to?"

She grinned, acted demure. "But you seem to respond to excess sunlight, for better or worse. And how's your diet? I'm still concerned about allergens."

I ran down my food consumption during my stay in Utica, and the only thing that sparked her to pause me was the steak I'd had at Delmonico's—a 16 ounce behemoth that overflowed the plate. Salad and baked potato on the side, barely touched. Glass of Merlot. Slice of cheesecake for dessert.

"That's excessive."

"Being a specialty of Utica, you know I was duty-bound to partake of it. And the steak was bloody. Rare is how I like it."

"Skinny guy like you? Where did you put it all?"

"The steak has already passed through me, if you must know."

Nothing else seemed amiss. I had a problem which did not seem to be a problem according to testing. However, the obvious remained: inflammation of my skin in no discernible pattern. And it was aggravated by exercise or sunlight or both. A bloody steak and a cold bath alleviated the symptoms. Five doctors in Oklahoma City had failed to nail it down. Lotion, they had all recommended. Lots of lotion. Now one doctor in New York had failed.

Leslie had a pad of paper in her hand, scribbling something.

"I want you to see a doctor in Rochester. Julian Cadbury. He's at the medical center at R.I.T., does research in autoimmune—"

"The chocolate doctor?"

"Not the same. He's an autoimmune specialist. We've worked together on a few patients, also we both presented on a panel last year. So I think he would be better for getting some traction on what's eating you."

"Oh, don't say it that way."

"Sorry, slip of the tongue."

She continued explaining her diagnosis. She promised to forward all the testing data to Dr. Cadbury in advance of my visit.

"Keep your sense of humor, Stefan. You'll live longer. We need to get you back to optimal health so you can enjoy your affair with the reporter, right?"

"I'm glad you approve. Besides, it's more than an affair. We almost got married."

"Almost?"

"It's a long story. The ring didn't fit."

"They can resize them, you know."

"The ring didn't fit her lifestyle."

"Oh. I see."

With a careful hug and a slip of paper passing from her hand to mine, we said our goodbyes.

☙

I did not know then if I'd ever see Leslie again. The city of Utica held fifty thousand other people I would never see again. Isn't it strange we think that way? Walking the streets, passing people, never wondering if we will pass them again some other day?

I was afraid to call Penny now, worried that she would either be involved in a report and be distracted and curse me for that distraction. Or she would not want to hear about all of my tests and the lack of results. She still seemed hurt that I just left on this trip without consulting her. What was there to consult? A week away to find a cure—or at least the source of the problem. What was that? I had promised to come back.

So I called her as I drove the rental car along the Thruway to Rochester, and she answered on the third try, ten minutes apart.

"Hey, stranger," she said, and her voice registered annoyance under her mask of friendliness.

I summarized the test results: nothing found. And the further diagnosis: autoimmune, not skin disease.

"The good news is it's nothing contagious."

"Well, that's something to be happy about, right?"

"That means we can still make love."

"But you're not here."

"—Ready ta go?" said a man's voice in the background.

"In a minute," said Penny, voice muffled.

"Who's that?"

"Tommy."

"Tommy?"

"You met him. My photojournalist."

"Your cameraman?"

"Yes. My Co-Wor-Ker." She punctuated each syllable.

My heartbeat quickened, and that surprised me. I took a deep breath, not wanting to show emotion. I had no idea why I would react that way. I felt confident in my relationship with Penny. But I'm also a man, and men are perpetually insecure. Except for the jerks. And jerks seem to rule the world. At least they seem to always be present when I need to do something important.

"I'm going to Rochester to see another doctor," I told her, and followed with the details.

"Hey, I got to go. The press conference is about to start."

"Press conference? What's going on?"

"I'm at the Capitol. The governor's going to announce the new education bill—"

"That's cool."

"Gotta go."

The line was dead.

And I nearly was, too, as first a semi-tractor trailer zoomed passed me with a loud horn blast and next a state trooper pulled behind me with lights flashing. I got a warning not to talk on the phone while driving. It was not yet a law, but I had hugged the lane line as I got more emotional in conversation. I do that, I said to the officer. I get emotional. I'm dying and my Beloved is back in Oklahoma with Tommy.

10

Dr. Cadbury had a ruddy complexion like a drunkard who had not been sober in twenty years. His face was a museum of bad complexion: pimples, blackheads, whiteheads, red lumps, and a scar down one cheek. He was grossly overweight, walked with a limp, and I detected the acrid trace of tobacco and/or marijuana on him as he entered the examination room where I waited, myself quite clean and sober. The man adjusted his girth as he plopped on the stool, spreading his massive thighs like redwood trunks to steady himself, and let go a belch that seemed planned.

"Sorry," he grunted. He scratched his belly as he looked over my chart, clipped with pages of test results.

"Well...?"

The doctor grunted, cleared his throat. "Not well."

He looked up from the clipboard, gazing over his glasses at me in as stern an expression as I've ever seen.

"Lupus? Is it lupus?" I asked.

"Not lupus."

"Oh." I'm sure I sounded disappointed to him, but actually I had the feeling of my gut being torn out of my abdomen by two clawed beasts of mythical origin. "What is it then?"

It must be like pulling teeth. I never understood that expression; you get a string, tie it to a tooth and a doorknob, slam the door, done. What I meant was the whole process of collecting samples, running tests, analyzing the data, comparing results, coming to some conclusion, and then deciding on some viable course of treatment.

I have followed that process as part of my job: analyzing blood samples. Upon order, I produce complete chemistry panels on a patient: glucose, cholesterol, and so on, and, if requested, also hemoglobin A1C, fibrinogen, DHEA, and the PSA for men, plus homocysteine, C-reactive protein, and a host of other tests. Whatever the doctor wanted. If I had thought my problem was a blood disorder, I could have run the tests myself. But ethics required that we not do our own tests. For skin disorders, I could never begin to understand all the possible diseases one could get.

"There is something going on," said Dr. Cadbury, "but it has aspects of several diseases so we cannot pin it down just yet. So I recommend a few more tests."

I sat, nonplussed. "What do you *think* is the problem?"

He went into a long explanation which I, having studied the science behind the biology, could understand. Then we debated; I challenged him on the interpretation of this number and that number. He took it all pleasantly enough and at times seemed grateful that he had a patient who knew medicine. I did not like what I was hearing, so I struggled to find the logic in what was happening to my body.

The only result was that the extra tests were ordered. That would also require that I extend my stay again. I would not be able to make the flight back to my Beloved.

"My best guess, and it's only my gut reaction talking, would have been one variety of *porphyria* or another," said Dr. Cadbury the next day that we met, new test results on cards in his chubby hand. "Your symptoms do fit that diagnosis, plus your genetic history supports it, as well. Your tests show no firm correlation. Something is wrong with you. Frankly, I'm puzzled. Something is happening that our tests are not detecting."

"Is that meant to be encouraging?" I asked.

"Take it as you will. Not any worse is encouraging to some people I work with."

"I see."

"Certainly it's not something easily treated such as psoriasis or eczema. I've seen psoriasis cases much worse than what you're showing. No, the tests indicate not a skin disease but instead a skin condition which is a *symptom* of something else. I suspect an autoimmune disorder. But test results do not bear out any common cause. I considered lupus, as you were thinking, but, again, not everything fits. So I had to dig in my manuals and read all night, trying to match your condition to any known disorder. And after several hours last night and today, I remain puzzled."

"That is encouraging."

"Is it?" asked Dr. Cadbury. "So puzzled is better than a bad prognosis."

"It's encouraging that you stayed up all night researching. I think it means you are sufficiently intrigued by my illness that you'll give me the honest truth, no matter how dark and dirty the truth may be. Not just some quick and simple diagnosis followed by a prescription."

"I can see how that might be encouraging."

"And so, what conclusion did you reach from your all-night cram session?"

"Well, Mister Székely, I came to the conclusion that it must be some form of porphyria. Maybe a rare strain, a new variant. That's the closest match to *all* of the factors. I mean, overall. It still could prove to be something else if we discount any one factor. Am I making sense?"

I nodded. "Go on."

"Now, in this situation, the symptoms and how they advance parallel what you have experienced. You've been saying that you fear becoming a vampire? Did I hear you right?

"I guess so. That's not so silly, is it?"

"Let me ask you first: Do you *want* to be a vampire?"

"No, absolutely not. That's what I'm scared of. My fiancée.... I don't want her to get anything from me."

"You shouldn't worry about that. These kinds of disorders are not contagious in the least."

"That's good. I wouldn't be able to live with myself if she...if she ended up...suffering...like me." My heart was beating quicker. "She is so good to me, I...."

"So you don't want to be a vampire.... Good. I think we can rule that out from the start."

"But I looked at my symptoms, and I read the reports, did my research. There's too many symptoms that fit.... I'm not an expert on autoimmune diseases."

"You're ahead of the game, then."

"I try to be. The game is so short, you know. Life or death."

"Hah, yes. I suppose so. Now don't be alarmed, but—"

"But I am alarmed."

81

"There is nothing you need to worry about in the short term."

I looked him square in the eye. "Oh?"

"Long-term is another story. It doesn't seem to be any skin disease, as I said. The skin problem is a symptom of whatever disorder is the underlying cause. Looking at your test results, I thought it had to be an autoimmune disorder, that is, when your body attacks itself because it thinks something that's perfectly normal is in actuality an invasive entity. But some factors do not match up. So I looked at your factors in light of blood diseases."

"And...?"

"And that brought me back to porphyria. But I want you to understand, we're not talking about anything related to the idea of vampires. That's just plain poppycock."

"But it's possible? If it's something new...."

"Well, you see, at first, people thought it's just a case of severe anemia, because of the low volume of red blood cells in the body. Red cells are the carriers of oxygen throughout the body. When a person suffers from extreme anemia, the symptoms are caused by not getting enough oxygen. Things in the body then die. The person would have a pale complexion, fatigue, fainting spells, shortness of breath, and digestive disorders. Certainly seems like the common description of your everyday vampire, am I right? See, in olden times, such a person having these symptoms would be seen as transitioning into a vampire—marked with the pale complexion and trouble eating food."

I began nodding my head at every point he made.

"Or there's *catalepsy*, which is a nervous system disorder that causes a situation much like suspended animation. There's a loss of voluntary motion, rigidity in muscles, and a marked decrease in sensitivity to pain and heat. A person suffering from catalepsy can see and hear you but cannot move. The breathing, pulse, and other functions are slowed so much that untrained eyes would think the person was dead. Except they weren't, and then *voila!* They cry out from underground and have to be either hauled out or they claw their own way out of the grave."

"Terrible way to wake up."

"And then we come to *porphyria*. You know, some people like to call it the 'vampire disease.' That's probably where you got this idea about a person turning into a vampire, Mister Székely. You likely know from your research that it's a rare hereditary blood disease with eight varieties, the most severe of which—and producing by far the most fearful appearance—is called Acute Intermittent Porphyria. It's when the porphyriac cannot produce *heme*, which as you know is a vital component of red blood cells. It can be treated, yes, but in olden times, like many diseases we understand better today, treatment was unavailable and sufferers were ostracized, much as lepers were."

"But weren't they real? I mean, they actually had the disease when they were sent away. It was not just in their heads."

"Yes, I suppose. Well, who knows? Just being odd-looking is often enough reason to exile someone from the community. Fear of the abnormal, right?"

"Then it must be abnormal to drink blood."

He focused his eyes on my face and I heard the clock tick on into the next hour.

"Is that something you do?"

I held my grin in check. "If I cut my finger. I lick it."

"Seems a normal thing to me. Now, ingesting someone else's blood...that might be considered abnormal to most. People must be careful not to risk any STDs."

"How about animals? Like blood pudding, and such?"

"I'm no cook, and I've never tried that delicacy. But there is a common misconception that ingesting another person's blood, and the *heme* in it, would replenish one's own supply. Anyway, recent studies do not back up that myth. You simply can't cure the disease by drinking blood. Doesn't work that way."

"Maybe not cure, but treat it? What if—"

"In the past," Dr. Cadbury continued, holding his hand up, "a porphyriac would have symptoms such as extreme sensitivity to sunlight, sores and scars that open and won't heal, tightening of the skin around lips and gums—and that makes the teeth more prominent, perhaps commonly misinterpreted as having fangs."

"I see where you're going with this. I'm crazy." I slapped my thighs, ready to go. "That's what you want to say. Isn't it? And I know you're thinking that being crazy is more of a problem for me than a skin disease."

"Not at all. You see, all of these diseases have been confused as signs of vampirism for a very long time, which have in due course led to a great many people being unjustly persecuted. What people know of vampires today pretty much comes from the movies—and books, if anyone reads them. I, for one, could never get very far in that Bram Stoker novel as a high school student."

"Me, neither."

"So you're not in bad company, Mister Székely. Lots of people have been fooled. You don't strike me as the type who would wear a cape and sleep in coffins during the day, then come out at night to cavort with a few lovely young seductresses just to get a chance to bite their throats and suck their blood. No offense intended, but you don't strike me as the urbane, worldly, well-dressed, seductive, deadly type. Am I right?"

"I see. You might be right. I'll have to ask Penny."

"Who's that?"

"My girlfriend—fiancée. She's a television reporter."

"Does she report on vampires? Or porphyria sufferers?"

"Uh...no."

"And you can forget all that hype about the Romanian prince, what's his name, Vlad the Impaler. So what if he put thousands of his countrymen on spikes to scare away the Turkish army? He didn't bite their necks and drink their blood. He was an impaler, not a vampire. The only thing Stoker got from that legend was the name: *Dracula*, in other words, Son of Dracul, and Dracul just means 'dragon.' So there's that."

"I know that story."

"You're of Romanian ancestry, aren't you? Ah, I see how you might be spooked by some odd symptoms."

"My family is Hungarian. But I admit they were some of the Hungarians who lived across the border in Romania. And, yes, that's the area called Transylvania. Okay, my ancestors lived in Transylvania. There: I said it. My conscience is clear. But it's not an evil place. Transylvania means 'across the sylvan land'—and 'sylvan' just means a forested paradise."

Dr. Cadbury regarded me, his mouth seemingly bunched up all in one corner.

"I read a lot," I said with a nod.

"I guess so."

"Lots of quiet time on the night shift."

He grinned. "And then there are the truly sick people. I mean mentally sick, who somehow believe they are vampires. That is, *psychic* vampires. They live in a fantasy world where they believe they really are vampires. I've even heard some of them file their teeth into fangs. You see that coming from people who watch too much TV—I mean, all those vampire shows. Sexy, handsome, seductive, always in control—who wouldn't want to be one of them? And don't get me started on that *Twilight* series."

"My fiancée's mother is into them. She thinks I look like that vampire."

"Like Edward? Not even close."

"Thank goodness."

"I can't begin to explain that...*comic book* away. Teenage love triangle. My daughter is so into them. It's cute, but not medically plausible. At least that

Interview with a Vampire was more in keeping with accepted mythos, but still, the longevity aspect bothered me. Eventually, a body will break down. And becoming a vampire just from being bitten by one? Come on."

"Not possible?"

"And garlic? I love it."

"My girlfriend's Korean so we eat a lot of garlic when we cook together—or if we go out to eat."

"One thing about garlic, since it's widely believed to ward off vampires, is that garlic lowers blood pressure. If you're a creature who has little blood anyway, why would you want your blood pressure lowered further? Of course garlic offends you if you're a vampire. The odor is based on sulfur—an agent used in olden times when burying the dead. For a healthy person, garlic is a very good thing to ingest. I recommend a clove a day."

"That won't be a problem for me, living with her...."

"Do you notice a rise in symptoms after you consume a lot of garlic?"

"I don't think it correlates." I thought for a second, shook my head. "Perhaps the porphyriacs from olden times, as you've said, were allergic to garlic."

"Could be." He cleared his throat. "As for that whole Christian fixation, that pseudo-medical factor is wholly self-serving. It's the odd ball of the community who is ostracized. He hates everyone because of it. They hate him more, so they want him gone, or dead. He must be evil, and evil must be anti-Christian. Hence, anything Christian—sometimes Jewish, or what other cultures around the world have, whatever the local religion is—it's used as a valid deterrent. So we find crosses, holy water, things like that...they supposedly scare away the vampire. Just metaphors. I'm sure if they were properly welcomed, even vampires wouldn't mind attending a church service or two. Free crackers and wine."

I laughed at how passionately Dr. Cadbury was arguing.

"My parents were Catholic," I said, lowering my voice. "So was my aunt, who raised me. But she never let me go into the church itself but I was taught to pray when I needed something."

"There you go."

"Now I just need a cure."

"First, the diagnosis."

"And that is...?"

The doctor got up, went out of the examination room but returned a minute later with a thick book in his hands.

He flipped through the book and found a page. Sitting again, he offered the book to me. It was a complete compendium of colorful skin diseases and their calling cards.

"Look at these images," said Dr. Cadbury, reaching over and pointing to several pictures. "These are porphyriacs. We see how the skin shrinks and becomes pale, losing its blood supply. At the same time, the skin is very sensitive to sunlight. Look at this fellow. It becomes more than a serious sunburn; the skin actually *does* burn. It dries and flakes, peels and, underneath, the dermis is raw. Additionally, you can see how the eyes of this example seem to bulge. The result of the eyelids pulling back against the eye sockets. This picture shows a typical case. In many cases, the sufferer cannot close his eyelids completely. Along with the loss of the blood supply, most of his hair falls out, both on the crown of the head and on the face."

The doctor turned the page, pointed at the top photograph.

"Look at this one: See how the lips are thin and retracted. It is against the person's will, we understand. He cannot completely close his mouth. That's not a toothy grin; it's the best the patient can do to hold his mouth closed. The lips draw back, rather like a rabid dog's yaw, and the gums and teeth are readily exposed."

"How do they eat?"

"They don't. At least, not in the way we understand eating."

He pointed to the next page.

"And see how on this one the nose has withered away, leaving wide open nostrils. No cartilage at all there. Quite startling, isn't it? The overall effect is a frightful appearance. Indeed, look how the canine teeth seem to project due to the gums withering to the bone line. The overall effect is a façade which quite closely matches something you would see in a horror film. Only these poor devils—pardon me, these *sufferers*—they're real. And how awful it must be for them to be cursed with this affliction, all the while remaining the same normal, rational person in mind and spirit. In olden days, what could they do? To become a circus monster virtually overnight must be...."

"Awful is the word."

"Yes, very awful. I've never encountered anyone myself with this kind of acute porphyria. But I must say, if there were to be a candidate, I would have to put it on you. It needs to be treated. Definitely. We can set up something. But that does not make you a vampire, Mister Székely."

11

All I could think of was Penny as I walked from my arrival gate to my departure gate in Chicago, bag in hand, feeling as though I carried the entire world in it, walking as though the soles of my feet were covered in boils. The passengers rushed past me like I was a rock standing in a stream, blocking the current.

Soon I would stand before Penny. She would stare at me, in that certain provocative way she has, part curiosity like *What have you done now?* and part *Come hither sweet boy*, and her eyes would embrace me. This time she would hesitate. She would wonder about me, about what part of me was touchable, what part might cause her grief or start an infection. I would be nothing more than mold on her wall, a spot of mildew to be washed away, disinfected, removed completely, as if it had never existed in her life.

I ground to a halt and leaned against a wall along the wide corridor, nobody noticing me, and sniffled back a tear. I felt the wetness roll down my cheek. More tears welled in my eyes, one dropped, the others I wiped away. I took a deep breath. I had to be strong, for her and for me. I was going to beat this, whatever it was. I was not going to let a dry patch of skin defeat me and make me miserable for the remainder of my life.

The first step was to pretend. Visualize it and it becomes so. I stood tall, back stiff, and pushed myself down the corridor, just like the others. My step was not as quick as theirs but that was only because I had a three hour layover before I continued on to Oklahoma City and my Beloved.

She would be out on some story, I knew, checking the time. Probably a report on government waste, fraud, and abuse. Or there would be a wildfire or a crash that people needed to be aware of. Or she would be finishing one of her human-interest stories, like how Miss Oklahoma gets herself prepared for the pageant—as she shared with viewers a few weeks earlier. Or she would be at the station editing video, telling of someone doing something, anything, possibly about a skin disease, about some unfortunate sucker who happened to pick up a bug that caused his skin to dry out and become like paper, then tighten and crack like a lake bed under the Oklahoma summer sun, the water that had evaporated, the lake mud caking, flaking, becoming dust, then blowing away like so much...dust.

Dust to dust....

I was becoming dust.

A chunky man in a wrinkled suit bumped into me when I stopped walking. He apologized, continued on, shaking his head. Yes, I was the weird one. Another man jostled me, muttered a curse as he danced around me, swept along with the others. I stepped to the side again, feeling forlorn. People still could see me, I realized. I was not a pile of dust yet.

Eventually I found a kiosk and browsed the magazines, found one on health that had an article about tanning and how to protect your skin from damage. I was the most pale person in the shop; the sun did not know me well. I grabbed two bottles of lotion and a bottle of water and went to the cashier. Waiting third in line, I scanned the shop for something else to buy and my eyes landed on the paperback carousel.

I stepped out of line and went to it, turned it and saw a copy of that novel: *Twilight*. The one they based that movie on, the book Mother Park liked so much. I looked at my phone: two hours to wait, then a two-hour flight. I decided to buy it and returned to the check-out line.

"Is that all?" the cashier asked me, regarding my collection of items on the counter.

She glared at me, and I could see in her face the thought that flickered through her mind: freak.

I knew my face was rough, dry and flaky, obviously a skin disorder. She cringed.

"That's all," I replied.

She took each item, holding it gingerly, scanned it, and with each, flashed another glance at me. She glanced from the corner of her eye, perhaps not aware she was doing it. She had to catch another glimpse of me—because I had such an odd appearance. When she finished the transaction and handed me the receipt, I saw her slip her hands beneath the opposite counter and apply a few squirts of hand sanitizer and rub her hands together, trying to avoid contamination from the things I had touched.

I took the plastic bag with all my purchases in it and headed toward my boarding gate. Near the gate, I visited the restroom and stood before the mirror. I could see what had alarmed her. To me, it had only felt like a slight itch but now I could see it clearly.

My face was off. That is, askew. Moreover, the cheek with the worst of the bad skin seemed to have slid down. It had broken free, as though I were a clay doll. Anyone seeing me would call me ugly. To an alarmist, it could be called hideous. No wonder she was struck so by my appearance.

I dabbed cold water on the worst area and felt nothing. It did not hurt; only the usual itchiness I had learned to accept.

Passengers entered, gave me a quick look, went about their business and exited. Whenever one paused to wash his hands, I knew there was a furtive glance at me. I knew they were thinking the same thing: What a poor diseased freak!

I continued my examination. Like a bad sunburn, my skin was flaking and I carefully removed the worst flakes. The largest one I pulled free was two inches wide by an inch long. It hurt. Another one drew blood when it finally let go. I washed with cold water and stopped the bleeding with pats from a dampened paper towel.

Checking myself, I found no other symptoms. I felt fine other than the state of my skin. I could only imagine how the problem continued under my clothing. No, I could not imagine; I needed to check. When the restroom was clear, I unbuttoned my shirt and held it open.

The same scaly pattern greeted me. Greeted is only a clever metaphor. Skin does not greet, does not welcome, does not make any indication of emotion or needs or desires; it simply is. It is a reflection of the environment it inhabits. My skin was accurately reflecting my horror. I scratched across my chest, my shirt open and untucked, leaving deep red lines in my skin.

"Whoa, looks like *you* got some sunburn," a hippie snickered as he sidled up to the counter to wash his hands and comb his long blond hair.

I nodded acknowledgement of his existence; I'm not unkind, even in my unholy state.

Then I retreated to a stall and stripped down to my briefs to continue the exam. My skin was crusty and with my fingernails I could dislodge flakes of skin. Rather than flakes, it was more like dust which would drift in tiny clouds out into the air and slowly dissipate like so many fireworks on the Fourth of July. The scaly patches continued across my belly and, feeling with my hands, also across my lower back and between my buttocks.

I pulled out some hand wipes from a packet in my bag, and began swabbing myself. The cool moisture helped, but I knew there was no way I could endure a two hour flight sitting in one of those cramped seats. I would go mad with itches I could not scratch.

I removed one of the bottles of lotion I had bought and began swabbing the goo over the worst areas: my chest, shoulders, lower back, between my buttocks, down my thighs, both front and back, and my shins. I worked a lot into my armpits, as though it were some kind of deodorant, and made sure my elbows and knees were covered. Then I took the second bottle out, a lotion designated for faces, and applied it with my finger tips to my cheeks, chin, nose, and forehead. I tried to shift my wounded cheek upward—about a half-inch—as I worked in the lotion. However, it would not stay in place and settled again in its droop, like I had some anesthetic at the dentist's office that had not yet worn off.

In those minutes locked in the prison of the restroom, I had taken the effort to think beyond the immediate first-aid I needed to treat myself. With body and face lathered up with medicated lotion, I stood staring at the stall door, hearing the sounds of society outside, fearing to go out into it. Would they allow me onto the plane? I might be quarantined. Thank goodness I was all right when I went through the security in Albany. I would probably be pulled aside trying to go through the one here in Chicago.

Please, just let me get home to my apartment where I can hide from the world and figure out what to do, figure out what indeed is happening to me!

As I hitched up my trousers and buckled them, I thought of what Leslie had said about my blood type. I knew I was AB and I knew that this type had both properties of Type A and Type B—hence the name. One who possessed Type AB tended to have more the characteristics of A or those of B. On occasion, it could change. Specifically, it could transition from the A side to the B side or vice-versa. During such a process of transformation, the body wouldn't know what was going on and would treat it like an infection. The immune system would go crazy trying to figure out what was happening and deal with the disturbance, hoping to kill the bad cells rather than the good cells. The effect would be a body at war with itself.

Suddenly, everything seemed to fit perfectly.

I was in transformation—a metamorphosis, like a caterpillar becoming a butterfly, or a snake shedding its skin. That was a better analogy. I was molting. Underneath would be new skin coming forth. Of course, it did not make sense. I only knew enough to put the idea against my skin and say *Ah hah!* Problem solved. Not exactly solved, but at least diagnosed. No wonder Leslie could not pin down my blood type: I'm in transition. No wonder Dr. Cadbury could not find the actual disorder I had. I was in transition. And like all transitions, it would pass—once I reached the next phase.

First, I needed to get on a plane and somehow make it back home where I would call in sick until I was normal. Then I would call Penny and assure her that I would be fine, that we could still be together, maybe even make some of that love we loved to make so much, maybe more of that. Then all of this dry, patchy, itchy, flaky skin would be only a bad memory.

Dressed again over a generous layer of lotion, I entered the real world and none who passed me seemed the wiser. I made my way to the boarding gate and noted I still had more than an hour before boarding would begin. I chose a seat in the corner, a spot where I could keep my eyes on the information signboard. I set my bag on the seat beside me and took out a bottle of water and slammed down a third of it in one long gulp. My hands were slippery from the lotion and the bottle fell from my hands, rolled on the carpet, leaked a few swallows before I could retrieve it. I needed to stay hydrated, I told myself, even if I would have to cross my legs during the flight.

I pulled out my brand new paperback and started reading *Twilight* by Stephanie Meyers, about a girl who meets and falls in love with a vampire.

With my eyes on the pages, lost in rain-shrouded Forks, I nearly missed the boarding call.

I had bought a cheap seat, stuffed at the rear of the plane, in order to gain an aisle seat. That was the result of my last-minute change after delaying my return because of extra tests. As long as I could return home and hide from the world, I would find a way to handle it. It was barely two hours.

As it was, I made my fellow fliers feel uncomfortable. It was probably best I was seated at the rear. That way, no one would be compelled to gaze at me. Even so, I was forced to make the journey down the aisle and everyone aboard got a good look at me. My appearance was clearly a sign of moral corruption. They would be wondering what sin I had committed to deserve this affliction. A bit of excess sexual pleasure in my youth? That was all I could admit to.

There was no one in the middle seat in my row, but a chubby girl in tanktop and jean cutoffs sat by the window. Her billowing arm rode heavily against her chest and her thighs stretched into the middle seat. She had good, clear skin, though. With ear buds stuffed into her ears and the bleed of hip-hop beat, she kept to herself and later fell asleep, not giving me any attention.

Across from me was a mother and child in the middle and aisle seats, an older woman at the window. The child, a boy of three or four, could not take his eyes off me, even as the mother sensed my consternation and tried to distract her son.

I faced forward as the flight attendant explained what to do in the event of a water landing. And I stayed stiffly upright as the plane roared down its launch path and into the sky.

I pulled out the magazine from the seatback in front of me and began flipping through it. At that moment, I felt grateful. Perhaps there was a God who really watched over me. After all, there had been no delays, no tortuous waiting on the steaming Tarmac for our turn to use the runway, no downgrade of the air conditioning as we sweltered in our seats. This time, as though I had prayed for it all night, everything was as it should be.

Except for me. I was not as I should be. In two weeks, I had suffered significant transformation. It was enough to cause me to want to turn away from the world until I beat the disease and emerged as a beautiful butterfly from my hideous cocoon, freshly reborn.

Then Penny would welcome me back.

Back....

I pondered Penny's back, from nape of neck to vale of butt, and I warmed at the thought of the sight of that smooth expanse of flawless skin. When her arms moved, when her shoulders twitched, I saw the squares of her scapulae do their dance, like two waffles kissing through the syrupy slippage. And her spine was so ruler-straight cartographers could set the horizon to her vertebrae. It ran perfectly down her back, the golden-beige hue of her heritage, free of blemish, a field with no trees, no rocks, only smoothness—a flawless yard for playing—for indulging in, say, naked croquet! I recalled how my hands loved pressing against her back, touching that supple firmness and feeling the beat of heart or the gurgle of kidney beneath. Sometimes I would put her on her belly and worship her back, kissing my way down from the nape of her neck to the purple spot at the base of her spine. If she were not an ace reporter, she could be a back model. 'A *back* model?' I imagined her asking. Why, yes, someone whose back is used in advertisements, such as the person receiving a massage—that sort of modeling career. I would go to any place, patronize any business, that advertised using her back.

I noticed an alarming rise in my lap and moved the magazine to cover it. My seatmate had apparently noticed the effect and grinned slyly, then turned and looked out the window.

At least my penis was still working properly. Yet who would dare to make use of it, or even come close to it, given how the rest of my body had changed?

In the end, the clan defeats the evil vampires and Bella is saved; it was inevitable given that other books follow. Sure, I skipped around, but I got through all of it and left the paperback on my seat as I got up to exit the plane.

Having only a carry-on bag, it was easy for me to exit the airport and find the appropriate curb to catch a ride home. It should have been easy, but I stood there thirty minutes and several limousines, vans, and taxis came and went despite my arm being raised.

Passengers from my flight eventually caught up with me, assembling around me with their collective luggage, each taking a taxi before I could stake my claim. Whenever my eyes met theirs, I could detect alarm; they did not enjoy seeing me there among them. I could identify that special emotion painted on their brackish faces. In the dirty reflection on a shiny sign, I could see I was red, brown-ish red, resembling a denizen of some third-world equatorial country, or someone with a rare disorder: ruddy, scaly, flaky, rough, dry skin across my face and down the length of my body. My clothing chafed and I was on the verge of ripping them off to be rid of the irritation.

Had I actually used the word 'stake'?

I closed my eyes, remembering my thoughts. Residue from that *Twilight* book, perhaps.

12

The early evening hour was hot and humid, yet I was chilled and dry. Extremely dry. I felt no sweat under my arms or down my back. No unsightly wet spots on my shirt. I was dry. Perfectly dry. Let's bottle this affliction and sell it as an anti-perspirant, shall we?

"Mommy, look at that man there," came a child's voice.

"Don't stare," said the mother.

"He looks like a devil."

"Shhh," the mother hissed. "Quiet, now."

I turned away, pretending not to hear them. After a moment, I strolled casually to the end of the taxi stand, as though I had meant to do that regardless of the remark.

Did I really look so bad?

I got a taxi, finally, driven by a South Asian fellow who agreed to take me the 24 miles home.

"You're coming home from vacation?" the driver called to me in a lilting voice as we exited the airport grounds and made for the highway.

"Business trip," I responded flatly, not so eager to be hooked into a conversation.

"Excuse me, sir, but are you perhaps from India?"

What? How did I look? Reddish-brown? Yet not from India!

"No, definitely not," I snapped.

That settled him for a few minutes.

"Pardon me, I only thought you resemble a cousin of mine," the driver spoke. "I thought you might be from the same part of India."

"No, I'm not," I said, much too tired to argue. "You must have mistaken me for someone with a skin disorder."

"Oh, is that it?" He drove on. "I remember seeing a lot of that in my cousin's village. Same appearance, the color, you know."

I looked up, focused my eyes on the rearview mirror so I could see the driver's face. He was brown-skinned like most people from India, but he had no apparent skin problem.

"What do you mean?"

"The village where my cousins grew up...."

"What about it?"

"Some of the people got this red skin disease."

"I doubt it's the same as what I have."

"It only looks the same, sorry. If you're a white man, it looks specially bad. Perhaps you should see a doctor?"

I had to chuckle, he was so innocent. "I did. This is the best he could do."

"Then I wouldn't pay him."

I could see the driver grinning in the mirror.

"No, there was no charge."

Actually, I had put the office visit and tests on a credit card. I had gotten some diagnosis, after all. I knew what it *wasn't*, if that helped in any way.

"So you've seen this problem before?" I asked.

"A few people, that's all."

"And what did they call it?"

"In the village they called it Red Scourge."

"That's a clever name."

"Those people, they got the red skin and it worsened. At last they died."

"Any doctor check them? What caused it?"

"They said it came to people who played with devils, and in the end a devil took them away."

"Folk tales."

"No, it's true."

"I'd like to read the medical report. I'm sure it's published in a journal somewhere."

"Perhaps, it is. Then good luck to you, sir."

"Thanks."

We arrived at my apartment complex and I paid the driver and got out. It was dark by then and none of my neighbors were out to welcome me home. Lucky them.

Once inside, I turned on the air conditioning and flicked the temperature level down to coldest. I practically ripped off my clothes, dropping them on the floor where I stood, and felt the breeze of comfort waft over me. My skin was burning. The lotion had long ago been absorbed and my skin was dry again. It was red, irritated, as though I had gotten the effects of a sunburn simply by the rubbing of my clothing against it.

I took a bottle of water from the refrigerator and drank it down. Then almost as quickly spit it up. Too cold? Too much shock to my body having so much cold water at once? I dropped to my knees on the floor and wiped up the mess. My knees hurt, pressed against the tiles. Upon standing, I saw they were red, as expected. Some skin had flaked off, leaving red patches of new skin on my knees. I really was molting.

Examining my hands, I saw they were rough, but too tender to touch anything, and swollen. My arms were similarly strained. Skin was flaking off: drying, curling into flakes, falling free.

I moved into the bathroom and with a deep breath I touched the light switch. Did I dare see my whole body?

My phone beeped. I had a text message.

It was Penny: Ur home? Hungry?

Yes, would have been my response to both questions, yet how could I meet her with my current appearance? Not even a child could overlook the shock. Ordinary passengers shunned me. And cashiers washed their hands after touching the things I touched. I was disintegrating, flake by dry flake. I did not know where it would end, how far it would go. Was it the Red Scourge? Would I eventually die from this affliction?

I texted back to Penny: Too tired but thanks.

U got a rain check BB!!! came her reply.

She still called me Buddy Bear, her huggable bedfellow. My heart warmed, more than from the burning sensation filling me. I doubted I had ever been more in love with my Beloved than at that moment, thankful she did not know how terrible I looked, or how worse I may become and thus gave me the full benefit of her doubt.

Taking a few breaths, I returned to the bathroom and stood before the mirror, my hand resting on the light switch, ready to illuminate my reality.

It seemed to have been a couple hours when I awoke, stretched awkwardly on the bathroom floor. I wondered if I had fainted. Dehydrated? Low blood pressure? Glucose imbalance? The light was on, so I had to have flicked it on. I recalled I was preparing to examine my whole body before the mirror. I flicked the light switch. I opened my eyes. Then I fainted.

From my prone position, I could gaze down the length of my naked body, my head against the baseboard and my feet against the ceramic commode. Yes, I was red: that same reddish-brown color which I noted my face taking on as I returned to Oklahoma City from Chicago. Had I really taken such a trip to upstate New York? It seemed like a bad dream.

Images flooded my mind, the sights of Utica and Old Main, my childhood home. I was born there in an asylum for the mentally ill and those whose appearance did not suit society. My parents had cared for those people. At some point I was sent to live with my aunt in Pittsburgh.

At some point....

Why?

At some point, did my parents experience the same problem that was attacking me now?

There were no photographs from those days, the days after I arrived in Pittsburgh—

The memory came to me of a Halloween party I attended in high school. I dressed up as Dracula, and it had felt so natural to me. I got into the part, doing the accented voice, being seductive, wooing the ladies, and everyone thought I was great. Some of the theater students tried to get me to join in the school play, saying I would be perfect. I took that as a compliment, but it did not draw me into thespianism. I had dressed in black, of course, and had a black cape. I had slicked back my dark hair and applied some white make-up to my face. I pushed plastic fangs into my mouth. I had smiled often to show off the teeth. I had pretended to bite several girls' tender necks. I had danced, too.

My aunt had taken a photograph of me in costume before I went out. She sent it to my parents in Utica. I recalled the angry response she received from my parents, something about not mocking the dark spirits. My aunt never showed me their letter, only gave me a summary. No doubt working with such decrepit inmates caused them to rethink such things. They had to have developed a keener sense of compassion and empathy than the normal citizen walking the streets.

I felt bad about that Halloween party and gave away my costume to one of my friends. The girls I had kissed at the party remembered me when we returned to school. I had many dates, many make-out sessions, and I realized I had a gift for seduction: look deep into their eyes, speak some poetic words in the right voice, hold them close, inhale their scent, lean in and...strike. They would swoon, fall in love, beg for more, and I would move on to my next victim.

The photograph of me in costume must have shocked my parents. What had they experienced that would have given them that reaction? Mocking monsters was an American tradition. We learn to laugh at our fears. It's how we get by. Everyone loves horror movies. We get a thrill from the fright. We like feeling the adrenaline pumping through us. Sure, we may not actually be interested in being cut apart by some chainsaw-wielding hockey player at an isolated campsite right after having sex, but if it is all pretend, we get the thrill but we still have the safety of going home from the theater afterwards.

Suddenly I wished I'd stayed longer in Utica, perhaps made a detour to Pittsburgh to try to find answers. Perhaps I could find an archive of photographs, journals, letters, anything to answer my questions. My many questions.

And question number one was *Why is this happening to me?*

Question number two: Is this what happened to my parents?

If what was happening to me now was what happened to them, was it also the reason they sent me away? To protect me? To keep me from seeing them change? Or to keep me away from whatever caused this affliction?

I gazed down the length of my body, my reddish-brown body, my skin sizzling with irritation, an unholy warmth burning along nerve strands like low-grade lightning. I could see I was inflamed down to my toes. I sent the command to wiggle and they responded. My hands were too tender to grasp anything. Did I have shingles? I did not know what to do: bathe in cool water to soothe the fire or bathe in warm water to wash away that outer slurry of dead skin.

Getting up was painful. Touching the wall, floor, and cabinet hurt my hands.

Standing at last, I stared into the mirror—as I apparently had before and fainted. I held myself steady against the basin.

I did not recognize the person I saw. My body was in full disintegration mode. My hair was thinning, falling out around me, upon my shoulders. The skin on my face hung in flakes from hairline to chin, like tissue paper. I pulled off some of the larger ones. My nose seemed to be retreating, the cartilage melting away. My eyes were either protruding or the skin around the sockets was pulling back, tightening. My throat was wrinkled like an old man's, hanging limply, coated in dusty skin residue. My shoulders and arms were reddish-brown, scaly, patterned, and bumpy like a reptile's skin. My chest was a desert of dried clay chips from armpit to armpit. Under my arms, hair had fallen out. Skin tags had grown, hanging like warts trying to escape the prison of my skin. My belly, a few days without a decent meal, was flat but the skin was crusty. The line of my belt had marked that crust, cut a path around my waist. My thighs had crusty skin and my knees were red and raw from having knelt on the kitchen floor. As I turned half-way before the mirror, I saw that the same skin condition continued down my back and across my shoulders and over my butt.

I was so frightened at my appearance that I wanted to cry. My eyes could not form tears, but the emotion of crying thundered through me, grabbing at anything before merging in my throat and all at once erupted in an anguished scream like nothing I had ever heard! Yet it was *me* making that sound! It was *me* who was filled with that pain! *Me* who was alone seeing himself fall apart, becoming a pile of dust, skin flakes, atop brittle bones—who would never again get to see his Beloved!

How could I ever let her see me now? How could I allow her to come close? I would never be able to endure her reaction to seeing me like this.

No—it did not matter what became of me; what mattered was that I could never be with Penny again.

Just rip out my heart right now and get it over with!

I went to the kitchen and took my favorite carving knife from the drawer, held it high over my head. My other hand located the entry spot, inside the ridge of my collarbone. Then a sharp thrust straight down into my heart—

But Penny would never know what happened to me, never know how much I loved her. She would never know that this act was not about her. This act was the result of having a dry patch of skin take over my life, bringing me to a horrible death.

"Aren't you coming in tonight?" asked Gerald, my snarly voiced supervisor, over the phone. The ringing had awakened me from my bitter sleep.

"Well, see, it's like this: I've come down with something."

"Yes, I remember you going off to a consult. And...?"

"Nothing conclusive. I still have symptoms, though, so I can't come in tonight. Sorry for the inconvenience. Call Sherry. She can use the hours."

Gerald was the last person I wanted to speak to, especially after a morning and afternoon of little sleep wracked by pain and shame and horror. I mocked him, condemning him to the fires of hell—yes: right over there, next to me!

It was evening, of course, since my usual shift was then beginning and Gerald had awakened me at dinner time. I had spent the day on my futon bed, stretched out naked, for pajamas would irritate my sensitive skin. I had slipped into and out of sleep a few times. Mostly I stared at the mottled pattern of the ceiling, interested in how closely it matched the mottled pattern of my skin.

I dropped the phone on the floor beside the futon, then thought to check for text messages from Penny. I rolled over to retrieve the phone and as my back pulled away from the mattress cover, I felt a tearing. I looked and saw my skin had stuck to the cover, ripped from my body. I tried to extricate the rest of my body from the mattress cover, inch by inch, until I managed to stand up beside the futon.

My foot touched something cold and I saw it was the knife, resting on the floor, unused. I bent to pick it up, my back stiff, my muscles weak as though I had completed two full marathons the previous day.

I shuffled into the bathroom, careful not to stare into the mirror. Standing before the toilet, I tried to let loose a stream of urine. Nothing. I *hmmph*ed, accepting my lack of piss as my poor hydration. I had tried hydration the previous evening, of course, but could not hold down the water.

I felt as though I was walking in my sleep. I imagined it was how it must feel to be a zombie. If I stumbled outside to check my mail from the vacation, would people in this apartment complex shout "Zombie!" and try to blow me away with a shotgun?

Instead, I contented myself to grab the remote and turn on the TV. I always left it set on Penny's station. As the TV came on, there was the 10 p.m. news broadcast in full swing. The story at that moment was another meth bust on the southeast side of the city. Next up, the anchor announced, a report on new technology the police department was using to monitor high traffic areas of the city. I stood stock still in the center of the living room, afraid to sit in my chair.

I stood through the commercials and then there was Penny, in a police office, pointing to a map of the city streets and talking about new software the department had purchased to help them track traffic flow to determine where best to place traffic lights in neighborhoods. Penny wore a red blazer over a yellow shirt with ruffles at the collar, black trousers, and in another shot I could see black flats on her feet. She wore her jet black hair full on her shoulders in the office shot but in a ponytail for what must have been an earlier shot along the busy street. For the outside shot, I noticed her lipstick: bright red. My eyes zoomed in on her lips. The story ended but I continued to gaze at the TV, in my mind still locked on her lips.

There had to be a way. Some kind of treatment. Something new that nobody had tried. I would do anything, no matter how risky, if only it would make me clean enough to be with Penny. At least make me look normal, at least my face, just so I can go out in public without people staring or throwing stones at me. Give me my face, enough that Penny might kiss me, and the Devil can take the rest.

During the night I tried to clean up my apartment, to get on with life, what there was of it. I made the kitchen and bathroom floors clean again. In the bedroom, I found the mattress cover had collected a ton of skin cells, flakes and hair that had rubbed off my body. I carefully unzipped and tugged on the cover to remove it from the mattress without scattering the debris. It seemed as though I really had molted: there was a body's worth of dead skin and hairs: a pile of fine, dust-like particles. I balled up the mattress cover and slipped a grocery bag over it, tied it securely. Next, I vacuumed the carpet to get rid of any of me that had escaped detection.

I sat at my desk, working at my computer, searching for more information, seeing what treatments existed somewhere in the world. I checked India first, the home of so many diseases both known and unknown, in that mass of humanity. If there was to be a cure, it would most likely be found in a place where many had suffered.

Despite a raging fever, I began to feel hungry and looked in the refrigerator and found nothing. A can of soup remained on the shelf in the cabinet, so I opened it, heated it in a pot, served it in a ceramic bowl. I mistakenly grabbed the bowl, knowing it was too hot in that first moment, but I felt nothing. No pain, no heat. I touched it deliberately again and I could not detect any heat even though I knew it was hot. Same with my other hand. Then, in my twistedly vain attempt to confirm something in a more or less scientific way, I applied my penis to the bowl and I finally felt the heat. I jumped back.

My trusty bathroom mirror was the measure of my fall from grace: drawn features, gaunt face, deep-set eyes, ghostlike. The rash, or however it would be described, had intensified. I was crusty and brown and itchy. My stomach was flat, empty, yet ached beyond hunger. My joints were swollen, painful. Bending my knees and elbows was agony.

I phoned in the prescriptions from Dr. Cadbury, had them delivered. I barely cracked the door to hand out a credit card for payment. I covered my head and face with a ski mask and told the deliveryman I had a rash.

After swallowing the tablets and injecting the liquid medicine through a syringe, I put myself to bed again.

Days passed.

My phone was full of messages I had not answered. I could hardly get to them, my fingers numb and unable to feel the keys. Work was calling, wondering when I would be returning. Penny called, wondering if I was all right. A few other calls from snake oil salesmen. I listened but could not think of how to reply. In voicemail, Penny was becoming alarmed. Text messages also showed her concern: more and more exclamation marks. The world did care about me, it seemed.

After another two days, I answered a call. I was feeling well enough to get something to eat. Soup again. As I stirred the concoction, the phone rang. I answered without seeing who was calling. It was Karen, the admin assistant. I confirmed I would be there for my shift but I'd be a little late. I wanted to wait until after dark, so nobody would see me. Sure, there was a camera at the entrance but I could pass quickly and not be noticed. I had to get back to work.

Besides, the laboratory was where I could find what I needed.

13

"Are you okay? Haven't heard from you."

It was Penny, my Beloved, calling to check up on me. It was after her 10 p.m. broadcast and I was alone in the lab, working.

"It's difficult to say."

"Why? What's wrong? Did you get it figured out?"

"I got all the tests." I listed them again for her and dismissed each disease. "I'm not a typical case, he said. I'm rare. In fact, he wanted to study me more, do a thorough investigation. I'd be famous, an important case study published in a medical journal. But I had to get back to my life. Got my job to do, which pays for my medical insurance. You get the irony?"

"Yes, it is ironic."

"I have my Beloved, too, from whom I cannot be away for too long. So I had to return. But my symptoms got worse on the way home. I barely made it back. I was on that plane for two hours, itching and burning...."

"Poor baby!"

"No, I'm serious. It's—it's advanced too much."

"What do you mean?"

"I don't look very good."

"You mean all that dry skin?"

"I wish it were only that. It's gone beyond that now."

"What could be beyond that?"

"It's well beyond lotion treatments. I got some prescriptions."

"Well, that's good. So it'll be taken care of soon, right? You take your medicine and you will be fine."

I started to rebut her, ready to say I wasn't so confident of the effectiveness of the medicine, but lost my breath. Emotions were welling up inside me and I could not hold them back.

"I want you so much," I cried, my heart pausing a beat, "but the way I look now I don't want you to see me."

"Oh, don't say that."

"It's true. I look bad."

"Define bad."

So I did: reddish-brown, flaky, peeling skin, hair falling out, inflamed joints—

"But I saw you with your dry, rough patches. I can handle it."

"You can't handle this."

"Buddy Bear, I need to see you," she said in her soft, cuddly voice. "I need *you* to need to see *me*. I can handle it."

I held my breath, on the verge of dismissing her again. Then I thought it might be for the best. My Beloved, as special as she was to me, was willing to take the test, a test of loyalty. Would she dare stay with me even with this horrid condition?

"All right," I said at last. "I will see you. But it better not be in a public place. I'm not going to put up with that again. I mean what I went through at the airport. I'm hiding from the world. Good thing I work nights, away from everyone."

"Oh, come on, Stefan. It can't be that bad. I'm sure you're just being dramatic. I had acne when I was a teen and I got through it. I got called a lot of names."

"I can't picture you with acne," I said, truly unable to imagine her sweet, clear face with such a condition. "Mine is worse. But, as you said, I need to see you. You need to see me. You need to decide if I'm worth hanging on to, or...."

"Or what?"

"You know...."

"If I'll dump you? Geez, you think I'm that shallow? If I love someone I'm not going to walk away just because he has some skin problem. Give me some credit for being a decent human being, Stefan."

I let out a sigh, my throat aching, my chest shivering.

"Yes, that's it. You took the words right out of my mouth," I said. "It's not a matter of loyalty, it's a matter of practicality. I would never insist someone stay with me if I had—have—with me having a condition like this."

The line was silent. I listened to her quickening breath.

"Is it curable?" asked Penny, just above a whisper.

"Good question. I hope so. I sure pray it is. The doctor was not sure what it is, so...we don't know."

"You don't know? Geez, what is it? What could it be?"

"It's a lot more than a dry patch of skin on my cheek. Now it's everywhere. I'm plain ugly. Hideous. I'm afraid to show myself to anyone. And I'm in pain, a lot of pain. And misery. I know this is going to kill me sooner or later, and the worse thing about it is that they will have to close the coffin because of how I will look."

Penny said something, and it might have been something positive, but my ears were ringing as my emotions overflowed and I could not make out her words.

"I'm sorry," was all I could say and clicked off my phone.

As I set my phone on the counter, emotion rumbling inside me, I turned slightly. And in that unfocused, confused motion, my elbow bumped the rack of vials there and the whole thing teetered on the edge of the counter. I held my breath, willing the rack not to fall, and then, as if the gods were having their joke on me, it tipped over and crashed to the floor. The vials rolled out but one of them had shattered, sending blood across the white tile floor.

I gasped—like when I was a child touring a horror house and the dancing skeleton jumped out in front of me.

That was a serious mistake, an amateur error, not taking care of samples. Carelessness. Not only could the ordered tests not be performed, but we had the embarrassment of calling the patient to give another sample.

It also made a mess on the floor that needed to be cleaned up immediately. Glass. Blood. And whatever microscopic debris that might remain on the tile floor after regular sterilization. My own shoes were covered in sterile covers, lest I track in any dirt. The lower hem of my lab coat had also gotten spotted in the splash.

I stared at the mess. I stared at my phone, playing the scene through my mind again. Turning to the paper towel dispenser, I stopped, thinking of the protocol for hazardous waste. If this was a sample from some drug addict or someone with a contagious disease, or teenagers in love, then it would be hazardous. I had latex gloves on already so I did not need to worry about that. But I hesitated. These vials had not been drawn by me. They came from the day shift and were left for me to run the panels. I stared at the loose unbroken vials and saw the handwritten scrawl on the label: TYPE AB.

Down on my knees, I leaned lower to read the label, hovering over the broken glass and spilled blood. It was from a woman, a Polish woman I guessed by her name. Sure that could be her married name, but even married she would not have changed her blood type. And AB was common in southern Poland—where it bordered Slovakia and, a little farther to the south, also Hungary. Therefore, I could only deduce she was of Polish ancestry—and possessed AB blood. Just like me.

Words from that *Twilight* book flickered through my head: something I recalled from the pages, a scene where Bella cuts herself and the entire Cullen family must bite their tongues to prevent their natural inclination to attack her from taking over. They could see the blood and, moreover, smell it. And yet, did her blood type matter? Were there different flavors of blood? Or was all blood equally tasty to them? In the book, they stated at one point that the blood of the wild animals they "lived" on, so as to not prey upon humans, was not as delicious as human blood.

When I was a child, one time I cut my finger on a metal can lid and before anyone could stop me I shoved my finger into my mouth and sucked the wound clean. The taste of the blood was neutral, flavorless. My action was merely efficient. It seemed to my child's mind to be the quickest way to solve the problem: soothe the cut and clean away the blood. I had no reason to fear my blood; it was part of me.

I extended my latex-covered finger and pressed it into that pooling sample of blood, and drew it back.

My fingertip was coated with that Polish woman's blood. I studied the way it oozed down my fingertip, then I plopped it straight into my mouth, like a lollipop, held it there, sucking off the blood, then licking the tip of my finger. It had no particular taste but it seemed to make my mouth burn. The inside of my cheeks tingled. I pulled out my finger and dabbed it again in the pool of blood on the floor, returned it to my mouth, knowing I was insane, fully and certifiably insane, to be doing what I was doing. I felt sick, disgusted with myself.

The thought of Penny seeing me flashed through my mind. Her face would show complete horror, then she would look away because I was so hideous, an animal, a monster to be scorned. That was my fate. I knew it instinctively, as surely as I could see my parents' faces in my mind. My father, frowning, his expression suggestive of seeing a son who had failed, failed to be strong enough to resist this nasty habit. My mother, eyes clenched as if crying yet unable to pull forth tears, mourning my erroneous choice. Both appraised me, speechless yet acknowledging I was now one of them: already a step or two down that path to immortality, to a chaotic, morbid, horrific life of death—

Who would care now?

I had no worry of STIs from an old woman who apparently had never been married. She lived in a nursing home, no doubt, pushing into her nineties. The worst I might ingest in that blood would be some free-radical keratins from her osteoporosis.

I stared at my clean finger and breathed deeply, as though I had just finished savoring a fine cigar. Perhaps at that moment I'd had a death wish; my actions were without care or prudence.

What did it matter now?

A stupid, childish act was all it was. Perverse, some might say.

Imaginary tears stung my eyes and my heart beat quicker as I swabbed up the spilled blood and wet my dry lips from the paper towel, licked off my lips, and swallowed slowly those droplets, as though it were a poison and I gladly awaited the first clench of my throat, the first catch of my heart skipping a beat, grinding to a halt. I would either awaken or die. And to be certain of it, since the patient would need to return and give a fresh sample anyway, I uncorked the next vial like a bottle of fine wine and sipped it all down with a satisfying, overly dramatic "Ahhh" before reaching for the next one. And the next one.

Part Two

14

SUMMER BREEZES DRIFTED ACROSS THE LAKE, warm and moist as they struck my face at the moment my Beloved crossed our agreed-upon finish line.

"I win!" shouted Penny, throwing her hands in the air as her bicycle continued on a short way. "I told you I could beat you!" she called back over her shoulder. "And by more than a couple lengths, huh!"

"Not fair," I cried out. "You know I'm out of shape." Certainly, I was out of breath. "And you're a lot lighter on your bike."

We coasted into the shade of the trees and hopped off our bikes, laid them in the grass, and went to each other, hugging, sweaty shirts and all. We didn't care. We had often mingled our sweat in less public activities.

"That Pilates class is paying off," she said, huffing and puffing.

We kissed, then went hand in hand to the base of that tree and stretched out under the branches. My Beloved scooted up against me, her head on my shoulder, my arm around her, both of us still breathing hard.

"It's much too hot for bike racing," I said. Nevertheless, I was enjoying being out with Penny, riding around Lake Hefner on a Sunday afternoon. The only thing I had to worry about at that moment was whether we had enough energy left for making love later. "That race wore me out. In fact, I might have gotten too much sun. My arms look kinda red."

She sat up as I held my arms aloft. "Maybe."

"Imagine if we had gone out riding in the middle of the day, like they always say to avoid."

"Hey, I don't want any sunburn, either," said Penny. "I've got to look good on camera, you know."

"You look perfect. Just a slight browning of your lovely skin." I rolled over slightly and kissed her forehead. "You really do have perfect skin. Flawless, in fact. Did I ever tell you?"

She just laughed.

"Did I ever tell you how much I love your back?" I asked. "I mean the skin on your back—how it's so smooth, from the nape of your neck to the vale of your butt."

"The what of what?" She giggled as only a serious news reporter would giggle. "You're crazy, Stefan!"

"Isn't that what it's called? The place where the lower back slides into the secret space between the buttocks. 'Butt crack' is so crude. I prefer Vale of Butt. More romantic—"

"Like you ever visit there!"

"Ah, but I *have* visited there. You've forgotten."

"It's not something I thought I should remember."

"But it's your butt."

"All right, enough of the butt jokes."

"But it's your fault. You make me crazy. But I digress...."

She play-slapped my ribs, then tried to rub the supposed pain away with her hand. Gazing up at me, she must have wondered if her rubbing had hurt my skin. I made no indication of it. She smiled quickly; I think both of us were thinking the same thing.

She climbed onto me like we were a couple of kids in some teen romance flick and the violins were swelling so lustfully. Or lusciously. Lushly? I can never keep that straight.

I reached out to help steady her, balanced on the point of my hip. She rolled onto my belly, settled into a comfortable position. My hand slid up her back, slipped under her shirt, caressing her spine. I worked my way to her shoulder blades.

"No bra?"

"No," she said, surprised. "Didn't you know that? You stood there watching me get dressed this morning. When I'm working out I'm more comfortable without it. Besides, you know I have no jiggle. I could go topless and nobody would blink. But you still accept me as I am."

"I do."

"And I accept you even with your occasional dry skin."

"You do."

"And even with all our faults we get along."

"We do."

"And since you're so focused on using *that phrase* today, I want you to know...well, I've been thinking. I mean, when you were away I missed you. I don't mean to get all sappy and such. I didn't think I would miss you. We're mature people so we don't get freaked just because a lover is gone a couple weeks."

"You freaked out?"

"No, I said we *don't* do that. But I did miss you. Surprised? Kinda surprised me, too. And ever since you got over your skin problem, I realized I really like hanging out with you. I mean, I know you're totally insane, but in a good way—"

"There's a good way?"

"Yes, there is. And I like having you around almost every day. I really look forward to our weekends together. So then I started thinking maybe *every* day would be even better. You know? So if you want—if you *still* want to—don't laugh, Stefan, and please don't faint, either—"

"I'm on my back anyway."

"If you want to, I think it might be cool if we, you know, if we went ahead and got married after all. I think I'm ready. I want to spend the rest of my life with you. What do you think? Ring and all. Do you still want that?"

"I do." The words caught in my throat, like that sliver of bone you never expect in a tender filet. "I did—I mean, I *do*. I still do. I want that. If you do, too."

"I do!"

"Then let's do it."

We embraced—so tightly I thought I was squeezing out her last breath, which would have been a terrible predicament to be in considering that she had finally agreed to marry me. And she was also pressing her clasped hands against my backbone hard enough to crack my vertebrae. I thought I heard a crack. Clearly we did not want each other to get away. We swept into a sloppy liplock that lasted several minutes, trying alternate positions, broken only when the next couple to ride past our tree called over to us as we were making out: "Having a nice day there?"

Penny wiped her hair out of her face, grinning like she had just stolen my heart and I had not yet discovered it missing. I licked my lips, as though savoring the best ice cream ever. The taste of her lips filled my senses. Or was it something else I had tasted?

We recovered and sat up, gazing into each other's eyes, studying the universe we found there. I could feel a burning sensation running through my body, but it was not the result of my former affliction. No, this time I knew the cause. It was that ever-eternal experience of complete and ultimate love. Yes, that kind. The joining of two souls. This woman was my Beloved! She was the One! And my heart was on fire!

My whole body sizzled, in fact.

Suddenly, I was worried.

We rode our bikes back to the parking lot and hitched them in the rack hanging on the back of the SUV.

Stopping off at the neighborhood Target, we picked up food for dinner. I remembered everything about a previous visit there months before: about the power going out, the food spoiling in the chill cases, and that disfigured devil child who frightened me. It seemed like a year ago, long enough for me to have shaken it off. Yet I could not. After all, I'd had my own sojourn in the land of the forlorn, trying to pass through the world of normal people. Whatever problem that odd-looking child had, I was a much more sympathetic person now. It seemed to be a lesson I was meant to learn. Although why I needed to learn it, I could never fathom; I had always been a fairly decent fellow with a modicum of compassion and empathy, perhaps even a bit more than the average Joe. Still, somewhere in the karma bookkeeping office I had been found wanting and a lesson had been assigned to me.

Sure, my eyes drifted across the soccer moms in their yoga pants and tanktops. They looked hot and seemed happy they had caught my eye. However, I was the lucky one now, for I had the lovely Penny Park to share my life with, and when she entered my field of vision, I dropped those old soccer moms like a bad rash. Penny was my destiny, after all. She had stuck by me during my darkest days, promised to stay with me no matter my health problems. And for that faithfulness, I had gladly done whatever was necessary to be able to stay with her.

Whatever was necessary....

Through the evening hours of that Saturday night, we had lounged in the bed, in the comfort of each other's aura. Love was made several times. I was good, Penny was good, we were good. No complaints about dry skin. No strange patch here or there. No red-brown scaly skin or burning, itching skin. Everything was as it should always have been.

In the morning, we stood naked before the wide mirror in the bathroom and were pleased by how healthy we appeared: two lucky people, hugging and kissing like silly teenagers. Then we dressed and went for a bike ride around the lake.

Returning to her apartment after our ride, we showered and went straight to the bed, unmade from our morning playfulness. With a line of kisses down her back, I preceded to massage her with my hands. I thought I knew what she liked but this time she balked. She said my hands were too rough. Not the firmness of my strokes but the friction of my hands against her smooth back.

I apologized.

"Probably they got rough from the grips on the bike handles," she said. "Mine are sore, too."

"Yes, that's it." I held up my hands, studied my palms: red and sore, hard and rough. I held them to my face. Yes, a little rough.

"We don't have to do anything," said Penny.

I pouted. "But I want to do something."

"You still got energy?"

She rolled onto her side, facing me and I dropped onto my back beside her, releasing a sigh to show my disappointment.

"I suppose I *have* hit the wall, as they say."

"Plenty of couples live perfectly happy lives not having sex." The syrup in her voice took away the pain of her words. "Doesn't mean they don't love each other. When you and I met, I never had any plans to have sex with you. That was the last thing on my mind. You were just a guy I met online."

"Not me. I wanted you right there in the Barnes and Noble. On that little table. I even had a condom in my pocket."

"I doubt that!"

"No, it's true."

"What a perv!"

"And I still am."

She offered me a brightly wrapped smirk. "But, as we got to know each other, it became a way to show you how much I care about you. I don't mean it was some kind of reward I was giving you, like for cleaning the kitchen or something. I just wanted to share some love with you. You were my candy store. I wanted to play and you were willing to play with me."

"Gee, I wish I'd know that sooner. About your, umm, play thing. Your candy store fetish."

"But there are other ways to share our love."

"Someday we'll be old and wrinkled."

"See? We need to be satisfied being together without always expecting it to end in some kind of sex. We're not a couple of horny kids. You're already forty-five and I'm going to be thirty-three next week. It's enough to just hold each other sometimes, don't you think? Now hold me tight."

She snuggled against me and I wrapped my arm around her shoulders, gave her a firm squeeze.

"Yeah, that's it. Like that."

"I am so tired from the bike ride," I said with a sigh.

"Go on, then. Rest. I'll watch over you, make sure nobody forces you to make love. I know you hate that."

My ribs ached as I laughed. "I don't actually hate it, but I'll give you a pass. It's been a great day—a great weekend. I love being with you no matter what we do."

"That's the spirit. We are a couple now. We can do anything. And we don't *have* to do anything, also. We have lots of time to be together. We have to keep getting along. Otherwise, there's no point in getting married."

We cuddled for an hour or so and I may have drifted into a nap a few minutes here and there. Awakening, we realized we had become stuck together, skin to skin, so we carefully pulled our naked torsos apart.

"Wow," said Penny sitting up, "you really got some sun today. You look redder now than when we got home."

I rose up on my elbows, scanned my chest and belly. She was correct. "You never see it right away. It shows up later."

"Maybe you'd better put some lotion on your skin before it gets too sore."

"Would you like to do the honors?"

She got the lotion from the bathroom and began rubbing it carefully over my shoulders as I sat up on the side of the bed. She continued down my back. Her fingers worked gently but my skin tingled. It was burnt. Despite wearing a knit shirt with collar, the sunshine had penetrated it and struck me. Here in Oklahoma, I was under constant attack. Only Penny's amateur nursing skills saved me. Her hands were soft.

She helped me pull on a fresh shirt from my weekend drawer and we said goodnight.

"Until next time, Buddy Bear."

We kissed for a few minutes outside her open door.

Sunday night. The weekend was done. Time for me to retreat to my little bachelor pad.

The result of my exposure to so much sun was apparent when I got home and stripped off my shirt and shorts. My skin had turned red, as Penny had seen, but for me it was different than a simple sunburn. My skin was drying out once more, tightening like a plum turning into a prune, becoming flaky, itchy, and unsightly.

At least I was able to get through the weekend with Penny. I didn't think she suspected anything was wrong. She thought the medicine had cured me, and I allowed her to believe that.

The truth is quite different, of course, which is my reason for needing to explain it. I want everything to be clear, if only for the sake of any future generation.

The truth....

First, let me make myself more comfortable.

(No, I'm not digressing; I really need to get this done without further delay. Please bear with me.)

I swing open the refrigerator and retrieve the glass bottle better suited for lemonade—something a little girl might pour from when selling a drink at a wooden stand at the end of her driveway. Instead of the pinkish liquid of lemonade, however, there is only a faint purplish hue, the dried residue of what once was inside, now reduced to the final portion. It swirls sluggishly around the bottom as I lift it from the shelf and hold it up to the light. It's rather discouraging to find my supply down to the last unit.

Yes, I do indeed take a kind of medicine to treat my affliction. The only problem, really, is that it was not prescribed for me. Not specifically. No, my medicine is a standard size bag of blood, Type AB, which has been mistakenly excluded somehow from the inventory at the blood bank where I've started working.

And what have you to say in response?

People drink a lot of strange things. People eat weird foods, too. Different tastes for different people, different cultures. And some find that what they drink renews harmony to their bodies. It's like the vegetable smoothie that restores nutritional balance. Similarly, my daily drink serves to bring my body into normal equilibrium. I look good. No skin problems. I have energy and feel no pain. For about 24 to 36 hours. Then the benefits start to wane. I can hold out maybe 48 hours—a good weekend with Penny, for one example. Then I begin to revert to whatever my body is trying to transform itself into, continuing that horrible process, if I do not actively work to subvert it.

This is my new reality.

I'm sorry to say it. I am not proud of myself and what I have done. Please accept what I say as a confession, a necessary plea for understanding. I do not wish to become a monster. I do not want to give up a life of happiness with my Beloved. I will not be transformed into something hideous that the world will hate. I do not accept that fate.

Therefore, I did what I had to do: I dared sip the blood of Eunice P. Kowalsky, a Polish immigrant, indeed, a Holocaust survivor, and so causing her inconvenience and discomfort. I was selfish, but also desperate. Moreover, she had Type AB.

Before she died, I was able to sneak some swallows from the pre-surgery supply she had been accumulating, creating a supply of her rare type to be used for transfusions, if needed. I cannot say with any certainty whether or not the supply intended to cover her needs during surgery was adversely affected by my casual siphoning. It wasn't so much: an amount barely noticed. Yet you will hate me for it.

Of course I did not consider her needs. I was not thinking clearly, nor was I particularly sympathetic to her plight. I had my own plight to worry about. I was dying—or worse, becoming one of the *undead* who roam the Earth unable to fully live or to truly die, shunned and exiled. Not made into those sparkly heroes of teen romances. Not like them.

It's a rare blood type, so when she passed on at her hospice almost two months after a successful operation, I was without a regular supply. I had taken a new job at the blood bank where her supply was being saved for surgery, after tracking her various medical visits through a long list of lab requests.

Actually, it was an additional job. First, it was part time, only to help out during blood drives. Then summer accidents, storms, and surgeries left the bank low in its inventory. I was good at bringing in business. I even dressed up as Count Dracula—the comedic *Sesame Street* version—just to liven the mood. I took my turns drawing blood from willing donors and none of them felt any pain. They liked my work and made me full time.

With a daily dose of this human Merlot, I was full of energy. I could work 24 hours without fatigue. I could go through a full night shift at the lab, then with a quick liquid breakfast continue into my day shift at the blood bank.

Mostly, I checked inventory. It seemed there was always a bag extra. It did not have to be Type AB; I chose A as my back-up. B came next, if that was all that was available. I avoided O like the plague. AB remained a rare delicacy, but occasionally I would be able to dine on the treat from some generous Eastern European donor. Those were the good days. Thankfully, it did not take much to restore me. A full mouthful was all I seemed to need. A bit more if A, even more if B. And as the summer slipped into fall, I noticed it was taking a slightly greater dose to maintain the benefits. All I really could ask for was enough to get me through the weekend.

Penny noticed only my propensity for a steady erection. She even accused me of taking one of those blue pills to maintain it. However, mine was all natural. The blood flowed quite well in me and I was always ready, always firm, and always interested in advancing our sexual appetites as far as it could be pushed. Even I noticed how my libido seemed elevated when compared to my youthful past. It was probably another effect of my treatment protocol.

My skin was good, too: clear, blemish-free, an even tone of pinkish-beige leaning toward albino. I did not yet glow in the dark but next to her summer tan the contrast was startling. We enjoyed that contrast, and she joked about me being a snowman. I laughed, of course, because anything my Beloved would say as humor deserved a sincere laugh. I was never happier than when I was with her, and being beside her in bed gave me reason to live. It was not simply about sex—or lack of sex, as she occasionally insisted—it was more: the hope and promise of our life together.

We had looked at wedding gowns, had checked caterers, and spoken with the minister at her Korean church. It was a go. We had a date set: the one year anniversary of our previous break-up, ironically. We got rings and they looked beautiful on her delicate fingers. Then I put aside the wedding band for that special golden day of heaven-on-earth. I put the ring box in the top drawer of the chest in the bedroom at my little bachelor apartment, hidden from the world until that day.

I closed the drawer, checking the ring, finding it still there, calm once more after confirming that it was not all a dream. Then I returned to the kitchen and poured a small cup of blood and sipped it much like I used to sip a latté in the café of the Barnes & Noble bookstore. It didn't feel so weird. I rinsed my mouth thoroughly, not wanting her to taste anything bad on my lips. I was perfectly normal. For 24 hours, at least. Then I needed to drink again. It was now a habit. Twice a day.

This could not continue. Once we were bound as husband and wife, living in the same apartment, where would I store my supply? How could I continue taking my daily medicine with her there? If she knew what I was doing, would she leave me? Or would she stick by me, accepting this strange habit, and help me live a long life despite it? I was nervous about the answers. I thought I could guess how she would react, but I had no idea what such news would mean to this wonderfully pleasant woman, Penny Park, ace news reporter and my Beloved.

I needed to find a real treatment, a permanent solution—a cure.

15

Nobody would disparage me were I to announce my intention to seek better treatment.

I panicked when Eunice Kowalsky passed on, but I was hired by the blood bank. I thought it was the right move in order to support my habit. Now I panic whenever someone checks the inventory and finds a bag missing. How much longer can I maintain my supply? I continue to wonder if reestablishing my blood antigens is the best, or only, way to treat myself.

I returned to the internet. The usual online search engines did not provide much of value. Popular hits did not translate into authoritative resources. I read many bogus websites offering spa treatments for a variety of skin ills. They looked nice, certainly, but the medical aspects were murky, at best, and downright false and potentially harmful at worst. I got into medical databases, as I had done to try to learn about my affliction. Treatments were specified in several scholarly articles. Yet they seemed logistically impractical or did not fit my particular situation. My symptoms fit more than a dozen diseases. Not even Dr. Cadbury could pin it down. If I could have stayed longer, he was quite eager to keep investigating my affliction.

My own research came down to two avenues: the health spa, usually located in a hot springs resort area or at a beach town where you could enjoy the view, or they were something that even a twisted mind would label as weird. Cross-referencing a few of them brought me to a short list, which I studied intensely for every bit of information, my skeptical radar flagging anything incongruous. I could not afford to take much time, expense, or run the risk of worsening my problem. However, I did want to live—and live comfortably.

I debated whether to seek such a treatment before or wait until after the wedding.

The wedding....

Was I really so crazy as to marry Penny? I mean, sure, I was crazy in love with her, but the other side of me dreaded sharing this deviant maelstrom with her. I didn't want her involved. My affliction being genetic, it was not likely. And yet, because I was charging down uncharted territory, I had no way of knowing what strange things were latching onto me and that I might then pass on to her. I had to protect my Beloved from myself.

We had gone to the Barnes & Noble one Sunday afternoon, getting lattés and perusing wedding magazines, and my Beloved forced my hand in the matter.

"Tomorrow's a holiday, so I'm off," she said so nonchalantly. "You want to sleep over tonight?"

I turned and gazed at her, saw the twinkles in her eyes. "You mean tonight?"

"Yes. Monday holiday. I'm not working."

A weekend I could handle. I loaded up on my "medicine" and everything was fine until Sunday night. Already, at 4 p.m., I was feeling a bit itchy. My skin was drying. I was merely being polite, staying with her as late as I could. Then she threw out this idea that I should stay longer. Do not be mistaken: I *wanted* to stay longer with her. But I could not. So I panicked.

"I have to work, though."

"Well, can't you get up and go to work as usual? You're a big boy. You know what to do. And you have everything you need already at my place."

"That's all true." I knew she could tell my voice was strained.

"Come on, it'll be fun."

"Fun?" What kind of fun would that be? Watching my body decay? Seeing me transform?

"We can make some of that love you always like to make," she said, her voice becoming sing-songy. "Tonight's a good night for that kind of whoopee."

"Whoopee?"

She frowned. "You're not interested?"

There was no way I could refuse without being rude, without her thinking I somehow no longer enjoyed making love with her. Nor without her becoming suspicious that I had alternative plans for the evening, maybe another woman.

I smiled, showed a big set of teeth, and at that moment I felt she might have noticed how my gums had begun receding. A swipe of my tongue let me know that more of my teeth were visible than a few months ago.

"All right." I thought for a moment. "I'll need to stop at my apartment for a few things."

She drove, we stopped, and she wanted to come in with me. I insisted she wait in the SUV, saying my apartment was a mess, which it was. She offered to help pick up while I gathered what I needed for the extra night at her apartment. Of course, you could guess I only wanted to get a sip of my fountain of youth elixir. I dared not let Penny see that.

"I don't mind," she said.

"Please wait here. I'll be quick."

I got out of the SUV and disappeared through the breezeway and into my apartment.

First, I took a bathroom break, feeling the need but not able to produce much. Not even after a venti-sized latté.

I went to the kitchen next, opened the refrigerator, and just as I reached for the bottle I heard the front door open.

"Oh, this isn't bad." It was Penny—who else? "You had me worried. You're okay at my place, I mean you're neat there, so I was imagining some huge catastrophe over here, but it's really not too bad."

I swung the refrigerator door shut, grinning like someone caught urinating in the park.

"What are you doing?" she asked, coming into the kitchen.

To feign insanity, I had dropped my pants when she entered the apartment. That would back-up my look of embarrassment. I kicked them off my feet, into the corner under the dinette table so I was only wearing briefs.

"You caught me. I was going to switch clothes tonight. Then I could go ahead and wear them to work tomorrow."

That made sense.

She asked if I had anything to drink. She was thirsty. How about that latté she had finished an hour earlier? Why was she making this so difficult for me? I was already feeling itchy. I had scratched my fingernails across my chest and one shoulder to ease the sensation. The red marks were visible.

I got dressed in fresh clothes with her as a witness, an eager fashionista, selecting a different shirt for me than what I first pulled out of the closet.

Then we finally went to her apartment, me following her SUV so we could easily go our separate ways in the morning.

Let me make a long story very short: we tried to make love and it was awkward, and we finally gave up. I told her I did not feel well. The usual problems. My hands were rough, she said.

She was sympathetic, repeating her mantra: "We don't have to do anything."

I hid in the bathroom with the lights off like a shy schoolboy.

The lights in the bedroom were off when I returned. Dressed in a pair of sweat pants and long-sleeve t-shirt. Summer outside, A/C inside. And socks.

"You're all bundled up?" she asked, touching my shoulder with her hand as I slipped between the sheets.

"I'm feeling itchy again."

She knew what I meant and hugged my shoulder. "Sorry. I should've let you stay home, like you seemed to want."

I insisted I wanted to sleep over some other night. Without a new dose of blood, I knew what was going to happen. I could anticipate it but I had never let myself go that long without the next dose. Yet I could not simply run out. Not now. Not at half-past midnight.

The morning was chaos. Penny's cries awoke me and my waking reaction to her screams shocked her even more.

"You're bald!" she shrieked.

Around my pillow lay bundles of my hair. It seemed half of my hair had fallen out and lay in clumps around my head. That was new.

I sat up, felt my head. Bare skin. Flaky, dry skin. Withdrawing my hand, a few strands had been caught in my fingers. And my hands! Like the hands of a very old man: gaunt and cruel, nails elongated, the effect of skin pulling back, and the tendons and blue veins distinct through the crisp, papery skin.

"Reaction to the drugs, I suppose," was all I could say.

"Drugs?" she asked, alarmed. "You're still taking medicine? I thought you were cured. I thought you were all right. You said you were all right."

I took a breath, felt my lungs ache for it, and from it. I tried to sit up, got one arm behind myself and paused in that position. The sight of her distraught face made me want to cry. But I could not produce tears. She was never supposed to see me this way. I had never seen me this way, either. Not this far gone.

"No, I still have to take medicine."

"For how long?"

"I missed the dose last night."

"Because I bothered you? Came in and distracted you? Why didn't you just say you had to take your medicine?"

"I was embarrassed."

"But this? *This?* This is what happens when...just overnight? ...if you miss a dose?"

"Apparently. I wasn't sure. I've never missed a dose before."

"So what is it? Cancer?"

"It's an autoimmune disorder. My body is trying to kill me. It thinks I'm the enemy. Funny, that."

"But it's not funny!"

"No, but it's ironic. A body trying to kill itself. A kind of suicide. And it's taking me down with it. I'm sorry."

"Sorry?"

"I'm sorry you have to see me this way."

"No, I mean.... I don't know what I mean, Stefan."

"Help me up and I'll get out of here." Emotion roared through me, like the shockwaves of a bullet. "I'll leave you alone. You don't need to deal with this. I'll get out of your life. You don't deserve this—me—all of this."

I pushed myself up, swinging my legs and feet to the floor. I saw her take a step to help me, then halt, hesitant whether or not to touch me. I teetered on the edge of the bed. I teetered on the edge of my life. With a few breaths, I managed to stand and my wobbly steps toward the bathroom made me feel as though I was a hundred years old.

"I have been looking for a better treatment," I grumbled from the bathroom, keeping the lights off.

Enough light came in through the small window to show me what she saw. It was too late. She had seen me at my worst. She could never unsee that.

"Doing searches online. Finding some place where this can be treated. Then I will be back to normal. I can't keep up this...this medicine protocol much longer anyway. I need to increase the dose to maintain its benefits but the steady increase is getting to be too much and that's causing side effects." I poked at a tooth, felt it loose in my jaw. "The main thing is that I revert quicker each time I go too long without it. Now you see what happens. I'm sorry you saw me this way."

I thought I could hear her crying out in the bedroom.

"Penny, I'm sorry."

"When were you going to tell me?" she called out.

"Hopefully never. I was sure I could beat this thing before the wedding."

"The wedding? Ohmagod! Oh. My. God. *The wedding?*"

I swallowed hard, felt a lump in my throat that was likely coagulated blood coming up from my stomach.

"Never did I do anything to hurt you," I called out to Penny. "I don't want this to be happening to me. I want to be cured. I want to love you forever. I *will* love you forever. But I know you can never be with me. Not now."

I saw some scissors in a half-opened drawer, part of her hair care tools. My hand wanted to grasp it, see if it was sharp enough to push through my papery skin. Maybe I could end it all now. I could demonstrate my sincerity to her.

"I will leave you and never bother you again," I spoke. "You don't have to marry me. I release you from any and all promises."

The cold steel of the scissors felt good, felt right in my hand but suddenly I could not do it. Not there in her bathroom. The hassle of calling the police to clear away the body and deal with statements would be cruel. No, I could not do it in her place.

"Let me get out of here," I said.

She came to the door of the bathroom, arms crossed over her chest. "That's not what I mean."

I looked at the dark image of her bouncing off the shadowed mirror. My heart shook, my hands trembled. I turned around to face her.

"Let me get my dose and I'll be good as new by tomorrow. I'll call in sick today and fix myself."

"Oh, Stefan...."

I pinned my arms to my sides and pushed past her, going into the bedroom to get dressed. I reached for my clothes.

"Yes, what about Stefan? Isn't he a fool? A fool! He finally got everything he deserved. He got his beloved Penny, the One, then he got this disease that will ruin it all. What a cruel fate!"

"Stefan, don't talk like that."

"It's true. Remember that dry patch of skin? That first time? It's spread. This is me. This is the best I can be—for today. It will worsen each day if I do not continue the treatment. Can you stand to look at me?"

With my back to her, I heard sniffling again, a sob. She never got emotional, even when covering a devastating tornado or a car crash or violent crime. She was steady, above the fray, a reporter delivering the facts: cold, hard facts. I had never seen her cry.

She did not answer as I gathered my things from the drawer.

"You can send anything else to me later. No hurry. Or give it to the poor. Or throw it all away. Who cares? It's all probably contaminated. Call in the haz-mat team."

"I care," she grunted as I headed toward the door.

"I'll find a cure. I *will*."

"I do care, Stefan."

"I'm going to find a place where they can treat this goddamn condition."

"But where?"

"I'm sure it will be far away. You needn't worry."

"But I love you, Stefan."

"Thanks. I wish it didn't have to happen this way."

"Please don't go."

"I must go—somewhere."

"Stefan, *nooo*—"

"I love you, Penny. And I'm sorry for everything."

16

New Orleans. The Big Easy. Though not as easy as I thought it would be.

I drove from Oklahoma, avoiding the hassle of passing through airports and sitting on planes. Took about twelve hours. I went overnight to avoid the masses of humanity who always seem to get in my way. I also did not want to be stared at.

And for each mile I covered, the more I cursed my fate. My foot was heavy on the pedal and I did not care if I was chased by highway patrol. I did not care if I lost control and crashed. I was sick, wounded by destiny. I did not care what happened to me. As I drove, I sucked on my bag of blood with a straw, like it was a child's juice box. And each sip brought me the realization that I had nothing more to lose. I could find a treatment but not likely a cure, and in those moments of realization, I thought I felt tears bunch in the corners of my eyes, but with a finger's wipe I found it was only a grain of sand. If I could have cried, I would have pulled over and shaken my fist at the sky, shouted at God to strike me down before I could suffer any longer.

Eventually, I arrived. But I was not a tourist, not allowed to be amazed or grateful or excited to be there. I was on a business trip, and my business was a matter of life or death.

I followed the map I printed out from Google, which got me to within a square mile of my destination: the French Quarter. Where better to meet up with some person operating a voodoo clinic?

Parking my car in a garage, I went to an old hotel that looked creepier than I did. The front desk woman, kerchief over her head and a jagged scowl on her brown face, seemed to know all my business. A glance and an "mm-hmm" to acknowledge my arrival. I had no reservation but I believed a back alley lodging would give me more privacy. I didn't want anyone looking at me or wondering about my business.

I took my bag up the stairs myself and found the room. The furniture was third-hand, the bed too soft, the TV twenty years old with a bent antenna. The bathroom might have been cleaned sometime during the preceding year. I had a lovely view of the next building: red brick and stucco, and a banjo-playing old man sitting at the open window there.

I stripped off everything and stood in front of the bathroom mirror to check myself. Not bad—made the trip without much decay. Looking respectable enough, I saw there were some red, scaly patches visible, spreading across my chest from collarbone to navel. How would the drive back be? My "medicine" would be used up shortly. The six-pack cooler I'd brought only contained one bag.

I sent a text message to Penny that I arrived but got no reply. Even by later that evening when I awoke from my daytime sleep.

With a few recommendations for dining, I went out in search of a snack. I was not too hungry. I walked past several eateries and selected the emptiest one, a brasserie, where I got a quiche when what I really craved was blood pudding. Bad joke.

Let me laugh while I can.

After dinner, as directed in email communications, I found a pay phone on the street and made the call. It was all quite mysterious. At first I was nervous contacting this strange entity I found on the internet one morning after work. Then it became a game, a chance for me to play along, figuring out who did what with what weapon and in what room. I was sure it was the butler with the wooden stake in a basement dungeon. Now I was here, standing beside what surely must be the last pay phone in the city, in a dark alley between two crumbling buildings, the noise of a bar in one direction and the music of a strip club in the other, the game becoming quite real. I plunked in some coins, a pocketful more awaiting use if the call went longer.

The person answering had a bass voice and spoke with a thick French accent, which did not particularly alarm me given where I was. I cleared my throat, said my name and gave a code word I was supposed to use. I felt dirty.

I could have called from the hotel or used my cell phone but they had recommended a public phone. Was this a legal operation? If it was a real treatment center, why all the secrecy? What were they really doing?

The website design suggested something more like a massage parlor—perhaps "massage" should be in quotes—rather than a clinic. The inner pages presented the treatments available, for "everything that ails thee," and more. A good, basic, therapeutic massage was listed. Probably just for show. What interested me was the reference to "preventing voodoo curses" which under normal circumstances I would have placed in the same category as séances and palm readings. However, I was desperate. At least I could go and see what they had to say about my condition.

The man on the phone gave me instructions: where to go and what to say. Now I was truly nervous. All this way to New Orleans just to hook up with some scam. Of course it seemed a scam from the website up to this moment. And yet I was drawn to it. I needed what they offered—if it really worked.

I didn't get much information via their website "contact" link. A few emails only, short and vague. The voodoo curses treatment they offered seemed to be for easing the fears of someone who believed he'd had a curse put on him. I certainly felt a curse had been put on me, but probably only by God. Such curses might lead to the person becoming...wait for it: a zombie. I vaguely knew that voodoo and zombies were linked. Haiti, I believe, and other Caribbean origins. A corpse was removed from its grave and reanimated, made to do the bidding of its master. Hardly the stuff of science-fiction thrillers. The list of symptoms was long and any handful of them could apply to just about anyone. A few seemed to describe me perfectly. I wondered if it was a zombie I was becoming, not a vampire. Was there really any difference? One searched for brains, the other for blood, both mindlessly, pushed by instinct. If I were someone like that and I had the requisite symptoms, perhaps this clinic could treat my condition, whether through FDA-approved medications or with some weird natural healing method.

So, following instructions, I took a taxi to Metairie, west of the downtown business district.

As we drove, I checked my phone again: no messages from Penny. I sent another text, letting her know I was heading to the "clinic" and might be offline for a couple days.

When we arrived at a certain address, I got out and watched the taxi drive off in the direction we had come.

It was dark except for the occasional streetlamp. It was a quiet street at that hour but I began to panic. I knew something bad was about to happen.

The neighborhood did not appear to be crime-ridden but I was from out of town and all I knew was what I'd gotten from TV news broadcasts. I still remembered all the crime after Hurricane Katrina passed over the city, desperate people clinging to life, and others taking advantage of an open, lawless city. And here I was standing on a street corner, looking for a date.

Yes, that was a joke. I needed a joke then. So I tried to see the humor in what I was doing. I could imagine Penny laughing in her skeptic's voice as I told her the story. Someday.

The sultry night air was oppressive and I could not breathe as easily as in my air-conditioned apartment. A little while longer, I told myself. My chest was tight and I had to force myself to take deeper breaths. I touched my face, felt my cheek: still soft and supple, normal.

"Where is my date for tonight?" I muttered, pacing a slow circle on that street corner.

Thirty minutes later, I checked my watch.

A car was approaching slowly. The headlights went off as it came beside me. It was a black stretch Cadillac, one space more than a regular version but not long enough that I would call it a limousine. The side window lowered and a black man looked out at me.

"Name?" asked the man.

Odd question for someone just pulling up alongside a curb to address a man standing there. That had to mean he was the right one. Who else would do that but the man I was supposed to meet? At least he did not ask "How much?"

I told him my name and he asked for i.d. so I pulled out my driver's license and showed him. Then the car door opened and I took the hint to climb in.

The rear seats faced each other and so did we. The driver put his foot to the gas and we drove on at a quick pace, probably late to our appointment.

My escort looked me over, grinning, a slight smirk playing in the corner of his mouth. He must have known I was desperate, desperate enough to take the risks: getting into a strange car with a strange man from a strange corner of a strange city in the middle of the night. Yes, I was certainly crazy. I could die any number of ways, I knew. Within 48 hours without my regular dose of blood, I might crash and burn—literally, as my cells burst and flooded my body with poisons. I said a prayer, an old ritual my aunt had taught me for whenever I was afraid: "Let it end quickly."

After several minutes, he introduced himself as Travaille. Mr. Travaille—pronounced Truh-veye. I got the spelling from the business card he handed to me. He worked for the woman I was going to meet. As he spoke, I recognized his voice as the one I'd heard in the phone call. French but in a rich bass that shook the car even at a low volume.

When we arrived at our destination, Mr. Travaille ordered me out. I got out of the Caddie and stood on the curb as he followed. He gave instructions to the driver, then waited until the car had departed before turning his attention to me.

He stood taller than me, like a basketball player, but I did not say anything to him about that. His hands were large and his grin was white-toothed. With a flip of his hand, he sent me on ahead, up the steps.

The house before me was an antebellum mansion that was showing its age. A portico and columns, set on a low rise, steps going up from the street to the front door. Double doors. No veranda; that would be in the back. My escort sent me up the steps alone and when I got to the double doors, I was not sure whether to knock or ring the bell I saw. I looked back and he was following me.

"Go in," said Travaille.

I placed my hand on the door handle and pushed. The doors opened and I stepped into an elegantly decorated anteroom, a foyer, the kind where you expect a butler to ask for your coat and hat. I had neither, given the haze of humidity outside. I waited as Travaille closed the doors behind us and waved me ahead.

The house was quiet and seemed empty. Was I the last visitor of the evening? Or perhaps I was the first.

About to exit the foyer for the grand ballroom—or whatever it was called, certainly not a living room; who would simply sit and watch TV in such a large, ornate room?—Travaille paused and turned to me.

"You better gimme the money now."

I don't know why I looked puzzled. I knew the amount. In cash. By then I doubted it was a robbery or a shakedown or even a scam. There would be a meeting with someone named Mama Mambo. Whether or not what she had to say was based on any true qualifications or not was yet to be seen.

Pulling out a wad of bills held together with a wide rubber band, I felt like a gangster, walking around with so much cash in my pocket, rolled up that way. Definitely a high roller.

"Here."

Travaille held out his hand and I set the rolled bills on it. His fingers curled around it and he withdrew his hand. He seemed to be able to weigh it and determine if it contained the expected amount. He grinned as if he was acknowledging another sucker had been born, then deposited the roll into his jacket pocket.

"Go on," he said with a push of his chin. "Go on in dere."

Through another set of doors, I felt I was entering the court of the queen. Indeed, it was close. The medium-sized room had walls covered in blood red and royal purple wallpaper in patterns of antebellum horses and riders, seemingly designed for nothing else but as fitting background for the dais in the center. A raised platform, covered in a burgundy carpet, sat in the middle of the room. Around the periphery of the room were straight-backed chairs, enough for a squad of patients, clients, or whatever we were called. With the chairs were a few small tables, some with small lamps, half of them turned off. On the dais was a great chair. I might even call it a throne but it did not have such a high back.

Occupying that grand chair was a rather large black woman whose head seemed hairless yet bore a tattoo of three tropical birds, their tails descending her forehead to her eyebrows.

This had to be the famous Mama Mambo.

"Come forth, mistah," the woman intoned as though she were in a trance. Her voice low and melodic.

I stepped forward, up to the edge of the dais, which rose six inches higher than the floor.

"What be yo troubles?" said this woman.

"It seems that I have—"

"Troubles aplenty...."

"Yes, my skin...I have some skin condition which seems—"

"I can smell it from here."

"Sorry, I—I showered before I went out this evening—"

"What be yo name?"

"My name is Stefan Sz—"

"It don't matter where you be from, only you need help."

"That's right. I've tried everything—"

"Did he pay? Don't bring me nobody ain't paid."

Travaille took a step forward. "He paid."

I looked closely at the woman's face, eyes squinted shut. Was she blind? She said she could smell me. I supposed the humidity had drawn sweat from me, a good sign that I was normal, at least for a while. Soon my skin would dry and no perspiration would occur. It would have been impolite to wave my hand to check her sight, so I turned back to Travaille.

"She's blind?" I mouthed.

"Since birth," he answered.

"Oh." I wondered how she could know about my condition if she could not see my skin.

"Relax. She gonna sniff you."

And that is what she did. With a few sentences exchanged to confirm what she was "sniffing" for, she stood on tree trunk legs and, with long burgundy dress sweeping around those legs, took a hard step off the dais. She was a head taller than me and three times as wide. Her chubby cheeks leaned toward me, her nose fidgeting, scooping up scents like a bloodhound.

She came right up against me, and her huge chest, held precariously inside her low-cut dress, bumped against me and nearly knocked me over. I stood stock still as best I could so as not to disrupt her "reading" of me.

"Mm-hmm," she repeated several times as she sniffed, stepping carefully around me.

As she moved around me, I could sniff her: lavender, with a hint of barbecue, the woody fragrance from the smokehouse, and something spicy, possibly cayenne peppers. I was thinking of Cajun food, and at that moment I felt hungry.

She stood behind me, sniffing closer, hovering above my skin: the back of my neck, the middle of my back, and then lower, as if searching for the lasting essence of any expelled gas left on my trousers. She stood up straight again and continued around me.

"Raise yo arms," she said.

I lifted both of them as best I could. That motion stretched my skin tight and it was painful, so I did not extend them fully.

She seemed to notice I did not comply. She moved in anyway, her nose pressed into my armpits, taking longer in the right one. After sniffing my left armpit, she returned to my right, perhaps to confirm her suspicions. What suspicions? I laughed inside, the kind a fool makes at the moment he realizes he has been made a fool and knows the whole scheme. For what I had paid for all the sniffing, I should get a kit of hygiene products.

Finally, she stepped back and I heard her humming and felt a steady vibration expanding from her throat to fill the room. I didn't know if this was part of the procedure or she was simply pleasing herself with a happy tune. She moved back onto the dais and plopped down in her throne with a thundering noise. She was breathing hard and took a moment to catch her breath.

"You kin drop yo arms," said Travaille behind me.

I lowered my arms to my side, feeling that I was about to hear some mumbo-jumbo that would comprise the totality of the experience I had just paid for. Then I would be sent merrily on my way, another satisfied customer.

"What it be, Madame Mambo?" asked Travaille. It seemed part of the ritual, following the script.

She wailed for a minute, a frightening sound, then humming a lilting tune and intoning another clever component.

"You eat of garlic?" was her first question.

"My girlfriend is Korean, so yes. Lots of garlic."

"No," she said firmly.

"No? What do you mean?"

"No girl. You send her away."

"Well, I—"

"You send her away because you got da curse."

All right, that was something new, something unexpected. I never told anyone, through this whole process, anything about Penny or me leaving her to protect her. Perhaps she was a mind reader as well as champion sniffer.

"I know about the, umm, curse. I've been to several doctors. They weren't much help. With all their training and the science, they—they—said it is porphyria. But I read about people with porphyria, that they can lead near normal lives. Besides, the onset of symptoms is too quick for me, so it can't be that. It's my symptoms that resemble porphyria, but it's not that. Can't be."

"No. It's da curse. I told you so."

"What is that exactly?"

"You got da curse. Now you come for help."

"Yes, that's right. What can be done—"

She called out for Travaille and he sprang to the dais.

"Yes, Madame Mambo?"

Was this more theatrics? I needed help, not a good show.

"Take this man 4-G," said Madame Mambo. I guessed then she really was a madame, not a mama. "Put him in number one. Start him in one."

"Yes, Madame Mambo." Travaille bowed his head.

"Wait. What is the curse? How can I treat it?"

"We gonna treat you," said Madame Mambo. "You got da curse. The mark of Cain. I smell it in you. You try to fix but you don know how."

"All right, that all fits, at least metaphorically, but what do I really have? What's it called? Do you know the scientific name for it? It's not that I don't trust you. I accept folk healing. I'm giving it a chance, but—"

"If you want a name, you call it by its old name: *revenancy*."

"What's that?"

"You turning *revenant*. I smell it in you."

"What is 'revenant'?"

"Yo skin shrivels away.... It burns.... Yo body falls.... Yo blood boils.... You start dying while you living."

"But what is this 'revenant' you speak of?"

"Yo skin rots away, like the leaves fall from trees, like you be dying, but you no die, only look like dead."

"That's the end result? How long does—?"

"Many people say 'vampire'—*oui*, vampire, the blood-suckers, the undead who walk the earth."

"Vampire? That's what I've heard before. I've been reading about it. Your diagnosis isn't anything new."

Feeling disappointed, I knew I had been taken for a fool. And I had *expected* it would be a scam. Just tell the victim what he wants to hear. That's easy. I had explained my symptoms when I set up the meeting, so I doubted there was anything she could discern by sniffing me. That was all an act—

"Believe...or no believe...."

"You have to die before you can become one of those."

"No. Possible."

"The un-dead must first be *dead*. I think that's how it works."

"No. Some people they become like dead and no have death first. They no buried and rise again."

"And that's the revenant?"

"*Revenant*...he who cheats death. But death it don't like no cheating."

"That's different from a vampire?"

"Not so different. Death first or no death. Same."

"That's the curse?"

"*Oui*, you got da curse. You know it. That's why you come to Madame Mambo. Nothing you do stop it."

"But it's a treatment that I want."

"We got da treatment." Then to Travaille: "Take him 4-G."

"What's 'four gee'?"

"Go downstairs."

"Downstairs? What happens there?"

I guessed she meant *for* G—whatever 'G' was. I could only imagine a torture chamber where a sadistic monster would enjoy hurting unamused guests, perhaps demand a ransom. And Penny would never know what became of me.

"We get you treatment. You pay for treatment, we give you treatment."

"So...." I had just one more question before I submitted to the next level of this game. "So then...I *do* have this disease you call 'revenancy'—right?"

"You got da curse. If you wanna treat, you stay for G."

My breath left me. I was trying to take a fresh breath but all the air I had left me. I gasped, then caught myself and took a gulp of air.

"I will become something *like* a vampire then. So all of this paranormal bullshit is...real? Is that what you're saying?"

"You already da vampire. You jus don know it, don accept it."

If I were seeing this scene in a movie, I'd laugh at the silliness of this conversation. The poor, desperate fellow visiting the old voodoo goddess, begging for a cure. However, though her words might have seemed comical taken out of the context of this baroque hall, they carried serious implications for me. I had already been suffering. She knew it. My skin was falling off. My blood was boiling. Just as she intimated. There was something real to her responses. It was not a scam, I began to realize.

"I'm already a...a vampire?"

"You already *revenant*. You wan treatment? You go to down da stairs."

"All right. I'll go. Anything. As long as it really works."

I was overwhelmed and exhausted. Regardless how much the show seemed like a scam, here was someone willing to believe me, taking my claim seriously. And she was offering me some kind of treatment. What that might be, I could only guess. I was already sipping blood to keep up my appearance. What could be more outrageous than that?

"Believe...no believe...."

Travaille waved me out of the room, out of Madame Mambo's court. And off to the dungeons.

"What's she talking about?" I asked Travaille as he led me through the rooms of the mansion to a door leading down below the house. "What's this treatment G?"

Travaille grinned, more than before. He raised his chin at me and when I acted dismayed, he pointed at my face. I raised my hand and touched my cheek: dry, scaly, flaky again. If Madame Mambo hadn't sniffed out my symptoms, she could have felt them. My dosage was wearing off. I needed to get back to my hotel, to my cooler of ice and bag of blood, before I deteriorated too much.

"How long is this going to take?"

"As long as necessary."

"How long can that be?"

"Depends."

"I'm sure it does."

"Come."

He waved his big hand forward and I opened the door, fully expecting that hand to give me a shove down the stairs, into the darkness, and that would be the end of Stefan Székely, the last of his line of revenants.

Instead, I saw a string of Christmas lights illuminating the way down a set of gray concrete steps with a metal railing to hold onto. Santa Claus would feel comfortable. Perhaps the massage tables were down there. Could I still be making jokes? Or was I the only joke here?

Penny would not be laughing. She would cry for me, and the thought made me feel more that I was doing the right thing. If I died tonight, I would die knowing she would be all right. And after a few weeks of mourning me, she would take up with that Tommy fellow and have a long, happy life with him. She would retain a memory or two of me which might pop into her head in stray moments when she least expected it, perhaps when she happened to enter a bookstore or order a latté. Only then would she remember me.

I descended into the basement of this old house in New Orleans. It seemed only slightly more insane than drinking a vial of a stranger's blood. Yet I had done that. All it took was desperation. Do that often enough and the soul withers, dries out like a stick of jerky, useless.

I felt a startling coolness halfway down the steps. After the humidity above ground, it was refreshing.

At the bottom, I stepped through a wooden door left ajar, followed by Travaille in his black mortician's suit.

The dark, musty basement was as bleak as the one my aunt had in Pittsburgh. She often spent time down there just to stay cool in the summers. She said the air was cleaner. She never wanted to open any windows with the factories belching their smoke.

I could not see well despite a few lights set at intervals around the walls. It seemed a fairly large basement with several columns supporting the weight of the house. In the far corners were horizontal lights glowing purple, providing only enough illumination to keep us from stumbling over the objects of the room. Laid out like an army barracks were several long boxes.

I blinked, strained to focus my eyes. It took me a moment to realize the boxes were caskets.

My muscles coiled, ready to flee, or fight.

"And what happens down here?" I asked, hesitantly.

"The treatment," said Travaille.

"And that would be the 'G' treatment?"

"*Oui.*"

17

When I opened my eyes I saw nothing. Complete blackness. I felt my body surreptitiously searching through my network of nerves for anything that might be amiss. My nose detected something pungent, rich, earthy, like a garden after a rainstorm. I moved my fingers and felt...*dirt*. I realized my toes also felt dirt. In fact, my whole body felt as though I was not wearing any clothing. My entire body lay in dirt. In a box.

No, in a *coffin*.

Suddenly, I panicked and swung my arm, crashing my wrist and hand against wood. I pounded hard against that wood above me and cried: "Hey! Let me out!"

After too long of a moment, a crack of light spread down the length of my container. The lid opened fully and a woman stared down. Her dark brown face contrasted with her white nurse's uniform. Her hair was in braids and tied up onto her head. I vaguely recalled she was the last person I saw before whatever happened to me happened. She had given me an injection of something to help me sleep.

Sleep...?

"Y'all right, honey?" she said. Her face showed concern.

I chuckled, everything flooding back into my consciousness. "I think so."

"Here, lemme help you up," she said and took hold of my shoulders, guiding me to a sitting position.

I looked around. The room remained dark, the purple lamps in the corners glowing faintly. Around me were a dozen more caskets, all closed. I could have been in a mortuary, in the room where the dead bodies were prepared for burial, where they were stored—as chilly as it was down there.

"Then, it's true...."

"Whudya say?"

"It's true. I wasn't sure. I forgot everything. I really did sleep in a casket full of dirt."

"Yup, yo shore did."

I lifted my arm and inspected my skin: beige-white again, a healthy tone, perhaps even a bit on the pasty-white side, and it was supple, full of moistness. I brushed dirt off my chest and felt the smoothness of my skin. No hair had grown back on my chest, but that did not matter. I touched my face, held my hand against my cheek and the skin there was also smooth and full, not dry and shrunken, flaky and itchy. But no whiskers yet. I could only conclude that this so-called 'G' treatment was actually effective. I understood then that 'G' stood for 'graveyard'—like being dead and buried, then rising again restored in mind and body.

"It's the dirt," said my nurse.

"Why? What's in it?"

"Mostly it's the nitrogen," said a voice I recognized. "And the phosphorus."

Mr. Travaille stood nearby, dressed elegantly as before: dark suit, like a mortician. He went to the casket opposite mine and, as if on schedule, knocked on the wooden lid, received a reply knock, and opened the casket.

An old man, also naked, bald and frail but with beautiful skin, sat up with less effort than I had. He brushed dirt from his chest and waved at Travaille.

"Good morning, Mister Travaille," said the old man.

"*Bonne matin*," Travaille replied.

A nurse came over and offered the man a drink of something dark in a clear plastic cup. The old man refused it. She set the cup down on top of the next casket and helped him climb out. He sat on the edge, balancing there. And between his legs rose his erection. He studied it a moment, then sensed I was awake and watching him.

"Good morning," he said to me. "Great day to be alive, eh?"

"Yes."

I was unsure if the old man was real or part of my imagination. I gazed through the dimness of the basement, faint clouds of dust making his figure obscure.

"I get a boner every time I wake here," he said with an off-key snicker, "and no lady ready to take care of it, yeah?"

I could only stare and wonder who this man was and what his affliction might be that caused him also to seek a treatment here.

"You seem happy," I said after a moment.

"Happy? That's not the question. I'm alive." He straightened up, stroked himself a few times.

"Ah! Ah! Ahhhh!" the nurse called, rushing over to him. "You be good. None o' dat pers'nal bidnez. We got a clinic to run here. Gotta keep it clean."

That made me smile.

The floor seemed covered with a layer of black soil. Inside the casket was enough dirt to cover a body: rich, black soil, like something I could use to grow some tomatoes in my apartment. It was a useless experiment; I cannot make anything grow. I am full of death, I now realize. And yet, a night in a box of that dirt and I felt great.

The man opposite me gathered his clothes from a different attendant.

My eyes followed the man as he exited.

The nurse returned to check on me. I felt fine. Not groggy, not dizzy. So she helped me climb out of the casket. I sat on the edge a few minutes, feeling the coolness of the air against my bare skin. I touched my chest and found no dry patches. I touched my face and again was pleased. Between my thighs, I also had an erection. Good blood flow. That was the least of my problems.

"Now don you be doin the piddly-diddly down theya," she warned me.

"Don't worry," I said. "I'm saving myself for Penny."

"Oh, you be worth more'an a penny."

"She's my fiancée...."

I grimaced, decided not to spend the breath explaining that Penny was my Beloved, the One, the reason for my visit to this clinic. I needed to make myself normal again so I could spend the rest of my life with her.

After a few minutes more teetering on the edge of the casket, I stood and mentally felt within myself, checking the gurglings of organs, the slush of blood, and the beat of my heart. My naked body, dusted with crumbs of dirt, felt pleasantly cool. I believed I had been reborn. Certainly, my long sleep had something to do with it. I'd been so drained during the previous months of living with nearly 24 hour wakefulness, leading my double life. I had to wonder. Was that all I needed? A good restful sleep? In a dirt-filled casket?

"It one o' dem miracles," another man spoke.

I looked through the darkness and found another man sitting on the edge of his casket, two down from me. He was older than me, at least by his body's apparent frailty.

"First time?" he asked me.

I could not even chuckle. "Yes, first time."

"You'll be back."

I squinted. Through the dimness he seemed handsome. What manner of horror might this fellow have presented prior to his sleep? I thought about myself. How bad had I looked before they slipped me into this box?

"How many times for you?" I asked him.

"I lost count. Bunches." He snorted. "Every week. Without fail. Elsewise I scare away the youngsters. And the ladies."

"Youngsters and ladies? You're a...grandparent?"

"Heck no. Parent."

"May I ask...how old are you?"

He laughed. "Now? Or before coming here?"

"Your true age, according to your birth certificate."

"Birth certificate? You some kinda reporter looking for a clue about what goes on here?"

"I did it, too. I'm not concerned with what might be legal or illegal. I do seem much better this morning."

"Actually, it's evening."

"Everything's the same down here in the dark."

"Exactly." He stood up, brushing himself with his hands.

A nurse came to help him, took a cloth to his back, removing the dirt.

"Easy, gal. Don't need to be scratched up. I got dancing to do tonight!"

The old timer turned to me, now that he had received his treatment.

"I got my eye on a lady.... Yep, my lady, she treat me right...."

"Your wife?"

"Hah!"

"You said you were a parent."

"That's truth. I mean my lady friend, the one I play around with."

"Even after this treatment you have sex? I mean, you can have sex? You dare do that?"

"That's the point, ain't it? Sheez, you are a first timer!"

"Sorry. As a first-timer, I'm not sure of the rules. Or what the proper etiquette is here. Forgive me, sir."

I saw a wave of his hand pass between us.

"You'll get the hang of it. Live your life. Take chances. Go to extremes. Then stop in here for a weekly refreshment. You can keep going strong. Like me."

"You never told me your age."

"So nosy! Awrighty, I'm forty."

"Forty? You look older, even after this treatment."

"How about fifty? Is that better?"

"I'm forty-five now. You look at least ten years older than me. But well-preserved. Vital, I mean."

"Yep, I'm vital, awright. Can I tell you a secret?"

"Secret? You don't seem one for having secrets."

"I got'em. Lots of'em. Number one is I'm a hundred-fifteen years old. Had a birthday last week. Celebrated in the bordello the next street over. Had three ladies at once. And they all got satisfied, if you get my drifting."

"Nice story. That's your secret?"

"It's the truth, young man. Look at me. Have you ever seen a finer specimen of a man?"

I did look; stared, in fact. His body was lean, lightly muscled, but without blemish. He seemed fit and what energy he could bring to an eager trio of ladies I could only imagine. If that was all he looked forward to after his treatment, I wondered what I would want to do.

"A shame we cain't sleep over on the other side, where dem women are."

"What?" I realized then that only men were surrounding me. "They have female patients?"

"Course they do. Women get da curse, too—"

Before he could end his sentence, a black and white image of my mother slid into my head, like the next slide in the projector: a ghostly portrait of her with a plain, pallid face, cheeks drooping a bit, her hair a frazzled white mess, eyes sunken, mouth agape, teeth exposed, gums decayed. It was the last photo taken before they began refusing. They agreed only because it was for some medical journal. The two of them, sitting side by side, gaunt and decrepit, yet full of love for each other. The two of them were the only remaining doctors there, still diligently treating the insane and the deformed, patients and doctors all hidden away inside Old Main in Utica, New York, easing the lives of their patients, even as their own lives diminished to nothing.

"Now what? I've had this treatment. I feel good. What do I do now?"

"You call for your clothes, you get dressed, you get yourself upstairs, and you check out. Then you go live your damn life!"

The old man accepted the nurse's armful of garments and began dressing himself.

"Life is too full of misery to jump back into that kind of life, with a job and work hours, responsibilities for other people, and ignoring my own pleasures. Ain't that right?"

"There you go! Live your life! It's all you got." He was right. "You live for somebody else and you'll wither away to dust in no time."

He buckled his belt, adjusted his shirt collar, then stepped over to me.

"We don't owe nobody nothing," he said, lowering his voice. "Not for somebody else's benefit. Nobody's gonna do anything for you 'less it benefits him—or her, yeah? Some of us gotta make do with what we can. Some of us got da curse and we gotta get treatment. Otherwise, we go on enjoying what we got left in our lives."

"And you're a hundred and fifteen years old?"

He burst out laughing. "If that's what you wanna believe."

Giving my bare shoulder a slap, he went to the exit.

I stood there puzzled, slowly brushing myself, finding a stray bit of dirt here and there on my body. I had to think about what he said. Whether he was truthful or not. Why would such a man lie about this treatment? I saw for myself his vigor compared to his apparent old age. And within myself, I felt refreshed. I turned to the nurse and bid her bring my clothing.

When I ascended the steps to the ground floor, I saw through a window that it was indeed night. My watch showed it to be 10:30, not so late that one could not have a rambling good time at the local bordello. However, that was not where my attention was. How long had I been held captive in a casket full of dirt in the basement of an old house in New Orleans? And did that now determine my complete insanity?

So I was here and, at least for now, I was alive and in a good condition. Much worse could have happened. Certainly, if it had been a scam, I could have been dead now; take my money and lock me in a box until I succumbed to asphyxiation, then dump my body somewhere—or run it through a meat grinder for the Cajun restaurants downtown. Weird thoughts can run through a man's head when he spends the night in a casket. But was it a night? I went downstairs and got in the box. Then I slept.

Then I awoke. Three days later, again in the evening. That's what my watch told me.

And Jesus rose from the dead after three days....

Perhaps there was something miraculous, after all.

I settled the bill with a clerk who closely resembled Madame Mambo. She could have been her grown daughter. With the cost of consultation and this initial treatment, I knew I could not afford to continue. Plus, my job and my life were in Oklahoma. There was no way I could keep driving down here every week or two for treatment. Even if I could get a new job down here, I could not pay so much for each visit.

Certainly my employer's health plan would not cover this kind of unapproved treatment—even if it seemed, at least in the first half-hour, to have worked quite well. Perhaps they could bill the insurance company as *therapeutic massage*. What's the ICD-9-CM code for massage? Is it 97140? Perhaps it's 97124. Not sure. What's the code for sleeping in a dirt-filled casket? Not likely in the book. So it's an out-of-pocket expense, all up to me. Cash—rolled up with a rubber band and handed to a man in a dark suit who pulls up in a limousine next to you while you stand on a street corner late at night. Ridiculous!

Outside, there was only the street lamp to light my way, but that was too bright and I held up my hand to block it. No taxi or limousine around here, it seemed, so I started to walk.

While I did feel full of energy, it felt awkward at first. My legs were stiff and did not obey my commands. After a couple blocks, I was in a rhythm and walked steadily. I did not know where I was going. My plan was to arrive in a business or entertainment district and catch a taxi from there.

I walked along a main avenue and eventually realized I was approaching the river.

Alone with my thoughts, I walked like a zombie but with a smooth, healthy gait, unaware of where I was, or what I passed. Dogs barked at me, then ran away when I glared at them. A few humans called to me and when I ignored them they grew angry, thought I was disrespecting them. I walked on, chased only by trailing curse words. I knew already I'd been cursed, so the words did not harm me.

A few vehicles passed me, none of them taxis. Soon I arrived at a bus stop but there was no service at that late hour. I walked on, smelling the river, the fishy odor mixed with spicy and greasy scents from the late-night eateries along the way.

I followed the road along the river until it turned away. I remembered my Google map showed a large bow in the river. I could continue following the river around that loop or I could cut straight across to the central business district. At Carrollton Avenue I turned, continuing on St. Charles Avenue, eventually passing Audubon Park.

Walking at a steady pace, I traversed the south side of New Orleans. I breathed deeply and the exercise was good on my body. I felt rejuvenated. Clearly the treatment had improved my condition.

I thought of Penny. She was pure and perfect, not one of *those* women.

Shaking my head, the image of a shadowy room with people rolling among the sheets evaporated. No, my Beloved was waiting for me, and I could return to her with clear skin. If the treatment lasted long enough for me to spend another weekend with Penny, then I could die in peace afterwards.

My cell phone showed no missed calls and no new texts for the days I was undergoing my treatment. Nobody missed me? I thought she would at least send one of her smiley faces. My job would likely call to see when I would be returning. I told them a week, but they go crazy when I'm not actually standing in the lab where they can see me. But not a thing from Penny. She's a champion texter and...*nothing?*

I walked quicker, feeling betrayed. Of course, I knew what I had done. I let her see my true face. She now knew what I was becoming, what my problem was, and that if she stayed with me she would have to put up with this hideous façade and frail, flaking body. Who would want that? A nurse, perhaps, someone whose profession required compassion. Penny was kind to me, but she was not one to be compassionate in that way.

No calls, no texts....

She had decided.

That reality hit me hard. It was for the best. No matter how upset she might be with me running away again, even for some kind of treatment, she would be wondering if I would be able to get over my problem, or if she would have to live with it, with me—if she could be compassionate. And yet, the compassion in *me* would not allow me to require, much less force, anyone to care for me or even associate with me while I had this ugly skin condition. I could only present myself and hope to make a good impression. It had worked with Penny at the Barnes & Noble the first time we met. I had looked good that day.

Lost in my thoughts I nearly bumped into a street lamp that was set out of alignment with all the others on the sidewalk. Like me, it did not fit, did not move in lockstep with the others of its kind. I stopped to check myself. No serious damage: a bump to my shoulder, a graze to my cheek.

Someone called out to me, inquiring about my intelligence in a tone implying that mine was very low. I thought it best to ignore the derogatory remark. I proceeded down the street. However, I quickly found myself confronted by three rather casually dressed young men. All of them possessed the standard Type B blood, it seemed. But it boiled to rage when I suggested they had better things to do with their late night camaraderie than hassle me, who had caused them no discontent.

They begged to differ. And thus began the confrontation: a shove to my shoulder, a tilting off-balance, recovery, and a clever remark intended to establish who was the more intelligent of us gathered on the street in the middle of the night. I was certain it was me. They again thought differently. The fellow in a tanktop moved to the side, then slightly behind me, and at an indication from the others, he kicked the back of my knee and I fell.

They laughed, for it seemed they wished for entertainment of a pugilistic bent. I had just been in a treatment program a little more than an hour before. I did not wish to ruin the benefits I had gained from it. I tried to explain that I was in poor health and I should be left alone. They were unsympathetic. Instead, it seemed that I was meant to become an even greater source of their night's entertainment and they proceeded to kick at me as I lay upon the dirty sidewalk.

Gradually, it was I who seethed with anger and whose blood boiled with rage, not only as metaphor but perhaps also in some strange biological manner. I sprang up, much to their chagrin, and stood defiant among them. They shrank back, fear upon their faces.

"I told you to leave me alone!" I shouted. There was tension in my muscles, like coiled springs ready to launch.

Then I did. My right fist struck the tanktop boy as my left fist crushed one of the other boys' nose. The third boy jumped back. Blood sprayed from the busted nose.

"Look at 'im!" the one who had jumped back cried out.

He pointed at me—

What? What did they see? I touched my face and felt some blood there. My skin had broken sometime during the fight.

"You kicked his fuckin' face open!" said one to the other.

I felt again. My cheek seemed to have slid downward and to the side, like a theater mask slightly askew. I shoved it back into place. The epidermis had separated from the dermis, like layers of a cake. My face was numb, my cheek muscles unable to twitch when ordered. It had to be unsightly, but also representative of my moral state. The young toughs could not understand that; to them, I was some type of monster to be vanquished. So they fell upon me once more and sought to thrash me soundly until I gave up and died.

However, I would have none of that and stood my ground, my hands held out as though they were swords. I had no training in the martial arts, but they were not privy to such information. I growled at them. I found saliva bubbling in the corner of my mouth. I let it foam down my chin and that further frightened them. A hellish howl erupted from my gut and blasted from my throat like Satan's vomit—just as I leaped upon them! My fists punched their chests, knocking them back.

They swore they were "gonna get me" and lashed out.

I skipped backwards a few steps, defying them, then turned and ran off down the sidewalk. I felt pain in my stomach and on my face. Perhaps I was bleeding inside. Their kicking might have injured my spleen. On my face, the skin was slipping.

They chased me a couple blocks, then gave up. I slowed to a jog, noticing I felt little fatigue from my physical efforts. Sure, I breathed deeply, but it was not debilitating, and within a minute I had regained my regular respiration rate. My fingers toyed with my face, pushing it back into place, pressing and holding it a few moments as though I were gluing it there. It felt like the proper position but, to be sure, I examined myself in a store window.

The lighting was substandard, but I could at least recognize it was me: the ghostly figure of a human being caught between the world of the living and the dead. Even brief treatment could not restore me for long. My skin appeared beautiful once more. Yet I was not cured; the best I could do was pass without notice.

And scare away young toughs with my rabid acting! Perhaps it was my sudden rage, my own call to violence which unraveled my careful restoration. Provoked, I had lashed out, and my blood surged as it normally would in such circumstances. I burst the seams. What my opponents saw was a man becoming a monster, displaying unusual abilities not apparent at first glance.

At the next major intersection were several nightclubs offering up jazz, drinks, and food even at that late hour. There were several taxis waiting. I caught one and got a ride back to my seedy hotel in the French Quarter. I was quite thankful that I had survived but fearful of the future.

Because I booked it for a week when I checked in, they were not alarmed at my disappearance. They had no reason to care; I already paid. The room was as fresh as when I first entered. No work for the maid.

I stripped off my dirt-stained, sweaty shirt and trousers. I was making *sweat* again! I sniffed myself, bent my nose to each moist armpit and took a long draw. A pungent odor! Immediately, I felt better: younger, fitter, ready to return to seduce my Beloved once more. I took a long shower, warm at first, then going as hot as I could stand, then dropping the temperature to as cool as I could handle. I toweled off vigorously and felt like inviting a lucky lady to share my bed. Just to see how fit I was now.

Instead, I checked my phone again and did not find any new messages.

I checked the puddle under the cooler I had left sitting on the desk. I knew right then that everything that could go wrong was going wrong. Inside, the ice had melted. The bag of precious AB was bad. I never expected to be away from it for three days; I would have replenished the ice if I'd been able to return sooner. Now I dared not try the blood. Besides, I had my treatment and seemed in good condition. My skin was clear, my energy high, my senses sharp. I could make it home well enough.

I carefully poured out the blood into the toilet and flushed.

Soon the sun would be rising over the city and I would be fast asleep in this bed. It was night that was meant for me. I would sleep all day, pay extra for the last hours that would take me through the afternoon, then start the drive back to Oklahoma, where I would begin my life again. I was interested to see how long this treatment would last. And if anyone would be there to welcome me.

Standing on the corner between my hotel and the parking garage, I heard lively music playing. I smelled food. After three days without food, I finally felt hungry. Turning down the street, I chose a place. Inside, I had a dinner of turtle soup, blackened fish with cornbread and greens. I finished with bread pudding. For the second half of the meal I wasn't sure I could finish everything, but my gut stretched wide and held it. I sat for a while, letting the musicians play on as I started the digestion process. Then I got into my car and drove.

18

They had followed me for almost an hour, first rushing at my bumper in their monster truck, then roaring past me and suddenly slowing ahead of me, forcing me to change lanes then blocking me. No sign of law enforcement vehicles at that late hour. I did my best to keep going, not willing to play their game.

Finally, they bumped me and even though I held the steering wheel firm, the truck pushed me onto the shoulder. I knew there was damage to my car. They continued pushing me off the road, then veered away as we came upon a concrete bridge buttress. It was too late for me. I turned the steering wheel sharply and my car slid down the embankment, coming to rest in the tall grass beside the creek.

I looked up the slope at the highway. No lights, no sign the truck had stopped. They would not concern themselves with whether or not they had caused a wreck or if my life was in peril because of their antics.

I had stopped for gas on the west side of the Dallas metro area, on the edge of the countryside, as the first thin line of dawn cracked over the horizon behind me. I went to the farthest set of pumps, expecting to swipe my card and go. Instead of quietly filling the tank and thinking of home, a monster truck pulled alongside the opposite pump and four young men tumbled out.

They seemed drunk. One tended to the gas while the others went into the store. When they returned, I was hanging up the nozzle and going for the squeegee to remove some bird droppings.

"What happened to you, man?" the guy pumping gas asked me with a snort and a laugh.

At first, I took no offence. Then I wondered why he would say that; I should be normal after my treatment. And after the brief altercation in the city, I had pushed everything into its proper place. I glanced at myself in the side mirror and saw that my face was patchy again. And it slumped—badly. It had only been a few hours since I left New Orleans, about 30 hours since I climbed out of the treatment "pod" and saw myself returned to normal. But who is kidding who? It was just dirt, very rich soil, what they called "Bayou mud"—high in nitrogen and phosphorous, good for growing plants and restoring skin.

His buddies thought I must be demented, stupid, someone not worthy of living. They proceeded to taunt me, using language only drunk country boys would understand. What I did take away from our conversation was that they perceived my affliction as a reason to torment me. Another group of toughs.

I got into my car, locked the door, and started the engine. I drove off, got on the highway and was breathing comfortably for a few miles. Then bright lights flashed into my rear view mirror, blinding me. I adjusted the mirrors. Eventually I saw it was the monster truck from the gas station. Then the antics began.

Could it truly be a matter of my appearance that triggered young toughs to act the way they did? I was not at my best but I was within the range of normal appearance. My skin was whole, though blemished. I was pale though not albino. My hands were red still from the punches I had thrown, my fingernails grown longer, my knuckles bruised. I looked as though I had been in a fight. That's all.

Yet as I climbed out of my car beside the creek to see what damage there was, I had the distinct feeling that what they saw was something beyond what their mortal eyes could detect. They somehow saw me for what I was: a monster masquerading as a human.

The side of my car was dented and scraped. I couldn't believe they would have wanted that scraping for their truck, as well. I guessed entertainment trumped practicality and logic. Insurance would take care of my car. I got on my knees and bent low to check the tires and wheels, to be sure it was drivable. I had to get home before I got too much sunshine.

With dawn growing into morning, I started the engine, heard it fudge a bit and resist, then turn over. I let it run a minute to clear whatever dust and sludge had been forced up under the hood, and backed up from the creek, turned it around and slowly maneuvered up the slope to the highway.

Cars and trucks swished past as I righted my car beside the lanes, listening to the engine. When there were no vehicles in sight, I pulled onto the highway and continued heading home, forced to listen to the rattling of loose door trim all the way into Oklahoma City.

Between Norman and Moore, south side suburbs, the mid-morning traffic slowed for construction and we were all down to 5 mph, side by side. A van was to my left and had its windows down. I could clearly hear the kid call excitely to other family members: "Look at the vampire man!"

I pretended not to hear but I shifted slightly to check myself in the mirror.

Not what I expected. My skin was dry, flaking again, peeling in spots, deathly white. The veins were visible, appearing as red lines across my face. A sweep across my scalp brought a fistful of loose hair. I looked again, more directly. My lips were parched, cracked, blood red as though I wore lipstick. Inside, my gums had receded, leaving my teeth looking rather fearsome. I felt hot, mostly from the sun beating through the windows. I was not sweating at all; instead, I was drying out, like a husk.

I cannot even make it back home without the damn treatment wearing off!

The traffic picked up, but I could not forget what that kid had said. I kept glancing at myself in the mirror, wishing it was night, wishing I could hide from everyone.

Suddenly, I knew what happened to my parents. I understood why they had kept to themselves, living and working inside that stone asylum, never going outside, never meeting with people from outside. I did not have any skin disease. I did not have an autoimmune disorder. I did not have any of a hundred possible diagnoses. What I had was rare; it was what my parents had: a genetic predilection. No wonder they sent me to live with my aunt—so I would not see them as they transformed.

Transformed? Into what?

"Look at the vampire man!"

Look at the vampire.

Let's call it what it is. There is no "vampire disease"; not even the dreaded *porphyria* is as quick and certain as what was raging through my body, what rages through my family line. There is no cure, apparently, no way to halt the march of the transformation. It is inevitable—

There was a honk behind me and I returned to the realization that I was driving a car along the highway, too slowly, it seemed. As the impatient drivers passed me they gave a honk or a shout and cursed me for getting in the way, indeed, for existing in their world. My presence offended them.

I sped up, as anxious to get home as never before.

When I exited the highway and continued through several intersections, waiting nervously at each red light, it was already past noon.

I pulled into my apartment complex and swung my car under the shade of the trees beside my breezeway. I looked around for anyone who might be out. Clear enough, I decided. I popped out of the car, grabbed my bag, and hurriedly jogged to my door, unlocking it and slipping inside before anyone could see me.

My heart was racing, my gut in knots. My throat was dry but I was not thirsty. Nor did I have a full bladder even by this point in my trip. My body seemed fit, tight, ready for action, but despite the long drive I did not feel hungry. Perhaps I was too distraught to worry about hunger or thirst. I did not even need to go pee—but I tried it after setting down my bag and stripping off my clothes. Barely anything exited: drops, mere drops of bronze liquid, the last of my fluids, I supposed, as I continued my march to husk.

In the refrigerator was a bag of A-negative, still fresh enough and inviting. I thanked my lucky stars, reached for it, and held it gently in my cupped hands. I kissed the bag, then prepared it and drank. I wiped my mouth clean and went to lie on my futon, naked and alone, wishing for a miracle.

Or for a quick death.

I huddled in dreams, a vagabond seeking bread, a panting wolf desiring blood, and in my romps through tangled forests and thorny fields I was hunted by a posse of townsfolk bearing farm implements and factory tools. One among them bore a rifle and when I was cornered against a large tree, he took aim at me and let fly the bullet. With my hyper-sharp eyes, I could see it clearly as it approached me. I could read the lettering on the bronze casing identifying the factory and city where it was made. Then it tore into me and I awoke in a cold sweat.

Sweat....

My skin held a thin coating of moisture, chilling to my senses and of a kind I had never before experienced. The odor of death filled the room and, at first, I thought I must still be locked away within my dreams. It was the odor of mold, of decay, a meaty yet sour scent spreading around me. My flesh was rotting away. Yes, as though I were in a casket. Muscles and fibers beneath my skin seemed useless sludge. My sheath of skin held in all the leakage. Opening my mouth, the odor wafted in a gray cloud out into the room.

I could not move, could not breathe deeply, or swallow, or blink my eyes. As I rested in my frozen state, I heard my phone go off twice, ten minutes between calls. I heard a beep indicating a text message had been left. I waited perhaps another half-hour before I tried to move again. Then I swung my arm up and over myself and touched my face, feeling for a dry patch of skin there and finding only smooth, supple flesh. I grinned, not believing it.

In a flash, I had sat up and felt my pulse racing, excited yet somehow fearful. I jumped to my feet beside the futon and took a few deep breaths, more to be sure of my mortality than to stoke myself for a fight or flight.

To the living room I went, to retrieve my phone.

It was the lab, as I suspected. No message left. The second missed call was the blood bank. No message. The text message was from my Beloved, and I shuttered as I held the phone, daring myself to read her message. I fully expected it to be some final comment on our relationship, the goodbye, the farewell wish, the 'it's me, not you' mantra which I myself had intended to use but missed the opportunity. My finger pressed the icon and the message appeared:

Im reporting on theft at blood bank. U ok???

At that moment, I had two thoughts and they fenced with each other for the right to command my will: first, the question of theft at the blood bank; second, the link between me and the blood bank that Penny had found. Were they only now noticing that some bags were missing? To that I might retort: It took you long enough! Penny Park was doing the story? That qualified as irony.

I supposed her message was to warn me: perhaps I shouldn't go in for my shift today, even though they were expecting me. I was already late—hence the phone call. And my main employer, the lab, also seemed to be looking for me—yet I had not taken much from the resources there.

As for me, I was back to my normal self, it seemed, thanks to my desperate opportunism and my self-inflicted quasi-medical treatment. Would any of them understand? Probably only Penny would. Then I wondered if she would somehow be linked to the story and be in trouble because of her relationship with me, the blood thief.

"We need you to come in," said Dunleavy, my boss. "Got some questions for you to answer."

"I see. What seems to be the problem?"

"You don't know? You can't guess? It's all over the news now."

"I returned late last night," I said, knowing I had arrived in the brightness of the afternoon. I had passed out long before the 6 and 10 p.m. news broadcasts where I might have seen Penny on the scene, reporting live.

"Well, it seems the basic story has been getting twisted into something ludicrous. They're saying a vampire has broken into the institute and stolen blood."

"A vampire?" I asked coldly. "That *is* ludicrous." I laughed to give my statement authenticity.

"Who else would steal a bag of blood?"

"Of course a vampire."

He wouldn't give me any more information over the phone so I had to agree to come in for a meeting. I knew then that I would be fired. Either because I was the thief they would looking for, or because I had been too lax with security protocols which allowed the thief to get a bag out of inventory. The truth was that I wrote down a different number on the inventory list, less than the true number of bags, thereby saving a couple for myself.

I would not be visiting the Blood Institute of Oklahoma any time soon.

I'm ok. Tired from drive. I <3 u!!!

That was my text message back to Penny Park, ace reporter, covering the blood bank story. I did not know why I added that last bit with the heart. Sentimentality? It was true, certainly, but did I add that thinking she would be impressed? feel a moment of nostalgia? a lingering trace of compassion for this monster?

I did not have to wait long for a response:

OMG Im worried about u!!!

I texted back: Must you cover THAT crime?

Its BIG- Vamps! Lead story at 6 & 10

Please be gentle.

WTF??? It was u???

I was desperate. Forgive me.

Serious?????????

You can break up with me now. I understand.

STEFAN!!!! I NVR BROKE UP where did u go???

New Orleans. Weird treatment. It worked for a while.

Ur skin problem? Thn Y steal blood?

Blood works better.

omg How?

I drink it.

OMG

I didn't know what to type back. As I thought, another text arrived on my phone:

They got sec cam of u

I started to type Sure? but another text arrived:

they dont want 2 go public & scare ppl abt blood supply

Stop texting. Call me PLEASE!

I set the phone down like it was a hot potato. Breathing hard, I listened for sounds outside, expecting the doors of a police car to be slamming shut any minute, the crunch of boots coming to my door, the knock—

"Hello," I said when the phone buzzed.

"You're scaring me, Stefan," said my Beloved.

"I'm sorry for that, for everything. I never meant to get you wrapped up in my problems."

"What *are* your problems? It's just a skin disease, isn't it?"

I took too long to answer.

"Isn't it?" Her voice was strained. "Is it more? What could be worse?"

"Penny...my Beloved...I have consulted with several doctors and I've tried several treatments. Some of it works...for a while. Yet nothing lasts long enough for me to carry on a normal life. It seems I cannot stop it. I can't hold it off."

"Hold what off?"

"My...transformation. I'm bec—"

"What are you talking about?"

"Listen to me, Penny! My body is changing—transforming—from whatever I was to whatever I'm...I dunno, supposed to be. I can't explain it. But I know it's happening. Everything I try works for a little bit, but then wears off. The time it takes to wear off is getting shorter and shorter. Soon there won't be anything that works to hold it off. Then I will become...I'll become whatever the hell I'm...what I'm supposed to become."

"But isn't—"

She couldn't finish her sentence and I could think of nothing else to say. I knew it was done. She and I were done. I was done. The police were coming for me. I stole bags of blood from the blood bank. How perverse! The public would enjoy this sordid tale of a vampire wannabe getting his blood fix every week. Only they would never believe it was true.

"Penny, I have to go. I better let you get on with your story. I can't let you be involved. Not with this crime, and not with me. I shouldn't have fallen in love with you. I'm sorry I met you that day at the Barnes and Noble. I'm sorry I sent you a message on Facebook. I should have minded my own business and shut up and done my job and never tried to find a friend, much less a perfect lady like you: someone who would love me for the first time in my life. Then all hell breaks loose to ruin it all! I meet my Beloved, the One, then I'm struck down by jealous gods! Can't you see that? The Fate I've drawn? This is the end for me. No more Stefan Székely!"

"You're acting crazy. Calm down."

"No, Penny! I'm not crazy. This is really happening. It's not my imagination. I'm becoming a monster."

"No, you're not."

"I'm all right now because I got to some blood in time, blood I still have here. Yet when I was driving back I was losing it, losing my composure. The treatment I got in New Orleans was wearing off. I was transforming into a monster as I drove back. I got stuck in traffic in Norman and they were pointing at me, calling me a vampire! I looked in the mirror: I *was* terrible looking. I *did* look like a vampire!"

"All sparkly and handsome?"

"Not like Edward Cullen! That's fake. I mean a real vampire."

"You mean like those sexy young people in that TV show?"

"No, not them. Not like that. I mean ugly. An ugly vampire."

"Oh, like what Buffy always slayed?"

"No, uglier."

"You mean like the old movies? The Count Dracula movies? Who was in those?"

"I don't know but I don't look like him. I was hideous, Penny. Absolutely hideous. I looked like the man I saw on one of those TV news magazine years ago when I was a teenager. He had *porphyria*. He had to cover his skin whenever he went out. Wore a hood and gloves and a scarf around his neck. But he had a wife and children, so it must have happened after—"

"He had what?"

"Porphyria. Some people call it the vampire disease. It's an autoimmune disease. Turns people into vampires. They *look like* vampires."

"Which kind of vampire?"

"Not a good kind. Their skin melts in sunshine. Eyes bulge, gums retract, teeth look longer, and their fingernails curl, the nose falls off, and they lose most of their hair. Their skin is pale but easily disfigured. Blood transfusions help. They're hideous. I—my parents—we have, or had...I don't know for sure...the genetic marker for porphyria. Or, I thought we did, but the tests didn't correlate. What I have is what my parents had, though. I know that now. They withdrew from society, kept to themselves, then went off to die. I told you about my trip to Croatia for their funeral, right? Then I—"

"Stefan, I gotta go now. They're ready."

"Sorry I talk too much."

"No, Stefan. Forget it. I'll call you later. Meantime, you should think about what you really know about your parents. Did they really have that disease or something else? I'll talk to you later."

The line was dead before I could utter a syllable back to her.

19

My head was spinning, both in a metaphorical sense and in a real way. I felt dizzy and sat on the floor. More accurately, I collapsed on the floor but landed cross-legged with a shoulder against the wall next to the desk.

The TV news showed the end of Penny's report on the "break in" at the blood bank branch and the theft of blood. She spoke on-camera with a supervisor who stated it seemed to be an inside job. Then she spoke with another person who wanted to assure the public that the blood supply was safe and secure and no one need worry if he or she were having surgery or if there was an emergency. Penny then reiterated the call for donation, as usual, because the supply varies throughout the year anyway and the supply is currently lower than what would be needed during the fall and winter.

"Reporting live outside the Edmond branch of the Oklahoma Blood Institute, I'm Penny Park, OKC News."

Nausea washed through me. It wasn't just from her report, a story which had no other conclusion than me. It was more. My stomach ached as if it was ready to vomit. Gas filled my gut. The pressure pain was agonizing. I pulled myself up and fell into the bathroom, my hands on the wall as I leaned forward and let go a surge of bloody sputum. Bad air erupted out the opposite end of me unlike anything I had ever sniffed before. It was noxious, like something derived from petroleum.

My mouth tasted of strange things, as well. Not only the taste of blood but something vile and bitter. I cupped my hand under the faucet and filled it with water, sipped. The water tasted bad—sour like rotted meat. I doubted it was from whatever I had eaten; I hadn't eaten much the past couple days, not since I left New Orleans. But the food there, my so-called last supper, had tasted fine.

It had to be my metabolism. Whatever had changed in my body must be causing these symptoms. I was transforming. What I didn't know was what to expect.

Think of my parents, Penny had said to me. Try to remember everything I could about how they transformed.

I had thought a lot about them when I was in Utica, but there was so much I still had no clue about. My aunt, who said little about them, had died long ago so I could not ask her. Besides, my aunt was not actually a blood relative of either my mother or father; she was a friend who agreed to care for me. My parents sent her money for my expenses, including paying for college. I had no other relatives that I knew about. Now I had only a few tokens from them stored away in a footlocker in the bedroom closet.

I had opened it upon my return from Croatia, and only long enough to put in the few items I had brought back that used to be theirs. The lawyer who arranged everything had given me a few envelopes of documents, letters, certificates, and so on, as well as some personal items: rings, pendants, coins, figurines, a scarf, a tie pin—small, insignificant things for which I had no use but for the nostalgia they provided me.

Retrieving the footlocker from the closet, I knelt on the floor and unlocked and opened it, feeling a surge of sacred fire being lit in me. On top were the items in question. I picked up one envelope and slid out its contents. A few letters between them, the early years of courtship, and many documents related to their medical training. I did not take the time while in Croatia to read any of them. There would be plenty of time once I arrived home, after all. I did not know what I was looking for anyway.

They loved each other, stayed together to the bitter end despite their transformation. How special was that? They could pretend everything was usual, normal, while looking out at the world. However, to look out of yourself and see your lover becoming so wretched, so full of decay and horrible to gaze upon—how awful a life could that be? This woman, this man, who they each took as spouse, to love and cherish to the end of their days, and then see that spouse day by day wither away. It must have been agony for

A Dry Patch of Skin

them. I had thought through all of that as I sat before their closed caskets in that church, the only one in attendance but for the priest. And yet, they dared to have a child: me. And then they gave me away to protect me from what was to befall them.

So they knew. At some point in their lives they realized what was going to happen—what *was* happening—as I, too, was now realizing. And what plans did they make for their later life? They had jobs, of course, caring for those similarly disfigured, the undesirable entities of New York state. They lived in the asylum where they worked. They had skills and knowledge, yet they could not save themselves.

A physician and a psychiatrist could not cure themselves....

What hope did I have?

I emptied the next envelope and more documents and letters spread across my lap. A small photograph slipped out, just 3 x 5 inches, black and white. The photograph showed two people who better resembled ghosts than humans. Deathly pale faces with papery skin in rags, dripping off jawlines, eyes seeming to bulge outward due to shrinking of the skin around the sockets, lips pulled back permanently exposing decayed gums and thus severely projecting teeth, fang-like, certainly fearful looking to most people's view, and a few dark strings of hair falling from the nearly bare scalps. My parents.

They sat shoulder to shoulder like lovers and I wanted to see in their faces some hint of humanity, not these chilly facades of carnival monstrosities. I flipped over the photograph and saw the writing there: handwritten names and a date. The last picture of two people who fell in love then fell into disease, and somewhere between made me, either by design or by error. For who would, knowing he or she possessed this affliction, dare to make a child who would carry it on? Who indeed?

I stared again at the image of the two people—rudimentary in form as humans. I gazed for a while into their eyes, frozen on the cold surface of that rectangle of cardstock, so alive yet so dead. They appeared a hundred years old.

My eyes shifted from the raised hand of Mother, attempting to brush back a stray hair when the camera shutter snapped, her fingers gaunt, nails pointed and long, to my own hand holding the photograph, my fingers normal and nails short, tendons and veins in the usual condition. And I wondered how much longer I had until I would need to hide away.

But what could I do in my hidden state? My parents had jobs, what one might call the perfect jobs for people of their condition. That was a different world; now no such jobs like those existed. Hard to keep isolated from the world in these modern times. Surely some people had to hide. What happens to those kinds of people? Where do they go? Where are they housed?

I slipped the photograph between the pages of my passport and put away my parents' final collection of belongings. It was strange that all they left for me were paper items. And a few small tokens which held pleasant memories for them. What was I supposed to do with them? I saw a certificate with an elegant border and pulled it out of the pile.

And just what am I supposed to do with all these letters and certificates?

The certificate I held in my hands was written in Hungarian, I saw, and I was not up on the family language. What I could make out was enough to cause me to set it aside. I would work out a good translation later. There was a monetary figure written on it. There were some dimensions written, also; numbers were easy to translate. A small map occupied one corner. It seemed to have something to do with property, that is, some real estate. My parents old home, I suspected at that moment. They had retired to Croatia, after all. Perhaps they had spent time at this other location, somewhere further inland. All part of their retirement.

Retirement.... It was difficult to think about the concept, that phase of one's life. The final years when one was too old to enjoy youthful activities. The final phase when one knows it's the final phase. Such a depressing thought. I was alive and I wanted to go on living! I did not want to retire. I did not want to give up and slip gently into that good night. I would rage and burn against the dying of the light!

Edwina! Béla! I will not follow your path into silence!

Somewhere there must be a cure!

I got up, legs numb, and rushed into the living room, flicking on my computer. I had a lot of work to do if I was going to save myself. I had too much to live for—no matter what people might think of me now, the blood thief the public was now calling the "Edmond vampire"—*thanks*, Penny!

Going to my bookmarks, I deleted the website of the clinic in New Orleans. There were others I investigated, but they were far away. The spas in Europe had dealt with this problem for a lot longer. They would know what to do.

I went back through the websites, reading everything again, comparing details as if I were arranging a family vacation. No more blood sipping. No more sleeping in caskets full of nutrient-rich mud from some bayou. No, this time, it had to be done right: a medically supervised and biologically viable treatment that would reverse all the symptoms and prevent reoccurrence. Forever.

Morning light was cracking through the blinds when I paused in my reading. The night was done.

I rubbed my eyes, felt how dry they were, withdrew my finger and saw the smudge there. My eyelid felt strange. My heartbeat quickened automatically as I stood on shaky legs and hobbled into the bathroom and flipped on the light.

There I was again: the face of a monster on the body of an invalid, as pale and red-veined as I'd seen myself before. A dry patch of skin had become a full body sore, a scab which had spread from forehead to chin, from collar to navel, from shoulder to fingertips—yet the sight did not shock me. I was becoming used to it, accepting it.

However, I still expected to beat it.

Whatever my parents had tried—if they had tried any treatment at all—had to have been superseded by newer treatments. My research online suggested there were some that could do the trick and return me to normalcy. Especially, stem cell therapies were becoming more widespread and showing great promise in repairing a variety of ailments.

My stomach rumbled and I spit up some black bile, bitter and caustic. I rinsed out my mouth with a handful of water from the faucet and the inside of my cheeks burned as if I'd drank acid. I spit it out and turned to the kitchen.

One bag remained: Type B. The least effective choice but the only one I had. Unfortunately, I could not return to the blood bank for more. Their security would be heightened now. I would be recognized and apprehended. That would make a great story! Edmond vampire caught red-handed! But I did not want to be the Edmond vampire.

Despite feeling miserable, I held off taking that blood. As long as I was alone, indoors, by myself, it did not matter how I looked. I might only have one chance to make a run for it and I would need to stoke myself with fresh blood when that moment arrived.

Where was I going? Somewhere far away, I knew. Europe. To a clinic where no one would know me, where doctors would treat me and save me from my parents' fate. Then I could return and continue my life with Penny Park, my Beloved.

There were seven messages on my phone when I next thought to check. They were all from Penny:

Report was good. U ok???

U at ur lab? Feelin ok?

Im sorry if I hurt u
I knw ur ok, just let me knw ok???
Please call me. I need to know ur ok
Ok I guess ur at work. Good. Then ur ok
U better get out. OCPD checking ur address!!!

The last was less than 30 minutes before I checked the phone. If the Oklahoma City police were really checking on me, they would have been knocking on my door about ten minutes ago—unless they were staking out the apartment complex, waiting for me to make a move. I thought of the incriminating evidence: a bag of Type B in the fridge and the empty bag of Type A wrapped up and pushed to the bottom of the garbage sack. Find those here in my apartment and that would seal the deal. That would be the end of Stefan Székely, locked up for life—irony! Put in jail until he withered away to a husk.

Perhaps it was time to flee, time to make a run for the coast, hop a tramp steamer to Liverpool or Calais and catch a train to Budapest. Must make a plan.

I called the lab, spoke with my boss, explained how I was not feeling well. In more detail, I had picked up a bug, something I could not shake.

"I was hoping I could take more time. I mean, use my sick leave days."

"That's fine. I was going to fire you, but let's be nice about it. Go ahead and use your remaining sick leave and then don't come back."

"You're a real sweetheart, you know? Has anyone told you that lately? I bet not."

"I'll be sending you your termination papers."

I punched the hang up button but it had such a mild effect I was not satisfied. It didn't matter. I could not go back to that job. What I could get was my last paycheck and then my retirement account funds. I would clear out my bank account. That would give me enough money for my trip. And my car? I only needed it to get to the airport, but a taxi would do that better. And my belongings here in the apartment? I would have to leave them behind, let the apartment management deal with them. Nothing of importance except the footlocker. I'd leave it with Penny—she could dispose of it someday if it bothered her.

After printing out a book's worth of webpage information and all my personal documents, I launched the program that would wipe the hard drive clean. Anything worth saving was already on a small flashdrive dangling around my neck, my papery-skinned neck, rubbing a red furrow around it.

This is the end of this chapter of my life.

The thought made me sick and I rushed to the bathroom to let out my latest stomachful of bile, gagging as I wretched and heaved, on my knees before the commode. Just as I felt there was no more to expel, my phone rang. Not a text beep but a ring.

Of course it was Penny, probably calling to be sure I'd seen her report on the Edmond vampire. I took the phone into the bedroom and dropped myself onto the futon before answering.

"Hello?" I said.

"Are you okay?"

"Sure. Why wouldn't I be?"

"Because your health problems...? You don't have to be clever with me, Stefan."

"I'm not being clever. With anyone. I'm just so...tired. Sick and tired. Just plain sick."

"That's what I mean. That's why I'm calling. I'm checking on you."

"Just like the police?"

"Did they visit you?" Her voice sounded genuinely alarmed.

"Nobody knocked."

"Then you're okay. No warrant to search your apartment."

"They wouldn't find anything."

"That's good." She did not sound too relieved.

"Whose side are you on?"

"I'm a reporter. I'm not on a side."

"I worried you would be involved and get into trouble. I mean, you're reporting on a crime committed by your boyfriend—or your fiancé. If we are still together."

"What's that supposed to mean? Yeah, we're together. Even though you keep taking off whenever you get the chance. I can't keep up with your schedule."

"I'm going to be leaving again. I'm going to try something new. I think it will be better."

"What do these treatments actually do?"

I thought of possible answers. She had the reporter's sense of questioning, not like me. Whatever treatments were available, they had to be better, at least no worse, than my visit to New Orleans. And I told her so.

She wanted to know the details, times and dates, addresses and phone numbers. She wanted to be able to track me down. It made her laugh. Then she apologized for laughing.

"I want to see you, Stefan."

"I want to see you, too." I took a breath. "But I'm really not at my best presently."

"Haven't had your Bloody Mary for this evening?"

"You think it's funny?"

"Sorry. But are you still drinking blood? Is that really a cure? Isn't there some way to buy it legally?"

She was full of questions, which was her training, but I could not convince her of the seriousness of my misery.

"I don't look good now. I'm ugly. I mean scary-ugly. I have one bag left and I'm saving it for the day I leave. It has to get me looking normal so I can travel."

"You got a real plot going there, don't you? Sneaking around. Conspiracies. Spies. Secret formulas. I'm going to write a book about you."

"Don't do that."

"Then let me come over and see you."

"I can't let you do that. If you see me now you'll never want to be with me again. I don't want that to be your last memory of me. Wait until I'm cured. Then we can be together forever."

"Forever is a long time, you know."

"Give me some time, Penny. Give me a break."

"I've been giving you breaks all year. You go to New York. You go to New Orleans. I don't know where you're going next. It's all a big secret. It's like you're in some bad movie. Is this all in your head?"

"No! Please understand. You saw me before, that morning when I stayed too long. Remember? Soon, without treatment, that will be the *best* that I can ever be. Is that what you want?"

"We've been together more than a year now, Stefan. I think I've earned the right to see you at your worse. In fact, I don't mind wiping your runny nose or bringing you chicken soup. It's part of the deal, I know. I can handle it."

"But it's not a simple cold or flu. It's worse."

"How bad can it be? I've been to hospitals and seen cancer victims, murder victims, car crash bodies. I've seen a lot of bad stuff. I can deal with whatever you have."

"And still love me?"

"Aren't we beyond all that love stuff by now?"

"Beyond? What do you mean?"

"We are beyond needing to confirm I love you and you love me. We don't need to do that. We understand it, without having to say it."

"I love you, Penny. I still like to tell you."

"And I love you, Stefan. I say it because you seem to want me to say it. But you still know it even if I don't say it, right?"

"I suppose. But thanks for saying it. I really need to hear that now…as I'm stretched out on my death bed."

"Oh, stop being so dramatic."

"It's the truth. I'm dying. But it's good to know you still love me. No matter how hideous I become. Can you kiss a corpse?"

"Stefan, listen to me! You're not dying. Maybe you feel like you want to but you're not."

"How do you know? Do you have medical training?"

"Not really. Had a First-Aid course in Girl Scouts, but—"

"Then you don't know."

"Let me come over and see. There's got to be something I can do to make you feel better."

"There isn't. Let me die in peace. I don't want you to see me like this, like I am now. I'm hideous. And I don't mean that in any metaphorical moral religious way. It's biological truth."

"Stefan, I'm going to come over there."

"No, Penny!"

"I'm coming to see you."

"I won't answer the door. I won't let you in."

"I have a key. Remember? We exchanged keys when we got back together."

"I'll call the police."

"Stop it. You're being stupid."

"There's nothing stupid about death. It is quite efficient, quiet deliberate, and it's forever."

"Again with the poetry. I know you're not as bad as you say. Not when you talk like that. I'm coming over."

20

We lay on the futon bed in the dark and I was more embarrassed about the old striped sheets, musty and wrinkled and needing a change, than I was about my awful appearance. Penny was rather playful, however, not believing I was unsightly. To emphasize the seriousness of my condition, I wore a gray sweatsuit and blue ski mask that covered my face so she could only see my eyes and my mouth through the holes.

"What, are we going skiing tonight?" she asked with a laugh, seeing me in my costume when she arrived.

She pushed me backwards into my apartment and swung the door closed with her foot.

"It's for your protection," I retorted, then turned away.

"You're really being dramatic, Stefan."

"There is drama in every man's life. Some people have more drama than others. This is my drama."

She came up to me, swung her arms around my chest, trying to stretch up as if to kiss me. My lips were dry, but she reached them and a quick peck brought a frown to her face.

"Not in the mood?"

"For love?"

"Love.... Sex.... Anything. How about a game of mah-jong?"

"What's gotten into you?" I thrust my hands to my hips. "Here I am dying and you're joking around."

"You're not dying." She hugged me, holding herself against my chest like an anchor, her face turned aside. "I missed you, Stefan, plain and simple. I worried about you. I was so scared. I mean, like maybe you wouldn't come back."

"From New Orleans?" I dropped my hands. "I almost didn't."

"Yeah, I thought...I worried you would maybe do something awful. You were so upset."

"Then why didn't you answer my texts?"

"What texts? I never got any from you."

We argued about that for several minutes before concluding the phone carrier was to blame, and agreed to dismiss the topic. I was dying, after all, which was much more important.

"Actually, I worried you might, you know, commit suicide, or something. Sorry to even think that."

I frowned inside my ski mask, my downturned mouth visible through the hole. "Is that what you thought?"

"The state you were in...I couldn't be sure. Now I want to be comforting. So you know you're loved. And so you know where I stand."

"Where's that?"

She feigned checking around us for a location. "Why, here, of course. In your crappy apartment. Next to you. I stand with you."

"Cured or not cured?"

She sighed, then took a step back but kept her hands on my shoulders. "Listen, Stefan. I know there's this problem you have, but I also think you're overreacting. Lots of people have skin problems and they get along, have families, lead normal lives. I've done reports on families living with a member who has a debilitating illness. Like burn victims and war veterans. It's difficult, sure, but they get by. They make it work. I just want to try—"

"So I should be lucky? Lucky I'm not like them?"

"That's not what I mean. People find a way. That's what I'm saying."

"As long as it's not contagious."

"I guess so. Yours isn't, is it? I remember you saying—"

"No, it's genetic."

"So what's with this sweatsuit and mask? You trying to scare me? Hide from me?" She pulled at the ski mask, stretching one eye hole open. "Is that really you inside there? I want to be sure who I'm making love to."

"It's me. But perhaps not for long."

She hugged me, assuring me she was real, then grabbed my hand, pausing to notice how rough and dry my skin was. I should have worn gloves.

"Come on." She meant to the bed, or, in my cheap case, the futon. "I hated doing that report about the blood bank, but they did not incriminate you. No police came by. But—"

"But I lost—"

"I guess you probably don't work there any more."

"—the job."

"So I want to cheer you up. You can move in with me. Save some money that way."

"Isn't that what we are going to do after the wedding?"

She knew that I knew where her hot buttons were and how to push them. She was ready, expecting a battle. She kissed my check, the woolly ski mask safely between her lips and my cheek.

"We don't need to talk about a wedding tonight. There's more important things to do."

"More important? Like what? Every damn thing I'm doing—that I'm about to do—is aimed at taking you down some kind of aisle and getting us to make some promises. If you're not going to be in my life then there's not much reason for me to go on living."

"Oh, poor baby...poor Buddy Bear."

She took my ski-masked head in her two hands, staring up at me, into my eyes through the eyeholes.

"This is the reason I am here, Stefan."

A smile tried to appear on her face. Instead, a tear formed in the corner of her eye and fell, followed by another.

"You are my Beloved," she said. "I care about you. I love you. I want you to be well and I want us to be together." She relaxed a bit. "There are problems, I know, but I'm here. I'm here now...for no other reason than to make you feel you are loved. Today is for us: afternoon delight. Are you with me? Are we together?"

I had to grin, even through the ski mask mouth hole.

"Yes, I'm with you."

She led me to the bedroom.

Like nervous teenagers we undressed each other. It's rather difficult to describe. She, dressed in a pair of slacks and a button blouse, sweater, and the usual bra and panties was difficult to sort. Me in my sweatsuit was too simple.

Once she was in bed, sheet pulled over her, I turned away and dropped the sweatpants. Wearing nothing under it, my bare butt revealed dry, patchy skin, pale and pasty. I sat down on the edge of the futon. The lights were off in the room but the light from outside bleeding through the curtains helped her examine my sickly body as I dared to pull the sweatshirt off over my head. I felt a soft hand touch between my shoulder blades. The ski mask had come partly off my head as I took off the shirt. My face was the worst part, but as I remained facing away from her, I pulled the mask back into place.

Holding my breath a moment, I swung myself backwards onto the futon, dropping beside her, staring up at the ceiling like a corpse in an open casket, arms at my sides. I knew I was not pretty.

"I'm sorry, Penny."

"Don't be sorry. It's not your fault."

"Perhaps God thinks otherwise."

"Let's not talk about God while we make love."

"We're going to make love? You know, we don't have to do that. Lots of people do other things together."

"I thought you.... That's why I'm here."

She leaned on an elbow, reached around to my belly, her hand falling on my rough thigh.

"Tonight, I want it."

"With me? That's much too generous of you."

"You are my Beloved."

Her hand went for my penis, which was erect. I never had a problem with blood flow since this problem began. In fact, the disorder seemed to enhance my readiness for sex.

"I don't remember you being so big," she said with a muffled giggle. "Sorry. I mean, that's supposed to be a good thing."

"Can you see me? Is it dark enough for you to do this?"

"It's just right. I can see enough. I can feel you more. Dry skin, I know. Don't worry about that. Or I can get some lotion and rub it all over you. Would you like that?"

"We can just lie together and hold each other," I offered, "if you're all right with that."

"But you're so ready. How can you hold back?"

"It happens a lot. I can't *not* have an erection, it seems. One of the, umm, side effects."

"At least this is one part of you that's still smooth."

Suddenly I felt her mouth on the head of my penis.

"You don't have to do that," I said, as my body grew tense.

"Just relax."

"Are you sure you want to do that?"

"Do you give your consent?" she asked, pausing.

"How could I not?"

"That's a yes?"

"Doesn't it sound like a yes?"

She resumed her game and after a while, she arose from that kneeling position and straddled me. She rose up and dropped down, her hands pressed against my shoulders, and got into a regular rhythm, her small breasts with their large nipples sailing toward me then away. And this mistress of mine!

She fell beside me on the futon, breathing hard, smiling like a schoolgirl winning the spelling bee, and gazed at me. For a brief eternity, I forgot I was wearing a ski mask. She could smile at me only because she had not yet seen my true appearance.

"I missed you." She poked at the dry skin on my shoulder. "It hurts when I do that?"

I shook my head.

"It's not so bad," she said. "Was it good for you, too?"

I had to chuckle. "Yes—the best I've had for a while."

"Since our last time?"

"Yes...."

Her smile sank somewhat, became more artificial, as though she knew she could not reveal her true feelings at that moment.

"I want to kiss you," she said, leaning over.

"Be careful."

"Can you take off that stupid mask?"

"I really don't want to."

"But I want to kiss you."

Under the ski mask, my face was as bad as it had ever been. Without the ski mask on, only the darkness of the room would save my dignity. Now she wanted to kiss. My lips were dry and sore, cracked, my mouth had an awful taste. My eyelids had pulled back, my eyebrows and lashes had fallen out. The hair on my head was reduced to patches.

"Please...."

"All right, keep your mask on."

Penny scooched up on the futon so she could bend over me. Her eyes were closed. I closed mine, too. Her soft hands cradled my wool-protected cheeks, held my head steady.

Then I felt it: her lips, touching mine, the sweetness of her breath blowing from her mouth like an autumn breeze, a joyous combination of caramel macchiato and peppermint Altoids.

"Thank you," I said as she rose from my lips. "That was daring of you."

"I'm a daring woman."

"I believe you. I really believe you now."

We spoke quietly, reminiscing on the episodes of our short life together, feeling wistful and winsome about our fate. Her hand held mine and her other hand caressed my chest, flicking at loose flakes of skin. She gazed at me in the half-light.

I breathed easily, like an old man whose final wish had been granted. If nothing more, he could die in peace.

If nothing more....

Penny got up to use the bathroom, stayed for a hot shower, returned with a towel wrapped around her.

"Whoa! You're still hard? Geez, it's been a couple hours."

Grinning, I wanted to be clever: "I've been thinking of you for two hours, that's why."

"I just showered."

I took her arm and swept her into my sandpapery embrace, folding her down upon the futon, and clamored over her lush body and took my place between her legs, alternating gentle with rough, sensuous with bawdy. Until we dropped in exhaustion.

When my breathing was returning to normal, she rolled over to me, placed her hand on my arm as though it meant nothing, and said "I'd better be getting home."

My mind, lost at the bottom of an oceanic trench, suddenly shot to the surface, gasping for air.

"Of course, my dear." My voice was flat and dry.

"I'm sorry to have to leave, Stefan."

I groaned. "Of course. It's inevitable. Life happens. And keeps happening."

"But we had fun, right?"

Despite the closed blinds, the sunlight filtered in and now filled the room enough that I could no longer hide from her eyes. I stared at her through the eyeholes of my mask.

"Thank you," I said, turning my face away.

She yawned. "Better than sleeping, right?"

"You don't have to pretend."

"I'm not pretending anything. You mean your looks, right? I see you inside that body. You are still there. Yeah, I wish your skin was in better condition, just like you do."

"But I'm hideous."

"Yes, you are." She sat up. "Is that what you want me to say? I made love to a horribly disfigured man. Is that it?"

"Well, that's what you did."

"And I'd do it again, too. Did you see that report I did about three weeks ago where the man, a firefighter, was severely burned. And his wife was just happy he was alive and able to function. And soldiers from Afghanistan—roadside bombs, missing limbs, you know. They are still loved by their wives and girlfriends. People stick with those they love."

"How about a skin disease? An autoimmune disorder?"

"I'm sticking with you, Stefan."

"Are you sure? Do you really want me this way?"

"I don't want you *this way*.... But I want you. Ski mask or no ski mask."

That made my heart warm a little. It had been cold for a few weeks. I had gazed into the abyss, but there had been nothing staring back at me. Now I could take a step back from the rim.

"I love you so much, Penny! You are my Beloved!"

So filled with joy, I kissed her, even with my ugly mouth, and then kissed down her throat, between her breasts, across her belly. She grabbed my ski mask and as I kissed my way down her body it slowly slipped off my head. She giggled at the tickles as I kissed around her belly button and through her dark pubic hair to the Vale of Golden Wings, as I liked to call it.

"The what?" she laughed. "Sounds like a chicken restaurant."

"What else to call it?"

"Vulva works well, don't you think?"

I was too engaged to reply.

Her legs opened to my oral advance, her sighs became excited huffs. Then the noise fell into silence.

"Oh, *shit!*" she erupted. "Dammit. I'm sorry."

She sandwiched my head with her hands, trying to push me out of my position. I held fast, determined to finish what I had started.

"No!" She gave me a rough shove. "I thought it was done."

"I'm not done. Lay back."

"No, not that."

I looked up and saw her face blanche in horror, seeing my true face in the clear light of morning. No ski mask shielded me.

"What's the problem?" I asked. "Are my cheeks too rough?"

"My period."

"Your...period?"

My face felt wet. I stroked my cheek and my two fingers came back red.

"I'm sorry," she said. "I thought it was done."

The thought hit me, like suddenly remembering the secret location of the key to the treasure chest. My face was covered in spots of blood. Menstrual blood—

"Don't," she insisted. "That's gross."

"Lay back," I pushed her down. "Relax!"

"No!" she shouted, kicking her feet out, then raising her knees. "Don't do that. It's gross!"

"You don't understand. This is what I need. Look at me: you see a corpse. You just fucked a corpse! Is that some kind of fetish for you? That's what's gross." I licked my lips. "Why did you come over here?"

She tried to sit up, hand between her legs.

"I wanted to prove to you that...that I would be with you...no matter what."

"Then stay with me. No matter what. If you want me to turn back into a human, I need to get blood. I don't want it, I *need* it."

"You can get blood from other sources, can't you? You have a bag in your fridge. Don't get it from me. Not menstrual—"

"It's the same," I said, filling with desperation. I pushed her down on the futon. "Now lay back and fuckin' relax!"

I pulled her legs out straight, pried them apart, resumed.

"No, Stefan! Stop! Stop it! Let me go! Leave me alone!"

I gazed up across her belly and saw not the simple disgust I expected but a mask of pure terror on her face. I was filled at that instant with a dangerous mix of rabid hunger and frantic desire. I had begun consumption, feeling the change burning through my body already. I could not stop.

She pulled back her leg, kicked at me with her foot, striking my shoulder. I slapped her foot, holding it away. She struggled to get her legs free as I spanked her hip, the first firm yet measured not to hurt her, the second a wild hit that made her cry, then scream in rage. I could not pause. I held her down, quivering and crying, as I lapped up what I could until it ceased.

I rolled over then, fell off the futon onto the floor, breathing deeply as though I had just been saved from drowning.

And she, exhausted from our struggle, sucked air, then curled up into a fetal ball, sobbing.

The tears I smelled on her face tore through me: the sting of prolactin and the pungent painkiller leucine enkephalim.

"I'm sorry, Penny...." My voice was weak, and did not sound sincere, though I was very honest in my apology. "I don't know what came over me. I got a taste and...and I couldn't stop. It's not normal—it's perverse—but it was like some shadow took hold of me and I couldn't fight it."

She did not speak, but suddenly rolled off the futon and began putting on her clothes. I remained on the floor, watching. My face was bloodstained, I knew. She did not look over at me. She did not bother to clean herself but slid her panties up into place. When she was dressed, she took her bag and left the bedroom.

"Penny!" I called, jumping up, grabbing my sweatpants and going after her. "Wait!"

She flung the door open, her bag hanging from her shoulder, as I got to her. I grabbed at her free arm but she broke away.

"Please Penny. I'm sick. You know that. Blood is what helps. It was just coincidence, sheer coincidence."

She stopped, as if she were going to shout at me, but pursed her lips instead.

I shook my head slowly, trying to step into the sweatpants.

"You said you thought it was finished."

"I thought so, yes," she growled, raising her fist and extended finger at me, "but that doesn't give you any right to do what you did! It doesn't matter if we already had sex. What you did—that was rape! You raped me with your—your mouth! I said stop and you didn't! That's rape, plain and simple."

I was stunned, knowing she was technically correct and feeling gutted for having done that to her.

"Penny, wait. That's not right. I wasn't trying to hurt you—"

"You're just using me, Stefan. I can see that now. You're a user, always choosing people for how you can use them." Her face was suddenly a mask I had never seen before. "You don't love me, not really. You just want someone to be your so-called Beloved. It's a fixation. An object to worship. Not a partner to share your life with. Geez, what was I thinking? And I was about to marry you?"

"Please let me explain."

"What you need, what you should be looking for, is some poor girl who wants, *needs* a daddy. Someone who will look to you for all her needs. And you'll provide all the smothering kind of love she needs. And in exchange she will give you all the attention you need, everything you want. And you will suck her dry. You will suck out all her emotions to feed your narcissistic soul!"

"That's not true, Penny."

"I was right the first time. You were so quick to try to get me married so I would be yours forever. Forever! Something to put in your trophy collection? That's what is sick, you know? Sick. It took me so long to see it. To see what you're really all about. But nothing is forever—"

"No, you're wrong!"

She turned to go and I grabbed her arm again, as though I had not just heard what she had said.

"Please, Penny—"

"Let me go!" she snapped.

In that instant of anger, she grasped my wrist, intending only to separate my hand from her arm. She twisted, stepped away, moving sharply forward, and her tight grip pulled my skin, tore it apart—away from muscles and the rest of the skin on my arm. She regarded what she held in her hand: a sheet of skin four inches long and curled as it had been around my wrist.

She immediately dropped the sheath of papery skin onto the concrete floor of the breezeway.

I screamed in pain and grabbed my arm.

She glared at me, no hint of shock, perhaps believing I deserved to have the skin ripped off my wrist. There was satisfaction in her expression.

Then she left.

"Penny...Penny...," I moaned. "I'm sorry...."

I sank to my knees on the concrete, holding my wrist—as if clenching it would lessen the pain—and watched her drive away, watched that SUV go out of view, lost in the glare of sunshine.

And my world suddenly began to flicker like an old light bulb about to expire, about to leave me in darkness.

Part Three

21

MY BED ROCKS FROM SIDE TO SIDE AND I AWAKEN, blanketed in the darkness that my soul has carefully constructed around me, the same darkness I have exhaled with every breath, and which fills this small cabin, as I think back over everything that has brought me to this sorry state of affairs. I realize now there is no more light in the world. I feel confident I could get up and flick that switch on the wall and no light would burn bright. My black aura would jam it, would block out the light.

And so I continue, as fated, living the remnants of my life, as this ship crosses the wide Atlantic Ocean with me as its cargo. Outside, life seems to press on undisturbed. Inside, I practice whispering in cemeteries. I recall the old prayers from my youth. I imagine digging graves. The odor of decay seems to be always present. And through these days afloat, I try to claim all the good things I have done in my life, yet they add up to a pinch of salt in the whole ocean.

Metaphors suck. I can think of nothing else, however. I put into words my states of emotion, the chemical sensations, the biological functions, and there is nothing more I can explain.

When we arrive, I will get off this ship and find my next passage, for I seek not only a true and just end but some small measure of redemption for everything I have done. I will never find it, but I will seek it. And as I wander the earth in that search, I will visit my fate with each step. I will shake hands with my destiny at each sunrise and wish I could weep at each sunset. Ironically, my eyes do not allow tears.

In my bag is my disguise, a clever mask which resembles the image of me in my passport. It is a cruel joke that mocks the person I used to be. It fits tightly, affixed with generous application of spirit gum, and I can speak and blink behind the thin covering with little notice. I am, in that regard, a bit of a phantom, either of an opera or perhaps a rock concert. No matter. A wig, wide-brimmed Homburg, silk ascot, and deerskin gloves complete my travel ensemble. For now, this disguise will assist me in moving through public spaces unhindered, and without alarming anyone.

I boarded this cargo ship, one of the twelve passengers, without any complaint; indeed, I'm just an eccentric old man wanting to travel to Europe romantically on the "tramp steamer"—though this vessel runs on diesel and has a scheduled route. Thus, I avoided the long lines at security checkpoints. There was no frisking, no rummaging through my bags.

My disguise holds true, yet in the privacy of my cabin I can undo myself and sit among my reality. One week out from the Port of Houston, my body has reverted to its true form. Hence, this disguise, courtesy of Oklahoma Movie Magic and their wonderfully creative prop artists. They believed I was making a psychological thriller during the coming two months: *The Magyar Mystery*. The script is entirely in my head. I play the lead, a man who seeks a hidden treasure at a therapeutic spa in Hungary. The mask itself is a crucial element of the plot. And money will get you anything you want.

I have read my travel guide to Hungary for the past hour and now sit back on the bunk to rest my eyes. They are endlessly dry. I squirt some medicine into my eyes and bat them a few times, then stare across the short room, like those rooms in my college dormitory. On the top of the cabin's narrow dresser is a small, round mirror I have turned down since I first entered and only raise when applying my mask. Next to it sits my special customer appreciation toiletry kit full of assorted skin care products from Bath & Body Works, which includes various lotions and creams, astringents, acne medication, as well as two tweezers and a set of hair care clippers. I feel well cared for. If all goes well, in a few weeks, I shall welcome the mirror's honest judgment and have no fear.

Then I shall return to Oklahoma and beg for one more chance with my Beloved. That is the most I can hope.

On this journey, and after I return, I mean no one harm. I wish only to pass by without notice. An innocent stranger of no concern to anyone. Let me be on my way. Let me pass and I will disappear from your view, from your memory, and your routine will resume—as I go further and further in search of this incredible end.

Have I wallowed enough in my waterless tears? Can the dry heaves cause me ill feelings? Can my shivering body put me at mortal distress? I think not. For no matter what I feel, no matter what my soul sluices from my body, I maintain a firm and resolute consciousness. It—whatever 'it' shall be called in some far-off day of literary reportage—compels me to advance, like a mouse after cheese, like a wolf after deer, like a bat after blood. I must keep moving.

I am fearsome. The word 'hideous' is no longer effective in description. An entire thesaurus cannot fathom the changes in my appearance these days of crossing, locked alone in my cabin, set along the waterline. And water, as my parched stomach reminds me, is a poison from which I must twist away. The irony impresses me. Were I to toss myself off the quarterdeck into that dark sea, surely I would burn like a witch in the Land of Oz.

My skin is paper-thin, tearing easily even in my meagerest movements, rendering the cracks bloody and postulant. From scalp to toes, not one inch remains unaffected by my disease. It is best for me to avoid clothing, which rubs so fiercely, raising welts and carving fresh scars into my flesh. So I stand in my cabin, one hand on the edge of the small table, the other grabbing the railing running along the ceiling. I shift as the ship beneath me shifts, a journey from New World to Old, a return to that which made me, made my family into what we have become.

And in the silences, ignoring the rumbling of the engines on the deck below mine, I call up memories that dared haunt me in another life. I hold them in my mind, study them, walk around them as though they were statues, a garden of mannequins bent this way or that way, acting out the scenes of my life, repeating what I have done. This ridiculous stagecraft is required so that I may judge myself.

Again and again.

For that is all I can do now—until we reach Rotterdam.

It is true, you know. Money can buy anything—anything but love. With the right amount negotiated, anything you want can be had. I had money, or enough of it. With the end of my two jobs I could collect all my salary, and severance pay, pension and 401(k) retirement plan funds. And my IRA accounts. I cashed them out. All of it, even with the penalties. And I had documents from my parents: their inheritance. There was an account in Hungary. And the deed to a property in Croatia. Medical tourist or not, I needed to visit Europe to claim it all. Then, after driving down to Houston, I sold my car and put that cash into my pockets. With all my apartment belongings stuffed into a storage unit in Edmond, I was free to go.

I touched my wrist, felt the raised remnants of stitches almost completely absorbed into the skin. Although it felt numb to my fingers, it looked better than the rest of my skin did. The ER doctor did an excellent job reattaching the sheath of skin to my wrist. He did not question my rough appearance. By the time I checked out, I felt vigorous and looked passable for a thug used to fighting, but one who had lost a few too many. That was my story.

Each day I spent some time wishing I were dead, thinking of ways to do it, and wondering whether such a method would do the trick or if I would find myself still quite animated, breathing or not. Dark humor, certainly. I reread *Dracula* and another book on vampires. I perused medical texts from the university library I probably would not be returning to the shelves. I wrote out all my thoughts and read them over again, looking for something that might be a small clue to a cure. However, nothing presented itself. Or, I might have stopped being clever enough to discern such things. I am not a solver of mysteries.

Penny is the investigator, trained to look where no clue exists and find solutions to problems. I was wrong to alienate her. I was wrong to dismiss her so quickly. Of course, it was she who left me. Granted, with good reason. I've learned that there is a special kind of hindsight which is far more painful than ripping flesh off bone. Even with a few hours' pause to calm ourselves, a chance to rethink what had occurred, all my text messages were ignored. I tried calling, left highly apologetic messages on her voicemail: "Penny, I'm terribly sorry. There are no words to express the depth of my sorrow and my wish for forgiveness. Please forgive me and please let me be in your life"—and several variations on that theme.

I saw her reporting on TV that first evening and it was painful to watch. There was the woman I loved. There was the woman I had hurt. There was the woman who had hurt me. There was the woman I wanted back in my arms more than anything—even more than my own renewed health, if that were the only choice. But I did not see her reporting on subsequent evenings. It was as though she had deliberately refused to show herself to me even on TV. She did not want me to have that small bit of joy, not be able to see her on the side of the highway telling about a fatal roll-over crash, nor a home break-in where the two thugs had beaten an old woman to within an inch of her life just for a television set and some petty cash in a coffee can. It seemed as though Penny would not allow me the opportunity to see her for the two or three minutes each story took.

Meanwhile, I took care of my business—my *travel* business. I did my research, made calls, studied maps, and finally booked my reservations, then prepared documents and packed my bags. I also packed up my apartment; I was leaving town and I might not return. A dull sensation of finality settled into my stomach. There was no way I could know what my fate would be. Either I would be renewed in health and return to confront my destiny in Oklahoma, or I would never find a cure and die alone somewhere, lost and abandoned. Or, worst of all, I might never die but also never improve. That would bring me full circle to how to kill myself.

At night, I could go up and walk the deck, free of wearing my disguise, and breathe in some salt air. On windy nights I cannot wear my hat. Then I dare to go with my head bare. I cannot say getting some fresh air does me any good. In fact, the salty spray seems a corrosive to my delicate, papery skin and once I return to my cabin I require some first-aid, some lotion applied judiciously to the worst spots where my skin has cracked, exposing the raw underlayer.

One night, walking the foredeck, I could see the lights of our destination along the horizon. It was nearing dawn so I returned to my cabin and packed, ready to disembark and make my way through the crowds, heading to my next passage: the train from Rotterdam to Budapest.

The commercial shipping docks were unusually dark and lonely that Sunday evening in mid-October when we arrived. The other passengers had noisily disembarked before me, immediately after the customs officer had come aboard and checked our passports. I delayed, hiding in my stateroom, and only when it was dark did I walk down the gangway. Twenty-eight days at sea and my legs were unsteady.

I saw car headlights ahead, out on a street running alongside the harbor. Knowing a ship was due in, a couple taxis awaited possible fares. I walked out to the street, waved and got one. I took the taxi to a cheap hotel in the red light district, where all the cheapest hotels seemed to be, and took a room there for the rest of the night.

"Sir, are you wearing—is that a mask?" the front desk fellow dared inquire.

"Yes," I responded sternly. "Is that illegal here?"

"I suppose not. We should, however, make certain of your identity as we assign a room."

"Agreed. However, sir, I am blessed with a skin condition which may seem quite unsightly to most people. And so I have had fashioned for me a covering which closely resembles my true face, so there will be no doubt as to who I am." I held up my passport, photo page open for his examination.

"Yes, I see. It is a good resemblance."

"Very well, then. My room?"

I was proud of my accent, unsure how authentic it might be but satisfied that I came off as foreign and exotic.

He handed me an actual key, not a plastic card.

"Good evening," I spoke solemnly.

There being no bellhops, I took my own bags and proceeded to the stairs.

From the dank closed-up room, I could detect the sour odor of marijuana wafting through the alley, more so after I opened the window to let in what should have been fresh air. Below was a well-lit entrance, a red light staining the window curtains. A couple of women stood on the doorstep, smoking and talking without regard to a traveler's need for sleep. I stuck my face out through the curtains to get a better look up and down the alley.

"Hey, lucky boy," one of the women called up. "You need a friend tonight?"

I had no idea why she would be calling me in English rather than Dutch, unless English was the universal language of love. So I shook my head at her and withdrew, the curtains closing.

That was not anything I needed for tonight. Indeed, were she to come to my room she might find herself quickly screaming in fear and disgust and slamming into walls in her frantic hurry to escape the clutches of this monster. However, I was not that kind of person. No matter my appearance, I knew who I was and I was not that person who would call up a nightwalker to a hotel room.

Yes, I was not that person—not the person who might burst into hungry rage and hurt Penny, not that person who scared her and slapped her, not that person who so disgusted her that she withdrew from being seen on TV. That was not me, and never could be me. And yet I knew my disfigurement, my disease, my desperation to overcome it had certainly transformed me into a monster.

I unpacked my toiletry kit, set it across the foot of the sagging bed with its cigarette-burnt quilt, and prepared to take off my face. I had worn it for more than five hours, waiting to finish the docking procedures and be allowed to disembark. It gets itchy after two or three hours and at five hours, I could not stand it. The stage make-up glue dries out, becomes affixed tightly to my skin, what there is of it, and at that point begins to pull my skin away with the mask if I try to adjust it or remove it. Application of the proper astringent with a mist bottle helps.

Once the mask is lifted off my face, I let my skin breathe for a while. Usually it hurts for a few minutes, something between the sting of a sunburn and the cringing pain of salt in a wound. Then I apply a foundation lotion and let that work into the skin. After that, I wipe gently any residue, then slowly work into the skin a rich night cream. If I am planning to sleep, I leave the cream on as I sleep, disregarding anything that smudges a pillow or blanket.

Removing my shirt, I follow the same protocol for my chest and shoulders. It's rather difficult to treat my back, even with the long-handled bathing brush I bought at Bath & Body Works. I repeat the treatment for my lower body. I stand with legs spread and mop my skin with astringent-soaked paper towels, dabbing rather than wiping. Yes, it is a tedious procedure but those parts, which are normally covered by modest clothing, are less affected by my affliction.

The particular environment to which my hands and face are exposed has great influence on my skin's condition. That is, clothing, as uncomfortable as it is to wear, nevertheless protects most of my skin from that corrosion. Then I sit upon my bunk or bed or a chair and apply medicinal cream between my toes and around my genitals. I do all this to gain some relief from the itching, burning, drying of my brittle, papery skin. If only I were able to carry along with me an electric humidifier. Then again, too much moisture and my skin begins to rot, literally turning blue-green and stinking, recoiling into lumpy mounds filled with pus. Not pretty. The alternative is extreme dryness, which seems a better choice. There seems no perfect balance: a stench-ridden mildewy corpse or a dried out mummy.

Yes, when the gods decide to give you what you thought you asked for, there is always a cruel twist, always a catch in what is delivered to you. Wet or dry? Both leave you looking like death, albeit different kinds of death. How clever! How profane!

I curse them all!

Because they have cursed me.

22

"*Treinkaartjes, gelieve,*" came the command from a male voice, accompanied by hard tapping on the door. He wanted to check my tickets, no doubt.

I had a private cabin with sleeping berth, worth the extra cost and, for someone with my health problems, a necessity. Inside, I could relax and take off my ridiculous disguise. Knowing the procedure, however, I waited to take off my mask for this ritual.

Opening the door, the man extended his hand and I lifted my rail pass booklet to him with my gloved hand. I looked away while he flipped the pages and stamped where needed.

"Final destination?" he asked.

"Budapesht." I affected my best Hungarian accent. I was a man of mystery, after all.

When the conductor departed and the door was closed and locked, I thought of the journey the Count takes from his castle to the port, then onward by sea to England. He slept in his dirt-lined coffin the whole way, all arrangements secured by his loyal assistants. Lots of preparation, lots of precautions. Perhaps lots of fictional license, as well.

I smiled to myself, quite pleased with making my own careful preparations and knowing I was taking a vastly more comfortable ride than that poor fellow of yesteryear. Twenty-one hours or so on three trains would get me to my destination. And rather than the courtyards and alleys of London, I would be visiting one of the finest medicinal spas in Europe. I would be thoroughly pampered and put back together again, ready to sail home to the warmth of my Beloved's arms—

The nightmare shook me and I fell from the seat, rolled on the floor and got quickly up again.

I was relaxing in the café section of our usual Barnes & Noble bookstore, my home away from home. It was more than half-filled with young people studying for exams, old people chatting, assorted others browsing magazines or books they had brought to their tables. I had a short stack of items on my table, as well. I shook my head, as though I had been napping on that table. I stood and stretched. At that moment, a man was getting up from his table. He stepped past my table and the top item on my stack of materials caught his eye. A map of Hungary. Without saying a word, with scarcely a blink of his eye, he picked up the map and took it with him. Just took it right off my stack of items!

"Excuse me!" I called out after him. Everyone looked at me, the crazy person. "I was going to buy that."

The man slowed, turned and, seeing me standing with an angry look, stopped and said, "But you haven't bought it yet, so it's available to anyone."

"What? Are you mad? Possession is nine-tenths of the law!"

But the man grinned as though he knew the law backward and forward, and stalked off to the cashier *with my map.*

So right then I gathered up my remaining items: travel books on Hungary and Croatia, a Croatian phrasebook, and a couple of magazines, presumably to read on the way, and took them to the cashier, too. I wanted to purchase them before anyone else could steal them. When I arrived, the man with my map had gone, but I continued with my purchase.

Then, as I took my bag of books and magazines back across the store, returning to the café to get a latté for the road, there was Penny Park, ace reporter, in her news station jacket, sitting at the same table I had sat at, her own latté in hand. Across from her sat the indefatigable Tommy, ball cap reversed on his head, a stupid grin on his face, his hand laid casually over the hand of my Beloved. I stood like a statue, frozen at the sight of them. As I watched, I saw her lift her hand and admire the ring on her finger. Tommy stretched across the table and she rose to meet his kiss—

The train was slowing, rattling, hissing, as it rolled into a station. I scooted up on the seat, and parted the curtains to see where we were. We rolled and rolled through the station. Finally, I saw a sign. We were only in Düsseldorf.

The dreams of a vampire are as dark as one would expect, full of the black and white of Gothic horror, and the various grays of a muted life that never quite blossomed. I recall the corridors of Old Main, the asylum in Utica. The walls were stone gray, the floors tiled in a darker shade of gray. The tall windows were grimy, limiting even the brightest sunlight. And so my days running through the corridors, laughing like a child who did not realize his fate, were always set in black and white in my mind. Thus, they are black and white in my dreams.

That all ended when I was about eight. Children at my school were teasing me because of where I lived—at Old Main—and the teachers thought it cruel to keep me enrolled there. I was taught at the asylum by a former teacher turned disfigured entity, much less than a person: unable to walk, her legs were fused together to make her like some kind of slug, always wheeled around on a gurney. I think her name was Doreen but I remember calling her Miss Doris. She showed me books, lots of them from the library in the asylum. I learned to read and I told her about everything I read.

When my parents finally realized their dilemma, they located a surrogate parent, my "aunt" in Pittsburgh, who agreed to look after me. She would raise me through high school. Then I would go off to university. My parents were pleased, as they never failed to state in the many letters I received from them. I wrote back many letters myself. My aunt insisted I write to them regularly. I was never allowed to meet them, however, engaged as they were with their professions. "We mustn't keep them from their very important work," she would say to me. It was enough I got letters, real handwritten letters on lovely stationary, and small gifts, tokens of affection, and cards with checks in them.

If it had been daylight I could have seen the magnificent view of the Alps in the distance out the windows of the train, but I saw only the scattered lights of villages here and there. It was easier to travel overnight, free of questioning looks, though I could not sleep well during the night, my mind full of past and present. In the daylight, the random noises of a train full of passengers made me toss and turn on the bunk. I could never sleep more than an hour at a time. The curtains were not thick enough, nor were they positioned properly, to block out the light, so I hung up my coat. I stuffed tissue into my ears to block the noise.

Because of that, I missed my stop in Frankfurt, where I was supposed to change trains. Instead, I traveled onward all the way to Würzberg before I realized my mistake. I then calculated that I could correct my situation by continuing on this train beyond Würzberg to Nuremberg. There I could take a local line south to connect with another eastbound main line.

When we were several kilometers out, I arose and put on my face, an ever so delicate task. After making myself presentable, I was ready to browse the station between trains.

In the crowded station, it was easy to blend in. Just another mysterious foreigner. I did draw a few quizzical looks from some passersby, especially from a young boy whose eyes followed me incessantly—until I had no choice but to give him the spook eye. He shrieked, causing the parents to apologize to me and hustle him away. Probably they scolded him and told him not to stare at such strange-looking strangers.

In the restroom, I felt embarrassed. I could produce only a little urine; what there was flowed like liquid bronze. Obviously, I was burning ketones by the handful. And yet I bore an erection which I attempted to hide from the gentlemen around me. I had entertained no erotic thoughts that would have instigated it. Such a proud steed was simply a side effect of my affliction. You see, the gods have deemed this my personal paradox: to have the potent means to satisfy a partner yet to be wrapped up in such a hideous façade as to repel one and all from my bed. I have read about this in books.

Stepping out of the restroom, I entered the public arena with my mask in place and overcoat on, with gloves, hat, and scarf, too, a perfectly coiffed mannequin seeking the next train. I was overly bundled for the cool October evening as I allowed myself to be swept through the station and onto the platforms, choosing my next train with some consultation of the timetable and maps. My Euro Rail pass was accepted on most train lines; I needed only to assure that I could get a private berth.

I was an eccentric gentleman, I wanted the world to believe, so I acted the part. How did I learn this demeanor? From a few old films? From the books I've read? I was only a caricature of myself. In fact, I almost did not notice the mask riding over my face now, so familiar was it to me. In a mirror, I might have seemed perfectly normal: reserved, certainly. Stoic? Absolutely; but mean, angry? Not really. From three meters, with the brim of my hat pulled down, hardly anyone gave me a second look. The moustache of real hair on the mask helped; I had a moustache when my passport picture was taken years ago, and so I had them add one to my mask.

I stepped onto my new train, the local line. Because there were no private berths, I took a corner seat at the front of the car, facing the forward end, my back to the rest of the passengers. When the conductor came through, I held up my Euro Rail pass. Once he passed, I pretended to snooze, leaning against the side of the car, hat squashed between my mask's cheek and the window.

Hours later, I was roused to exit. I stiffly stood and noticed my mask had come unglued and was hanging precariously. The nearest passengers stared at me. I pressed it back into place but it did not stick. With one hand, I held it in place and I threw my small bag over my shoulder and grabbed my larger bag with my other hand.

Inside the station, I pushed into a toilet stall and peeled off the mask. I got out the cosmetic kit from my bag and reapplied the spirit gum, then placed the mask onto my face again. It was becoming routine now; I could do it in the dark—with a wild horse dragging me through the gates of Hell.

I exited and two police officers stood before me.

"*Haben Sie ein Problem, Sir?*"

Shaking my head slowly, I believed I should've grinned although my mask was unable to.

"*Ist das eine Maske, die Sie tragen?*"

I pointed at my face. "Oh, this? Yes—*Ja.*"

"*Aus welchem Grund haben Sie eine Maske tragen?*"

"I'm sorry but I do not understand—"

"Why are you wearing a mask?"

My hand automatically reached for the inside pocket of my overcoat to retrieve my medical certificate.

"I have a skin condition. It would be...let's say unpleasant for everyone...for me to go in public without the mask."

I handed them my papers and they opened them and looked them over, spoke between themselves, and handed the papers back to me. It was a real certificate; I had filled out a perfectly good blank form and signed it with the name of my boss. They asked for my passport and I offered it for their inspection. One held up my passport to compare my picture with my mask's clever duplication.

"*Was eine clevere Sache,*" the other chuckled, amused by the match.

My passport was returned to me.

"You are free to go."

"Thank you. I mean, *danke.*"

Their glances back at me did not leave me with confidence, but I was, at least, able to go about my business. With almost no good sleep since I'd disembarked from the cargo ship, I was dragging. I suddenly feared making a serious mistake. Already I had missed a train connection. Were I to become lost in the middle of some wilderness region of Austria, for example, speaking little more German than some medical terminology, and needing treatment in order to go on, I doubted I could survive.

On the next train, I could not get the thought out of my head. If I made a mistake and found myself alone, I would be lost, for sure, wandering helplessly. To villagers who encountered me, I would be nothing more than a monster. They would attack me. At best, I would be cornered and have to face the constabulary. I might end up in some kind of asylum based on my gruesome appearance and wild behavior, behavior that would be my natural, frantic, desperate actions, in fear for my life.

The local line train had shaken and rattled, and stopped every few kilometers, making the journey take forever. It was good that I was neither hungry nor thirsty, nor did I require any restroom visit. In that way, I was the perfect traveler. I was my own cargo, carried from point A to point B. Others got off and others got on. Scarcely anyone gave me a look, keeping quietly to myself in that last seat. Finally, we had arrived at my next destination and I was happy to get off that small train and go in search of a room at the nearest inn. I had to get some decent rest. Then I could continue my trip to Budapest.

Stepping from the station and shaking off the confrontation with the policemen, I saw a wide plaza with markets and tourists spreading before me, an elegant main avenue leading into the bustling city. Taxis were lined up along the curb in front of the station. Buses moved past. I knew I was not in a place where I should be taking a rest, not in the large city of Munich.

I had no choice: it was morning and I needed to get out of the sunshine. There had to be somewhere I could hide out for a few hours before I got on the next train. Crossing in front of me was Frauenstraße, the sign showed, and on the opposite side of the boulevard was a small park with a gazebo and a pond, and plenty of shade trees.

I was walking slowly toward it, feeling stiffness in my legs, my feet numb and tingling, pain in my left foot, when I noticed a strange odor. The breeze curled around me. The smell was stronger: a raw, putrid whiff of something dead or dying. A dog followed me and, at first, I suspected the poor animal had stepped into something nasty. However, as I walked, then began to limp as my legs' fatigue became more severe, I came to the realization that the bad smell was coming from me. Of course, I'd had on the same clothes for more than two days.

Three more dogs joined the parade. Sniffing and growling, they impeded my steps, causing me to dance across the plaza, almost loosing my balance. I tried to shoo them away but they were not afraid of me, not with my handsome stage mask glued onto my horrible face. I realized then that I had not seen my true face for more than twelve hours, captive as I was aboard the slow train from Nuremberg.

Then one dog decided to make his move, to claim his portion, and bit into my ankle. I tried to shake the dog from my ankle but he held fast. I stumbled, then fell, and the other dogs did not hesitate to attack me—

23

When I awoke—again; yes, always weak, always passing out—I believed I had finally managed to die and was now ensconced in a glitzy kind of heaven. There were angels surrounding me, after all, a sure sign of divine providence with their pure and pretty faces and dark flowing hair, white gowns, soft voices. Of course, the world knew I was easily fooled.

In the next several minutes, I felt my past come barging into my present consciousness. I quickly reached for my face and was shocked to find no mask there. That left me feeling quite naked in front of these angels. What awful things they must be thinking of this monster, this hideous creature of the night! What a poor wretched thing, surely the pet of Satan!

Indeed. How dare I believe I could cross half the world and find a clinic that would heal me from the curse of my family. Not clever enough for that. The last thing I had going for me was a smidgen of hope for a cure. And I got so close....

Living is so much better than dying. Poets and lyricists have said so, and they have convinced me. Truly, the coursing of blood through our bodies is so much more delightful than the opposite possibility: that is, the immoveable corpuscles, sheltering in place like a line of moviegoers standing on queue, huddling, the formation of plaque and the blocking of those avenues of liquid sustenance. It's a metaphor, of course, and yet were it not for such wordplay, I could not describe what I felt as my weakened veins collapsed or clogged up, my arteries narrowing and filling with toxic sludge and outrageous cancers. It is not the end for me, oh no; it is the beginning of death. And death is yet another beginning. A life lived as one of the undead—

"*Nein*, you are not dead," said a woman's voice. Too low, too rich to be one of these angels surrounding me. I could not see her from my prone position on the bed. A hospital bed. "I must say, you came to us looking like death."

"You speak English...."

"Aren't you American? Your passport says you are."

"Yes, but.... Where am I? Germany?"

"That's correct. In Munich. You apparently came here by rail. Don't you remember any of that?"

I was not sure what I remembered, nor what I should tell or withhold. She and her team of angels had to have seen me at my very worst. When they removed my mask.

And yet this doctor was rather upbeat.

"How—how do I look?"

She set down her computer tablet and leaned far over me, eyes blinking. Perhaps she was looking for something of interest to comment on. At that moment, I saw her nametag: Dr. Gloria Gottlieb—'Beloved of God.'

"You look well," she said, straightening up.

"Really?"

"Much better than when you arrived. You lost so much blood. You were given a transfusion." She smiled down at me. "You also had surgery to repair the damage done to your legs and feet."

"My legs and feet? What happened?"

"You do not remember?"

Pursing my lips, I decided to make up a story, a good one.

"I felt sick, tried to get off the train and stay in a hotel for the night. Then...a dog bit me. I think that's what happened."

"That is correct. We cleaned the wounds and stitched the skin together in two places."

"Oh, thank you, Doctor Gottlieb."

"There is more. You developed gangrene in your feet. We were able to treat it but, I'm sorry to tell you, we had to remove three toes. Two on your left foot and one on the right foot."

"Gangrene? But how? Are you serious?"

"You mustn't wear your shoes so tight, or for so long, without airing the feet. The blood supply was severely reduced."

I knew what she had said was not a common cause of gangrene, but I understood that, from her perspective, she had seen my feet encased in the leather shoes, which, granted, I had not taken off for days, and thus come to that conclusion. The truth was far less radical. My continuing transformation likely reduced what blood flow I did have going to my feet, especially while sitting so much, which caused the flesh to die. I was walking on stumps as I tried to cross the plaza. I could not feel my feet.

"...coagulative necrosis," she was saying, "which is the reason we had to remove tissue well past the extent of putrefaction."

"Putrefaction...." I sighed; something of me had died. "I get it."

"You'll need some time to heal. Then you can be on your way. Or perhaps you'll wish to return home after a traumatic injury."

"Ja...."

So close....

Staring at the ceiling, I dared to touch my face. The skin there was smooth, supple, ready to be kissed. I ran a hand over my scalp and felt my hair was growing out again, already a field of stubble. My chest also had hair growing. It did not take me long to make the connection. The transfusion was what did it. Fresh blood. I was certain I had gotten Type AB. If they had looked at the papers in my travel portfolio, they would have easily gotten all my medical information as well as my travel insurance documentation.

While I knew the real reasons for my horrid condition, these dedicated physicians saw only a man with circulation problems which resulted in the same kind of foot problems as a diabetic. In my misery, I had gotten a boost that would save me and allow me to continue on to my ultimate goal.

But there had also been sacrifice. Three toes in exchange for a transfusion. Fair enough.

I raised the sheet and looked down my body to my feet. They were bandaged so I could not see what remained. If I were still able to walk, I would need to get to Budapest in as simple a way as possible. That would mean flying, which was what I had tried to avoid. Too much scrutiny for a man with my unique problems. However, having been given a transfusion, I was back to normal: I looked normal. I could skip the mask and fly to Budapest in an hour. The gods had not defeated me yet!

Or, rather, should I refer to God, the one and only? God, who keepeth me on the narrow path and fills me with cursed genes, then tests me time and time again and finds me forever wanting. For I have never been a follower or true believer of any religion. I was a boy immersed in science. And with my parents' joyful end, I knew there was no God directing the fates of the people of this world. For why should children suffer? Why should people die? Why have floods and storms? wars and famines? earthquakes and drought? and so much inexplicable death and destruction? I have questions and He does not answer.

I measured my fate hour by hour, and at each interval, a nurse entered the room to check on me. I was still alive and the nurse would always seem surprised. As was I.

Finally, the doctor returned to fulfill her duties to this injured vagabond. She made pleasant small talk, then inquired how I was feeling. I had no answer. She glanced at the window.

"You keep the shades closed?" She started to open them.

"Please leave them closed. I'm sensitive to sunlight."

"Very well." She closed them.

I asked what my condition was, whether or not I could leave.

"You should stay a few days," said Dr. Gottlieb. "When the ambulance brought you, you very dehydrated and undernourished. At first we thought you were a homeless person but then we noticed the travel documents."

"Yes, I'm on my way to Budapest."

"Tell me, how long has it been since you had a good meal?"

"Days. Perhaps weeks. I feel very little hunger."

"Also your urine was quite dark and very minimal. How much liquid have you drank the past several days? Or weeks?"

"I have not had time to get many drinks."

"You have wasted away. Almost skin and bones. If not for the dog biting you, you might have died somewhere from these conditions. You are lucky we were able to catch you before you fell too far."

"Fell? I was tripped by a dog—the dogs, four of them, I think, all biting at my ankles."

"You don't need to think about that now. You are on the road to health. Let's get you mended. Then you can decide what to do next."

"I must get to Budapest."

"Oh? And what is there that's so important? More important than your health? Or your life?"

"First, there's a bank to visit. My parents...."

"A bank account then? I see."

"They died and left me some funds."

"I see. That's no reason to run yourself to the edge of poor health. Banks will wait for customers."

"That's not what I meant. I took the wrong train. I should be there today, not stuck here in a hospital."

"You need to be in a hospital. You had wasted away to nothing. Your skin was paper-thin, your muscles also wasted. Badly malnourished. The human body is not meant for that kind of abuse. We usually only find these conditions in long-term drug addicts. Your blood work showed no sign of illegal drug use. We suspected at first you were some kind of addict, possibly heroin, the way you were wasting away. You were close to death. You might have died before someone found you."

"Close to death...." I laughed, shaking my head against the pillow. "I know I'm dying. That's my entire reason for going to Budapest. I'll get my money, then travel to Croatia. I'm due at a spa there. A medical spa. You see, I have a skin condition—or an autoimmune disorder, actually. It's like porphyria. Heard of it? They can treat it and I'll be good as new. Then I can return to a normal life. I mean, a life with...with my Beloved...with Penny...."

Tears formed in my eyes and unexpectedly rolled down my cheeks, startling me. I wiped them away, then studied my moist fingers. I was back to normal, it seemed.

"I'm not familiar with that disease you named," she said. "Your skin is fine now, anyway, now that you've gotten some nutrition." She reached for the IV bag, checking its level. "Soon you will be completely back to normal."

"How much longer?"

"It depends on several factors. Already you've been our guest for three days. Perhaps another three and we will see if you can be released. If you had family here.... You could go home with a family member."

"I'm all alone."

"So you say."

"If I'm well enough, couldn't I just fly to Budapest instead of going by train? How long would it take?"

"Oh, it's about two hours, I believe."

"Cost? One-way, that is."

"I'm not sure. Perhaps two-hundred Euros."

As long as my appearance was respectable, I could pass easily through airport crowds. I could pass through the security and customs gates, as well, without needing my mask—and without any hassle.

"You mentioned someone...your 'beloved'? Is she waiting for you there?"

A grin spread across my face like morning sunshine across a windowpane.

Dr. Gottlieb smiled. "Ah, I suppose so."

"She is my destination...my ultimate destination. But I must go and slay a dragon first. Then I'll have proven myself. Then she might take me back."

"How romantic!"

"Yes, romance. What a ridiculous thing mankind has created."

"Although it can also be beautiful."

If I had planned to stay longer in Munich, I would have summoned a priest to my bedside to baptize me and make me curse-proof. Surely, it would be good to have God on my side rather than fighting against me.

My aunt in Pittsburg was a religious woman and often prayed in front of me. She never insisted I pray with her but always left open the opportunity. In hindsight, she probably believed my parents had been cursed by God for something they or their ancestors had done long ago. Praying would not have mattered. And I, even as a boy, carried that curse. She had gone to the St. Nicholas Orthodox church almost every Sunday but never took me inside. Perhaps she was afraid I might pollute the place. She would be blamed. Thus, I waited outside, where I passed the time role-playing stories of the Bible.

I knew if I stayed any longer in Munich, all the benefits of my wonderful transfusion would wear off and I would return to my degeneration. It would be better for me to go on to Budapest as quickly as possible while I had a normal appearance, whether or not I was completely back to normal per their medical criteria. They did not know the details of my affliction, but I had no time or inclination to explain it. I had only two goals: heal myself and return to Penny.

So in the middle of the night, I slipped out of bed and dressed in the clothes hanging in the closet. They seemed to have been cleaned and pressed, wrapped in plastic. I checked the contents of my travel bag. My mask was there but it stank and was sticky on the surface where the glue had been applied. I washed it off in the lavatory, dried it thoroughly with a towel, and replaced it in the bag. I checked the bandages on my feet, felt the missing big toe and second toe on my left foot, the missing little toe on the right. A little painful but I could walk on them with my shoes to support them and cover them. I put on two pairs of socks and my shoes, kept them loose. As I did so, I saw the line of stitches circling half way around my ankle and another up my calf—surrounded by yellowish skin and purple bruising.

I snatched the little bottles of lotion and shampoo from the rack by the basin, slipped them into my coat pocket. Then I took my bag and my backpack and went to the door. Checking each direction, I hurled the backpack onto my shoulder and stepped out, tiptoeing down the hallway to an exit door. I went down three levels of stairs and escaped through a laundry area that led to a garage door and loading dock. I hopped down and began to jog out to the side street, limping after only a few steps. I walked as quickly as I could along that street until it intersected with an avenue. I continued on, limping, and waved at three taxis driving by before one pulled up beside me.

"Airport," I said and the universal word was understood.

I waited all night in the airport, sitting on a row of hard seats opposite the ticket counter. I tried to drink down a coffee but my stomach could not handle it and I gave up before it was half-empty. I bit into a too-dry apple streusel and ate only half. A man worse off than me accepted the remaining portion and wolfed it down in two stuffings. He stared at me, as though he had seen a ghost.

So I was charitable. That was something God would notice.

With dawn coloring the terminal windows orange, I awoke from my brief nodding off and prepared myself for the flight. A stop in the restroom and a minute standing before the urinal made me feel that I was doing the right thing. Little urine came out but it was a beautiful yellow. Posing before the mirror, I considered that my face was rather handsome: I remembered it from many times shaving ear to ear, nose to throat. Whiskers had grown. Nevertheless, I could tell there was a change. The skin was dry, needed some lotion, and was discolored in spots. I took some lotion from the bottle in my pocket and applied it where needed. I combed my bristly scalp, covering as much as I could with the longer hairs, then set my hat on my head.

I returned to the ticket counter and purchased an Economy Saver ticket on Lufthansa flight 1674 for just 75 Euros. It would depart from G19 at 7 a.m. Then one hour and ten minutes later, I would be landing in Budapest. After using a limo service to go 11 kilometers into the city, I would be able to resume my journey.

I got through the security checkpoint with little trouble. My passport picture matched my present appearance well enough, though my once-full moustache was now reduced to a five-day band of whiskers.

"One-way?" the security inspector asked.

"Yes." I showed him my Euro Rail pass and he understood I'd be returning by train.

I was passed through with barely a second glance and went on to the boarding gate.

Soon I was plopping into an aisle seat beside a girl dressed all in black: t-shirt and skirt, leg tights, what I thought was the Goth look, maybe Grunge. I can never keep fashion trends straight; after all, my job deals with what's inside. With fangs, she could have been a vampire herself. She did not sparkle. In fact, her skin was entirely too white. She gave me a once over, shrugged a bit, returned to gazing out the window, rock music bleeding from ear buds whose cords streamed out from under long, black hair. The black boots with silver buckles she wore looked uncomfortable. The buckles matched the rings in her nose and lip. Oh well, only an hour's flight, I thought. To her, I was nothing special. That assessment calmed me, made me feel more as if I was one of those normal people you hear about.

Once airborne, the pressure of the cabin began to affect me. I scratched my nose repeatedly and eventually drew blood. The skin there was flaking. My nose was dry when I took a deeper breath. Please let this flight go quickly, I prayed. It may not be too soon for the transformation to be resuming. A panic swept through me.

The Goth girl next to me muttered something in a disdainful tone. Clearly, I had upset her with all my fidgeting. I recognized her words as Hungarian, so I felt a bit at home. It was mostly my aunt who had taught me, and although my ability in the family's native tongue was old and unused, I managed to catch some of it—something about being calm, not being afraid.

Of what? The steadiness of the aircraft? The sureness of the landing gear? The availability of the airport shuttle? Or simply of God? I could not believe God would push down an aircraft full of passengers just to get at me for a lifetime of lax devotion. Was I so special?

"*Köszönöm,*" I spoke, thanking her, after a minute to find the word in the back of my head.

She gave a scowl, shook her head, and her silver nose ring flapped. There was an idiot sitting next to her, she would tell her friends. This man who was afraid of flying. He had a crusty face, kept poking his nose until he made it bleed, and would not sit still. It was a miserable flight. That was what she would report.

"*Bocsánatot kérek,*" I said, after I'd taken a few more minutes to pull the words from my brain. I was apologizing.

She giggled then, perhaps amused at my American accent.

"*Ne aggódj. Ma nem a te napod, hogy meghaljon,*" she said, an edge to her voice. We were still not going to be friends, I sensed.

That made me smile, however: 'Don't worry, it's not your day to die.'

I had to believe her. Then I wanted desperately to find a calendar so I could confirm the date. Perhaps God had another day marked.

24

With a nudge to my ribs, I knew we had arrived. In fact, I did not even notice we had landed. I had fallen asleep in my upright position, my head cocked awkwardly to the side, saliva running off my lip.

The girl in the seat next to me spoke, almost too faintly to hear, and I guessed she was telling me it was time for me to get up and move out of her way so she could exit the plane.

I yawned and tasted blood in my mouth, an odd metallic flavor that was disagreeable. Once I was in the city, I promised myself, I would get some of the famous plum brandy. I grabbed my bag and started up the aisle. The flight attendants nodded and wished us a pleasant day in Budapest.

The Goth girl followed me off the plane, followed me through customs and immigration, then waited curiously while I got my checked bag, my old barely used backpack, from the carousel. She did not seem to have any luggage of her own coming down the line. I caught her looking at me, so I waved an innocent farewell gesture and headed out to get the limo.

Standing on the curb waiting, I noticed the girl about twelve meters down from me. Every time I glanced in her direction, she quickly looked away. Was there something disagreeable about my appearance? I walked to where she stood and asked her in my broken Hungarian if she needed a ride. No, she would take the shuttle, she mumbled. I offered to share my limo and she thought about it all of half a minute, then agreed.

We were exiting the airport in great comfort and grand style when I asked her a favor.

"Do you speak English?"

She grinned, as if she had expected a more difficult question, then said, "Little."

"That's probably more than the Hungarian I can speak. Well, I know some but it's been a long time...since my childhood. If you can speak some English, how about you help me for half a day? I'll pay you for your time."

"Sex...?" she asked softly. It was obvious she did not want the limo driver to hear her.

"No, absolutely not." I was shocked.

What kind of girl was she?—even though she did look like some kind of Goth hooker, with the whole death-is-wonderful theme, the nihilist fashion statement. Indeed, that 'We're all going to die anyway so what does anything matter?' mantra was rather pathetic. Listen, sister, if you had what I have, you'd appreciate your life a lot more. That's what I was thinking.

"No, I need someone to guide me around in the central business district. If you can read the signs, point the right way...."

"*Igen*," she replied. 'Yes.' Then "O-kay," but did not smile.

"What's your name?" I asked.

"*Az én nevem* Alma," she said. Then switched to: "Mya name iz Alma."

"I'm Stefan Székely." We shook hands. "Nice to meet you."

To get her warmed up, I asked her to tell me the story of her life, starting with her trip from Munich. Boyfriend. Naturally. He was in college, studying electrical engineering. She was returning from a weekend visit, she said. Her family was ethnic German. In fact, her parents had a German restaurant on the south side of Budapest. She was studying Biology but didn't have good grades. It was Art she preferred—drawing images of death, I guessed. My facial expression to that remark cracked her straight face, made her laugh, and she seemed less Gothic: just a young woman in search of herself.

I asked Alma about the banks in the city center. That was my first order of business. Indeed, I could have saved myself a lot of trouble if I had taken the trip up to Budapest while I was visiting Makarska for my parents' funeral. I had gotten all the documents at that time but thought nothing of them until more than a year later when I reached this current crisis. When I got them out and read them, I learned I had an account waiting for me in Budapest. And some kind of a house, according to a deed. I was so absorbed by my romance with Penny that I had ignored the important papers my parents left for me.

"I must be quick," I told her, but perhaps more for myself. If I waited even until tomorrow, it could be too late. My appearance might be too changed by tomorrow for public display. Then I would have to wear the damned mask. I had to take care of my business today.

I showed Alma the business card I carried with my passport:

Magyar Fejlesztési Bank Zrt.
1051 Budapest, Nádor utca 31

"Can you take me to this bank?" I asked.

She agreed to guide me and told me the directions.

The bank was near the famous Parliament Building—behind it, actually, considering that the wide Danube River was on the opposite side, the 'front' side. The bank was near Szabadság Park, and at the far end of the park, she said, was a tourist information center. She correctly guessed I would want to make a stop there, considering I had never been in Hungary before.

I leaned forward and asked the limo driver if he could drop us off at the address of the bank. Of course, for an extra tip, he could—because it was off the normal route. Normal route? It was a limo: door-to-door service. He was expecting to deliver me to a hotel, but I had no hotel reserved in Budapest. No problem; he would call around, find me a cheap place...but fancy enough for a gentleman with a hooker.

I understood his tone as Alma cursed him in her quiet voice.

"She and I were on the plane together. She's only guiding me to this bank. That's all. I have a fiancée back home in America."

The driver laughed. Best joke of the year. Getting some final moments of joy before the old habit begins, eh?

No, it's not like that. I tried to explain but broke it off, not caring what this oaf thought of my personal business. Be glad you're not similarly afflicted. Let your skin turn to paper and fall off. Then see how funny life can be.

He made two calls on his car phone, arranged a room for me near the bank I was seeking.

"Eighty-nine Euros one night," he announced proudly. "Also near Nyugati station. NH Hotel. Maybe six, eight blocks from MF bank. So you get money, then you have good time with young lady, hah hah."

"Just take us to the Magyar Fejlesztési Bank—*kérem*."

I felt I should add 'please' so we would actually arrive at my requested destination. Too much stress just getting into the city. My skin was drying out already. I needed some of that plum brandy and maybe a slice of *szilvas pite*—

plum pie. Where to get it? Certainly, Alma would know where. I asked her, offering to treat her but only after my banking business was concluded. If she would wait for me.

We pulled up to the curb in front of the elegant nineteenth-century gray stone building and got out, settled the fare, and carried our bags into the bank. Alma found a seat and chose a magazine to leaf through, the ear buds back in and music on. At the information desk, I handed the business card to the young man sitting there. He looked me over; I was not in my finest banking garb, plus the long trip, plus the hospital stay.

Right then I felt weak, as though I was not really back to full strength. My goodness, I was in a hospital bed a few hours earlier! They were probably still searching for me. I was wearing down, however, running out of fuel.

I gave the fellow my passport and he checked a computer file for a few minutes, then stood. He had me follow him across the long, eight-columned hall to another row of desks.

The young man introduced me to an older man sporting a long moustache and a high forehead, squinty eyes that probably should have benefitted from glasses. He was dressed in his best banking suit.

"Good morning!" said the bank account manager, rising and coming out from behind the desk with hand extended. "At long last you come to us—as your parents said you would."

I smiled politely. "They passed away almost two years ago."

"Ah...yes." He released my hand. "Of course they did. My condolences, Mister Székely."

He paused before speaking each sentence, as though he needed to choose the right words. I became suspicious. However, this man seemed to know my parents well and all about their business. So we sat down and chatted about their affairs. We went over the accounting for their estate. We discussed my holdings. The usual stocks and bonds. Some real estate. They had made a sound plan for leaving a legacy to me, their only son—their only child. Therefore, I was wealthy, as it turned out. Comfortable, at least. A great position to be in exactly when my body was failing me so miserably.

I fidgeted in the chair, scratched at my throat, my cheeks, my nose. The manager had a secretary bring a glass of water for me but I was not thirsty. Water would not quench my thirst. After clearing my throat, I offered an apology which was waved off. I blamed the long trip and the manager was courteous and patient.

He went through everything thoroughly, had me sign more documents, then brought an envelope of Hungarian *forint* bills for use in Hungary and another of Euros for my travels outside of the country. That combination would serve me well, what with a simple meal in Budapest costing 3500 to 6000 *forint*—or 22 to 30 Euro. I pulled out 5000 *forint* to give to Alma for helping me. Then I packed up all the documents into the portfolio the bank account manager presented to me.

Getting up, I waved to Alma we were going and she smiled as though she was happy to have something to do today, showing this foreign man around the center of Budapest.

A fresh, cool breeze blew as I tried to hail a taxi, not wanting to walk out in the brilliant October sunshine, but she insisted it was not far, even with bags to carry. She only had a large, floppy bag hanging from her shoulder. I had my rolling carry-on bag and the backpack.

We had walked only half a block before I felt ill. My head was spinning. Hunger and fatigue—and my feet hurt. I stopped in the middle of the street and she had to pull me to the side to avoid a truck rushing past us.

She cursed at me for not paying attention, then noticed I was not the same happy-go-lucky person I had been a short while ago. Sitting me down on the edge of a brick flowerbed wall along the street, I took several deep breaths and felt my lungs burning. I was not sweating. My hands were red.

Alma said my face was red. "How you burned so fast?"

I shook my head. "It's a curse."

"We go taxi."

So we rode the eight blocks to the hotel and Alma helped me into the lobby of the modern conference-style hotel and up to the sleek front desk, then took a seat to wait for me. I held on to the counter as the clerk checked me in. After asking each question and writing the answer on the registry forms, he gave me a quick inspection. I did not look well.

"Long day, long trip," I said. "And some bad food, I think."

He smiled, nodded.

With key card in hand, I went to the elevator and the bellhop took my bags. I motioned to Alma to join us and she jumped up and hurried into the elevator before its doors closed.

"My guide," I said to the bellhop's curious eyes.

After the room was checked and approved, bags set on racks, the bellhop handed back the key card and waited. I pulled out a few *forint* for him. When he exited, closing the door behind, I handed *forint* to Alma and thanked her for escorting me to the bank and to the hotel.

"I'm not feeling well," I said, dropping onto the bed. "So we will have to get that *szilvas pite* another time, all right?"

"You got bad food?" She seemed concerned, examining me. "You look...red. Very red."

"Yes, it's my curse. My skin is sensitive to sunlight. And it's a really long time since I've eaten anything."

"You want food?"

"Eventually, yes. But not now. I'd probably throw it up."

"I get food...for you." She held up the money I had just given her.

"No, that's for your help today."

She went to the door, opened it. "I get *szilvas pite* for you and me. And food for you. *Gulyás*. You like *gulyás*?"

"You mean goulash? My aunt used to make that a lot." I fell back on the bed and chuckled. "That's probably too rich for my stomach right now."

Then she was gone. The door was closed, locking behind her. I saw her bag resting next to mine. She would have to return for it. Meanwhile, I was hurting.

I took off my shoes and felt my toes. The socks were moist—from blood not perspiration. I pulled off the socks and examined the bandages. They were a mess. I reached for the phone and got the concierge on the line. Yes, right away. He would send up a first aid kit.

Ignoring the stench of my rotting feet, I took off my shirt and trousers and noted my skin was dry, crispy, already reverting to the form I was meant to have. Disgusted, I pulled on the white lounging robe hanging in the bathroom and tied the cloth belt around me.

A hotel staff woman brought the first-aid kit and, after she left, I repaired myself. The stitches were healing well but the general condition of my feet was awful. I sure needed to soak them in something, then scrape away the dead skin. I took out a spray bottle from my bag and hoped to freshen the air in the room, to cover my decaying skin's vile odor.

I went to the bathroom, started a warm bath. I poured in some shampoo, stirred it to make soap bubbles, then sat on the edge of the tub with my feet in the water. It was too hot at first, but that was a good sign. I could *feel* the heat. It was agony for a few minutes, then soothing. Satisfied my feet had soaked long enough, I got up and toweled them off.

I teetered a bit when I stood, but grabbed the towel rack for balance. I caught my breath and stumbled out of the bathroom into the main room.

My eyes were blurry but I saw someone had come into the room. A girl. It was Alma and she had two paper sacks in her hands. She held them up to show me, then dropped them as she screamed—

CR

"We have to stop meeting like this," I was whispering to Penny, sitting at our usual table in the café area of the Barnes & Noble bookstore. I reached across the table and clasped her hand. We gazed into each other's eyes and a smirk played on her lips. She was thinking of something sarcastic. I could tell by the way her eyes changed colors. Brown then hazel then brown again. In a second or two, a joke would slip from her mouth and we would snicker together. However, her eyes changed to blue, instead, then red, then white—no irises or pupils at all. I became alarmed and asked her if she was all right. "Do you need to see a doctor? Or perhaps an ophthalmologist? I know a very good one, just in case."

"*Hívjon orvost!*" a woman called out. I doubted Penny knew Hungarian, so I guessed it must be a Hungarian girl who was the one wanting a doctor. That would make sense.

I opened my eyes and found myself on the floor beside the bed. A girl was kneeling beside me—her name was Alma, I recalled—and she was swabbing blood from my face and my chest as a maid was handing her white paper towels.

Tiny beads of blood from a thousand pinpricks spotted my face and body like a case of measles. My skin was rejecting the blood that was put in me, trying to get rid of it. In addition, my rectum was inflamed, expelling bloody diarrhea. It was not a pleasant situation. This freshly prepared, newly cleaned room was now completely ruined.

"I'm really not prepared to spend another night in a hospital," I mumbled as I was carted away by medical people. "I know what's wrong but there's no cure." Of course, they either did not listen to me or they could not understand my words.

I heard a siren, then I did not, and again I was bundled into a hospital room, surrounded by people wearing masks over their faces. This time it was not Halloween, I was not playing the infamous Count Dracula, and my friends were not laughing as I tried to speak with the huge plastic fangs slipping in my mouth. Did you know you cannot effectively eat candy corn with plastic fangs in your mouth? In fact, you're likely to choke on the candy corn, as I did, which of course, prompted a similar rush to the hospital. Yes, I, the Count, was choking on those brightly colored candy corns—or blood, in this case, which seemed to be in the present, not the past. Strange how memory works.

The lights overhead blinded me. I closed my eyes, could only hear frantic mumbling, and these people deciding my fate.

I awoke in another hospital room and saw immediately the staff of five watching me, clothed completely in rubber suits and masks that covered their heads, as though they were in astronaut training. I was the alien landscape.

"You are in quarantine," said one. Looking alike in their coral green suits, I could not determine who had spoken. "We are running tests to determine what disease you have."

I grunted and spit out some mucus and blood, which one of them stepped over to swab from my cheek and the pillow.

"Where am I?"

"This place is Szent János Kórház," said one of the doctors. "It is research hospital. You know it?"

I shook my head. Not that it mattered. I had not known much about where I was for nearly two months now, ever since I drove out of Oklahoma City heading to Houston to get on that cargo ship. In the greater scheme of things, this was God's final joke: to make me suffer in various ways so I am taught a lesson. Then I would either awaken and be blessed for surviving, or I would be cursed and, after all of these trials, still be exiled from the world of humans.

Yes, I could see it all so clearly now. Everything was part of a grand plan, a major scheme to bring me back into the fold. I was supposed to suffer and thereby seek God to relieve my suffering. I was tossed overboard into stormy seas to see if I would float or sink, and the only lifebuoy anyone could throw to me was named God. Therefore, I was forced to choose the only choice given to me. So I did. Thank you, God, for this valuable lesson. I have learned it well. Now, will you be releasing me from these terrible tribulations any time soon? I'm ready to be cured and go home.

They mumbled among themselves about this plague and that epidemic and speculated which one I had. However, they did not know that I had none of the above. Rather, my scourge was self-inflicted. It was the genetic time-bomb my mother tried to warn me about. According to my parents' plan, I was supposed to live my life as long as I could, being happy and healthy, and when the moment arrived just as it had for them, when the transformation began, I would simply accept it, as they had. Seventy years was long enough. That's what they seemed to have decided when they chose to commit suicide together. No more living in fear and agony, no more being ostracized by their disfigurement. They chose their time and place of exile.

"You've got dry rot in your foot," one of the masked, hooded doctors told me from the side of my bed. It may have been the next day, but I could not be sure. "You had toes amputated for that, it seems, but it continues. Probably you did not get good care. The bandage was badly arranged. Are you in pain?"

"Yes, I think so," seemed a good response whenever my head swam to the left. When my head swam to the right, I could think of nothing to say. Storm clouds again.

"It has spread further. If it continues, you will lose that foot. Otherwise, it will continue up your leg, all the time releasing its poisons through your body. This is the sickness you feel now. We have given you antibiotics. Now we need to wait for your body to get stronger and fight the infection."

I gave a weak chuckle.

"My body will not get stronger," I muttered. "My body won't fight any infection. I am dying. I am meant to die. That's what God wants. Another notch on his holster."

"No, you will live. We want to save your foot, if we can. There is no question you will live...unless we do nothing."

"Please do nothing."

"We cannot do nothing. We are doctors. We pledged to heal the sick and treat the needy."

"Please make an exception for me. This is what God wants."

"Don't be silly, Mister..." She picked up my file. "Mmm...Mister Székely. You are Hungarian?"

"Yeah, like fourth generation. I came from America to visit a spa in Croatia. To cure my affliction."

"And what affliction is that?"

"Some kind of porphyria.... You know, the vampire disease."

The doctor repressed her laughter, hiding behind the mask, under the hood. Her laugh reminded me of Penny's laugh: very cool, silvery, like a tiny bell dinging in the night, like gentle wind chimes, very small wind chimes....

"Like the bell that rings when an angel gets her wings."

"Pardon?" asked the doctor.

I started to laugh, overcome with ethereal joy. Heaven's gate was opening for me. I could see angels there, on either side, waving me to enter. I heard harps or lyres or lutes playing and I felt so calm. I was ready for this final step, prepared at long last to meet my maker, the one who has cursed me in my final years.

"Hello, God. It's me: Stefan. I believe you now."

25

The heater was on and the room was stuffy. Outside, autumn rain patted the windowpanes, like a clicker counting my sins. I lost track of time and could only guess what day it was.

The door to my room opened and a girl entered.

"Alma!" I cried in surprise.

She was dressed in skinny black jeans and a too-large black leather jacket with many silver studs over a black t-shirt featuring a large white skull. She still had the ring in her nose and lip, and rings on her fingers, two necklaces around her neck. I was a little frightened by her.

The paper sack she was carrying she set on the side table.

"Hallo," she said.

"I'm sorry for all the emergency."

She pouted. "You...very scared."

"Yes, I suppose it was very *scary* for you."

Picking up the paper sack from the side table, she held it up and slid out a small brown box.

"Here is *szilvas pite*."

"Wonderful! Oh, thank you. You are so good to me."

I stared at her, saw the large bruise on the side of her face, as she handed me a plastic fork, urging me to taste the plum pie. The first bite was heavenly—just right: the sweet and the tart perfectly balanced. I *mmm*ed for a few seconds, smiling, then took another bite.

"This is fantastic—absolutely delicious." I finished chewing and swallowed. "I owe you something for bringing my bags here. Did you make use of the room?"

She seemed puzzled. "Hotel room...no."

"No? But I told them it's yours."

"Only get bath there. Clean blood...off my body."

"Oh, right." I took the last forkful of the *pite*, lifted it to my mouth. "I need to buy you a new shirt. I'm sorry I got sick. Thank you for helping me...uh, when was that?" I slipped the fork in and enjoyed the last bite as I watched Alma think about my question.

"Today is *péntek*—Friday?"

"Yes, that's it. Friday. So I've been here three days."

"You want more food, I get for you," she said, folding up the paper sack and tossing it into the trash basket.

She sat on the chair at the foot of the bed. There, the lighting showed her purple bruise more vividly. I wanted to ask her about it but decided she would tell me if she wanted me to know what happened.

I tried to sit up more in the bed. It was not comfortable. My back was sore—too long in my coffin, right? Alma got up, pushed the pillow behind me, shoved it in so it supported my back.

"Actually, I need something more from you. I mean, if you can help me one more time. There's an envelope in my bag...."

I directed her to find it and give it to me. It was still sealed. I was pleased. An honest person is hard to find. And I was wary enough of Goths. With me taken away to this hospital, my bags were left in my room. My bags and all my papers and money and the special toiletry kit of Bath & Body Works products. Somehow, they had been brought to the hospital with me. That was Alma.

I held up the envelope. "This is yours...if you can do me one more favor."

Her eyebrows pinched together. "What is favor?"

"I need a guide. Yes, again. I need to travel to a spa. It's near Sárvár—out west, beyond Lake Balaton. The thermal baths there are similar to where I was going in Croatia. That is, before I was...um, diverted here."

Again, she seem puzzled. I was not sure whether she didn't understand me or she was hesitant to get further involved with a strange man like me. Who was I, anyway? A sick man she met on a plane. But he'd promised her money for guiding him around. Then again, he was never supposed to have been on that plane, anyway. Fate. God was playing it close to the vest.

"Of course you want to know what the favor is. I get it. Well, it's nothing difficult. I just can't do it myself, you see. Not since I'm stuck in this bed."

She stepped up to the bed. "What you want me do?"

"I need to go to Sárvár. Is there a train that goes there? Or do I need to take a bus? Whichever transportation I need, can you purchase a ticket for me? That's all. Oh—and help me get from here to the bus station or train terminal, whichever. Help me get on that bus or train and the whole envelope is yours. Minus what the ticket costs. Okay? Can you do this for me?"

I watched her pursing her lips, thinking.

"You and your boyfriend can have a very good time with that money."

She smiled, then suddenly frowned. "O-kay, I help you. I get ticket for you, Meester Székely."

She lowered her eyes.

"What's wrong?" I asked, seeing her upset. Then I was careful to choose easy expressions in asking her more.

She pulled off her jacket and brushed the t-shirt a few times with her hand, delaying. Actually, she had no boyfriend. She made it all up, she said, and wiped a tear from her eye. Another tear slid down over her bruised cheek. No, I misunderstood. She *did* have a boyfriend in Munich, but they broke up. She was flying home, leaving him, no longer living with him. He had slapped her around too many times even for simple things like not having dinner ready. But not on her face.

She slipped into Hungarian when emotions overtook her. It was difficult to follow.

As she was already upset, I went ahead and pointed to her face and asked what happened to cause that bruise. She covered her cheek with her hand, and turned away.

I apologized. She did not have to say any more, I told her.

"*Az apám,*" she whimpered. 'My father.' He had never liked her running away to live with the boyfriend. Her coming home was not a joyous reunion. Her father had called her many bad names and told her to get out. She erupted into a full sobbing, and I envied her for that ability. It all stopped after a minute, though. She got angry then, cursing her father and her boyfriend and punching her fist into the bed.

Leaning against the bed, she seemed to want to be hugged, even dressed for a killing as she was, but I patted her shoulder instead.

❧

I seemed to take my naps in the strangest places and at the most inopportune times, but now that I was involved in a chess match with God, I needed to conserve my strength whenever I could.

The rumble of the bus shook me awake when we hit a rough patch and the vehicle veered sharply as it made its turn, barely passing without a scrape a small flatbed truck loaded high with vegetables. Rutabagas? Gazing out the window at the truck, all seemed well, and the farmer waved at the bus driver.

We were far from Budapest. I waited patiently for a road sign as the bus continued on the narrow two-lane highway, passing through flat farmland with tree lines. Other than being greener, the landscape was not too different from Oklahoma.

I looked over at Alma. She was asleep. Her head was pressed against the window on the opposite side of the bus. Her long, black hair was bunched under her cheek, no music seeping out of her ear buds.

After a half-hour, the bus slowed and entered the town of Balatonaliga, situated at the head of Lake Balaton, the largest in Hungary. It was a long, narrow lake, which reminded me of the Finger Lakes in upstate New York. But the road turned to the northwest and went along the short end of the lake for a few minutes before the bus pulled off the highway for a rest break.

The passengers piled off for restroom and food. I did not feel as spry as they did. My foot was hurting, sending a knife of pain up my leg.

Alma awoke, smiled when she saw me, and stretched her arms out.

"Feeling okay?" I asked.

"O-kay," she muttered, pulling herself up from the seat.

"Can you get me something to eat? Anything. A sandwich is all I need. And a bottle of tea, perhaps." I dug in my pocket and pulled out some bills, handed them to her. "And whatever you want for yourself."

She nodded, visually counted the money, and went up the aisle, bounding down the steps as a younger girl would. As I watched her standing in the line leading into the café, she pulled out her cell phone and checked it. Only for an instant. Evidently, there were no new messages or calls. I could sympathize with her.

I was lucky she had stayed with me. In fact, she had insisted on going with me. Perhaps God had sent her to help me. Or to test me. It was also possible she was put with me for God to test *her*. I've heard God likes this kind of conundrum. In fact, whenever any two people meet, one of them is likely a test for the other.

Getting out of the hospital was trickier than before, but with Alma's help, we managed to escape. She arrived early, before official visiting hours began, wearing a short black pleated skirt and knee-high black stockings, the same thick-soled black boots, she had worn on the plane, and the black leather jacket. The gap between skirt hem and the top of the stockings left her white thighs uncovered. She set down her big purse and stood beside the bed, talking with me—saying barely a dozen sentences over more than an hour. I did not say much either.

Nurses checked on me twice.

Then we left.

I was hobbling because of my foot bandages, but she got me on a yellow and white tram, which eventually delivered us to the bus station. There was a train that went there but we had missed it. We also would need to change trains along the way. With my foot problem, I agreed with her that I should take the bus, which would go all the way to my destination for half the price. Like a professional guide, she led me through the station via the most efficient route and over to the right bus.

She faced me as I was ready to climb aboard. Again, I thanked her for helping me. We said goodbyes, which seemed a good deal friendlier than our few hours together would seem to have warranted. The way she gazed up at me reminded me of Penny after we'd gotten back together, when we accepted that we both had quirks we'd need to learn to live with.

"Please, Meester Székely," said Alma, her soft voice wavering, "I am go with you? Please?" If I did not know to be patient and listen carefully, I might not have heard her.

I was surprised and ran down a list of reasons for her not to tag along with me. My health problems were the big reasons. She insisted she could continue to be of service. She had nothing else to do, nowhere to go.

"I am...go with you. Helping. O-kay?"

With the driver calling for us to either get in or stand back, I nodded at her, she nodded back, and the deal was done. At the last instant, she climbed aboard after me and the driver closed the door.

There was a lot of money in that envelope, so perhaps she simply wanted to earn more of it. I guess she saw how much help I really needed. I was an invalid. My illness had subsided and I began to feel somewhat normal, but my foot was killing me—literally. I paid her ticket when the driver came down the aisle checking everyone. She had no luggage, only that big floppy bag that served as a purse. It did not include any change of clothes, however. When we arrived, she could buy more clothes with the money I gave her.

As we rolled through the streets of Budapest, she pointed to this historic building and that old bridge, the royal palace on the hillside across the river, and the magnificent riverside parliament building—landmarks of her city. She expected I still wanted her as my guide. If only I had time to be a tourist in Budapest. I decided I would return for a visit once my medical treatment was completed.

We chatted for the first few kilometers once we were out of the city. She asked more about my life, my reasons for coming to Hungary. I had no cause to suspect she was any kind of threat to me, not a scam artist, so I explained how my parents left me some money and property when they died. However, soon after that, I started to be affected by this health problem. Yes, I tried remedies in America but nothing worked. The only cure I could hope for now was to be found at this spa. They had experience with my kind of medical situation.

I noticed then that she had nodded off. So much for telling my story. The uneventful trip across the *Puszta*, the great plain that occupied most of the country on either side of the Danube River, caused me also to seek a nap—

Then we stopped for a rest break. After a few minutes, Alma came back aboard the bus. In her hands was a full meal for two.

"This is *halsaláta*," she said, handing me a bowl. In it was a mixture of vegetables like a salad, with small chunks of fish. Herring salad. She handed me something long and narrow wrapped in paper. "This is *parasztkolbász*," she said. It looked to be a paper-wrapped sausage.

"*Köszönöm*," I said, thanking her, trying to keep to the spirit of using foreign words. I accepted the bottle of tea she handed over and studied the label, seeing what words I knew.

The sausage was spicy with paprika and garlic. My nose knew it immediately and I worried whether or not my stomach could handle it. I could not afford to get sick on this bus in the middle of nowhere. The fish salad was even more questionable. Certainly, her selection of food would have been good for lunch if I were in a normal condition.

I ate slowly, watching my guide eat the *lángos* and *libamáj*, twice reaching into the paper sack between us to retrieve a *kifli*. The oil-fried pancake, fried goose liver, and the small crescent rolls made a good lunch for her.

Alma was telling me something I couldn't really follow, half in Hungarian, half in English, laughing in spots. She seemed like a different person. I was happy she was enjoying this excursion from her usual routine. After leaving Munich, she had no routine in Budapest, so I understood her willingness, eagerness, to accompany me on this three-hour tour. It would be something special. Then she could return to Budapest.

For dessert, she showed me two *rétes*, holding them up as if they were precious gems. The flaky pastry filled with apple, nuts, and raisins was a little messy to eat but tasted great. It seemed Alma had not eaten this well for a few days. I certainly had not—yet I believed I should hold back a little longer.

Once everyone was aboard, the driver checked us again and we continued on to Sárvár, rising into low hills as we went west.

We stood forlornly in front of the glass façade of a sleek, modern, classy hotel, in every way a resort: the famous Sárvár Fürdö. The extensive hotel complex was surrounded by a variety of pools for swimming and baths for soaking. Inside awaited a full range of services for both families with bored children and adults in need of relaxation or therapeutic mineral bath. It did not give me much confidence I could find an ancient cure for an ancient malady here. It was too much water park and not enough voodoo treatments. This was a hasty change in my plan, I admitted, an ill-thought detour. I hated Plan C as much as Plan B.

The uniformed doorman held open the door for us.

"We go in?" asked Alma.

Her tone seemed to reflect my disappointment.

I should have gone to my original destination in Croatia—the clinic I had called from Oklahoma, the spa where I had actually spoken to a clinician and gotten my questions answered. They could help me with my condition. My health was failing in Budapest so I thought perhaps this closer facility might be good enough. To get me by. To save me.

My feet hurt tremendously, especially my left foot, which was numb. My back was sore from the bus ride and my stomach was still deciding what to do with the lunch. As for my skin, I was feeling itchy and scratched myself frequently once we got off the bus, as though I had contracted a swarm of ants. My nails came back stained with blood.

"I suppose we should go in, yes," I said.

We entered and were immediately greeted by two resort staff who made no note of my poor appearance. So who was this odd man wearing the wide-brimmed hat and sunglasses, bundled up in bulky overcoat on a wonderful sunny, unusually warm autumn afternoon? That was what this resort manager was thinking. And who is this serious little friend, the black-haired waif? Perhaps a girl of the streets he picked up in the city? Or perhaps his daughter, along for a weekend before she goes off to university? I knew their thoughts as surely as if I could hear them spoken.

In fact, my hearing was somehow extraordinary and I turned around in the lobby to track down the source of various snatches of conversation. When I did, my eyes met theirs and they paused in their talking, realizing I had heard them across the wide lobby. They stared at me and my guide and I knew their thoughts. Yes, here was someone who clearly needed special treatment. Look at him: a disfigured monster all wrapped up, hiding in plain sight among his victims! He and his poor assistant, not too much better herself: look at that hair, the dark cosmetics around her eyes, the rings in her nose and lip, the spider web tattoo on her neck. Surely, this one has already wasted her life, the poor creature. And now to be the lover of that cretin! How dare they come to pollute our fine establishment!

The front desk woman was speaking to me.

"No, I do not have a reservation," I said, torn away from my concentration on the cacophony of conversation. "Excuse me, but I'm hoping there is a place available, as I am in need of certain treatment. I noted in your brochure that you—"

"What seems to be the problem?"

It was a smartly dressed man, clearly the senior staff member in the lobby. He addressed me and, when I turned to him, he grinned like someone who was putting on a pleasant face. Gazing at me, the manager was struggling to restrain himself from a well-deserved wince.

"Good. You speak English. I want to ask for only one certain treatment, which you offer, at least in your brochure. That is all I require. That, and a room for the time I'm here."

"Unfortunately, sir, we are full this weekend. There are no more rooms."

"No problem. I'll stay somewhere else in town and come over for the treatments. Is there someone on your staff I could speak with who handles particular treatments? I would like to know more about the—"

"That person is off this weekend. Terribly sorry. Called away to a funeral, I hear. Quite unexpected."

"Yes, there's a lot of that going around."

"So you see...we cannot accommodate you."

"But you do not know which treatment I'm referring to. How do you know if that person is.... Never mind. I understand. I am not welcome at your resort. I don't have the right look. I might, let's say, cause some disturbance to your other guests."

"We do apologize for this inconvenience." He never stopped smiling, as if he wore a stage prop mask. "There are other hotels in the area...."

"I'm sure there are."

He gestured to the front desk woman. "Perhaps, we could call and arrange a room for you...elsewhere...for this evening?"

I stared him down but knew it was useless. If I were in his shoes, my feet would still likely hurt. He was protecting his turf, shielding his guests from this hideous monster who dared seek refuge within his walls.

"Yes, thank you. Find us a room somewhere else," I said with a smile he could not see with my wide hat brim shading my face. All the better to hide my dry skin and toothy grin. I knew I was changing already. I needed to get out of public view very soon—before I went mad and started biting everyone.

26

The drawing board is not my friend. In fact, I feel betrayed and cheated and kicked in the teeth by that drawing board. That is the reason I abhor returning to it. However, if that is the only choice, I will accept the old inn in the far corner of the town, off the tourist guidebooks, the one with the rat and the spiders, and the torn and badly stained antique quilt on the one double bed that slumps in the middle. The cheap room in the back, across the alley from the garbage dump, with a view of a hill, its forest, and the darkness full of monsters. Perfect for an odd couple.

Throwing off my coat and hat, I stomped back and forth in the center of the small room.

"I should've expected this!" I roared so loudly that the frumpy innkeeper likely heard me downstairs. However, I did not want to be cast out of this last choice of rooms, so I tried not to let my anger overwhelm my perspective. "I know I'm ugly, falling apart, and so frightening to women and children, and their stupid little dogs. He's right to keep me out of there. Someday I will haunt him—all of them!"

I paced the room and turned at that instant to catch Alma, sitting on the corner of the bed, concern on her face. Seeing her, I realized the drama I was exacerbating.

"*Nem probléma*," she muttered when I paused.

"I get that I'm being irrational. But for me it is rational. I'm dying. I want a cure and I'm turned away at every door."

"*Ne aggódj. Ma nem a te napod, hogy meghaljon*," she said, as though she were reciting a famous proverb. I remembered her saying that on the plane. It is not my day to die. So don't worry. Sure. Let's see what God has to say!

"That's easier said than done."

Shaking her head, she fiddled with her phone.

"You're frightened, no doubt. Aren't you? I dragged you halfway across Hungary to be my...*playmate*. That's what they think. Maybe they're right. But I don't want you. You're not my type. It fills me with rage to see you dressed that way, like you're trying to scare somebody with this whole death motif thing. But it doesn't work. It's a pathetic look; I mean sad-looking. You're just a young lady who doesn't know what to do with herself. You can't find your path. So you dare to latch onto someone like me who was kind to you. Just a beaten down old man who showed kindness. That's all it took to get you to come with me. Now what do we do? Geez, I gotta send you home."

I knew she could not follow my words, not as quick and fierce as I shouted them. Besides, I was not sure I meant what I said. Perhaps everyone in the small inn could hear me, although we seemed to be the only guests tonight.

Alma looked ready to speak, then returned to her phone.

"Look at this room: one bed," I continued. "What is this, their honeymoon suite? Is this what I'm worth? I have a hundred-thousand dollars to spend, courtesy of Mother and Father, and they treat me like I'm some kind of worthless vagabond with a couple bucks in my pocket. Like I'm the scum of the earth. Like I'm a pedophile who loves little girls! That's what they think."

"I not little girl," she muttered, looking up at me from under her thick eyebrows. "I have twenty years."

I almost bit my tongue. Perhaps she understood everything I had said, after all.

"I know. Sorry, Alma." I stopped pacing. "I hate this place."

Alma sat on the bed, checking her phone, finding nothing to respond to. She turned off her phone with a huff.

"Nobody wants us," I said, seeing her disappointment.

"No," she mumbled. "No-body."

"I'm sorry to get you involved with my problems. You've been a great help, a good companion, and I have enjoyed meeting you. But let's be realistic. There's no reason for you to be here. You should head back tomorrow, get on with your life. Definitely forget about me." I went on like a stuffy career counselor, listing the options for a woman, pros and cons, deciding everything for her. "Or you could be a journalist. You know…like on TV."

She listened patiently, being polite. I stared at her.

"Well, maybe not…. Heck, do what you want."

She said something in Hungarian, but it seemed she spoke to herself more than for me to understand.

"You know…." I paused. Finally, she regarded me, a scowl on her face. "If that's your only set of clothes, we should get another outfit for you to wear. I don't mean you look bad, or that your style is inappropriate. But you're going to need something fresh for tomorrow."

She looked herself over: the black jacket, jeans, and t-shirt.

I laughed and she grinned. If it were only me, I wouldn't care whether or not I wore the same clothes a second day. With the weather cool and with my peculiar skin condition, I did not sweat. For her, there was already a trace of body odor.

"If you want to shower, maybe you'll feel better," I said, then did not know how to proceed.

"*Vegyünk egy zuhany*?" she asked, surprised.

"Yes, take a shower." I waved toward the bathroom. "I'm only suggesting. After, you could wear a t-shirt of mine. It may be like a nightshirt on you. Then you could wash your shirt and it can dry overnight. Tomorrow we'll get you some new clothes."

She showed no reaction, perhaps wondering what I meant.

"New clothes?" I knew I sounded like a creepy old man who offered candy. "Let's get you some new clothes tomorrow."

"O-kay," she said with a nod.

She stood. Grinning with embarrassment, she tilted her head down to the right then left, sniffing.

"Sor-ry," she muttered. "I get clean."

She pulled off her boots and went into the bathroom.

"Alma," I called after she closed the door. "I'm sorry. I didn't mean it that way. Everybody sweats. It's been almost twenty-four hours since we left that hospital…. It's quite normal…."

I heard the shower running.

My heart ached at that moment, feeling bad for what I had said. I would explain and apologize when she came out. Until then, I had to find a shirt for her.

I went to my backpack and dug in it for whatever clothes were left that were clean. I was not a good travel companion, I knew; I never intended to have a companion on this journey. I found only a regular button-down shirt unworn and clean.

As I bent over the backpack, my shirt was sticking to my back and I sensed my skin was flaking, becoming fixed to the cotton fabric. I unbuttoned my shirt and delicately slipped my arms out of the sleeves. I had to rip my body away from the fabric, causing a dozen spots of pain. I clenched my teeth through the effort, then tossed the soiled shirt on the floor beside the bed.

Yet another sign of my rapid disintegration. I would never get better. I could not even get treatment at this spa clinic. No treatment, no cure, only the same ugly skin flaking, only the same horrible appearance, a face only a ghoul could love. Penny certainly would not love it. I had to wear a ski mask the last time we—

There were no mirrors in the bedroom, but there was a small handheld one in my toiletry kit. I grabbed the bottle of lotion, too. After slipping off my trousers and laying them on the bed, I saw that my legs had a similar problem: scabs. I knelt on the floor, using the bed as a table and spreading out my skin care materials. I dabbed some lotion on a cotton swab and tried to reach back to apply it to the spot where skin had torn away.

I would be especially cruel if I were to force Penny to live with me while I had this skin condition. Who would want to touch me? I knew Penny would not be the one. I could not do that to her.

Knowing the choice was not mine, I fought back a laugh. She had already made her choice clear. We tried to be kind to each other, but I am, like it or not, a monster, a ravaged revenant.

The bathroom door opened behind me and I froze, arm bent behind me, holding a cotton ball.

"You...o-kay?" asked Alma.

I explained the situation, half-turning to face her.

She stood wrapped in a white towel, which covered her from armpits to knees. Her feet and skinny legs seemed like a child's and were so pale, down to her black painted toenails. Her long black hair was still wet and combed straight down to her lower ribs. At that instant, she seemed to want to smile but was determined to hold it back.

Now she could see the real me: my skin condition, ugly as it was.

I apologized for everything I said before. "I was angry, but not at you. It's just that this is not what I was expecting, not at all where I thought I would be tonight. And I never thought there would be someone with me, someone in a towel, fresh from the shower."

She grinned, after a heartbeat to translate my words, perhaps. She stepped toward me as I sat cross-legged on the rug in only my socks and shorts.

"You...hurt?"

There seemed real concern in her voice. The thought flashed through my head that perhaps her natural talent would best be served as a nurse. She had been studying Biology, after all.

She knelt behind me and took the cotton balls and the lotion bottle from my hands. She began pushing the cotton to each spot where skin had torn. My injuries were as though fishhooks had caught my back and then had been yanked free, leaving the open wounds. She worked carefully on twenty spots, some painful, others tolerable.

As she worked on my back, I felt I was slipping into a dream, something dark, with a wolf and two bats, a castle on the hill. I began talking about everything I feared and she continued her gentle work. Finally, I returned to the reality of this room.

"I don't know who you are, Alma Jónás—or who you think you are or want to be—but I presume you were a little girl once upon a time, a cute baby, a precocious toddler with a dimple on your chin, a princess your parents loved very much, the apple of their eyes. And then a black rose fell into your garden and you picked it up, held it in your tiny, tiny hands and perhaps pricked your finger on one of the black thorns. You thought it must be a sign from God that you were unfit, that you were not one of the chosen. Maybe that black rose had thorns that cut you."

She dabbed another wound on my back. It stung.

"Now you go around reminding people," I continued, "people who think their frivolous lives are so perfect, so blessed but actually rather banal. You remind them that they will ultimately die someday. And, who knows? Perhaps they'll die in some particularly gruesome way."

She tossed the used cotton ball on the carpet, beside my bare leg.

"Your job is to remind everyone about death. Is that it?" I half-turned, trying to see her face, but couldn't. "Or, is it something God has assigned you and you do it reluctantly, hoping for a 'get out of jail' card you can play on your next go-around? You were created to be a reminder. At least, that's what I think whenever I look at you: when I see your dark heart behind your white flesh, and when you dare to touch my disgusting skin with such gentleness, when you look into my eyes and keep reminding me I'm not dead yet, when you insist on going with me each damn time we come to a moment of parting."

She pressed the last cotton ball to the last spot on the back of my neck. I had lost count how many wounds she repaired.

"What is God trying to tell me? You are a reminder of something...."

I felt her fingers press into the shoulder muscles at the base of my neck, some kind of massage.

"It is o-kay?" she asked.

"Oh, that's so good now," I said, adding a grateful groan. "If not for you...I don't know how I'd manage. You are...an angel."

Suddenly, like a great flurry of snow, a white towel flew over my head and onto the bed in front of me.

Her hands reached around me, tossing the lotion bottle and bag of cotton balls to the bed. From behind me, her arms wrapped around me, pinning my arms to my sides, her small hands pressed flat against my chest. I felt her chin, then her cheek, press between my shoulders. A long exhale warmed my skin.

"Are you all right?" I asked.

Her breaths tickled my skin. In front, I saw her arms crossing before me. I saw the lines of cuts on her forearms, rows of them, and the tattoos of wilted flowers, black roses, on her upper arms, and the pewter rings on her fingers, silver chain bracelet dangling around her right wrist. I felt the ring in her nose against my back, then the ring in her lip as she kissed my neck.

I laid my rough hands over hers, clasped them against my chest.

"Thank you," I said, just above a whisper.

She responded with another embrace, like she was worried I'd leave. Relaxing, she rose behind me, me still in my sitting position, and swung to the side, in two tries sliding around to my front, wedging herself between me and the side of the bed. The cool sensation I had felt against my back I saw then was a large silver ring with a miniature gem pierced through her nipple.

She lifted her leg, bent at the knee, and extended it across my lap to the other side, dropping her knee to the carpet. She placed her hands on my shoulders and lifted herself up, then dropped herself onto my lap so we were, in only three seconds, face-to-face and bare chest to bare chest.

Her hands remained on my shoulders.

"Alma...."

She grinned, a little embarrassed, it seemed. "Meester Székely...."

"This is not what I was expecting, either. I thought we were—I think of you as a friend—a new friend—who helps me."

My throat became tight as I stared into her dark eyes, at the same time noticing again the rings in her nose and lip and the spider web tattoo on the side of her neck. It matched the spider ear rings fixed to her lobes, visible when her long black hair was tucked behind her ears.

"It is...o-kay?" she asked.

I stared into her sapphire eyes, noticing at the same instant how she had the fragrance on her of the soap and shampoo. I felt her heartbeat gradually matching mine.

She closed her eyes, leaned forward until her lips met mine. Her kiss was surprisingly tender.

Her hands remained loosely clasped behind my neck as our lips parted. Her weight, what there was of her, filled my lap. She must have been able to feel the firmness in my shorts.

"Alma, dear, I know you might be thinking of something that probably isn't true." At that awkward moment, I believed a speech was due, but I wasn't quite sure what to say. "You are a lovely girl, and thank you for helping me. I keep saying that, I know. But I do mean it: thank you. But not for this. Not for whatever you think we are going to do next."

"Next?" She pouted. "What we to do next?"

"Tomorrow, we need to leave here. I will go on to the clinic in Croatia and you...you should go back home. To Budapest. That's where your life is, where you belong."

"No," she said with a grumble. "I go with you."

With her sitting naked over my lap, over the slit in my shorts, it was difficult to refuse her. She kissed me again, several pecks to my mouth.

"You had to know this adventure could not go on," I told her. "You and me, we were always going to part from each other.... All right, forget that. Instead, just look at me: I have this skin condition. I'm ugly. So how can you stand to touch me? Are you not afraid of catching what I've got?"

She shook her head, lowering her face as though in apology. "It is o-kay."

"No, it's not okay. I have to undergo medical treatment. And then I must return to America, my home. Your home is here: up in Budapest. Sure, I know you had troubles. I'm sorry for that. I'm sorry for all the men who treated you badly. I want to take care of you, but I can't—"

"Please...I go with you." Her hands cradled my face, held me like a naughty child. "I got no-thing. It's...only you."

"But Alma...."

"You and me."

"It can't be that way."

Her hands returned to my shoulders and she lifted herself up, her knees digging into the carpet, and reached under herself, digging into the slit in my shorts. As her fingers maneuvered me, her eyes focused more intensely on my eyes, blocking my will. She took hold of my erection and lowered herself little by little on to it. She rose and lowered herself, keeping her eyes focused on mine until she knew I had finished. She hooked her chin on my shoulder then, cheek to cheek, breathing hard.

I fell back on the rug, holding her on top of me.

Her fingers played with a flake of skin on my shoulder as I stared at the ceiling. I wondered what part of God's plan this was. Was he testing me or her? From that NH Hotel in Budapest, she could have disappeared, taken my envelope of cash and never returned. Yet she showed up at the hospital—with pie. And a bruise on her face. She couldn't part from me at the bus terminal, either. No better option? There was nothing special about me, but I seemed to represent whatever she thought she needed.

"Oh, Alma...." Her heart beat weakly against mine. "What have we done? Are you my Beloved now?"

Her chest rose and fell against my body, and with the tickle of the nipple ring, I pitied her and swung my arms around her, held her for a long time there on the scratchy carpet, beside her black boots.

"Are you sure you want to go with me? Are you willing to be my Beloved? I mean, forever?"

"*Igen*—I go with you. Any place go is o-kay."

"Is that what you really want? To go anywhere with me?"

"*Igen*—yes."

"Anywhere?"

The road was no longer a superhighway with wide medians. It was curved and hilly and there were no shoulders. Night was falling and no moon lit the way. I roared ahead anyway, unconcerned about the headlights approaching through the mist and the forest, lights that had to indicate the biggest tractor-trailer rig ever constructed was barreling toward me—with a sign warning of the one-lane bridge practically lost in the darkness. And I was crammed into a small sports car with an extra can of gasoline in the back seat, and there were no brakes, no air bags, no insurance. I knew that. Yet my foot weighed further down upon that pedal.

"Oh, Alma," I whispered, my fingers feeling her spine beneath her smooth skin, "you are my big rig."

27

Darkness spread outside the open windows, the curtains waving from a cool breeze. For October, I estimated it must have been close to nine. We had stayed on the rug for a half-hour, carefully measuring our heartbeats against the rhythm of the earth, or the footsteps of the husky innkeeper in the room beneath ours, then moved to the bed. We repeated our experiment there and it seemed like she could not get enough.

The last time, holding our final exhausted pose, I noticed her hand, arm extended, holding up her phone. Before I could speak, there was a snap. She had captured us in the act: a horrible old man worthy of the grave forcing himself on a young waif. A few deft clicks from her thumb and she set the phone down beside us on the bed.

"To György," she said with an evil laugh.

"Who's that?"

"Boyfriend."

I chuckled. "You sent him a picture of us? I'm sure he'll like that."

"And...father." She actually giggled.

"They'll be looking for us for sure now, you know."

I stared at my watch like it was a police scanner and saw we had missed the dinner hour. Of course, hunger did not affect me, perhaps not my skinny companion, either. I thought I should give her the chance to eat. I asked if she was hungry.

"Little," she said, too relaxed to move.

Rolling off the bed, I stood and felt my foot roar with pain as I put my weight on it.

"You o-kay?" asked Alma, sitting up.

"Apparently not."

I checked my foot. The bandage was stained and needed to be changed. I grabbed my trousers, crumpled on the floor.

"There's a café down the street," I said, digging into the rear pocket of the trousers for my wallet. I pulled out a few bills, handed them to her. "How about you get us some food we can call dinner while I repair my foot? Who knows? Maybe they also have some *szilvas pite*. Get whatever you like."

Her smile brightened and she got up from the bed, gave me a quick hug, and dressed again in her worn clothes. She took the money and reached for her jacket.

"Bye bye," she said cheerfully, and left.

I retrieved my first-aid kit, cleaned my foot, and applied a fresh bandage. Then I got dressed, putting on the stained shirt, refusing to start a fresh one until the next morning.

My skin felt better, but I still looked awful. In the bathroom, the wet towel she had used was hanging on the shower curtain rod. On the towel rack hung her bra—black with lace.

In the mirror, I saw a corpse. That girl must be blind, I decided. Or, is it just an unholy compassion for an ugly old man? Some kind of fetish? There might be some people who get aroused being with a creepy old man, calling it a challenge or a dare. With her death theme going strong, it made sense for her to be attracted to a disfigured man like me.

I sat on the chair, propping my feet on the side of the bed, and leafed through a news magazine I found in the drawer of the nightstand. There was a Bible in Hungarian there, also, but I already knew the stories.

After a while, I looked up. It should not have taken very long for her to go down to that café and buy some food, whatever they had left. This was not fast food America, however. I thought the café might have closed, now that evening was deepening. Perhaps she felt obliged to find some kind of food and had gone further into the town.

I started to worry. I got up and paced the room, then put on my shoes and coat, grabbed my hat, and went out.

It was dark along the street but a few lamps on storefronts gave enough light for me to gaze as far as I could in each direction. The way to my right went up a slope and seemed to go past a cemetery and into the forest. So I went to the left, down the street.

The shops were quiet and locked up for the night but I could hear some partying going on further into the town.

Hurrying down the street, my limp increased.

In an alley between two shops, more like a narrow parking lot, was a girl pulled back and forth between two young men. Some kind of love triangle gone bad, I initially concluded.

"*Az a nöci túl csontos,*" one said. The words 'too skinny' was all I caught.

"*Szerentném megdöngölni,*" said the other—saying he wanted to 'hammer' her into the ground.

I smiled to myself, remembering the slang expressions I had learned first which stayed with me longer than all the proper vocabulary. But this was not a language lesson.

"*Akarsz baszni? Akarsz baszni?*" the first kept asking her. Clearly, the girl did not want to fuck, not according to her attempts to tear herself away from their grasp.

"Hey!" I shouted, wanting to startle them enough so the girl could escape. "What are you doing there?" Despite my using English, I expected they would understand that I had seen what they were doing. They were caught. "Let her go!"

"Meester Székely!" the girl cried out, and only then did I know the girl was Alma.

She struggled to get free and in her fight, her shirt was ripped open and torn from her arm and shoulder. I pulled off my overcoat, dropped it on the ground for her.

Then I rushed at them, not thinking what I was going to do, but in one motion I pushed the taller one in the padded ski vest on the right against the wall there and the shorter one in leather jacket on the left backwards away from her. My sudden strength surprised me. The fellow on the left tumbled hard to the ground, rolling on the concrete, scraping against some gravel and was slow getting up. The one on the right stumbled dizzily and grabbed the back of his head where it had slammed against the stone wall of the building. Even in the glow of a street lamp, I could see the darker shading on his hand that must have been blood.

"*Rohadt turisták!*" the bloodied guy cursed. Always blaming the tourists. That angered me.

His comrade got to his feet, shaking his head, and they stood together in front of me. Alma was behind me, watching the two young men from around my shoulder.

"*Az isten bassza meg a büdös rücskös kurva anyádat!*" the one bearing the bloody head shouted. That was the worst he could do? You want God to have sex with my mother? That would make me Jesus, wouldn't it? And Jesus was a badass.

I filled with rage. My skin tore open along my back and my shoulders, and my face was a mask of red death. They cowered. Their eyes widened, bodies shaking as I lunged at them. The shorter guy I threw to the ground again but this time with such force that I heard something snap when he struck the pavement.

I shoved the bloody-head boy so hard against that same wall that my hand broke his nose and his blood sprayed onto my shirt. His hands went to his face and he heaved for breath, a raspy, wrenching noise that echoed between the buildings. He slid away along the wall, disappearing into the darkness.

His accomplice, rising to a knee on the ground, regarded me: my hands red with his friend's blood, challenging him to fight. Instead, with his other knee apparently hurt, he hobbled off into the darkness, too, a stream of swear words trailing him.

Lights came on in the neighboring homes, and I saw a face peer out through curtains. I turned and fell into the shadows of the building, my hands covered in blood, my shirt stained red. Half of me was shocked by my behavior, thrilled with my burst of strength, but the other half was fearful that I had gone too far in this chess match with God.

"Oh my God," I repeated again and again, hardly out of breath. I had no doubt that God was already tallying my card with black marks. How did that even happen? It was all so quick.

I stood frozen. And there was Alma, staring at me from the street, my overcoat around her shoulders. I wasn't sure what she could see in the light from the street lamp. Additional lights blinked on with the noise, and I knew people were coming out to investigate what had happened to disturb their evening.

Starting toward her, I passed into the light and she let out a shriek at the sight of me. Her eyes stayed fixed on me as I moved into the next shadow.

"You need to go," I grunted.

I stumbled over the box of food she had been carrying when she was accosted, crushing it beneath my shoes. As I reached her, I wiped off my bloodstained hands down the sides of my shirt and pointed up the street, indicating the way to our quiet inn.

"Go on," I said, waving my arm forward.

She was aghast, seeing me as I was. "You...hurt?"

"I told you I would be scary, when you see me at my worst."

"I help you."

"No, you can't. No one can help me."

"Please, let's go...go there."

I shook my head. "You go. Tomorrow, you take the bus back to Budapest. I better leave tonight for...for somewhere."

"No, we go...you and me."

In the lamplight, I saw wet streaks down her cheeks.

She tugged at my sleeve. "Please, let's you get clean."

We heard people approaching and she grabbed my arm firmly, pulling me after her. Without a second thought, I gave in and we hurried away, ducking between two other storefronts a couple blocks up the street.

The conversation at the alley escalated into a frantic murmuring until one voice emerged from the chorus to call for the police.

Inside our room, I barely got my shoes off before Alma rushed me into the bathroom and made me stand in the bathtub while she unbuttoned my bloodstained shirt, yanked it off my arms and shoulders, and dropped it at my feet in the tub. She got me to step out of my trousers then pulled off my shorts and socks.

She turned on the shower and pulled the curtain around us. As she started to get wet, she jumped out, stripped down to her skin, and returned with a couple of washcloths. She applied soap to the cloths and scrubbed my chest, then worked on each bloody hand and finally, with more gentleness, on my face. The shower water ran down over my head, washing everything away, a red pool swirling at our feet. After a few minutes, it seemed I was in a dream and nothing had actually happened.

She took a washcloth and brushed my body like a painter. As she worked, I saw the parallel cuts across her arms again and wondered what had happened to cause her to take a knife or razor to her arms. They seemed to have healed well, at least, even the ones that looked recent.

When she turned, I saw the tribal design tattooed around her thigh and the Baroque sun gracing her left calf and the moon on her right calf. Three stars arced across one buttock. I smiled. She was obviously the sun, moon, and stars to someone, it seemed. Now she was complete darkness.

Because of me.

She noticed me inspecting her body but only blinked.

"Are we clean yet?" I asked, worried and fatigued.

Despite my appearance, she wrapped her skinny arms around me and held me tightly a moment before releasing me. She parted the curtain and stepped out, grabbed a fresh towel and exited the bathroom.

The shower was turning cold but it made me more alert. As I turned off the water, I realized that the blood on my hands and shirt could have served to sustain me a little longer. Now it was a wasted opportunity. Perhaps it was enough that we were able to slip inside the inn and go quietly up to our room without a stray drop of blood being left on the floor, rugs, or stairs. I was thankful it was an old family-run place with no night guard.

I dried myself, took another towel to wrap around my hips. I wrung out my shirt as best I could, until the water ran clear, then knelt and cleaned the tub, pushing any remaining residue to the drain, making sure there were no spots or stains remaining in that white ceramic basin. I reached for my first-aid kit on the shelf and re-bandaged my foot. I saw in the mirror that my face was reddish like a sunburn, scaly, and seriously flaking in places.

The light was off in the bedroom. From the lit bathroom, I saw that Alma was already in bed, sheet and blanket pulled up to her chin, and the towel she had used now draped across the chair. I could not determine whether or not she was asleep, but I had no choice in the sleeping arrangements.

I stood in the middle of the bedroom, listening to the sounds outdoors, the usual night noises. No sirens, no crunch of boots on the front steps, no ringing of the nightstand phone. At that moment, the whole universe was asleep, and everything had been either forgiven or forgotten.

Alma rolled over, eyes open, watching me. She turned back the sheet and blanket, opening the bed to me. I tossed my towel over the chair, turned off the bathroom light, and slid between the sheets.

She moved against me, nipple ring poking my ribs. Her arm reached over my belly, stayed there. I curled my arm around her shoulders but I was unable to fall asleep. My mind was too busy.

What have I become these two months trying to save myself?

I thought of an answer for a while, any answer, but found none that fit.

Just as I was slipping into sleep at last, the pounding on the door awoke me. The key rattling in the lock beat my ability to leap out of bed and put on some clothes.

The door flew open and three men entered, flicking on the lights, followed by the innkeeper.

28

At once, I knew that my first instinct had been correct: to leave the girl and flee immediately. However, I had given in to her urging and, at least in that first hour, it seemed to be the right choice. I was able to clean up and get rid of the bloody shirt. My guide had unexpectedly become my nurse. We could have sought comfort again in this slumping bed, but there had been too much drama already. The first time was a mistake, obviously. It was the next test God had set for me. I knew that the instant these men barged in.

"You see there is only one bed," I said to the policemen, the innkeeper standing close behind them. "How else do you expect us to sleep? We were fast asleep. We're tired. We're here for the spa, after all. In fact, we would've had separate rooms if we had been able to stay there, but they wouldn't—"

More questions from the captain, his hands on his hips. The combination of Hungarian and broken English made it difficult to communicate. He grew frustrated.

His assistant rummaged through my papers and Alma's bag, retrieved my passport and her ID card, and gave them to the captain. The other assistant turned on the bathroom light and stood in the doorway, scanning the room. I could see the pile of wet towels on the floor but he did not touch them.

"No, it's not illegal or immoral to sleep nude," I said. "She did not have a change of clothes, so of course she would sleep nude. I could have given her one of my t-shirts to use as a nightgown, yes, you're right. However, none were clean. Besides, she was already in bed asleep. I didn't want to disturb her. But the issue is not our sleeping arrangement, is it? It's something else."

They agreed. The more important issue was the attack that happened in the town. A young man had had his nose broken. Another young man had suffered a busted knee but had managed to hobble away. They both described a tall, strange man, possibly a foreigner, who confronted them while they were completely minding their own business, walking home from their friendly neighborhood pub. The man started insulting them, calling them names, and when they insulted him in return, only in jest, of course, the man attacked them.

"I don't know anything about that. Didn't even hear anything. I was here, in this room, the whole damn time." I jerked my head to the side, indicating *with my young friend here.* "Besides," I said, lifting my leg from under the sheet, showing them my bandaged foot, "I'm not able to walk easily, certainly not able to get in a fight."

They asked what happened to my foot and I explained that it had required surgery. Dog bite.

Yes, in Munich. Well, I came to Hungary in search of medical treatment at this fine spa you have on the other side of town. But they turned me away. I suspect it was due to my appearance, a bit too rough after several days of train travel and a hospital stay before I showed up there. I'm able to recuperate here in this inn, however.

The captain pointed to me, to what I guessed was my face, and asked what happened. Why did I look so terrible?

I explained about my skin condition. It was unsightly but not contagious. I had hopes of curing it with the mineral baths at the spa, but...again, that did not work out.

"I'm sorry to say, but what you see on me tonight is almost the worst I've experienced. It's been a long trip and I've been stressed. And stress makes it worse. If I could get the right medication...."

He waved me silent, wincing at my appearance, and asked more questions about my guest.

Yes, I know. This girl surely must be well-kept, especially to get her to sleep with a man who has this terrible problem. That requires a special degree of compassion, does it not?

I agree: this girl should get herself a new set of clothes today. That will definitely be our first priority once we finish our sleep and get up for the day.

And get some breakfast.

"So we had nothing at all to do with that attack." I tried to repress a grin. "Perhaps it was a...a vampire."

"*Vámpír?*" the captain asked, his face reflecting amusement.

His assistants glanced at each other, stern-faced. The captain spoke to them and the assistants laughed.

The captain studied me a moment, then asked Alma if she were all right, in any distress, if this man was holding her hostage in any way. She had pulled her knees up to her chin when they burst in and she continued to keep the blanket there, covering herself. Her plain face, nose ring and lip ring, and dark stringy hair made her look innocent. The captain coughed. Who would want to attack her? Yes, a poor girl from the poor side of town, earning some money by being kind to an ugly old man.

"*Jól vagyok,*" she replied in a low, flat voice. 'I'm fine.'

The captain did not believe her and asked again.

"*Csodálatos este volt,*" she said, an edge to her voice. In fact, 'It was a lovely evening' did not exactly fit her dark tone.

With the captain glaring at her, waiting for her expression to melt and give away her secrets, Alma turned in the bed and put her hand on my jaw, then stretched over and kissed me. Parting, she insisted we had been in bed all evening. She chuckled for effect, holding my hand atop the blanket as though we were lovers.

The captain shook his head, handed back her ID card to his assistant who replaced it in her wallet and the wallet into her bag. She was of legal age, the captain understood, although she looked a lot younger.

One of the assistants called the captain's attention to the plastic mask in my bag, holding it up for everyone to see.

"*Mi ez a dolog?*" asked the captain.

"I told you: I have a medical condition. I don't want to scare little children with my appearance."

Yes, like this. Terrible, isn't it? If I were to go out in public, I would probably wear the mask. When I arrived, I did not wear the mask. I was not as horrible as now. Although bad enough. That's the reason they wouldn't let me—let us—check in to the spa. They probably didn't want me polluting their precious mineral mud bath.

The assistant returned the mask to my bag and the captain tossed my passport on the bed. He wanted us out of his town as soon as possible. The first bus or train would do.

"*Gyerünk,*" said the captain, turning to the door. 'Let's go.'

The second the door caught, Alma let out a long exhale and I felt her shiver against me. She grabbed me, threw her arms around me as if she were afraid.

"*Mit tegyünk most?*" she asked.

"Hah! 'What do we do now?' I don't know. I haven't given it much thought. I was sleeping. Well, trying to sleep."

I glanced at her: her face was tense. I thought she was about to cry but her lips remained firm, her eyes dry.

"I'm sorry—*sajnálom*," I said, taking her hand to reassure her. "We have to leave in the morning. You heard him."

"*Mi történik velem?*"

I let out a sigh. "It's much too late for me to keep translating. Can you use English?"

She slapped at the pillow. "Me—what happen to me?"

That was a good question. In fact, resting beside her, our bodies touching, I felt even more doomed. The devil often comes dressed as a Goth girl, after all. I thought I heard God laughing somewhere outside, up in the clouds. Might as well confess everything and wait for the end, the final blow.

"We were lucky," I said. "Maybe we need to get away before our luck runs out. We're safe for now. I mean, for tonight. In fact, if we rushed out now, we might look suspicious." I wondered how much she understood. "Anyway, we still have a few hours until morning. We better get some sleep."

"What happen morning?"

I shook my head. "We leave. You should return to Budapest. I'll give you money for the ticket, of course. And thank you again for your help. And sorry for all the trouble. As for me, I will continue on...on to I don't know where. I feel lost. I've come so far and now...nothing. God hates me."

Gazing at her cheek, I caught sight of a strange reddish patch there. It matched the one on the opposite cheek, I was relieved to see. They were red from embarrassment or from crying, not from a skin problem. Thank heaven!

"I was supposed to go to a clinic in Croatia. They do stem cell research. As you might guess, also stem cell therapies of various kinds. The best in Europe. It's near where my family has some property. That's the reason I stopped in Budapest: to settle all the business. That property is mine now, now that my parents are dead. But I'm from the U.S., so I'll probably sell the damn place and be rid of it."

I turned onto my elbow, facing her.

She laid her hand over mine. "Please...I go with you?"

"How much longer can you go with me? Won't someone be looking for you? You sent those pictures...."

She shook her head—slowly, then with more vigor.

"We have to go separate directions. We have different lives. I must go to Croatia, finish my original journey. I don't want to be a hideous monster. Like now. Without treatment, this will be worse. I am late for treatment." I took a couple deep breaths. "In Munich, I had a blood transfusion and it made me like new. And the hospital in Budapest, too. I was fine then. But those effects have worn off now. Look at me. I'm dying, getting worse, looking like...like a vampire."

She sat up in bed, concerned. "*Vámpír?*"

"At least I look like a vampire. Not very pretty, am I?"

Again, she shook her head but refocused her eyes on mine.

"I will be worse in the morning..."

She hugged me, pressing her head against my chest.

"...unless I get some blood."

She looked up, held my face, gazing into my eyes. "*Vér?*"

I nodded, as though I was confessing a crime and could not say the words. Then, I swallowed and spoke: "*Vér....* Yes, blood."

"*Nem aggasztó,*" she whispered. 'Don't worry.'

She climbed off the bed, went to her bag, dug around inside, poured out half of its contents, selected a small tube. She returned to the bed, opening the gray plastic tube that resembled a cigar case. Inside was a small razor.

"Wait! Don't!" I cried, but she put the razor to her arm.

A red line appeared. I stared hard at it, at her. She raised her arm to me and gave a curt nod.

I cradled her arm in my hands and lowered my face, pausing over the line of blood, watching it starting to run down to her elbow, and then lapped hungrily at the cut. She squeezed her arm to keep the blood flowing. Behind me, I could feel the heavy hand of God pressing on my shoulder, pushing me further into that dark grave, nodding appreciatively as I took yet another step closer to Hell.

It was not really a reward of any kind, but perhaps it should have been. I had promised her before I had gotten my fresh fix of blood. With her shirt torn by the two neighborhood jerks and me having no spare shirts, she simply zipped up her leather jacket over her black bra.

Once we arrived in Szombathely, the next bigger town west of Sárvár, I sent Alma into the first women's clothing store we found, giving her some cash and instructions to get a couple nice outfits and something to sleep in. It was not a store catering to young Goths, but perhaps it was my duty to set her up properly. A young woman needed good blouses, sweaters, and some slacks or at least fashionable jeans. She could have something pretty to get herself started in a new life...

"...something to remember me by, as you head home."

"I not go...to home," she said with a pout, standing forlornly outside the store with her shopping bags.

"You just can't keep tagging along with me."

"I go with you," she said. "You...need me."

She was right, I knew. However, despite what she did for me, the situation was overwhelming. I could not play through this time. What was I supposed to do with this girl now? Take her home with me? There she stood: black skirt and skinny white legs, the black boots and the black jacket matching the black lipstick. Next to her, I looked like a desperate old fool.

"But, Alma, I have important things to do. Medical things. It's a private matter. You don't want to wait for me, maybe wait for weeks. Besides, you're Hungarian. You don't by chance speak any Croatian, do you?"

"No," she responded. "I speak to you English."

"I know. But now it's time for you to return to your home."

"You my home!"

"I love the way you helped me last night, Alma."

"You help me, too."

"But that can't be the start of a beautiful friendship. I mean, it was just sex. It was a mistake. You understand, don't you?"

"Mis-take?"

"It was wrong. Yes, you helped me. Not the sex, the blood."

"I help you, Meester Székely."

"You might as well call me Stefan now."

She pulled off her jacket then, standing on the side of the street with her bra showing, and held up her bare arm, the white bandage obvious.

"I help you. You help me," she said, putting her jacket on again.

"But there are people who want you to come home."

"I got...no home."

"There must be somewhere you can go. I mean in Budapest."

"I got...no family."

"No one? No aunt or uncle? Friends? How about school? You were going to go to school, study art...? You should do that."

"I got...no-thing."

While she was in the store, I had taken care of renting a car, a small dark gray Opel Astra for my trip to Croatia. She placed her hand on the sleek side of the car, stroked it as though she had never seen a shiny new car before.

"You...good to me," she said, sliding her hand along the top of the car as she stepped against me. "I...good to you."

"All right, I get it. I'm the sugar daddy. We have to be clear, Alma: I'm only thanking you for taking a few days to help me, a stupid foreigner who doesn't know his way around. That's all. The clothes are for helping me. That's all."

I flashed back to her sitting in my lap the previous evening, rising up and dropping down like she was riding a carousel. But what was that? Eight and a half minutes of animal instinct?

"That's not a relationship." I knew I was a hypocrite, of course, but God enjoys watching hypocrites hang themselves. "That was not some kind of payment. That was sex. Only sex."

"And blood. I give you blood." She slapped the car's roof. "*Adok vért!*"

"Yes...."

I thought of what to say to convince her to take the train back to Budapest with her sacks of new clothing. As I did, I rubbed my forehead. I noticed how much more smooth my skin was. In fact, my cheeks were also returning to normal appearance.

"Please," she said.

I gazed at her, my chest tight. "I can't take you with me. It's not right."

And yet.... What is right any more? Did I finally make God blink? Did I feel guilt? And if I did, why now and not earlier in my sordid life? Was it because I now cared about someone, someone back home? Although Penny might hate me for my bad behavior, I did not hate her. I still loved her. Thus, guilt burned through me. I would never speak of this part of my trip to her.

"Come on," I said. "I'll take you to the train station."

With a tired sigh, I opened the door for her and she frowned. Setting the shopping bags on the backseat, she climbed into the front passenger seat with a huff.

"Listen to me," I said, staring ahead out the window, "what we did, what happened last night...that wasn't supposed to happen, you know. I don't know what to say, Alma. It's understandable that two people who happen to meet would...would find comfort...."

"To-gether," she muttered.

She turned in her seat, tucked her knee under herself, and raised herself up. She leaned toward me. Her hands reached for and held my face, then her lips came firmly against mine. The devil's kiss. I could see that now: God had sent this girl as a test. Whatever she mumbled after parting and sitting down again, I could only guess at, but it sounded apologetic.

"We all make mistakes," I said. "And we move on. We get on with our lives."

I continued my sermon as I started the engine and turned the car around in the street, heading back and following the signs for the train station. Two left turns and a right, then around the central business district loop, and there we were: train station.

The engine hummed and I knew I should just shut it off and get out. I knew I should help her with the shopping bags, and pay for her ticket, then wait with her on the platform, and give her a hug before she stepped onto the train, and then wave at her, her hand pressed to the window pane, gazing back at me as the train slowly rolled away from the station—

I couldn't do it.

With a shift of gears, I backed up and turned away from the station. I faced forward, stock still, as we zoomed back through the town streets and veered onto the highway south.

From the corner of my eye, I saw her half-grin, as though she knew she had gotten away with something. I knew we had gotten away with something, too. God was weighing the balance. Some shopping and a little trip through the countryside would certainly balance everything.

The Astra handled well and I increased speed—until I slowed through the town of Körmend, slowing more as I passed an old stone church where a crowd was celebrating a wedding. The bride and groom were ushered out by family and guests, some wearing traditional costumes. I whispered a sincere prayer for a long and happy life for them, then said one for myself.

I thought of my own Beloved, the one named Penny, who still visited my dreams when I least expected her to. With every other beat of my heart, I was certain she would never welcome me back. All this trouble I was going through was exclusively for me, just to be able to live without fear of exile. I wanted to be able to go into a grocery store without everyone clutching their children or grabbing something to use as a weapon. If I could defeat this disease, I repeated in my head over and over as the kilometers clicked by, then I could return and persuade Penny to take me back. First things first.

Guilt came first. Somewhere, God was chuckling.

My foot pressed on the accelerator as I approached Őrség National Park, buttressed against the ridge of mountains forming the border with Austria. I turned the car onto a lesser road running due south toward Slovenia.

Glancing over at Alma, asleep there, I thought of the last time I called

Penny. I pulled out my cell phone and saw there was no service for it. Nor could I even see my text messages. I knew that; I had put it away once I was aboard that cargo ship and barely thought of making a call after I took the train from Rotterdam. I knew I would not be able to connect once I was in Europe. I had tried enough to contact her before I'd left town. I had tried but there was never any response.

The road became a dream and I was stationary in my car seat as farms and trees and cows rushed past me. Next was Zalalövő...then Zalabaksa...Lenti... Lovászi, the quaint little villages I passed through on the way to the town of Tornyiszenrmiklós, where I connected with M70, the big highway running southeast along the border to Letenya—where we would cross the border. It felt like I was driving on the New York State Thruway again from Utica to Rochester. Only a few years ago armies crossed this plain, I knew. Centuries before that, more armies crossed here; before them, more settlers; further back, nomadic tribes. Perhaps, also my ancestors.

Now I was crossing the border, driving across the bridge over the Mura River into Croatia, formerly Yugoslavia. In Croatia was my destiny, it seemed. My parents had vouched for it when they chose to make it their final destination. After purchasing a house somewhere among the hills south of Zagreb, near the Plitvice lakes, they had decided to go out to the coast, to the sunny subtropical coast, and see out their last days together. I decided I would visit Makarska again after I concluded my business in Zagreb, where the clinic was located—before I got sidetracked in Germany and chose to take the plane instead of the train, and met the Fate that God had planted there for me: this girl, Alma Jónás.

I glanced over at her, asleep in the passenger seat, the back laid down, as we rolled up to the customs station. Her face was beautifully pale, her hair black, shiny, and uncombed, her jacket zipped up. Wearing that short skirt, her legs bare, I had turned on the heater to make her comfortable, to protect her from the October chill.

"Wake up, Alma," I called softly. "We are at the border, entering Croatia. Get your ID ready."

29

"Yes, I see that, what you speak of," said the clinician, Dr. Kovačević, as he leaned in close with a magnifying lobe to examine the rough, dry skin on my face. "There is very much damage, especially these outer layers. You cannot continue this longer or there will be permanent, irreversible damage. Then you will be, as you like to claim, looking like a vampire. That is not what you want, if I may guess."

"No, it's not."

I felt confident now that I was in the hands of this portly, balding man in white lab coat. This clinic in Zagreb, KLINIKA ZA MAKSIMIR, was the place I had hoped to visit originally—before everything started going wrong.

"But this is only the best I've been able to achieve with my own treatment."

He regarded me. "And that treatment is...?"

"Blood. I consume it. A little. Every few days."

"Yes, I have heard of people doing this."

"And it seems to keep me somewhat normal."

"Looking normal, you mean. The problem still exists."

"That's what I fear."

"Then you have come to the right clinic. This is the best clinic in all of Europe, I would say, for treating this problem." He went on citing studies and critiques, listing all the good points of his clinic, as though he still needed to convince me. I had already decided, and here I was. "Therefore, I can assure you that we have the most advanced treatment system. If you are ready, we can set up your personalized protocol. How does tomorrow morning sound?"

Sitting back in the chair, I crossed my arms. "I have nothing else planned."

"Excellent. First, we will address the skin problem with our patented skin regeneration therapy. This involves extraction of platelet-rich plasma—what we call PRP—containing autologous white blood cells which has a superior PRP enrichment rate of about six- to ten-fold—that is, about three to five times higher than for the conventional method—which makes our clinic the best in all of Europe. Our method contains white blood cells, which are not contained in the conventional PRP. This therapy, therefore, has much greater efficacy in rejuvenating skin, eliminating wrinkles, and reducing all of the irregularities from the acne marks, for example, compared with conventional therapy."

"I'm not exactly concerned with acne or wrinkles—"

"You see, in conventional cosmetic medicine, hyaluronic acid and collagen are commonly injected. Now that our platelet-rich plasma skin regeneration therapy has been perfected, the patient's own blood may be used to improve all the symptoms."

"That's great, but suppose there's some kind of problem with the patient's blood? What if it can't be used? I mean, what if it's poisoned? Don't we need to address the underlying issue? The *cause* of my skin problems?"

"Yes, very much so. I shall get to that momentarily. First, I want you to know all about how our program of regenerative medicine using the patient's own blood, specifically components in the blood called platelets, used to rejuvenate the skin."

"I'm actually a phlebotomist by training, so I know blood—"

"The therapy is performed by injecting components collected from the blood. There is no risk of allergy or infections. It has been studied very much and applied in a variety of fields. Best of all is this therapy requires only one injection."

"So you're talking about a kind of stem cell therapy?"

"Not stem cells, only platelets."

I frowned, feeling my face sag a bit. "But you have a stem cell therapy program, don't you? I read about it on the website."

"We do, yes. You see, a selection of cells are drawn from your own body and manipulated in the laboratory to the desired directions, then reinserted into your body. The result is a growth of healthy cells that replace unhealthy cells."

"That's what I want. My problem is genetic. I need new genes. For that, I'm willing to try it."

"It's not that simple. The process can take months."

"I don't have months. My body is fighting me every day. The way things are going, I could be dead in a few weeks. If I don't get treatment, I will die. Dead! Do you hear me?"

He held up his hand. "I hear you."

"So help me." I could sense my face drying, tightening.

"The science cannot be hurried."

"What can be done in a shorter timeframe?"

"The only thing to try would be a compressed protocol, but without any safeguards in place, rigorously checking each stage, there is no guarantee of success. The procedure may give you the same result: death. Not good for you, not good for us. We do not want a patient to die. It is bad for our reputation as the best clinic in all of Europe."

"I continue to get worse no matter what I do. Each treatment helps for only a short time, but when it wears off I always revert to wherever I was: somewhere in the process of becoming whatever I am meant to become. You see, doctor, I'm at war with God, and I do not have any ammunition, only a new treatment every week or so, in every country I visit. God is winning."

Dr. Kovačević rubbed his hands together, scratched his chin.

"And what do you think God is doing to you?"

"God wants me to die...or, perhaps as an even better joke, to just have me look and feel as though I am dead."

Dr. Kovačević laughed but not in a comfortable, amused way.

"I'm sure it's only...only a test," he said. "It's like Job. Remember the tale of Job? He loses everything when Satan tested him, having a contest with God, but in the end Job is rewarded with more sons, more cows, more everything."

"He still lost the sons he loved."

"Yes...it is an interesting story. We know that God works in so mysterious ways, yes? Please understand, Mister Székely, we are not at all any kind of a Hollywood glamour spa. Aside from our reputation as the best clinic in all of Europe, we do not get movie stars here. If we had movie stars visiting us we would be rich. We would charge them what the procedure costs and much more, and they would be happy to pay."

"I don't have a lot of money. I'm no movie star. But I need help a lot more than any of them do. There has to be some way, something, uh, more modest yet still beneficial, something that could be done for me? An abbreviated protocol?"

Dr. Kovačević let out an explosive sigh. "I'm very sorry, Mister Székely. Perhaps you've come to the wrong place."

"Not the wrong place. I may not be here for one of Europe's best beauty treatments, but you do the stem cell therapy I need. But mine is to keep me alive, not just look like I'm alive."

"I understand your concern," said Dr. Kovačević. He adjusted his position in the chair to be able to point to the chart on the wall. "I want you to look here. This is the procedure." He raised his hand, pointing at the first drawing. "You see, first blood is pulled out of the patient and processed with a few special ingredients, then it is centrifuged at a particular speed to get the growth factors to start. The blood is then injected back into the person."

His finger moved to the next drawing.

"The cells have two key components, which play a role in the growth of new cells and the production of collagen, elastin, and other elements. When it is applied to the skin—this chart is about skin therapy, of course—these help firm wrinkles and slow the development of new lines."

I grimaced. "I don't care about wrinkles. I care about death. How about my problem?"

"Yes, death.... You see, as we age, there is slowing as well as breakdown of the skin collagen, the blood vessels, and all the supporting, connective tissues. When stem cells are applied to the skin according to our special protocol, along with use of the electroporation and ultrasound devices, it reduces cell damage, as well as it starts new tissue formation. Furthermore, increased blood supply is important for the rejuvenation process, so it's like a renewal of the skin."

"That's all fine and good," I said in a harder tone, "but my skin problem is only superficial. The underlying problem is serious. It's my genes. I need to swap out my genes, my DNA, my blood, damn near everything, or I will die in a few weeks."

He seemed not to hear me, or not care what I had said.

"Both safety as well as efficacy have been questioned in news media, as you must likely know, and it is essential that the treatment is done under proper supervision of an expert. You see, the topically applied stem cells are usually derived from plant cell sources and there are very few side effects reported, but most of the safety questions are about the systemic injectable stem cells as well as those of fetal or other animal origin. Topically applied stem cells are usually safe. Cases of allergy in the form of itching, redness has been noted nevertheless—"

"I don't care if you use fetal stem cells or whatever. I need to live! Just do it! Somehow."

"I wish you to know what is possible and what is not possible. Stem cells are being used in beauty treatments everywhere, but you have to be careful of the source that is used. If you want stem cells used for more of the invasive treatments, you should go to a clinic in.... There's one in Shenzhen, China. That is near Hong Kong. They have done the leading research on the kind of therapy you seem to want."

"Need, not want—"

"You see, you cannot use stem cells or growth factor from an unknown line—that is, stem cells that can grow something else than what you want. The simplest way to assure the efficacy of those stem cells is to derive cells from your own body fluids. It is very expensive because not many clinics offer it. In China, the regulation is very lax. To maintain safety, always go to a credible doctor, such as myself or my colleagues here. Not to China."

"Not a problem. I'm here. I don't have time or money to go to China. This is the best clinic in Europe, like you said."

"Yes, it is. You see, our stem cell therapy is used effectively for treatment of wrinkles and fine lines, also dry skin, acne scars, skin lightening, and similar problems. There were protocols designed for maximum effectiveness. These protocols require the client to visit every four to six weeks, which is the skin renewal time frame."

"Four to six weeks? I can't keep coming here. I have to return to the States. I got an inheritance, but I'm not made of money. Tell me, Dr. Kovačević, what can you do for a hundred-thousand dollars? That's all I have."

The room was silent. He pursed his lips, perhaps waiting for a sign from God that he was allowed to unlock the vault of secret procedures. He began fingering an invisible key.

"I see. We certainly can offer you any of our skin treatments. Something more *invasive* will be more expensive. And more time is also involved."

"What would that be?"

Dr. Kovačević rubbed his hands together, nodding.

"You see, stem cells can be injected into the body to treat any number of problems. The concern we have is over the legal and ethical matters."

"I don't care about legal or ethical matters. I only want to live and look good doing it."

"Yes, I completely understand. Our reputation as the best—"

"The best clinic in all Europe, I get it."

"We cannot take the chance to do any procedure that is not legal, or especially if not ethical."

"I don't care. Let the people who care try to stop me from living. I'll haunt them from my grave!"

"Mister Székely, we have...." He regarded the door a moment, continued in a lower voice. "We have some treatments that are not on our list, so not on the website. Stem cell therapy, yes. I think something good can be done for someone such as yourself. With your special problems."

Dr. Kovačević leaned forward and started to tell me about the options when the knock on the door cut off his explanation. The nurse entered with a few questions. He looked at a chart she handed him, then signed or initialed a few pages, and as the nurse exited, he continued with his previous spiel:

"You see, our platelet-rich plasma procedure provides guests with ninety-nine percent of the results they seek. We have many who need this treatment due to trauma, such as burn victims or, as you indicate, porphyriacs. You see, our procedure maximizes the regenerative potential of PRP, which then has the effect of potentiating your body's innate natural healing power—"

"I get it. It kick starts the healing process."

"Exactly. It is more than cosmetic medicine; it is full tissue reorganization. It's cutting edge. The therapy uses the patient's own blood and, thus, poses no risk of allergic reaction."

"You get the stem cells from my blood?"

"Yes, but it must be from bone marrow, in this case. Or, from umbilical sources. For this procedure—if you truly want to change your blood. It is a painful method, I must tell you."

"I'm already in constant pain."

"This is much worse, I think. Everyone reports this fact. If this is what you want, we will do our best to limit the pain. It is from these stem cells that we can manipulate them into anything your body might require. Heart muscles. Stomach lining. Nerve tissue. We can even make sperm cells from your stem cells, but they likely would be sterile, suitable only for cloning—that is, if you want a twin." He chuckled.

"But can you *make* stem cells from sperm?"

Dr. Kovačević choked, then he could not decide whether to laugh or speak.

"That, Mister Székely, has not been attempted by this clinic. Yes, I think it could be done. In a theory. I must warn you that you would be our first case. So, right or wrong, legal or not legal, ethical or not ethical, the responsibility would be all on you, who authorize this clinic to attempt such a procedure."

"Maybe I have no choice. Maybe it's my only option. Maybe I must try it or die. That's where I'm at in my life: the end of it."

"We would draw up papers stating such. It is to cover our—the issue of liability. You understand. Because we are the best clinic in all of Europe and cannot risk any negative publicity."

"The risk is all mine. Live or die. Either I die or, worse, I do not die but go on as though I had died. God will be proud of his creation, either way."

"Oh, I'm sure it is not so dire as you claim. I have read all of your medical record file. This is serious, yes, and you should get therapy. I don't expect you would die with or without this special procedure."

I sat up. "And if you are wrong?"

"Mister Székely, we are professional here. We are doctors. We care about all of our clients. You are no different to us. We offer a service to you and you accept it with the outcome we expect. We withdraw some of your cells—in this case, as you suggest, the spermatozoa—and follow the standard protocol for manipulating the cells, and then we would inject them back into your body. The transformation should begin soon after that. It should require only the single injection, so repeated clinical visits are not necessary. We would like to check on you, if you could return later, certainly. Being the first trial of this kind, we have interest in your progress. We would be interested in reporting on our success."

"And this would treat the underlying cause of my problem?"

"I believe so. The cause of your body's breakdown is clearly related to the regenerative formulæ innate in your blood. It is not functioning properly. Hence, the constant breakdown you experience—"

"Like some kind of cancer of the blood."

"Cancer implies an unchecked growth of cells. Yours, on the other hand, are not growing at all, not at normal rates. Yours are diminishing. Hence, your need to replenish the *heme* at regular intervals. If I may, it seems a case of extreme anemia. You do not have the volume of blood in you necessary to sustain life. I do not know how you are alive, sitting before me."

"Neither do I."

"It's either a miracle...or a curse."

"How am I able to keep going as though nothing was wrong? I eat almost nothing, drink hardly anything. Water is like acid to me. And yet I have amazing strength, uncontrolled when I'm angry. I am quick and always alert. But I grow weak every three days or so and need recharging—with a fix of fresh blood. And there is this side effect of having a most fantastic erection. 'Seek a doctor for an erection lasting more than four hours' my ass; this thing goes on for a couple days, softens only as I'm entering my weaker phase where I just want to sleep. I'm unconscious for a couple days or more. It's crazy, but that's what I'm experiencing."

"Not so crazy.... Tell me, how old are you?"

"I'm forty-five. No, forty-six now. Last month. Why?"

"You look younger. How long have you been forty-five?"

"A while."

"Hmmm, it could be true. You have all the traits."

"Traits? Of what?"

"Considering that, I wonder if you really could be...."

"What? Say it." I stared into his eyes until I saw fear reflecting back at me. "Out loud. Say it."

"A vampire."

I looked away, releasing him from my intense gaze.

"You think it's true? Were you afraid?"

"Not afraid. Concerned. I know we can treat your condition. Indeed, you have come to the right clinic, after all, the best in all of Europe, possibly the whole world. Shall we go ahead?"

He smiled at me as though he had done this so many times before. What were the chances that someone like me had sat here discussing the exact same problem with him? He nodded a few times, apparently thinking through the protocol.

I nodded twice. "Yes, let's get started."

"The procedure will take some time, so we should start right away. I'll send the nurse in to collect the sample from you. Soon you will be able to start again and have a new life."

30

I found Alma in the waiting room, asleep in a corner chair. She looked angelic with her pale face and dark hair. Her cheeks were golden rather than rosy. The way she was bent in the chair, knees drawn up, her short skirt did not cover her black lace underwear. A man older than me in a nearby chair had a toothy grin as he watched me sit beside her. Others stared at us while I tried to rouse her.

She was slow to awaken. I considered that was because of our irregular schedule and lack of food. After all, she probably weighed about 95 pounds. I gathered her into my arms and, with one arm around my shoulder, escorted her out of the clinic. She stumbled beside me, legs wobbly and uncoordinated, as we crossed the parking lot to the car.

I dropped her down inside the car, tucked her feet in, and closed the door.

"Alma, are you all right?" I asked with growing concern as I buckled my seat belt. I reached over and fastened hers.

She shook, not like a seizure but like someone who did not wish to be awakened, fighting me off.

"All right, you keep sleeping." I started up the car. "I need to find a priest. Why? you're probably wondering. Right, Alma? I want to make everything right with God before I go through this procedure. In case it kills me." I gave her a glance. "Did you hear me, Alma?"

I drove to the parking lot exit, checking traffic on the avenue.

"Did you hear me, God?"

Pulling out into the closest lane, I was nearly hit by a charging truck. There was a horn blast but I did not hear it. I veered into the next lane to escape the truck. God surely sent that truck as a warning. It was not there on the avenue when I first looked.

Find a hotel for a week, check in, get Alma to bed.

She did not look very good. Her once pure white skin, which when I saw her the first time on the airplane seemed part of her Goth persona, was now yellow. I suspected it was jaundice. Her liver was fighting some infection. But from what? Not from our high living, certainly not alcohol consumption. I thought back through the past two days.

We arrived in Sárvár, tried to get into the spa, were rejected, went to the small inn, slept in that broken bed. And, of course, the incident. Perhaps she ate something, drink something, took some drug before I encountered her in that alley. She had gotten food for us then was stopped by those two boys. I fought them. Nothing happened to her. Back to our room, we went, afraid of being questioned or arrested. In fact, the police had come in the middle of the night. Nothing obvious.

In the morning she seemed normal, quiet but in good health. She was usually quiet so I took no particular notice. She had been lethargic in the taxi to Szombathely to get the rental car, only waking to shop for clothes, and slept almost the whole drive to Zagreb, only awakening at the checkpoint. Her ID was in order.

"My girlfriend," I had told the customs official, smiling as if I were some kind of lucky fellow.

The official frowned, not believing I had chosen very well, but if I was happy with such a plain girl with piercings and tattoos, then good luck to me. He let us pass.

"Alma dear," I called to her, my lips close to her ear.

She stirred a bit on the bed but her eyes remained closed.

"I'm going out for a while but I'll be back as soon as possible. Then we'll go out for something to eat. How's that sound?"

She mumbled something I could not make out. I took it as a positive sign. She was just tired, exhausted from our ordeal, so it would be good for her to continue sleeping. I was the opposite: I could not sleep, too anxious, too energized, afraid to relax.

ભ

It seemed unlikely that I could get what I wanted at the largest cathedral in Zagreb. I drove patiently around the city looking for something more modest, an out of the way church, following the map I got from the hotel concierge.

Svete Katarine, or *Crkva sv. Katarine* in Croatian, the Church of Sainte Catherine, seemed to fit my criteria: a Roman Catholic Church in a backwater district on the north side of Zagreb. The quaint old building was small, had white walls with red trim.

I parked and straightened my shirt and coat, brushed off my shoes. Running a hand over my scalp, I felt stubble growing there and was satisfied. I touched my face, felt my skin was supple, and I breathed easy.

The sanctuary was empty for this weekday morning, but I was not there too long before the priest came out from a door behind the altar and greeted me. I assumed it was a greeting. I knew no Croatian so I waved and smiled. As he drew close, I extended my hand. He shook it.

According to this priest, who immediately began his tourism lecture, the church dated from 1620 and was completed in 1632. Later, arriving Jesuits found the existing Dominican church to be run down and unserviceable, so they built their own on the same spot. A monastery was built adjacent but it had since become the Klovićevi dvori art gallery. The church had also changed from Jesuit to Collegiate, the priest explained. To my eyes, though, the church was elegant and amazingly ornate, the vaulted ceiling covered in decorative motives and paintings of Biblical scenes. Never had I truly seen anything so beautiful, so profound. My aunt had never allowed me to enter her church. I stared up at the stained glass windows until the priest fell silent, lecture ended.

He called my attention to the altar area, explaining its various aspects. It was all in Croatian.

I waved him to stop and he seemed puzzled.

"I don't know any Croatian, sorry." I bowed my head, trying to be humble.

"You are welcome, none the less," said the priest. "I'm Father Mirko. You're American? Call me Father Mark."

"Thank you for speaking with me. I hope English is all right. I don't know any Croatian and my Hungarian also is not too good. I know medical German, if that's of any use."

"It's fine," said the priest, adjusting his collar as though it was too tight. "I spent a few years in the States, so I had to speak English. Not so bad, I think."

"Really? Where?"

"It was in my youth, shortly after seminary. I was in Buffalo, New York. You know it?"

"Buffalo! That's close. I grew up in Utica. We visited Buffalo a few times when I was a child."

"Then it's a small world."

We discussed everything about Buffalo and upstate New York in general for half an hour before getting down to business. We sat in the pew near the rear of the sanctuary.

"So it's possible to have a baptism here? In this church?"

"Yes, certainly. When was your child born?"

"My child? No, it's for me."

"Your parents were Catholic yet you were not baptized?"

"I was so young."

"Yes, well, we usually perform the baptism for newborns."

"If I was baptized when I was a baby, I sure don't remember." I gave a little laugh but the priest did not seem to find humor in my remark. "Besides, I don't think it took. I mean, it may have not been official. What I'm trying to say is I doubt it had the desired effect on me, or on my life. I've had, let's say, some difficulties...."

The priest studied me, no expression crossing his face.

"It's possible to baptize an older person."

"Will it work as well?"

"Work?"

"Yes, will I be covered? You know, protected."

"What is it you wish to be protected from?"

"Well, first of all, death. Second, I have a medical condition. I am going to be undertaking—well, that's a bad slip of the tongue, especially for a day like today. What I mean is I'm going to have a medical procedure, an operation, and I want God to be on my side. If that makes sense."

He nodded. "It makes perfect sense."

"So you'll do it?"

"Me, or one of my assistants."

"I'd prefer *you*, if possible. The senior priest."

"My young apprentice is quite capable, I assure you."

"I'm sure he is, but...I would prefer you perform the baptism."

"Very well. When shall we schedule this baptism?"

"How about this afternoon? Is that possible?"

"Today? That's rather quick. Don't you need time to invite your family and

266

friends?"

"I'm all alone. My parents died two years ago. I'm their only child. And I am unmarried and have no children. So you see...I'm a rather forlorn figure. I'm all alone. And even God, I think, does not speak to me."

"I understand your situation. There is something we can do, if you need it done today."

"Oh, thank you, Father!"

He smiled at last. "It will be my pleasure...though I do not do it for my pleasure. I am pleased that someone such as you comes to me for advice and connection with our Heavenly Father."

"That's exactly what I'm doing."

We stood and shook hands.

"Oh, and if it's possible, Father...would you be so kind as to also perform the funeral service?"

"Funeral service?"

"Yes. For me. If the operation...."

"I understand. But you must not think that way."

"If it becomes necessary, Father. I'd like to be cremated. My parents left me some property near Bihać—in the Plitvice lakes region—and my ashes can be scattered there. I have the location, address, everything you need to know, on papers in my bag. I'll give you copies."

"It seems very serious. What kind of operation are you having that would have you so worried?"

"Not that it's a great secret, but I need to have a complete transformation of my genes. Or I'll die. I'm talking about a kind of stem cell therapy."

"Then it is serious. I've heard of the stem cell research. Are they going to be using stem cells from fetuses?"

"Oh, no, Father. The stem cells will come from me. They are working on them in the laboratory right now."

"I see. Then it will be permissible to God."

"I hope so. We've already had so many disagreements...."

"We...?"

"Me and God. Which is the reason I want to be baptized."

"Yes. First, the baptism. Then your operation."

"Then, if needed, my funeral and cremation."

"As you wish."

We shook hands again and made a 5:00 p.m. appointment. Father Mirko gave me a trifold brochure which told me everything I needed to know about baptism. Not being a baby, I did not need any baptismal gown. Nor did I have any Godparents. All I needed was the basic, yet official, sacrament.

Then I would be ready to face death.

"Alma, my dear," I whispered into her ear once more, "you really do need to get up and rejoin life. You should be rested sufficiently by now. You need to eat something."

I was already dressed in my only suit, dark blue and heavily wrinkled but better than street clothes for this solemn occasion. A white shirt and red and blue striped tie made me look rather suave, ready for a lavish date at a posh restaurant or possibly a night at the theater.

I lightly tapped her cheeks until she squirmed. Her hand tried to flick my hand away. After a moment, she rolled away from me and continued sleeping. Typical teenager, I thought. But she was fully an adult at twenty.

"Aren't you feeling well?"

No response.

I went around the bed and sat on the edge, next to her, then gathered her up into my arms. She was limp as I held her, but I felt her heart beating, felt breath from her nose. Her skin was yellowish and I worried about the cause. I wondered if she was a drug user and had somehow slipped herself something when I was not looking. I lay her down again and searched her bag, that big floppy purse of hers, and found nothing drug related.

"Alma, what is the matter?" I watched her for a few minutes, then checked my watch. "I have to go now. I have an appointment. I'll be back soon and then we can get something to eat. All right? How does that sound?"

Nothing made any sense. I thought back over the day once more. The only thing out of the ordinary that occurred to me was when she awoke at the border checkpoint. She had indicated my face was showing signs of decay again. I had checked myself in the rear view mirror and found she was right: my cheeks had the telltale dry patches again.

Our eyes had met the moment I looked down from the mirror. Without saying a word, she seemed to understand. From her bag she produced the razor blade and, with sleeve rolled up, she swiped her arm, drawing a line that bubbled red with the essence I needed. Her eyes gave consent, told me what to do, so I leaned over, the customs office still in plain sight behind us, and I licked up the blood that ran from her cut.

I licked until the bleeding stopped, then dug into my bag for the toiletry kit and retrieved a Band-Aid. She smiled faintly, as if she was acknowledging she did her duty—like a mother who had successfully breastfed her baby.

I had mouthed 'thank you' but said nothing and we drove on to Zagreb.

Checking her arm where she had cut herself, both the line from the cut she made in Sárvár and the cut made at the border had become black, each cut encircled by a red rash. The skin around the cuts was yellow. They did not look normal. Perhaps the razor was dirty. I wondered if she had gotten an infection.

I paced the room, which seemed to be how I summon God for a consult. Maybe blood poisoning. Somehow. She needed to see a doctor, yes, I knew that. But I had an appointment. Perhaps I could be baptized *then* take her to the ER. Alternatively, perhaps I should drop her off on the way to my baptism.

"Alma, my dear, I must be going now." I brushed her head, stroked her hair. "Will you be all right for an hour or so? I promise I'll be right back. Can you hang on a little longer?"

I drove to the church, trying to remember the more direct route but getting lost in the older neighborhoods and fighting one-way streets going the wrong direction. Finally, I arrived and parked, jumping out and hurrying inside as though I might miss my turn.

"Good evening, Mister Székely," said Father Mirko, dressed in his finest robe.

"Thank you so much for doing this for me."

His smile was so pleasant I had to stare a moment.

"I do this for God and for Our Lord, Jesus Christ," he said, his hand on my shoulder. "As much as for you, my son. Shall we...?"

He escorted me to the altar and two other priests appeared to assist him, more as witnesses than to actually participate in the sacrament. I nodded to them, Father Velimir and Brother Zlatan, as they were introduced to me. I acknowledged my appreciation of their time and effort.

Father Mirko set me beside the baptismal fount and had me kneel. If I had been baptized as a baby I would have been held beside the baptismal basin. As an adult, however, he would dab the holy water on my forehead and paint a cross there with his thumb, all the while saying the words, some scripture or official liturgy. I was not sure since it was all in Croatian.

He bid us all bow our heads as he spoke a prayer. He ended with a few English words: "And help our brother, Stefan, serve you as best he can, for all his remaining days...."

Father Mirko held up a ceramic flask and applied the holy water to my head. He wet his thumb in the holy water on my head and pressed his thumb to my forehead to draw the sign of the cross there. A stream of holy water ran down my forehead alongside my nose and pooled against my upper lip. He gave me a look as though he were saying 'Don't worry, it's normal for that to happen.' However, it was not an expression of mirth, I realized then.

He seemed at that moment in distress.

His assistants became alarmed, rushed to his side, calling to him. They lowered him to the floor where he fell into a seizure, shaking against the floor. His hand was burnt, as though he had dipped it into boiling water. I felt my forehead and nothing seemed out of the ordinary.

"You!" shouted Brother Zlatan, pointing to the door. "Go!"

I got up off my knees and stood aside. "What happened?"

"*Otac Mirko je udari od zla duha!*" Father Velimir cried in fear. "*Pogledajte palca. To je izgorio!*"

"What's wrong?" I asked.

"Father Mirko...he is struck...by evil spirit."

"What? How can that be?"

They glared at me. Father Velimir dared touch the spilled holy water, mere drops on the tile, and quickly drew his finger back, his face reflecting pain.

"*To je kiselina!*" he cried. "Acid!"

"Acid?" I snapped.

"You are evil!" Brother Zlatan cursed. "Get away!"

"Me? But I—"

"Out! Go out!"

I scrambled down from the altar, tripping on the steps. I ran up the aisle, looking back over my shoulder at the three of them.

There was not much I could do, not with God cursing me in ever more callous ways. Now it was not only me but also everyone I came in contact with. I had been given the curse of turning holy water into acid. What next?

I returned to the hotel room, shaking in fear. There were only two things I needed to do: get through the stem cell therapy and see that Alma was taken care of properly.

"Alma, my dear," I said, standing at the foot of the bed, "you must get up now. In fact, you should be going home. There's got to be a train that can take you back to Budapest. This is not the way you want to continue your life. You can't follow me. I'm a dead end for you." The thought made me chuckle; a bit too morose in my word choice, perhaps. "I mean, the situation now is much too grave." I shook my head. No better. I should have been a poet. "Sorry. Bad turn of phrase. But even if you are dead tired, you—"

I paused, thinking I should just stop speaking.

However, there was more to say: "No matter how tired you might be, you have to have gotten enough rest by now. So let's get up and get you packed—and before I go in for my procedure tomorrow, I want to see you aboard a train heading north. You've been very helpful and I've given you plenty of money in exchange for your help—enough to get a ticket, certainly. I'll write you a check to cash in at that bank in Budapest. Then you can start a new life doing whatever you want to do and forget those people who hate you."

At that point, I jostled the bed and she stirred.

"Did you hear me?"

I went around to the side she faced and placed my hand on her shoulder.

"Alma?"

I caressed her cheek, which caused her eyes to open. They seemed lifeless, sleepy or drugged. Her skin was cool and deathly pale except for the yellowish patches. I gathered her into my arms and felt how small she was: her ribs and spine were boney. I could not recall when either of us had last eaten. Her heartbeat was steady but slow.

"Aren't you well? We need to get some dinner."

She exhaled a foul breath as I tapped on her cheek. Her eyes focused on me, meeting my eyes. Her throat wretched, coughed, and she needed to spit. I caught it in my hand.

"Better now?"

I got up and washed my hand in the bathroom, returned to her. Sitting on the edge, I lay my hand on her shoulder.

She spoke in Hungarian, mumbling so softly I could not make out her words. I asked her to repeat them. Though a little louder, it was not much better. I asked if she could tell me in English.

"I go with you," she finally said.

"That's not possible. You heard what I said before? I meant it. You've been very helpful but where I'm going, you can't follow."

"I go with you," she repeated in a stronger voice.

"No. I need to be sure you're going to be all right. I need to be sure you're going home. You know what happened. If we hadn't met.... If you weren't tagging along—"

"I go with you," she cried out, slapping the bed for emphasis. "I give you blood."

"After this procedure, you won't need to do that. I'll be all right then."

She tried to sit up, made it to her elbows. Her face was tense, but also dry and rough. Like mine.

"I go with you," she muttered weakly. "No home for me."

"Listen, Alma." I took her hand, held it. "There's a story, a very ancient story, about a man who was condemned by the gods to push a huge stone up a mountain every day. But every night the stone would roll down to the bottom. And every morning he had to push the stone up the mountain again. He knew it would roll down at night but each day he did his best to push it up the mountain. The man's name was Sisyphus. And do you know why he never gave up? why he didn't stop pushing that stone up the mountain even though he knew it would roll down again each night? Because he was cursed. He could not give up because he was cursed. I'm like that. I am cursed—by God himself. And now everyone around me is getting hurt. That's why you can't go with me."

Her eyes seemed to show understanding, maybe sympathy.

"No matter what I do, I can't stop myself from changing, transforming into whatever I'm fated to become. I try to treat my condition. I try this cure and that therapy, but whatever I try works for only a short time but then it stops working. I continue changing, as though whatever I did made no difference at all. It's like I'm pushing that big stone up the mountain day after day after day. And every night, so to speak, I change a little more into what I am fated to—"

"Sor-ry," she muttered as though it was all her fault.

She pulled herself up into a sitting position, her back against the pillows and headboard.

"No, I'm sorry. I should have left you in Budapest. Shit, I just met you on a plane. How in the world did you get mixed up with me? And then we...we had sex. I am not that kind of man. And I have a fiancée, too.... Maybe."

"Sor-ry," she muttered.

"So much has happened, and I don't want you to get into trouble because of me. At least we've been lucky, I mean, up to now. But it's better if you go back."

She tried to stand, fell back on the bed. "I go with you!"

"Alma, there is no place to go with me! That's what I'm trying to tell you. I am a dead end. I am literally a *dead* end for you."

I glared at her, but she did not back down, defiantly engaging my eyes. From the corner of my eye, though, I saw that my hands were dry again, skin peeling. Her skin was not supple, either, and was yellowish. I thought again of what kind of infection it might be. Malnutrition? Her body was wasting away. She needed medical attention as much as I did. But first,

"We need to eat something," I said. "At least, you do. Let me go get the food this time. My foot feels all right now. I need to walk a bit, get some air, anyway."

"I go with you." It was a soft, pleading voice.

"I'll be back, don't worry." I gave her hand a squeeze. "I don't know what I'll find in this neighborhood. I sure wish they offered dinner at this hotel instead of just breakfast. But don't worry. I'll look for something simple. Your stomach probably can't handle anything too rich or exotic to start. Bread and soup, perhaps. How does that sound?"

Her face was placid, her eyes fixed on me.

"Is that all right?" I asked.

"O-kay," she muttered.

"I'll bring you some dinner and meanwhile you pack your bag so you're ready to go. You can probably catch an overnight train and be back in Budapest by breakfast."

I started toward the door, yet paused when my hand was on the doorknob. Something I did not expect suddenly filled my senses—like an exotic perfume, but it was not a scent, only a feeling. Like the memory of a scent. Or, a premonition. Something evil, it seemed. Perhaps I was the evil stinking up this room. Perhaps this room previously had been occupied by someone who had died. That could be the kind of thing that left the trace I was feeling.

"I'll be back as soon as possible," I called to Alma, shaking it off.

I stepped out of the room and pulled the door closed between us.

31

"Oh my God!" I cried, rushing to the bed. "Alma! Alma!"

Both her arms were stained with blood, marking the flow in streams from cuts she had made in her wrists. I looked closely: she had not gotten too deep. Her skin was white, however, and her eyes dilated. She was unresponsive, so I called the front desk and they sent for an ambulance.

I sat at her bedside in the hospital room, holding her hand, her pale, limp hand, at once so delicate and childlike but also imbued with a strength I had never noticed. Her cuts had been bandaged and she was resting with an IV feeding her fluids. She had not lost too much blood and did not need any transfusion, thankfully, but no one there could determine what caused her to sleep for so long. Between my consumption of the blood she offered to me and what was lost from her wrist slashes, she should not be so critical, and yet something was going on inside her.

They were running tests.

"Perhaps you should also run an STI panel," I told the nurse. "You never know. Kids today. A lot of sexual activity and plenty of infections possible."

The nurse nodded. Whether I was a concerned father or an alarmed lover, she passed my request on to the doctor, and he authorized the tests.

"Please be all right, please be all right."

I lay my head on her hand, said a prayer that felt weird and insincere. But I meant it.

Thunder outside answered my prayers and the rain slapping the windows served as my tears. I could not make any myself.

Despite the brief touch of holy water and a priest's thumb in the sign of the cross on my forehead, I doubted the ritual took. Unfinished, as I guessed it must have been, it would not protect me during my procedure in the morning.

Word came back that she had toxins in her blood. Some kind of blood poisoning. No sexual diseases but her condition was serious enough. Yet she had not eaten anything strange. She'd had no blood contact. She had washed me off, sure. Some could have gotten into her through the self-inflicted cuts on her arms. Or...when she climbed on top of me and we fucked.

There's the poison, God snorted inside my head.

I sat up all night with Alma, praying for her to awaken instead of preparing myself for a complete change of essence and the start of a new life.

"Let the poison clear," I whispered. "Let her be all right."

By the pre-dawn rounds the nurses were making, I got up from the bed, letting go of Alma's hand, and refreshed myself at the washbasin in her room. A nurse came in to check on her and take her vitals.

"No change," I muttered, standing and watching.

The nurse wrote the stats on a chart. We both noted the appearance of her face, especially the dry patches of skin that had formed on her cheeks and throat.

"I have to go now," I spoke, my voice wavering, "but I will return later. I have my own, uh, operation today. I'll be back as soon as possible. It could be twenty-four hours, though. I just want you all to know I'm not abandoning her."

"We will care for her," said the nurse.

I made sure they had the information about our hotel, in case she was released from the hospital before I could return for her. The hotel room was paid for the whole week, anyway. That was the best I could do for someone who did not deserve to be hurt—by me or anyone else.

Leaving the hospital, I walked briskly a few blocks over to the clinic where I would have my operation.

"God—*dear* God," I spoke aloud, although it was merely a whisper against the cold autumn wind hitting me, "you know it's me calling: Stefan Iaon

Székely. You know it's me so you'd better answer. I never asked for anything—nothing, except you leave me alone. Now I am alone, but not quite. Alma is my friend. It just happened to be that way. Maybe you set her up as a test for me. Maybe I'm a test for her. Either way, she is sick now. Maybe because of me, or maybe she was always fated to fall sick no matter what, some other kind of test, who knows? And now I'm going under for my own medical procedure. You know that; you always know. I'm trying to get rid of this disease, the one you gave me, the one you *let me get*, the one that has cursed my family for centuries. You know the one: this damned *porphyria*-thing, or whatever variation you and your minions have devised. This is Stefan Székely, the arrogant fool you love to trick, and I'm asking—*begging*, dammit—for one, only one, *favor*. Here it is! Listen carefully because you know better than me that I may never get another chance to ask for it. Please, please, *please*, if only one of us can live and be healed, if only me or Alma can survive this day, please God, I ask—*really*, believe me, I'm being honest; I've never been more sincere—please let it be Alma Jónás who lives. *Please* let her go on living. She was never meant to cross my path. You know that. I take back every bad thing I ever said about you if you will heal Alma and let her live her life as though she never met me. That's all I ask, God. For that, I will surrender. I will be whatever you want me to be."

A flake of snow alighted on my nose, then more flurries fell around me. Probably it was God sending me a sign, but as usual nicely disguised and suitably vague. But I did not stop to gaze at the snowflakes. I knew they would melt. They always do.

And become someone's tears.

I checked in at the clinic and was called back after only a few minutes and met with the doctor. We went over the procedure again, step by step, and then he left and an administrator came in and had me fill out more forms and sign them. A nurse took my vitals and left.

I waited in the little room, staring at a poster featuring an anatomically splayed body, all the inner organs visible. I focused on the heart in all its glory: red arteries and blue veins, yellow fat deposits, a fine miracle of design, forever pumping, never resting, indeed the eternal clock.

Dr. Kovačević returned, looked over the stats.

"I'm ready," I said, without him asking.

"That's good," he responded absently, skimming through the clipboard's papers.

"I know it must have sounded crazy...I mean, what we talked about before. The reason for this procedure. I hope it will cure me of this curse. Fresh blood, as you said. More like fresh cells. The big reset. Start over."

Dr. Kovačević looked up, then turned to face me. "You mean the vampire curse?"

"Yes, that. I hope this will solve the problem."

He chuckled. That was not something I wanted to see before going under anesthesia.

"It's such a fanciful idea," he said, "but if you want to do the procedure, we can do it. No guarantees it will keep you from turning into a vampire. Personally, I think that is only in your head. This procedure is only for your body, not your mind."

"That's what I want."

"Your paperwork seems in order. Financing arranged. And I see you have signed everything. Excellent. The nurse remarked on your erection, too. I bet she was thrilled to give it a shake, eh? The lab has worked to prepare the stem cells. Everything is ready."

He regarded me, perhaps expecting an affirmative response. But I felt nothing. I was empty. It would all be in God's hands now. Or the devil's. Perhaps it made no difference now.

I looked up at him, my face grim, my skin rough and dry.

"My friend...she's in the hospital now. Right now. The one down the street from here. She cut her wrists. Maybe she felt.... Maybe I.... I'm not sure I should do this now. Also, she's got some infection. I need to wait to see that she lives."

Dr. Kovačević looked up, eyes pinched together.

"Mister Székely, at your order we have prepared everything. We cleared our schedule in order to fit you in this morning. Now you wish to cancel the procedure?"

"Not cancel. Just postpone."

"That will not be possible. Timing is of the essence."

"Yeah, essence. I get that." I put my head in my hands, afraid of myself. "Everything is about essence, isn't it? In the end that's all we have. That's all anyone has."

"Then shall we proceed?"

With a frown stitched across my pallid face, I nodded once, and in that simple gesture the fuse was set. Everything I knew and everything I had ever experienced was about to vanish like a sniff. Tomorrow would indeed be a new day in a new life.

Two nurses helped me disrobe and pull on the gown, then sat me on the bed to wait for the cart that would take me into the treatment room.

"Wait!" I cried, jumping off the bed.

"What is the problem?" asked Dr. Kovačević.

"Before we do this, I need to make a call. Long distance. If there's a phone I could use for that. I get no signal on my cell phone in Europe."

"A phone call? We can arrange that," said Dr. Kovačević. He spoke in Croatian to the nurse, then to me: "After phone call we go ahead with the procedure?"

"Yes. Thank you."

A nurse showed me to an empty office. It was filled with an impressive oak desk and walls full of medical books on shelves. She moved the phone to the corner of the desk and gestured for me to use the side chair.

"Dial zero," she said as I took a seat, "then the international number you want to connect to."

Instead of going to voice mail, it rang three times before Penny answered.

"Hello?"

"Penny, it's me. Stefan."

"Where the hell are you? It's like you fell off the face of the Earth." By her tone she seemed more surprised than angry. I was glad of that. Perhaps two months was enough to soothe any disagreements. Or mend broken hearts.

"I—I'm in Croatia. I told you this was where I was going."

"You told me that? When?"

"Doesn't matter now. I got into some trouble."

"Trouble? You? Why am I not surprised?" She had a lovely, refreshing chuckle. "Anyway, happy Halloween."

"Is it?"

"It's tomorrow. But are you going to call again tomorrow?"

"I'm sick. You know: the same problem I've been having for the past year. It's much worse now. I almost died."

"Died? What happened?"

"Like I said, I got into some trouble. And I'm about to have a procedure. Call it an operation. It's something new and radical."

"Geez, Stefan, what is it?"

I told her the name of the clinic, its address, and my doctor's name, just in case anything bad happened. In case she needed to see about my belongings. I told her where she could find keys to a storage unit in Oklahoma City. I no longer had the apartment. I was leaving everything to her, whether she wanted it or not. If she didn't want any particular thing, she could give it away or sell it. I would be gone.

"Is it really that serious?" she asked.

"I could die during the operation. Or, if I live, I might want to die because I won't be any better. I mean, something like a living death...if that makes any sense to you."

"Actually, it does. Stefan, listen: I'm working on a story right now about those people you were telling me about. The people who have porphyria. Is that what you have?"

"Not exactly. There's a lot that overlaps but—"

"I interviewed doctors and two sufferers. It's going to air next week, six and ten. It's Health Week, don't you know? I thought of you and decided to do some research. I'm sorry y—"

"Penny, I can't talk long. It's long distance. I just wanted to tell you what I told you. In case anything happens. I want you to know I'm sorry—sorry for what happened. Everything. I'm sorry for what happened between us, and for what I did to you. I'm so sorry for everything—"

"I'm sorry, too. Forgive me?"

"I have to forgive you. You didn't do anything wrong."

"Hey, Stefan, I got some news for you. When you get back, I want to take you to a new tea bar that opened in Edmond. It's like a Starbucks but has mostly tea, lots of exotic teas. It's owned by a Korean family."

"You mean there's enough Korean people in Edmond to keep it running?"

"Lots of people like tea, Stefan, not only Koreans. But I do see a lot of Korean-Americans hanging out there. You'll like it. We can make it our new hang out place. First tea is on me when you get back. Now the second piece of news I want to tell you—"

"I've got news to tell you."

"Stefan, mine is important."

"No, mine is more important. Mine is about this procedure I'm having in a few minutes. I had to beg them to hold off so I could make this call. I'm in one of the doctor's offices right now, using their phone. This might be the last call I get to make. To anyone."

"You're being dramatic, as usual. Stop it."

"Do you hear me? I'm trying to live. To go on living and not be hideous to the world. This is my only option—my last option."

"I know, I know. But I'm sure everything will turn out fine."

"You don't know that."

"I have confidence. Besides, I know you'll pull through. You have to you. You have a lot to live for. I need you to come home. I will love you even with your skin problem—"

"It isn't just a skin problem. My body is killing me! I'm dying, Penny! Can't you get that through your head?"

"Sorry. Yes, I know it's serious. I wish I were there with you. But you have good doctors, right?"

I caught my breath, shut down my cruel words. If this were to be my last conversation with her...with my Beloved.... My heart was pounding. How could I leave her with that angry tone, that rude remark? Must leave a good impression. No matter what.

"Penny, I'm sorry. I'm so stressed. I'm sorry for getting angry. Shit, just like I'm sorry for every damn thing I said and did before going on this fucking trip." My voice quivered. "Before leaving you. Before I—"

"Stefan, wait. I know you're sorry. You're always sorry. But for what? The last time we were together? Is that what you mean?"

"I guess so. When else did I hurt you?"

"I'm over that, okay? It's been two months, you know. You did hurt me. But lots of time, lots of thinking. You ready for my second piece of news?"

"What news?"

I heard a big inhale followed by an equally significant exhale.

"That I'm pregnant."

The hum of international airwaves seemed to fill the room, making it feel like I was speaking through a dream.

"Did you hear me? ...Stefan?"

"How could that be? Didn't you get your period when we...when we were together that time."

"I know. That's what I thought, that it came back. But my ob/gyn said a little bleeding can happen even with conception. My producer, Jennifer—you know her? She experienced the same thing. It wasn't menstrual flow, it was—"

"Abort it."

"Excuse me?"

"You should abort it. Don't let my damaged genes continue in this world."

"Are you serious?"

The nurse ducked in to hurry me.

"I must say goodbye now, Penny. It's time for my operation. I don't know what will happen. If it's a success, I'll come home. I mean, to Oklahoma—"

"Are you *serious*, Stefan?"

"If it's not successful, please remember I really did love you."

32

The universe is coal black, except for scattered starfire and the usual pesky anomalies that ruin any grand metaphor. So it was: my eyes closed, or completely blind, or encased in a nailed-shut box, or buried under a rich mound of earth—all the same as my consciousness flooded through me. The first thing I recalled were words I did not understand. Some foreign language. I knew they were not from God. Indeed, though I had traveled through many galaxies and right up to the edge of madness, I would recognize God's voice anywhere. There is a certain gravelly quality to it, a stirring of bemused passion with a hint of cynical whine on some phonemes. It is unforgettable. And then, suddenly, between an exploding supernova and the birth of a tree frog, he spoke to me. He said: "Done."

And so it was that after three days comatose, I awoke.

I awoke screaming like a burning banshee.

My body was fighting whatever was done to it. I was about to explode, as full of toxins as I was. Organ failure was imminent. Dr. Kovačević swore he had never had any patient experience rejection at this level of severity. I was a special case. They should not have tried to rush it, to push the protocol. Supposedly, I had muttered that it didn't matter, that I was used to rejection, and laughed hysterically.

The pain overwhelmed me and I could no longer joke about what was happening. My body felt as though a whole barrel of pins and needles had been pumped into it through an IV. The tingling and pricking and stabbing increased hourly until I was far beyond any screaming. Not even the usual drugs could shut it down.

Then it all stopped.

I awoke in the middle of the night, alone in the silent hospital room, strapped into some kind of bed. It was 3:33 a.m. by the clock on the wall. Perfect time for the dead to rise. Those late-night owls can stay up until 2 a.m. and early risers might awaken by 4 a.m., so my timing was ideal. Jesus himself likely arose at 3:33 a.m., but I was quite ready to dismiss this pointless exercise in one-upmanship with God.

Game over.

It took a few minutes to orient myself, to remember where I had been and what I had done the previous week. Somewhere on the other side of the world was a woman I loved but had hurt. I fled to this clinic seeking relief from my on-going delusion that I was turning into a vampire. I knew it sounded crazy, but that's what I recalled. It seemed to be the truth, but what really is the truth at 3:33 in the morning?

I threw off the sheet, saw it flutter to the floor. There were no wires, cables, sensors, or clips fastened to me. No monitoring equipment of any kind was attached. There were no machines turned on, none that I could see around the dark room. How could they not be concerned with my well-being? I had paid a lot for this.

I swung my legs to the floor and sat on the edge of the bed for a minute, then stood. All seemed well. I stepped across the cool tile floor with my bare feet, steady despite my missing toes. My body moved well. There was no pain. Realizing I had completed the protocol and felt fine, I decided to leave. No reason to stay. It seemed best for me to depart before dawn, before the earliest rounds of the nurses. I certainly did not want to alarm anyone.

So I dressed in the clothes I found hanging up in the closet, grabbed my overnight bag, and slipped out. I was getting used to leaving hospitals in the middle of the night. This hospital, however, I was able to escape without leaving a mark upon the mirror.

The night was cold, almost frosty, but clear. An autumn half moon hid behind cadaverous clouds. The streets were empty at that quiet hour, and the distance to the next hospital was short. I could see well enough. I knew the way—as though I had been there barely an hour earlier. And in my dark blue suit and white shirt, the necktie rolled up in a side pocket, overcoat and hat on, I strolled like a gentleman down the street to the hospital where I had taken Alma for treatment.

"Where are you, Alma?" I spoke to myself as I walked.

The rental car was still in the parking lot, just as I had left it what seemed like an hour before. I tore the parking ticket from under the windshield wiper and tossed it into the air, watched the cold wind blow it away, like a wayward angel being recalled to heaven.

With a glance at the dark windows of the hospital, I sensed she was no longer there. What happened to her? Had she died? It felt as though I had left her there only a few minutes earlier. But I could not deny my senses. So I unlocked the car, got in, and started the engine.

It was easy to drive to the hotel where a room should still be waiting for me. The hotel staff would be happy to charge my MasterCard for whatever extra days my name was associated with the room. At least I could get a cold shower there and change into fresh clothes. Then I would decide what to do next. After all, life is full of choices, I often told myself. But, then, so is death.

Inside the room, only the small lamp on the nightstand was on. Stretched out on the bed was a girl. One corner of the sheet and blanket covered her legs. Her feet showed. Her shoulders and arms, breasts and belly, too. She was asleep, her naked body seemingly tossed upon the bed in that haphazard position.

I smiled, pleased that she had been released from the hospital and again appeared healthy. Her skin was wonderfully pale, smooth and supple. Normal. There were no longer bandages on her wrists, either. I was satisfied. At least she'd had this room to return to for recuperation.

I closed the door behind me.

"You survived...."

I meant my first spoken words to be ironic, a joke. After all, she should easily have survived her mishap. I, on the other hand, had probably died and not accepted it yet.

I took off my coat and hat, sat them in the chair by the door.

She stirred, then stretched out her arms, yawning.

When her eyes beheld me, she jumped back hard against the headboard, struck in terror. Her eyes were wide, mouth twisted, ready to scream. She did not recognize me.

"I'm sorry to awaken you," I spoke softly.

I dared step forward then, out of the shadows and into the farthest edge of the small nightstand lamp's illumination.

She called out to me, challenging me. Who was I?

285

At first I was hurt that she did not know me, or that she was frightened by my appearance. Ghastly as I was, I had to be scary to anyone who encountered me. But to awaken in your room to this monster, especially if you were a petite, frail girl? It had to be a horrible fright.

Yes, there I was: my dry, flaky, peeling skin, covering a gaunt, veiny, pale body, with hairless head, cracked lips, bulging eyes. Indeed, I bore a hideous, ghoulish façade.

And yet, despite her reaction to my appearance, she was fairly arousing. I was ready to pounce upon her—

A sharp pain struck me then, like a stake to the center of my chest and the pain grew and rumbled through my body. Accompanying the sensation was a vague remembrance of words I had uttered, a prayer sent up to heaven, a text message to God.

I stepped back from the bed, an artificially obvious motion designed to diffuse the tension in the room, to let her know I would not attack her, yet she did not relax.

"I made a promise," I said to her, then tried to think what the words were in Hungarian. "*Ígéretet tettem*. You understand?"

Digging in my bag as she continued cowering on the bed, I found the envelope I was looking for and pulled out the brown bank portfolio. I took out the ledger, set it on the dresser and scribbled a number and a date and added my signature, tore the paper loose and set it on the dresser.

"I must be going." I packed up my bag and gathered up my coat and hat. "That's a check, a bank draft, for you to turn into cash when you get back to Budapest. Ten-thousand Euros. You should go to the same bank we went to. Remember that bank? The name is on the bank draft."

I pulled out the keys from my trouser pocket.

"*Ki vagy te*?" she asked from the bed, sounding more baffled than fearful. 'Who are you?'

The slightest of grimaces fired briefly around my face, brilliant like the gleam in God's eye, then faded to black. Done. I shook my head and stepped toward the door.

"I'm taking the car, but you have enough money from what I gave you already to get a taxi to the train station, then a train back to Budapest. You cash that bank draft and enjoy your life, Alma Jónás."

"Who are you?" she asked, finding the English words. "How you know my name?"

"I'm someone who sat beside you on a plane. That's all. That's all I will ever be to you."

I opened the door.

"Where you go?" she called, sounding desperate.

"There's a house I own. It's mine now—ever since my parents died. It's somewhere near the Bosnian border. I'll go there."

"So I go...with you?"

Something was starting to make sense to her. A memory or two burning into her consciousness. So I shook my head again.

"You can never go with me. Not now. Never again, Alma. I'm sorry—*sajnálom*. Please forget me."

She tensed, folded her hands into fists in protest. Her naked body flushed, skin smooth and youthful, healthy once more. Her eyes released two tears and in that moment she became beautiful.

33

I am not ancient, not in the way many of us have been depicted in literature or legend usually claim to be. Living forever is vastly overrated. It's a perpetual retirement. Fun at first, then boredom. How many sunrises can one adore? How many sunsets? How many lives can be lived? How many books read? It is pure myth. All evil needs a *cause célèbre*. All evil needs a victim.

I carry the gene, the marker of our madness. This is the curse many have spoken about over the centuries. I am not a monster, however. I have no desire to inflict harm upon my Beloved, or anyone else. I desire only to survive. Yet survival is problematic, for we must endure constant debilitating discomfort. Many of us wish we could die. It is a matter of expediency.

In all honesty, I continue to have common desires and I hunt for ways to fulfill them. A well-stocked library would be a good start. Though I know my time does have a limit, I won't be living for hundreds of years, as so many stories might suggest. I believe I have the normal lifespan yet those years are sure to be cut through with my curse, rendering me undesirable, loathsome, fearful-looking, hideous, and in the frightened eyes of those who may see me comes the hatred that has become our greater curse, worse than a gene, worse than a hunger for warmth, for blood—for love! Therefore, I require someone who would have me as I am, without fear or reservation, someone who could accept me and everything about me. Yet I find none to take the challenge, so I must march on. Alone.

The cold air kept the foggy forest silent except for the dull, colored leaves crunching beneath my boots. Ravens caw from the trees, warning of my presence. My pack is heavy as I walk the winding road up the hill, which spirals twice around. I hike the path as it rises through the trees, until I break free of the forest and stand in a small courtyard. It is large enough for a wagon or carriage and its team of horses to sit idle while the lord and lady exit and are ushered inside by a staff of attentive servants. In a past era, that is. Now, the gravel plaza sits undisturbed.

Setting down my bag, I gaze at the main doors, two large wooden structures more resembling barn doors than something from its elegant past. It has been reconstructed to preserve the building during its long demise. Nobody had bought it—until my parents did. Nobody wanted it, haunted as it was by the echoing cries of women tortured within its walls during the recent war.

The knocker on the door is a bronze stag head, antlers broken off. But it has rusted tight and I cannot lift it to knock on the door. I walk to my right, looking up at the windows, seeing if anyone spies down upon me, this hideous vagabond in search of his fate. Then I go to the left in search of an entrance, around the end of the masonry base of the building. Nothing.

I return to those main doors and test them.

With some effort, I pry the doors apart. Only age and the weather seem to have sealed them. There is no lock, no key. Nobody would venture up this hill to check on an old dilapidated villa likely to be haunted by crimes done two decades earlier.

I enter and find the main hall smoky with dust and the slants of sunlight breaking through the clouds outside trying to slice through the grimy window panes. Covered with gray cloths, the furniture is arranged as though a grand ball had been presented only a week before. A large chandelier hangs from the ceiling, its candles burned low. A huge fireplace commands the side wall. I make my way across the room to the next doorway.

Somewhere there has to be a kitchen, though I doubt there is anything to eat. Even with a hike of several days I am not famished. Nor am I in need of drink. I could walk forever, it seems. I do not fatigue. Nor do I need the usual kinds of nourishment.

Up the grand staircase would be the bedrooms. I wonder if there would still be beds there, and whether or not I could make myself comfortable after shaking off the dusty sheets. Wouldn't the previous owners have taken such belongings away rather than leave them to fade away over the years? And who were these past owners? I wonder about them as I ascend the grand staircase, my bag in hand, my pack on my back.

At the top of the stairs I drop my bag and set down my pack, stretch my shoulders and breath deeply, ignoring the dusty corridor.

I hear a noise. A soft shuffle, like slippers moving across a wooden floor. The sound comes from my left. Perhaps it is in the room that beckons there. I momentarily freeze, wary of encountering someone. But who would be the more frightened? A squatter making use of this magnificent villa or a member of the undead? I neither want to scare any person nor be identified and then hunted and killed by fearful villagers.

I take a deeper breath, stoking myself for what I might find inside that room, and step toward the door.

Again I hear sounds from within the room.

Then nothing.

I weigh the possibilities. The old man in the village, who swore he knew everything about these woods and this villa, said nobody ever visits here. He stated firmly that people thought the place was haunted. Too many bad happenings here, what with the war and those women suffering so much. People kept away. It would be empty and I was welcomed to stay here if I were not too nervous. His voice, even with his lilting Croatian-accented English, reflected his amusement that I would want to find this place. I told him I was an archeologist.

He offered me an old mare to ride, saying it was a good day's hike from the village. However, the horse was spooked by my presence and would not let me brush her head. So I elected to walk. It was a golden autumn day.

I paid him for the map and went on my way, certain that this was the property on the deed my parents had left for me. If it was truly mine, I had no reason to be shy. With an old villa to my name, I could be a lord. Granted, a very poor, very ascetic lord, flawed in many ways. Those were minor details. This would be my home. A place for my final years.

When I open the door to the room, I see only darkness. My eyes adjust and the heart-shaped stained-glass window at the far end of the room allows in enough light for me to make out what the room contains. I study the window a moment: mounted hunters in pursuit of a stag, cornering it with two hounds against a tree. The end of the hunt, apparently. And death would come next, come quickly.

There is a long table before me. To the sides, against the walls, stand a pair of armoires. Other cabinets, chairs, a bench, old trunks are all that the room contains.

Suddenly, I see a figure stand up from one of the chairs deep in the room, in the shadows. At the far end of the table, another person rises. Together the two of them step toward me.

The man wears a rough suit, something any country gentleman would wear to pass the day. The woman wears a frumpy, patterned dress with an embroidered vest. She clasps her hands in front of herself.

As the man takes a step forward, I get a better look at them.

They are not easy to gaze upon.

"You've come," says the man. "At last you're here."

"Welcome," says the woman.

Together they step toward me, moving smoothly from the shadows into a wide stripe of light that shockingly reveals their ghoulish, ragged, torn faces.

"Welcome," says the man.

"We have missed you," says the woman.

The man extends his hand, expecting me to shake it. I hold my breath, knowing what I face, knowing what my future holds, knowing in that instant who these people are—

In the center of my gut burns a fragment of truth. It ignites and begins to consume me in a cleansing fire. I feel the universe shifting like a kaleidoscope into a profound yet delicate balance. I stop spinning. The dizziness falls away.

"Hello, Mother.... Father...."

The words catch in my throat. My eyes might be deceiving me, much like so many mirrors have of late. Yet it has to be true, this family reunion, this end of all journeys, this...*fate*.

The tall, gaunt man clasps my hand, pulls me closer. The woman sidles up to me, lays her arm around my shoulder, and gives me a hug.

"We've been waiting for you," says Father.

"Now we're together again. At long last...." My mother's voice wavers, suddenly awash with emotion. "We shall have a long life together, my beloved boy."

Father gestures to the dark end of the room and only then do I notice a young man calmly sitting there. His arm is outstretched, with some medical equipment standing in awkward silhouette against the stained-glass window.

"Don't mind him," says Mother. "He's our...."

"Our guest," Father finishes. "Our guest for this week."

He extends his arm, ushering me over to the person hooked up to the IV. From a tray, he lifts up a vial dark with blood.

"We know it's been a long journey for you." He gestures at me, at the chair.

"So sit. Take a rest. You must be thirsty."

I breathe deeply and everything tastes bitter. Touching my side, my hand resting protectively over my spleen—where all regrets are stored, as the poet Baudelaire has written—I imagine a mirror hanging on a wall somewhere on the other side of the world. No face appears, and my heart stops cold. The end has begun.

Acknowledgements

Although actual businesses are mentioned in the novel, no disrespect is intended, nor is suggestion made of any actual impropriety or poor service by these businesses.

Thanks go to my daughter, Marta, who suggested the cover art design and, as a budding medical student, also answered my many questions and cross-checked medical references in the book.

I always use music to assist with my imagination. For this novel, I used the music of Adrian von Ziegler, BrunuhVille, Carter Burwell (the first *Twilight* film soundtrack), the choral works of Eric Whitacre, selected songs of Coldplay, Evanescence, Tokio Hotel, Muse, and In Fear and Faith, as well as the First Movement of Symphony #3 (Opus 36; "Symphony of Sorrowful Songs") by Polish composer Henryk Górecki. Thank you for your inspiration and amazing aural scene support.

About the Author

Stephen Swartz grew up in Kansas City where he was an avid reader of science-fiction and quickly began emulating his favorite authors. Even after veering from science-fiction, his stories still usually feature exotic lands and foreign languages, strangers lost in familiar places, and the occasional breakfast menu.

Along the way, Stephen studied music in college and, like many writers, worked at a wide range of jobs: from French fry guy to soldier, IRS clerk, and TV station writer, before heading to Japan for several years of teaching English.

Stephen is now a Professor of English and has taught writing in New York, Pennsylvania, Kansas, and Oklahoma. He lives just to the side of tornado alley in Oklahoma, where he can be found working on the next novel most evenings and weekends.

Other books by Stephen Swartz

AFTER ILIUM

A BEAUTIFUL CHILL

THE DREAM LAND TRILOGY

I. Long Distance Voyager

II. Dreams of Future's Past

III. Diaspora